SEVEN DIALS

THE PERFORMERS

CLAIRE RAYNER

SEVEN DIALS

Book 12
THE PERFORMERS

WEIDENFELD AND NICOLSON
London

Copyright © 1986 Claire Rayner

Published in Great Britain in 1986 by
George Weidenfeld and Nicolson Ltd
91 Clapham High Street
London SW4 7TA

ISBN 0 297 78823 X

Printed and bound in West Germany by Mohndruck

For Esta Charkham,
who is quite a Dame in her own right.

With love.

ACKNOWLEDGEMENTS

The author is grateful for the assistance given with research by the Library of the Royal Society of Medicine, London; Macarthy's Ltd, Surgical Instrument Manufacturers; the London Library; the London Museum; the Victoria and Albert Museum; Leichner Stage Make-up Ltd; Mr Joe Mitchenson, theatrical historian; Miss Geraldine Stephenson, choreographer and dance historian; Miss Rachael Low, film historian; the General Post Office Archives; the Public Records Office; the Archivist, British Rail; Mr Edmund Swinglehurst, archivist, Thomas Cook Ltd; the Curator, National Railway Museum, York; Historical Records Department, British Transport; Meteorological Records Office; Archives Department of *The Times*; Mr David Mancur, IPC Archives; Borough of Westminster Libraries; the Lodgekeeper, Albany, Piccadilly; the Archivist, Guildhall School of Music and Drama; the Imperial War Museum; and other sources too numerous to mention.

THE LACKLANDS

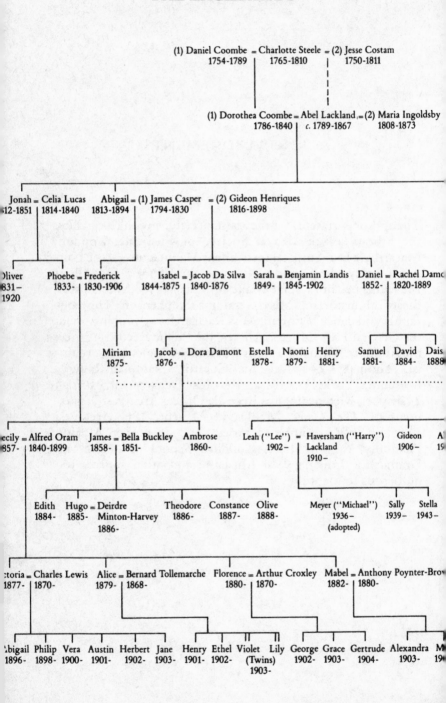

(1) Daniel Coombe = Charlotte Steele = (2) Jesse Costam
1754-1789 | 1765-1810 | 1750-1811

(1) Dorothea Coombe = Abel Lackland = (2) Maria Ingoldsby
1786-1840 | *c.* 1789-1867 | 1808-1873

Jonah = Celia Lucas   Abigail = (1) James Casper = (2) Gideon Henriques
12-1851 | 1814-1840   1813-1894 | 1794-1830   1816-1898

Oliver   Phoebe = Frederick   Isabel = Jacob Da Silva   Sarah = Benjamin Landis   Daniel = Rachel Damc
831-   1833-   1830-1906   1844-1875 | 1840-1876   1849- | 1845-1902   1852- | 1820-1889
1920

                        Miriam   Jacob = Dora Damont   Estella   Naomi   Henry   Samuel   David   Dais
                        1875-   1876-   1878-   1879-   1881-   1881-   1884-   1888

ecily = Alfred Oram   James = Bella Buckley   Ambrose   Leah ("Lee") = Haversham ("Harry")   Gideon   A
857- | 1840-1899   1858- | 1851-   1860-   1902 –   Lackland   1906 –   19
                                                                      1910 –

              Edith   Hugo = Deirdre   Theodore   Constance   Olive   Meyer ("Michael")   Sally   Stella
              1884-   1885- | Minton-Harvey   1886-   1887-   1888-   1936 –   1939 –   1943 –
                              1886-   (adopted)

ctoria = Charles Lewis   Alice = Bernard Tollemarche   Florence = Arthur Croxley   Mabel = Anthony Poynter-Brov
1877- | 1870-   1879- | 1868-   1880- | 1870-   1882- | 1880-

bigail Philip Vera   Austin Herbert Jane   Henry Ethel Violet Lily   George Grace Gertrude   Alexandra   M
1896- 1898- 1900-   1901-   1902-   1903-   1901- 1902- (Twins)   1902- 1903- 1904-   1903-   19
                                                       1903-

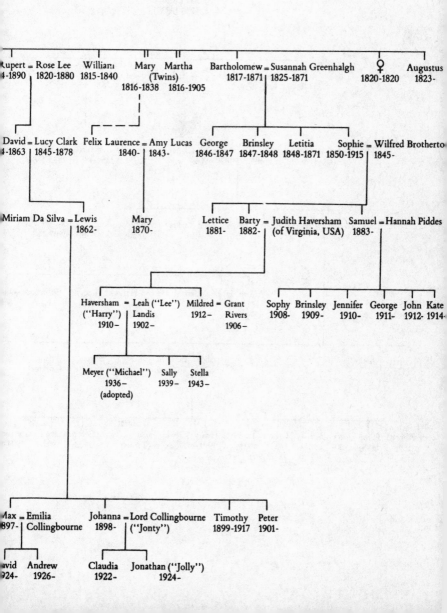

Rupert [...]4-1890 = Rose Lee 1820-1880 · William 1815-1840 · Mary (Twins) 1816-1838 · Martha (Twins) 1816-1905 · Bartholomew 1817-1871 = Susannah Greenhalgh 1825-1871 · ♀ 1820-1820 · Augustus 1823-

David [...]4-1863 = Lucy Clark 1845-1878 · Felix · Laurence 1840- = Amy Lucas 1843- · George 1846-1847 · Brinsley 1847-1848 · Letitia 1848-1871 · Sophie 1850-1915 = Wilfred Brotherton 1845-

Miriam Da Silva = Lewis 1862- · Mary 1870- · Lettice 1881- · Barty 1882- = Judith Haversham (of Virginia, USA) · Samuel 1883- = Hannah Piddes

Haversham ("Harry") 1910- = Leah ("Lee") Landis 1902- · Mildred 1912- = Grant Rivers 1906- · Sophy 1908- · Brinsley 1909- · Jennifer 1910- · George 1911- · John 1912- · Kate 1914-

Meyer ("Michael") 1936- (adopted) · Sally 1939- · Stella 1943-

Max 897- = Emilia Collingbourne · Johanna 1898- = Lord Collingbourne ("Jonty") · Timothy 1899-1917 · Peter 1901-

David 924- · Andrew 1926- · Claudia 1922- · Jonathan ("Jolly") 1924-

THE LUCASES

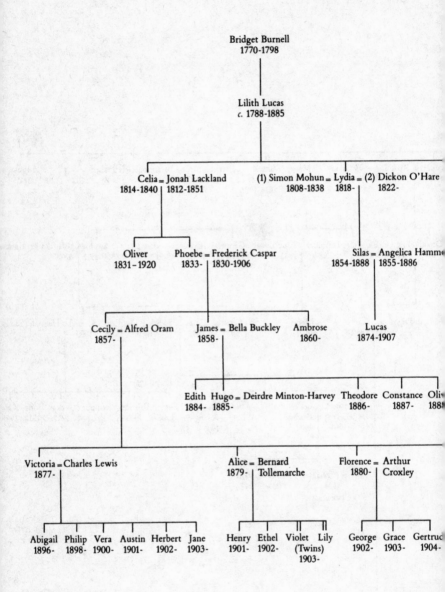

Bridget Burnell
1770-1798

Lilith Lucas
c. 1788-1885

Celia = Jonah Lackland
1814-1840 | 1812-1851

(1) Simon Mohun = Lydia = (2) Dickon O'Hare
1808-1838 | 1818- | 1822-

Oliver
1831-1920

Phoebe = Frederick Caspar
1833- | 1830-1906

Silas = Angelica Hamm
1854-1888 | 1855-1886

Cecily = Alfred Oram
1857-

James = Bella Buckley
1858-

Ambrose
1860-

Lucas
1874-1907

Edith
1884-

Hugo = Deirdre Minton-Harvey
1885-

Theodore
1886-

Constance
1887-

Oli
188

Victoria = Charles Lewis
1877-

Alice = Bernard
1879- | Tollemarche

Florence = Arthur
1880- | Croxley

Abigail
1896-

Philip
1898-

Vera
1900-

Austin
1901-

Herbert
1902-

Jane
1903-

Henry
1901-

Ethel
1902-

Violet Lily
(Twins)
1903-

George
1902-

Grace
1903-

Gertrud
1904-

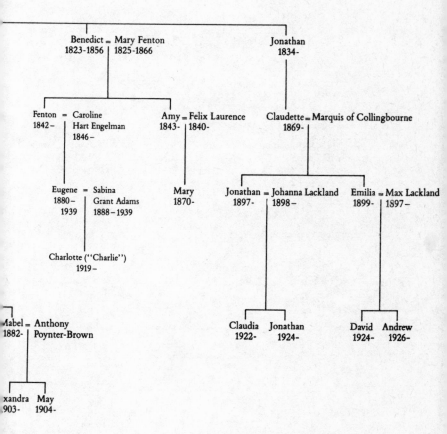

It really was remarkable how often it rained on the second Friday in the months of October, January, March and July, Billy Brocklesby thought. He peered out of the big double doors of the hospital into Endell Street at the chattering gutters and gleaming slate-grey pavements as people went splashing by with expressions of long-suffering martyrdom on their faces and shook his head disapprovingly at the dull sky. It really was too bad of the elements to show so little respect for that august body, the Board of Governors of Queen Eleanor's Hospital. On the four days a year when they foregathered London should at least be dry, if not actually sunny, but there, what could you expect these days? Ever since the War had started everything had been out of kilter; before 1939, Billy Brocklesby told himself as he hooked back the great doors to show the world that Nellie's was, as always, ready to do business with the halt, the sick and the maimed, before the War everything had been different. Plenty to eat and drink, sensible people running the country and sunshine every day. Now, in spite of the fact that peace had broken out over a year ago, you couldn't get so much as a packet of fags to bless yourself with, let alone any decent scoff. And it always rained on the Guv'nors' Day.

'Bloody Government,' he muttered under his breath as the first bewildered patient of the day came splashing into his newly washed front hall, dripping water all over the shining black and white terrazzo squares. 'Bloody Government' – and then, loudly, 'Round the side, missus. First left and then left again for Outpatients – and mind where yer putting yer feet – just been washed, this place 'as, and got the Guv'nors comin' any minute – ' And he sent her hurrying on her way, his brass buttons glittering imperiously as he ushered her out.

There was no doubt that he looked the part of Nellie's Head

Porter most satisfactorily, in spite of the fact that he limped so badly and that his blue serge uniform was so thin and shiny, and his spirits lifted perceptibly, despite the rain, as the woman shot a scared glance over her shoulder at him and went scuttling away. That was better; a bit of respect, something else that was in short supply in this brave new peaceful world. They'd done more than throw out Churchill in last year's disastrous election, Billy Brockesby was fond of saying to anyone who would listen to his dyed-in-the-wool conservative views. They'd thrown out decency and tradition and good old fashioned respect for your betters as well.

There was another flurry at the door and he turned back from his little lodge, where he had been about to settle himself with the *Daily Sketch* and his first cup of tea of the day, his face scowling in readiness to send another venturesome patient round to the rear entrance where she belonged, but at the sight of the new arrival his expression at once became ingratiating in the extreme.

'Morning, Dr Lackland, sir,' he said, beaming widely. 'Nasty morning, sir, very nasty – let me take your coat, sir, very wet it is – I'll see to it that it's dried nice and ready for you when the meeting's over, sir –'

'I can manage, thank you, Brocklesby, I can manage perfectly well –' Max Lackland tried not to let his irascibility show in his voice, but he wasn't too successful, and Brocklesby stepped back, his face blank now, and said woodenly, 'Yes, sir, as you wish, sir', and watched him go hurrying up the wide curved staircase, his damp coat tails flapping. Not the man he was at all, he thought, not the man he was by a long chalk, and getting nasty with it. You had to make allowances, of course you did, losing his wife like that and them as close as a pair of pigs in mud, but all the same, no call to go biting a man's head off when all he wanted to do was be helpful, was there?

No, Brocklesby told himself, no call at all, and went limping back to his lodge and his rapidly cooling tea. Dr High-and-Mighty Lackland wasn't the only one to lose people to them bloody doodlebugs. Hadn't his own old girl got hers two years ago this very month when three of the buggers had dropped down at Croydon? Not that she was all that much of a loss, to tell the truth, wicked tongue that she'd always had on

2

her, but all the same, he'd lost her and had to look after himself these days, in consequence, and did he go around biting people's heads off over it? He did not, he told himself righteously, as he folded the *Daily Sketch* into an even smaller wodge and peered at the results of last night's dog races. He did not, bearing his losses with dignity, not like some he could mention; and still muttering under his breath he checked off the names of the winners – and he hadn't napped a bleedin' one of 'em – and sipped his tea noisily and tried not to care about Max Lackland's bad temper.

Max himself, standing in front of the window in the big Governors' Room at the top of the stairs and staring sightlessly out at the rain, was thinking much the same about himself that Brocklesby was. There had been no need to be so unpleasant, damn it; the man had meant well and probably couldn't help his oleaginous manner. They had been lucky to have had a Head Porter at all during the difficult war years when every able-bodied man there was had had better things to do than guard a hospital's main entrance. To have found Brocklesby, with his left leg torn to tatters by World War One shrapnel, so making him useless for World War Two, had been Nellie's good fortune and he, as a senior member of Nellie's staff, should be able to tolerate the man's less than pleasing personality better than he had this morning.

But it had started off a bad day. He had woken to a sense of desolation that was even greater, it seemed, than it had been at the beginning of his private hell, dragging himself out of the rags of his sleep with a conscious effort, trying not to remember that today was their wedding anniversary. But it had not been a memory he had been able to evade and he had stood there in his bathroom, the tears for Emilia coursing down his cheeks and the hard racking sobs tearing his chest as he contemplated, yet again, the agony of the long years that lay ahead without her. His life had been destroyed that afternoon in 1944 when a late V2 rocket, weaving its erratic way across the West End of London, had coughed and died just above the Regent Palace Hotel and the nearby shop where Emilia had been trying to buy a new shirt for him, and now he had to go on living that destroyed life, breathing, working, eating and sleeping while inside he was shrieking his pain and his loss, hour after impossible hour.

3

And today was no better. It was still only nine o'clock; there was the rest of the day to get through somehow, another twelve hours to exist before he could again claim the temporary respite of sleep, which even though it brought such agonizing dreams, at least passed the time quickly.

Behind him the door rattled and he turned away from the window, grateful for the interruption, and saw his father standing there leaning on his stick and staring at him from beneath eyebrows that seemed to go on getting more and more shaggy with every year that passed, as though they had a vigorous and personal life of their own and had chosen out of some quirk of ridiculous humour to grow on this wreck of an old face, as moss grows on old walls.

'Well, m'boy?' the old man said and set his head on one side as he stared at the hard-faced man with the thick grey hair who was standing there looking at him. 'Well?'

'Well enough,' Max said, not ungently, and came over to lead him to the chair at the head of the table as Victor came in behind him.

'That man down there don't deserve to wear that uniform,' he grunted, and came and slid a practised hand under old Sir Lewis's other elbow so that both the younger men could lead the shaky old figure to his place. 'If I've told him once I've told him a hundred times – it don't do to sit there drinking tea for all and sundry to see you, not when you're Head Porter! Got to have a bit of dignity.'

The old man turned his head towards his son and gave him a sketch of a wink and Max, without thinking, smiled back, almost hearing his face creak at the rarity of the experience and felt, just for a moment, a lift of his spirits. In the old days, they had all laughed at dear old Victor, he and Emilia and Father, laughed at the constant rivalry that existed between him and the man who had taken over his job at Nellie's when he had agreed to become old Sir Lewis's housekeeper, nurse and general factotum after Lady Lackland had died back in '41. To laugh now, without Emilia to share it, felt odd; wicked, almost. But that was a thought that had to be dismissed, and the psychiatrist part of his mind lectured the personal part of it, as it so often did these days. It was normal to feel guilt, but not necessary. It was not healthy to wallow in his loss, he must work at restructuring his life, make a new pattern for himself,

4

make it possible to live without Emilia. Bereavement was a commonplace experience –

'Big agenda today,' Sir Lewis said, and waved away Victor's fussing with the rug he was wrapping round his thin knees. 'I just hope they don't make too much of a meal of it. Women – ' And he sniffed noisily and rubbed at his nose with a flourish of a large white handkerchief. 'You got any special business for us today?'

'Nothing special,' Max said and sat down beside him, opening his briefcase to spread his papers neatly in front of him. 'I can't stay longer than eleven anyway. I've got a Board at twelve – chap's been refused his job back because he was diagnosed as an anxiety neurosis, and I'm not letting them get away with that. Anxiety neurosis – ', and he half sniffed, half snorted. 'Poor chap was trapped on Sword Beach with a broken leg on D-Day and once they got him out had a few bad dreams for a few weeks. Entitled to! Any sensible man would, but some half-wit of an army psychiatrist labels him as an anxiety neurosis. I ask you!'

'What job are they trying to do him out of?' The Old Man squinted up at him. 'Does it matter what his war record was?'

'You've got it in one. Librarian, for pity's sake, librarian! A good peaceful life, ideal for a chap who's had a bad war, and they're trying to say he's not fit. Bloody bureaucrats – '

'You might as well get used to 'em,' Sir Lewis said. 'The way they're trying to run things now, we're all going to have bureaucrats livin' in our pockets. Nationalizing everything that isn't bolted down, they are: Bank of England, coalmines, civil aeroplanes – bloody everything. Can't stop 'em doing it to us as well, much longer – '

'I don't care what they do,' Max said. 'Nationalizing isn't such a bad idea in itself. I quite approve of it. It's time the people who make the money had a share of it, and as for the health service – well, you know my views. No, it's the individuals who get up my nose. Jumped up little Hitlers, some of 'em. And this Board is a whole bunch of little Hitlers and I'm not letting them refuse this chap his job back. So, I can't stay after eleven. D'you mind?'

Sir Lewis laughed, an agreeable cracked old sound that made Max's lips quirk again. 'Mind? Why should I? I've nothing else to do than sit here today, so I might as well do

5

what has to be done and let you young ones go about your business. Of course I don't – ah, here we are! The only reason I come here at all these days! Pretty ladies, pretty ladies! Hello, my dear! How are you? How's that lucky husband of yours?'

Lee Lackland, neat and charming in a green tailored suit and a frilled cream-coloured blouse that looked as though it had been made from a saved-up length of parachute silk smiled widely at him as she came in, and pulled off her froth of a hat, clearly a precious pre-1939 relic, as she came over to bend down and kiss his papery old cheek.

'Very well, thank you,' she said and smiled at him, and her face fell into soft and rather endearing lines. She had been a good-looking girl always, but now, as she moved into her middle forties, her looks seemed to be ripening and improving. Remembering how she had appeared on her wedding day, a dozen years ago, all snow and frost and floating gossamer hair, and seeing her now in the full glow of her maturity, Lewis approved. This was how a woman was supposed to look; so much more interesting than these worried bloodless girls one saw about these days. And he peered back down the long corridor of his memory to seek out his Miriam, seeing her as she had looked in the 'nineties as a giddy girl, when he had first found her – or rather, she had found him – and how she had looked in those later years, with her rich creamy roundness and her soft-cheeked sweetness, and his old eyes filled with tears. Not that anyone paid any attention, for that often happened to the Old Man these days.

'And the children?' he said gruffly and at once Lee became animated.

'Oh, splendid, really splendid! Michael is working *so* well at school – they say he has the makings of a really fine scientist, you know, and he says already he wants to be a surgeon like his Daddy, and the girls are so sweet! Sally can read really well now, and Stella is trying so hard to be as clever as she is, and pretends she can read too – it truly is so sweet to see them together, and of course the way Michael lords it over the girls when he's home – it's too funny, and – '

'Hello, Papa.' Again the door swung and there was Lady Collingbourne, her head on one side in unconscious parody of her father's most familiar posture and Sir Lewis peered across the room at her and greeted her with relief. Delightful though

6

it was to talk to Lee, she did become rather boring on the subject of her children.

'My dear Johanna!' he said and held out both hands towards her. 'Why didn't you come to see me last night? I made sure you would.'

'I'm sorry, Papa.' She came and kissed his cheek and sat down beside him as Lee settled herself a couple of chairs farther along the huge round leather-covered table. 'But Claudia wanted me to go with her to choose some clothes for her trousseau and to see what we could do to get some more clothing coupons for her wedding-dress and by the time we were finished I was beyond anything but a bath and an early night.'

And she did indeed look tired, with violet-grey smudges under her eyes and her cheeks a rather sallow colour over the black dress and coat she was wearing. It had been four years now since Jonty had died at the battle of Tobruk, but still she wore mourning for him, seeming quite unable to bring herself to show any signs of recovering from her grief. Looking at his sister now, Max felt a sharp stab of anxiety. Was she at risk of sinking into chronic grief? Was this a family tendency that he would have to watch for in himself? And he stared at his sister and thought confusedly – are we a blighted family? First one of us killed in the Great War, and now two of us widowed in the Second and Peter so changed – a blighted family.

And then he shook his head at himself, angry at such fanciful thinking. He was a sensible man, a psychiatrist, a man of science, not a mystic; he should be ashamed to think such stupid negative thoughts. Yet all the same, it did seem that they were uniquely cursed, in a sense, and he too looked back down the long pathways of his memories to their joyous childhood, he and Johanna and Peter and Timothy who had been so young, so very young, when the trenches of Flanders had claimed him – and again he shook his head and tried to concentrate on what was being said.

Johanna was talking now about Jolly, having exhausted her discussion of her daughter's coming wedding, and the Old Man was listening with every sign of interest; talk about children might become boring when they were other people's children, but these were his own grandchildren and that was quite different. Always a family man, deeply absorbed in the

7

care of his brood, Sir Lewis enjoyed nothing more than to hear of his young people's doings, and Max looked at him and once again managed a smile. It was good to see the old man so animated and happy. He would have to find some news to give him of his own sons, David and Andrew. He'd enjoy that.

But now he turned his attention to the newest arrivals for the meeting of the Governors: James Brodie, the Bursar, and William Molloy, the Administrative Secretary. They always arrived together, not because they were in any sense good friends – indeed, they were often at daggers drawn, since Brodie was the most parsimonious of bursars and Molloy the most ambitious of secretaries who believed that the spending of money on the hospital greatly enhanced his own importance – but because when faced with a committee of Lacklands they tended to draw together for mutual support. And Max couldn't blame them.

To run a hospital that was on the one hand meant to be an independent body, but which on the other still employed so many of the descendants of the original founder of the place among its staff, was no easy matter. The Lackland clan – and how many of us are there here now? Max asked himself, and rapidly did a mental count; apart from the Old Man there was himself and Harry Lackland, and Herbert Lewis and George Croxley and both David and Jolly now medical students and walking the wards – the Lackland clan was indeed a formidable force. Poor old Molloy and Brodie, he thought and nodded at them and they nodded back, jerkily, for all the world like a pair of mandarin dolls, and for the fourth time that morning Max found himself smiling, albeit briefly.

Perhaps, after all, today wouldn't be as bad as he had feared when he had stood there in the steam of his bathroom, weeping for his lost wife. Perhaps there was some left-over life worth living. At least he could be useful here at the meeting this morning – and as the Old Man rapped his gavel on the table as the last handful of members of the Board of Governors took their places, he took a deep breath and pulled the Agenda sheet in front of him. There was work to be done, and thank God for it. Work never let you down, no matter how bad you were feeling inside.

2

Charlie finished her round of Bluebell Ward, wrote up her notes carefully, and refusing Sister's magnanimous offer of a cup of tea – a rare treat in these days of ever more stringent rationing – on the plea of extra patients over in Spruce, made her way as slowly as she could towards Spruce and her male surgical duties.

Maybe if she timed it right she could catch Max on his way out of his meeting? His secretary had certainly been unhelpful in the extreme about her request to see him when she had put her head round Max's office door this morning.

'Board of Governors' meeting,' she had said in a tone of shocked awe, making it clear that she was deeply unimpressed by any member of Nellie's medical staff who hadn't realized it was the second Friday in October. 'I can't possibly interrupt him before he goes to that, not on any account! And he's got an important Board to go to after that, so all you can do is try to catch him on the wing – '

Max's secretary nurtured a fond image of her chief as being a man of such huge importance as well as superhuman ability that he had literally to fly everywhere he went, and enjoyed nothing more than blocking any and every attempt by other people to talk to him, and Charlie had tightened her jaw at the sight of the woman's self-important face and said nothing. But she'd made up her mind that catch him she would, and now, lingering on the first-floor landing looking down into the chequered hallway beneath and the foreshortened figure of Brocklesby – another self-important Nellie's employee who irritated her profoundly – she sighed suddenly, and resting her arms on the balustrade leaned over so that she was looking down directly onto the head of the Founder's statue.

What would Brocklesby do, she wondered dreamily, if I spat on those bronze curls? Would he explode or collapse? And

9

for a moment she felt like a naughty ten-year-old child again, sitting in the front row of the balcony at the movie house in downtown Baltimore, her parents on each side of her, yearning to lean over and spit on the people beneath in their feathery hats and round black derbies. She had never dared to do it then, and she didn't suppose she'd dare to do it now, but it was amusing to think of it, and to imagine the effect such behaviour would have on these stuffy Britishers if she, an outsider, a foreigner, a pushy *American*, did anything so outrageous.

Not that they were all stuffy, she had to admit, and remembered, as she so often did, Cousin Mary, who had been so meek and demure an old lady on the surface and yet so wickedly funny and acerbic of tongue when she felt herself to be in safe company, and her lips curved. Dear Cousin Mary; what would she have advised her to do about Brin? Wouldn't she have had some sharp little insight to offer her, have found some stiletto of a comment that would have punctured the bubble of absurd excitement Charlie felt whenever she thought of him? I'm sure she would have done, she thought, and sighed again. Losing Cousin Mary had been more of a blow than she had realized, and even now, almost three years after Mary's death, she could still feel the pain of it.

Her mind slid backwards, memory pushing in. Mary, she thought again. How funny it had been, that first meeting. She had been a rather gawky twenty-one-year-old using most of her meagre inheritance on a recuperative visit to England, prickly and aggressive in all her dealings with everyone she met, finding that was the only way she could cover her deep grief over the loss of her parents within a few months of each other. Father, dying in a stupid argument in a saloon down by the docks at Sparrow Point, and Ma just not bothering to go on living without him; they'd been a racketty pair, always in debt, always in trouble, but they had loved each other wholeheartedly and had doted on Charlotte, their only child, and she had been missing them dreadfully, as well as feeling furious with them for daring to die and leave her as they had. So, she had gone to England on an impulse mainly, and then, out of curiosity (for wasn't she Charlotte's only living relative on her father's side?) had gone to see Mary Laurence.

But it had not been only that; she had also wanted to hit out at someone, anyone, for her sense of loss, and to visit a British cousin and be rude to her had seemed something worth doing, absurd notion though that was, and she had gone marching behind the butler into Mary's handsome drawing-room in her house at Lancaster Gate and said loudly, 'I don't know why the hell I'm wasting my time coming here, but I'm your Uncle Fenton's granddaughter', and had stood and scowled at the rotund but neat figure sitting so upright in her chair beside the fire.

And Mary had looked at her benignly over her glasses and then laughed aloud and said, 'Heavens, of course you are! You look *exactly* like my Mamma in a temper and she always told me that she was the image of her wicked brother. *Do* tell me – are you as bad a person as your grandfather was? I do hope so, because I'm fearfully bored, and I'd relish a bit of wickedness to speed the days by – '

And Charlotte had tried to go on scowling and not been able to and they had both laughed and got on famously from then on; and now, standing leaning over the first-floor balustrade at Nellie's in 1946 she looked back at the seven years that had followed that first meeting and sighed yet again. It had all seemed so right somehow; to stay in England and live with her elderly cousin because she wanted to, and not only because she had been trapped here by the outbreak of war, to do her medical training at Nellie's rather than at Johns Hopkins at home in Baltimore, which had been her first plan – it had all seemed so sensible and it had indeed all worked beautifully. Until the Blitz and Mary's heart attack during one particularly noisy raid.

That had been a dreadful night, dreadful, and though it had left her comfortably provided for, for Mary had willed her a handsome fortune as well as the big Lancaster Gate house, it was a lonely life for a girl. She had her work, of course, and was good at it; to be a surgical registrar at the great Queen Eleanor's Hospital at the age of only twenty-eight, and a woman to boot, and to have so excellent an income, was splendid, but she often found herself counting her blessings, and asking herself what more a girl could want. And that was a bleak way to be.

But what more *could* a girl want? she thought again and then, without realizing she had done so, murmured aloud,

'Just Brin', and a passing nurse said politely, 'I beg your pardon, Miss Lucas?' and Charlie felt her face redden furiously.

'Oh, nothing, nurse,' she said quickly. 'Nothing at all. I was just thinking aloud.' And the girl went rustling away, leaving Charlie standing chewing her lip and staring at the door of the big committee-room.

To hang about for Dr Lackland or to give up for today? That was the question. And if she gave up, what would she tell Brin? There he was sitting on the edge of his bed in Spruce Ward, no doubt, watching the door for her, waiting desperately with that look of eagerness on his face that always had the effect of making her belly tighten, because she'd promised him she'd talk to Dr Lackland, and – 'Damn,' she said aloud, and then more loudly, 'Damn and *blast*!'

'Dear me, you *must* be peeved.' The voice behind her made her actually jump and she turned quickly and felt her face harden as she saw Harry Lackland standing there, his hands in his pockets and his square face carved into a wide grin. 'Swearing? Don't let Sister Spruce hear you – she'll drag you off to a Bible meeting and convert you as soon as look at you if she hears that sort of talk.'

'Hardly swearing,' she said, trying to be light and knowing she sounded stiff and ungracious. 'Just a touch irritated – '

'Now, why should so charming a girl as you succumb to irritation?' he said and she felt her face harden even more. If only he wasn't so dreadfully arch, she thought furiously. It's bad enough he thinks it's clever to flirt, without thinking he has to do so in so heavy-handed and obvious a fashion.

'Because there are a great many reasons for irritation,' she said sharply. 'Not least the time one has to waste tracking down consultants. I'm waiting to speak to Dr Lackland.'

'Won't *Mr* Lackland do?'

'It's a psychiatrist my patient needs, not another surgeon – thanks all the same,' she said and turned to go. 'I'll come back, and try to get him after the meeting – '

'Ah, it's the Governors,' he said and turned to walk away with her. 'I'd forgotten. It's the second Friday of the month, isn't it?'

'Yes. Didn't your wife mention it?' she said, knowing she sounded spiteful and not caring. 'She's a Governor, isn't she?'

'Oh, yes, Lee's a Governor,' he said easily. 'Good lass – did it to get me off the hook. I'd have to be one if she wasn't. I'm very grateful to her – tell me, why do you want to talk to old Max? One of your patients gone mad at the sight of your beauty and running amok all over Spruce and frightening poor old Sister?'

'Of course not,' she said and now the anger really showed and he shook his head at her and said even more easily, 'Just teasing, my dear. You'll never get used to me, will you? And me a fellow American, too – we really ought to understand each other better than we do, you know.'

'Indeed we should,' she said, sharper than ever. 'And I have to say I wish you'd understand that I really don't enjoy these jokes. I'm here to do a job as much as anyone else and I really would prefer it if you treated me the same way you treat all the other resident medical staff.'

'But they aren't as pretty as you are,' he said, unabashed, and put a hand on her arm. 'Really, Charlie, you are very pretty, you know, and I do wish you wouldn't be so – well, chilly. I'm a harmless soul, you know, just friendly and cheerful and – '

'So your wife always says,' she said savagely and pulled away from him firmly and went hurrying through the big double doors into Spruce, letting them swing back in his face, and leaving him outside in the corridor. He really was getting impossible, she told herself furiously as she marched into Sister's office, and sat down with a little thump, and if he doesn't stop it I'll tell him exactly what I think of him and I won't be polite about it. And she reached for the pile of notes Sister had left ready for her, and pulled them towards her with a savage little gesture. Indeed and indeed, she would tell him *exactly* what she thought of him.

Harry watched her go, standing there in the same easy posture with his hands in his pockets and a faint smile on his face, but he was hating himself. Why the hell did he *do* it? He knew she disliked the sort of badinage he used, knew that the look she gave him spelled disdain and not enjoyment, but all the same, out the stupid words came. As though someone else were speaking and not him. When would he find the way to get her to look at him as though she found him interesting rather than merely irritating? He didn't have this effect on other women; when he smiled at the nurses, offered them his little jokes and teases, they smiled and sometimes laughed, occasionally blushed, and always looked approving even though he wasn't necessarily interested in going further with them. He just teased nurses because that was his way with pretty girls, and always had been. But now here he was, dealing with a woman he'd really like to impress, would really like to get to know better, and all he could do was behave like some sort of hobbledehoy. It really was too absurd; and he turned sharply and went clattering away to Elm, to see the gastrectomy patient he'd operated on yesterday.

Maybe, he told himself as he went, maybe I could make even more out of the fact that we're both Americans? He sometimes forgot that fact; he'd been living and working here in London for over a dozen years now and his youth and early manhood in Virginia seemed sometimes not to have happened to him at all, but to someone else he had known in a vague sort of way. Yet for all that, he reminded himself as he arrived at Elm Ward and Sister, bridling with pleasure at the sight of him, came surging forwards to greet him with all the deference due to his status as a senior consultant, for all that I *am* an American, and so is she. Perhaps I could ask her to come to see a film? – must remember to call it a movie, of course – say *The Best Years of Our Lives* – everyone was saying it was the best thing to come out of Hollywood ever; ask her to that, seriously, not jokingly, and see what happens?

And he stared unseeingly at the chart in his hands and imagined the scene; he stopping to speak to her as she sat having her solitary lunch in the medical staff common room – she always sat alone for lunch, so that would work well enough – and saying casually, 'I'm going to this splendid movie – several of my other American friends have told me it's superb. Perhaps you'd care to see it? And then we could go on and have a bite at a rather nice little restaurant I know in Soho where they actually manage to fry chicken the way it ought to be done, Southern style.' And she'd look up at him with those considering narrow green eyes under those straight brows and after a moment she'd smile and say, 'Of course – that would be lovely – '

But there his fantasy shivered and collapsed, and he smiled brightly at Sister as she handed him another chart, and tried to

14

banish Miss Charlotte Lucas and her disturbing effect on him from his mind in order to concentrate on the matter in hand. But it wasn't easy. The senior registrar on the other surgical firm piqued him and fascinated him in equal measure and that was a heady combination, and the last thing he needed. He was quite susceptible enough to women without one who owned her upsetting qualities coming along to make matters more difficult for him.

He did his rounds, punctiliously checking every detail in every patient's notes, inspecting yesterday's gastrectomy's wound and drainage tubes, removing stitches with his own hands from the very difficult bilateral hernia he'd repaired last Friday and going over with Sister the treatment charts and medication lists for every one of his patients, for no one could ever complain that Mr Haversham Lackland was anything but the most careful of surgeons into whose hands any and every patient could safely be entrusted. He knew himself to be less than reliable in matters to do with his private life, but when it came to his work he was good and no one would ever be able to deny that.

After he'd left the ward and was sitting in the shabby surgeon's room in the main theatres, waiting for his first case of the day to be anaesthetized, he let his thoughts go back to Charlotte Lucas. Why was she able to creep into the interstices of his concentration so easily, disturbing his thinking, getting in the way of work? It wasn't that she was so remarkably good looking, after all. A rather gawky girl in some ways, with a long lean body and a small neat head on which she wore her dark hair piled in a rather severe chignon. Her face was a long oval, with a thick pale skin that looked translucent in some lights and she had a full, slightly drooping mouth and a rounded chin that were far from obviously beautiful. Perhaps it was her eyes, those odd narrow green eyes which looked so oddly dramatic because their lower lashes were of the same length as the upper ones; a strange quirk, that, and one he wanted to look at a lot. Yes, he decided, it was her eyes that captured him. Or maybe it wasn't; maybe it was that drooping mouth after all, which looked as though it could be a sensual one and –

Damn it all, he thought furiously, there I go again, thinking about that wretched woman with her cool stares and her look of scorn; why let her get under my skin this way when there's that staff nurse on Casualty who's shown me every way she knows how that she's interested, and she's a good five years younger than the Lucas madam. Why do I let her do this to me? I must be mad –

In more ways than one. Why did he tomcat around this way with women at all, when there was Lee at home? Most of the senior men around Nellie's deeply envied him his Lee; he knew that from the way they looked at her when she arrived at hospital functions, as she so often did these days now she was a Governor. And when he looked at her himself he knew why; she was a lovely woman, absolutely lovely, and as good as she looked too, warm and responsive and cheerful, a superb housekeeper – no man could be better cared for than he was – a loving and attentive mother, and a charming hostess. Yet Harry looked at other women, and often did more than look. He pursued, he wooed, and there were times when he won. More than one of Nellie's student nurses had suddenly decided that she didn't want to train after all, and had left in the middle of her second or even third year, unable to cope with seeing Harry around the hospital treating her like a stranger – albeit a charming one – when he had decided the affair was over. He knew he had spoiled more than one promising nursing career, and was ashamed of that, but it made no difference. He still did it –

And why? He sat there in the surgeon's room amidst its sagging armchairs and scratched linoleum and piles of old *Lancet*s and coffee cups and listening to the distant rattle of instruments and the anaesthetist's booming voice as he soothed his patient into acceptance of mask and ether, and shook his head at his own behaviour, not finding himself at all an attractive person. Though it isn't all my fault, is it? he asked himself, self-pity rising in a comforting tide. If Lee hadn't been so – well, the way she had been those first years after we married, it would have been different. If she hadn't been so obsessed with her own longing for children that she had shut him out, if she had been all a new wife should have been instead of sending him, as she undoubtedly had, headfirst into Katy Lackland's arms – but now he refused to think of himself and his affairs another moment. With Katy Lackland back in London and likely to fall under his feet at some family function or other any day now such thinking was dangerous. As dangerous as thinking about Charlotte Lucas, so he would think instead about something else.

Like the difficult bypass of the duodenum he was about to do. A jejunal anastomosis demanded great skill and concentration; he had plenty of the first, and it was now up to him to make sure he supplied enough of the latter. And he pulled his cotton theatre suit into more comfortable creases, tied his mask over his mouth and nose, and went into the anteroom to scrub up. Later today he would come back to the matter of Charlotte Lucas. One way or another he'd find a way through that young woman's absurd defences. One way or another.

3

In the boardroom cigarette smoke was beginning to wreathe around the ceiling, wrapping its tendrils round the handsome plaster work and muffling the fading colours even more than the long years of the War had done, when no one could possibly justify spending time and money and effort on mere repainting. Lee tried not to cough, not wanting to seem to be criticizing the smokers, but it wasn't easy, and she blinked down at the papers in front of her, trying to concentrate. But it was hard because Brodie's voice was so very soporific. He was droning on still about the costs the hospital had had to meet in the past three months, since the last meeting of the Governors; about the price of drugs and bandages and sheets and blankets, when, that was, they were able to get them, for the Ministry of Supply had been less than helpful – and now a note of indignation crept into his voice – in spite of the fact that they had lost so much of their stock when the flying bomb had made such a mess of the pathology and pharmacy block.

'We shall have to find more money, I'm afraid, a lot more money, if we're to avoid the need to close down a ward, or even two. I do all I can to make ends meet, but even I can't manage the impossible. With most of our original legacies running out – after all it's over a hundred years since we were founded and excellent as some of our benefactors were, and their gifts well administered, nothing lasts for ever – well, money is hard to come by. Unless we get a sizable injection of new funds the patient, poor old Nellie's, you know – the patient is liable to take a very nasty turn for the worse.'

And rather incongruously he giggled at his own joke and then sat and stared lugubriously at them as they stared back or shuffled their papers and tried to absorb what all the numbers he had thrown at them actually meant.

'Closing wards is, of course, out of the question,' Max said

18

after a while, as no one else seemed inclined to say anything. 'We have waiting lists for operations, I'm told, and that is something I can't imagine we can possibly tolerate for longer than we must. It's high time the old block was rebuilt anyway – we lost the whole of our isolation unit with that bomb, didn't we? – so it's really a matter of some urgency, if our finances are as parlous as Brodie tells us they are.'

'I'm not prone to exaggerating, Dr Lackland.' Brodie seemed to bridle, and Max shook his head at once.

'I wasn't suggesting you are, Brodie. I'm just saying – look, have you a total of our needs? How much must we have to rebuild the pathology block? And how much to replace the missing linen and so forth? Tell me that and I'll have a go at the Ministry about it – I've one or two friends there – and add on a moiety for some redecorating. The War's been over long enough now – no more excuses. So, how much, Brodie? Err on the side of extravagance so that we really know what we're up against.'

Brodie sniffed, consideringly, clearly enjoying the attention he was getting and Molloy threw a look of pure hatred at him and said loudly, 'I venture to suggest that whatever Mr Brodie considers enough we add at least fifteen per cent. I personally know of all sorts of expenses still outstanding that he hasn't even mentioned. There are some new types of trolleys we could use very well here, and some developments in the surgical instrument line that Mr Harry Lackland has been telling me about, and that I'd like to see us getting. After all, this is *Nellie*'s, not one of your tuppeny ha'penny establishments! We ought to be at the forefront of modern ideas, not equipped like some second-rate cottage hospital – '

'Of course I can't be made responsible for every – ah – exaggerated notion of justifiable expense that other people round the hospital think reasonable. I'm just a simple bursar, concerned with the realities of day-to-day costs in these hard times – '

'Yes, yes,' Sir Lewis said irritably, rousing himself at last from what had seemed to be a light sleep. 'Let's have some hard numbers, man, some hard numbers. We're well capable of deciding for ourselves what we need and what we don't need to buy. So, how much?'

'You'll not get much change out of twenty-five thousand

pounds,' Brodie said baldly and leaned back in his chair, well satisfied with the effect he had had, knowing he had shocked them as they stared at him, even Molloy, blankly.

'Twenty-five thousand pounds?' Lee said after a long silence. 'My dear man, where on earth are we to get that sort of money?'

'You asked me what we needed,' Brodie said. 'That is what we need. With the fifteen per cent addition Mr Molloy here suggested. And even then, as I say, it won't go as far as it might – even without any crackpot spending of the sort that so often afflicts us.' And he shot a malicious grin at Molloy.

A little hubbub broke out as the Governors assured each other that it was quite out of the question to attempt to raise so enormous an amount, until Sir Lewis banged his gavel again and they subsided and he sat and glared at them from beneath his hedge of eyebrows.

'Twenty-five thousand pounds,' he said consideringly. 'Hmm. A lot. But not impossible.'

'Not impossible, Father?' Max said, startled. 'Of course it is! Where on earth are we to – '

'Pooh,' Sir Lewis said airily. 'I've a few pounds of my own I've not much to do with. Nothing to do with people's inheritances, of course – ' And he coughed, embarrassed, and looked at his son briefly and then at Johanna and then down at the gavel in his twisted old hand. 'That's all settled, d'you see, trusts and so forth. No, I've some left over from income. I live low on the hog, don't you know. Abstemious, that's me, and I've more cash around than I need. I'll give five thousand to any pathology block fund. As long as we can see how to get the rest of it – '

There was another little hubbub as the Governors, with the exception of Max and Johanna, broke into another rattle of talk, this time of thanks and admiration for their Chairman, and the old man shook his head and said irritably, 'I said, it's only there if we can raise the rest. I'm not about to throw money away – never was. But it's there for you if you can find the other twenty thousand – so it's up to you. What are you going to do?'

'I'm not sure what we can do – ' Max began and then Lee coughed, a little shyly, and said, 'I went to the theatre last night.'

20

Max turned and stared at her, puzzled, and she went a little pink and said quickly, 'That's not as silly as it sounds – let me explain. It was for the war orphans – you know that charity my friend Hannah Lammeck does some work for? It's to find homes and so forth for children whose parents were killed in the War, especially those in the Blitz. Her husband was killed, you see, and – well, anyway, she gave me tickets for a benefit night last night. It was rather good – singers and comedians mostly, but very agreeable. And I'm told that it raised almost eight thousand pounds! Well, if we could do something like that, only perhaps bigger, and raise ten thousand, say, then we could do the other things we do – flag days and appeals and so on and perhaps manage the rest of it. Didn't someone say that the year before the War the appeals we had made fifteen thousand pounds and that was enough to keep them ticking over for the next two years, until we got those special wartime allowances from the Government? Well, couldn't we do that again?'

'It sounds a good idea, Lee, but really, it's enormously difficult,' Johanna said dubiously. 'I heard about that show you saw last night. Any number of people were trying to get me to buy tickets and I did contribute. I paid for a page in the programme – you know the sort of thing – but they all said that it was taking ages to get the work done and that poor Letty was run off her feet with it and – '

'Letty?' Max said, lifting his head.

'Letty Lackland produced it, did all the direction and so forth,' Lee said. 'I should have said that, I suppose. I'm sorry. Anyway, she did, and that was another thing I thought about – I mean, I know she's not a Nellie's person, but she is a Lackland and – ' And then, as she caught a look exchanged between Molloy and Brodie, she reddened and stopped.

'I doubt she'd do another show all on her own again,' Johanna said. 'I'm sorry to sound dreary, Lee darling, but I do know she was so exhausted and she's getting on a bit, after all. She was almost retired, wasn't she? To ask her to do this for us, so soon after the one you saw last night – '

'She wouldn't have to do it on her own,' Sir Lewis said and they turned to look at him. He was sitting much more upright than he had been all morning, and staring down the table with his old eyes glittering a little and Max thought – he's not looked as excited as that for years – and was puzzled. Until the old man said, in a rather high voice, 'I dare say Peter'd be glad enough to help her, hey Max? If we asked him, explained the problems?' And then Max understood.

'It's possible, Father,' he said cautiously. 'You can't be sure of course. But it might be worth a try –' And his father looked at him with a sudden watery glint in his eye and Max felt his throat tighten. Dear old man, who loved all his children so very much, and was so distressed about Peter –

Not that they weren't all distressed about Peter. He had gone off to Europe just before the War had started, and disappeared into silence. A few letters and cards had arrived for the first few months, and then, just before the Germans marched into Poland, there had been a terse postcard to Sir Lewis that had said only that he was well, that he wouldn't be able to write for some time, and please not to worry, he'd come back when he could, but for heaven's sake to make no searches for him and do nothing till they heard from him.

And then nothing, not a whisper, not a message, never a letter, and the years had drifted away as the War had gone grinding on its course and the old man had grieved and fretted and seemed physically to diminish as he obeyed his youngest son's command and did nothing about making enquiries about him. But he had been convinced throughout even the very darkest days of the War when it seemed that the whole of Europe was overrun by the German armies, like a byre full of plague rats, that Peter was alive and would come home. One day.

And so he had, walking almost casually into his father's house in Leinster Terrace late in the autumn of 1945, as though he had never gone away. But he had gone away, and come back a very different Peter. Taciturn to the point of surliness, thin and grey and a little stooped, he looked not much younger than his own father and certainly a great deal older than his brother Max, who was in fact his senior by some four years, and flatly refused to say anything at all about what he had been doing.

That it had something to do with the German persecution of the Jews they knew; Lee had been able to tell them that much, for she and Peter had worked together to rescue just one of them the year before the War, the child who was now her

22

much loved adopted son Michael, but even she had not been able to tell them much. That Peter had probably been helping to get Jews out via some sort of underground was her surmise, and that was all they had, Sir Lewis and Max and Johanna, to help them when they looked at the wreck of the youngest member of their family; the knowledge that he had done some incredible work, performed some unbelievable actions and was now in need of love and peace and – what else they could not know.

But Sir Lewis fretted and worried over that question and looking at his eager face at the head of the Board of Governors' table at Nellie's this morning Max could see that he believed he had an answer. Well, he thought, maybe he has. Peter does need to do something, anything to keep him occupied. For the past months, since he had returned to London, he had sat around the Leinster Terrace house, reading, playing interminable Patience but mostly just staring into the distance, silent and alone. To get him out of that was essential, and the psychiatrist in Max lifted with hope as he grasped his father's train of thought and he nodded vigorously.

'I agree. We'll talk to Letty about the possibility of a Benefit of some sort, and suggest to her that she'll need help and see what we can do to see she gets it. Will you talk to her, Lee? You saw last night's affair, so you'll know better than any one of us what it is we're asking – '

'Tell her it's got to include Peter, won't you, Lee?' Sir Lewis said urgently and his voice was sharper than it had been all morning. 'It's important, that – '

'Of course I will,' Lee said, gently, as aware as any of the family of Peter and his needs, and the amount of distress the old man felt about him. 'And I'm sure Letty will be delighted. She's very fond of Peter, and of course she knows as well as we do – anyway, I'll telephone her tonight. And I'll let you know what she says – '

'If we are to agree that we are to try to raise this money,' Brodie said loudly, 'we really must do it all constitutionally. We're all delighted, of course, that the family feels able to do so much, but all the same we really must have a proper subcommittee and plan it all as it should be planned. I dare say you could all do it on your own – ' And he managed another forced little laugh. 'You have a long history in the family of

23

making things happen, this very hospital for a start, but all the same – a subcommittee, I'd venture to suggest, Sir Lewis – '

'Yes, well, as you wish, Brodie. Just propose the motion, put it to the vote, we'll do it all as it should be done. I'll give you five thousand for the fund, Mrs Harry here will set about starting a Benefit Night and you can get on with your usual appeals and flag days and so forth. Who's to sit on this subcommittee then – '

The remainder of the members of the Board who had clearly felt somewhat excluded from the discussion of ways and means into which the Lacklands had launched themselves now became very animated and Max leaned back in his chair and watched them a little sardonically as they began to jockey for places on the subcommittee, all trying to get themselves nominated without actually offering so that they could put on a show of polite diffidence and be coaxed to accept, and thought about his father's scheme for Peter.

It was an excellent one, and he only hoped it would work. Because if it didn't, and Peter refused to be pulled out of his clearly desperately deep slough of despond, something more active would have to be done, whether Peter liked it or not. It was one thing to leave a man who had clearly suffered a great deal in peace to lick his wounds and recover; quite another to allow him to crawl into a hole and rot. If he refuses this, Max thought, I'll have to start to bully him. One way or another we'll get Peter sorted out, and he sketched a faint wink at his father and then looked at his watch.

'I'll have to go, I'm afraid,' he announced as the talk sagged for a moment. 'I'm not available for the subcommittee so you don't need me, and I do have to go to a special Board for a patient, so if you'll excuse me – ' And he collected his papers together and made for the door.

'Dine tonight, m'boy?' Sir Lewis grunted at him as he passed his chair and Max nodded.

'If I can, Father, I'll telephone. Depends on how the day goes.'

'Good. You're looking better –' And Max realized suddenly that for the past hour he had thought of many things, but never once of Emilia and a great wash of guilt filled him and he nodded sharply at the old man and made for the door as fast as he could.

Damn him, damn him, damn him for a stupid old fool. Why had he had to say that, to remind him? And the guilt flooded up again, this time for his anger at his father and as he closed the door behind him he managed a wry grin. He really was becoming fit to be one of his own cases, with such waves of absurd and irrational feeling overwhelming him and he shook his head at himself and then turned to make his way to the stairs. He had work to do, thank God, and that would sort him out –

His secretary came panting up the stairs towards him as he reached the end of them, her face quite puffed up with the importance of her message and he looked at her with his usual mixture of irritation and gratitude. She really was incredibly efficient and helpful; if only she wasn't also so doggedly adoring and pompous, and he schooled his face carefully and said as colourlessly as he could, 'Yes, Miss Curtis? A message?'

'That Board, sir – they've had to postpone for an hour. I told them they'd be ruining your entire day, that you had a great many appointments all carefully slotted in, but they were adamant, really adamant. They have to wait for this wretched man from the War Office, it seems, and he's tied up, so there's nothing they can do – I was very terse with them, I can tell you. Very terse. But there it is – '

'Have I got so many appointments?' he asked and she pursed her mouth and smirked slightly. 'Well, actually, sir, it's not as bad as it might be. Your next is a call out to Friern for Dr Samuelson, who wants a second opinion on that schizophrenic child, so it could be worse. But still, it's not right to mess you about that way –'

'Then I could go back to the boardroom I suppose – ' Max said, hesitating. To go and sit in his office and do his letters, as he would have to do some time in the next week, was possible, but suddenly the thought of being confined up there with Miss Curtis fussing round him was more than he could bear.

'Well, one of the registrars wanted to talk to you,' Miss Curtis said unwillingly, finding it going deeply against the grain to oblige Miss Lucas but knowing Max's moods well enough to realize that there was no way she would get him to come and do his letters, as she wanted. 'She's in Spruce, I believe – said she wanted to talk to you about one of her patients –'

'Miss Lucas?' Max brightened. 'Oh, well, that's settled then. I won't go back to the boardroom. I'll be in Spruce till it's time for the Board, Miss Curtis, and then there'll be lunch and then I'll be on my way to Friern and Dr Samuelson. You can leave as early as you like. I won't be back here till Monday morning.' And he went away towards Spruce leaving Miss Curtis alone and yearning at the top of the stairs.

One of these days I'll have to replace her, he was thinking. Poor soul sees my widowed state as altogether too interesting and I can't cope with that for long. And again the guilt rose in him as he thought of Emilia and irritably he pushed the ward doors open and went in search of the surgical registrar.

'I see,' Max said at length, and put down the chart, centring it neatly on Sister's desk. 'I see. A reactive depression following injury – not unusual. I've dealt with a great many similar cases this past few years, Miss Lucas.' Including myself, he thought, looking down at the chart. Isn't that my problem? A reactive depression after the appalling injury of losing Emilia? 'I doubt you need worry unduly. He'll recover in time. There's little I or any other psychiatrist can do to hasten that recovery, I'm afraid. Patience has to be the only prescription.'

'I haven't given you the whole picture, I think, sir,' Charlie said carefully, and reached for the notes. 'Perhaps I didn't write it as clearly as I might have done, and – '

He put out his hand and stopped her before she could reach them. 'Never mind the notes, Miss Lucas. You tell me, in your own words, why it is that you're so worried about this young man. His case doesn't seem to me to be so severe, nor is his injury sufficient to justify the significance you give it, unless that photograph is a particularly poor one. I thought it seemed clear enough. Of course I'll look at the man myself in a moment, but meanwhile – *is* the injury so very disfiguring, do you believe?'

'Perhaps not to you or to me, sir,' Charlie said and pushed her hands into the pockets of her white coat, so that he wouldn't notice how tightly she had them clenched. It was getting more and more difficult to get the importance of the situation across without telling him why she was so worried; yet she'd promised Brin she wouldn't do that; it had been medically wrong to make such a promise, but it was understandable that he should demand it and – she took a deep breath and looked up at Max.

'The thing is, sir, that he's an actor. You must know quite a lot about him actually – after all, he is a relation of yours and – '

Max laughed suddenly. 'We're a large clan, my dear, and I sometimes think that half London is related to us! Let me see, who is this chap? I know his name of course, but not all his links with the family – '

'I think he's a distant cousin of yours, sir. His sister is Katy Lackland, the actress, you know? His home is in Yorkshire – I mean, that's where his father lives, and he has another sister and brothers there, but now he lives in London, or has since he started on his career as an actor. That was just before the War. Well, he was in that flying bomb raid that did so much damage to the Regent Palace Hotel. Do you remember? It caused rather more fuss than usual because there was a direct hit and –'

'I remember,' Max said, his voice expressionless. Emilia, he thought, his voice screaming inside his head. Emilia, buying me a shirt. 'Well, he was in that raid. And then what?'

'A piece of shrapnel of some kind, sir. Caught his cheek on the right. There was a good deal of contamination with brick dust and other debris and though the wound was carefully cleaned at the time – once they got him out, that is, and that took several hours – and it was tolerably well stitched, there is a degree of keloid about the scar. He's got some shrinkage of the musculature so that his smile has been altered – the corner of the mouth on the right lifts slightly – '

And when it does, a little voice deep in her mind whispered, when it does, your belly turns over.

'– and there's a slight pull on the eye on that side. You may not think it all that bad, and it wouldn't be perhaps if he were anything but what he is. Doctor, lawyer, Indian chief – their faces don't matter so much. But an actor?'

'I've seen some actors with less than perfect faces,' Max said drily. 'And I believe that there are some who make an excellent living mainly because they have rather odd faces, rather than because they have perfect ones.'

'Perhaps they were born with such looks and learned to get used to them,' Charlie said. 'Brin – Mr Lackland – started out with considerable good looks and regarded them as a definite asset to his career. He's now lost them because of this injury and the effect has been to make him very – to cause considerable disturbance.'

Max looked at her shrewdly. 'Tried to do some damage to

himself, has he?'

She went scarlet. 'How did you – I mean, I really can't – '

Max shook his head, amused at her naïvety. 'My dear girl, you really must give me some credit for having experience in my own speciality! I've been called in by more surgeons and dermatologists and what-have-yous because their depressed patients have made a suicide bid and listened to them waffling around the issue in a state of sheer funk, terrified I'm going to call in the police and have them hauled off to court. But do be reasonable, my dear! I'm a psychiatrist, one who is concerned with the psychological well-being of my patients. I'm the last person to help the police uphold a law I consider appalling! I've kept the police at arms' length in more attempted suicide cases than you've removed appendices. So let's stop making silly evasions and get this story sorted out properly. What did he do?'

'He swallowed a handful of Nembutal.'

'How many?'

'I'm not sure. He was rather vague about it. I was on duty late one night and I went to do a ward round and – '

Went to do a ward round? jeered the little voice inside her mind. Went to see him, you mean. You're besotted with him and that was why you were on duty late, just for the chance of seeing him.

'I was doing a late round,' she said more loudly, looking very directly at Max, aware of her still heightened colour and furious with herself because of it. 'And I went to the ward to see him. I'd been trying to do a neatening of the mucous membrane inside the mouth and was going to see if we could reassess the possibility of excising the keloid to tidy his scar, and that was why he was in the ward. I found him very dozy and – ' She swallowed. 'He was flushed and agitated and I asked him why he was in such a state and he told me he'd been saving up his Nembutal because he was so unhappy and – '

She stopped and stared down at the floor. How could she tell the hard-faced man sitting there looking at her so coolly how she had felt when it had all happened? How there had been that lurch of sheer terror as she had looked down on that flushed face she loved so much and seen the tears in those dark eyes, and how her hands had shaken as she had pulled back the covers and unbuttoned his pyjama jacket so that she could set

29

the bell of her stethoscope to his chest?

His heart had been pounding strongly but dreadfully fast, and she had stood there listening, trying to remember all she had learned about how to treat people who swallowed overdoses, aware all the time of the trouble there would be if anyone knew what he had done. Attempted suicide was a crime. How often had she seen patients in Nellie's wards with policemen sitting stolidly beside their beds, watching them in case they tried to commit their pathetic little crime again? How often had she heard of people being discharged from hospital to be taken to stand in the box at court to trot out their pathetic little tales of desolation and despair to a bored magistrate? Far too often, and she wasn't going to let it happen to Brin.

She had told the night nurse on duty – happily a rather foolish girl, not given to thinking much about what she was told to do – that she was taking Mr Lackland down to the theatre for some special dressings she wanted to do, and had demanded a wheelchair for him, and with the nurse's help had got him out of bed and safely out of the ward. And then had spent the rest of the night walking him up and down to keep him awake, feeding him with stimulants and doing all she could to make him see how unnecessary it was to be so desperate. His face wasn't so dreadful, really it wasn't, she had told him over and over again till she was hoarse with saying it, as she dragged his weary drooping body from one side of the small operating theatre to the other, praying all the time that no one would come and see them, no one would push the door open and demand to know what she was doing there. '– really, your face is a splendid face. No need to be so despairing about it. No need at all –'

And at last he had emerged from his dazed sleepiness and she had been able to take him back to his bed in Spruce Ward to sleep off his exhaustion, while she had had to spend the day walking through her usual work in a state of total confusion about her patient. What was she to do with and for him? She just didn't know, and that had been when she had decided that the time had come to call in an expert – but not to tell him why. Brin had begged her, with tears in his eyes again, to keep his foolish behaviour a secret and she had of course promised – but now this man with the direct gaze had got it out of her and – it took every atom of control she had not to let her own eyes fill with tears.

'I see,' Max said. 'A fairly florid but hardly life-threatening episode.'

Her brows snapped together. 'I beg your pardon?'

'You say he'd swallowed a lot of barbiturate, but since he is still, I gather, with us, and you say nothing about having needed to wash out the stomach, the overdose must have been minimal.'

'It took me several hours of walking him about and pouring coffee into him to make sure he had stayed awake,' Charlie said stiffly. 'So – '

'Oh, my dear, you've seen too many of these Hollywood films! The treatment of overdosage with noxious substances is rather less dramatic and a good deal more messy. If he survived the night of walking with you and then slept off the drug – as I imagine he did – '

'He slept for most of the next day and night – '

'I imagine he did. But for all that I doubt he took more than enough to alarm you, but certainly not enough to do any long-term harm. What is it he's trying to persuade you to do?'

Charlie was very angry now and she knew it showed and didn't care. 'I don't think, Dr Lackland, that you can make quite so firm a judgement till you've at least talked to the patient. It seems to me rather to be jumping to conclusions to – however, I'm sorry I bothered you. I shall deal with him in my own way, and can only ask you now to – to honour my request for confidentiality,' and she got to her feet.

Max shook his head and lifted his brows at her. 'Oh, come, my dear, no need to be so touchy! All right, I accept your rebuke. I should indeed see the patient before making any judgements. I was leaning a little more than I have any right to on my previous experience. Very well, lead me to him and we shall talk again. I'll see him on my own, I think, after you introduce me – '

'It's really not necessary –' Charlie began but he interrupted her, albeit gently.

'Now, I have apologized, so please, let us not be absurd over this. Which bed is he in?'

'Seventeen,' Charlie said unwillingly. 'But – '

'Then lead the way, Miss Lucas, and we shall consult over

your patient', and he moved towards the door of Sister's office and held it invitingly open for her.

She hadn't felt so self-conscious walking down a ward since her very first day out of medical school when, resplendent in the shiny new short white coat of a first-year clinical student, she had joined the rest of her set on their first round. The men lay in their beds, neatly and quietly, as well schooled as any soldiers, for Sister Spruce was a martinet in matters of neatness – woe betide any patient who lay about in sloppy postures on her ward – but they watched with interest all that went on around them, unless they were too ill to care; and there weren't many in that state, for this was a surgical ward and most of the inmates were lively enough, unlike those on medical wards. Charlie felt their eyes on her and her companion very keenly indeed. Did they realize that this stocky man with the still face and the square shoulders was a psychiatrist? It would be dreadful if they did make such a guess, for there could not be one among them who did not share the all-too-common belief that there was a stigma in having something wrong with your mind. Brin would never forgive her, she thought, if the other patients guessed and treated him differently in consequence.

But none of the men seemed to pay her companion any attention at all. It was herself they were interested in, and she managed to relax a little as she went on down that interminably long ward beside Max Lackland. Of course she was being silly; these men cared only about their own health, and she, as the registrar who was responsible for this ward, was a person of consequence in their eyes. They wondered, each and every one of them, if she was coming to their bedside; once they realized she wasn't, their interest switched back to their newspapers and magazines and library books. So by the time she reached Brin's bed and reached for the curtains to pull them round to offer some semblance of privacy, she was once more in command of her own anxiety.

'Good morning, Brin,' she said. 'This is – '

He was lying against a pile of pillows, a newspaper open on his lap in front of him but quite unheeded, his hair a little rumpled so that a loose lock of it lay on his forehead, and his pyjama jacket partially unbuttoned. His skin looked a pleasant brown against the white of his pillows, and his eyes glowed

32

even more darkly. He looked in fact absurdly well to be occupying a hospital bed and her lips curved involuntarily at the sight of him because he looked so agreeable.

'You don't have to introduce us, Charlie,' he said and his voice, as ever, sent a small tremor of pleasure into her; it was a rich deep baritone with a lift of laughter in it, and was one of his greatest assets, a fact she suspected he well knew. 'We met on VE night, sir, do you remember? My sister Kate and I were invited to your sister's house to dine and you were there as well and –'

'Yes, of course, I remember,' Max said, his voice relaxed and friendly. 'Not that I was feeling too festive, as I recall. Still, we had to mark the occasion in some way, I suppose. I'm sorry to see you here as a customer of the family hospital.'

'I – I'm not all that thrilled about it myself, sir. But –' And he lifted his right hand and touched his cheek and then let his hand fall on to his counterpane again, never taking his eyes from Max's face. It was a relaxed and unexaggerated gesture, but a very effective one, for it said more than any words could have done. There was pain in that small movement of the arm, and anger and ruefulness and tears and attempted bravery, all wrapped up together, and Charlie felt her lips tighten as she saw it. How could anyone doubt for a moment how much this man was torn apart by his disfigurement? Whatever it seemed like to others, to him it was a massive blow and he needed all the aid he could be given to deal with it.

'You're here for treatment of that scar?' Max said, brutally breaking the small spell that Brin had managed to cast and leaned forwards to stare at the right cheek. The scar indeed looked startling there, a much lighter colour than the surrounding skin and rather thick and raised from the surface of the face. It ran from the corner of the eye which it dragged down slightly, giving his face on that side a rather comically lugubrious look, to the corner of the mouth which, while it seemed natural enough in repose, twisted a little incongruously when Brin spoke, and even more when he smiled.

'I hope so,' Brin said, still keeping his eyes fixed on Max's face. 'I hope the scar could be made less – bulky. Charlie thought it might be possible to remove the overgrowth and leave a finer, less raised, line. I – what do you think?'

'I'm not a plastic surgeon,' Max said. 'My opinion is

33

worthless on such a matter.'

'But you must agree it needs doing?' Brin's voice had sharpened.

'Nothing surgical *needs* doing, unless it's life-threatening,' Max said mildly. 'You may *want* to have it done, but that is a different matter –'

'It's essential that it should be done!' Brin said and now he was speaking more loudly and Charlie shook her head at him in covert warning, very aware of the rest of the patients listening eagerly on the other side of the curtains. In a long dull hospital day, any activity was of interest. Brin caught the warning and spoke more quietly. 'Of course it's essential,' he said, and the lowering of his voice made him sound a little sulky. 'I would have thought anyone could see that. It's the most essential thing in my life right now, I can tell you that.'

'Yes,' Max said consideringly and after a moment sat down on the edge of the bed. 'Would you leave us, Miss Lucas? I think it might be better if I talk to Mr Lackland quietly for a while. Perhaps you could wait for me in Sister's office? I'll try not to keep you too long.'

'Of course,' she said. 'Brin, you can be quite – honest with Dr Lackland, you know. He – we all treat all of our patients in total confidence.' Listen to what I'm saying, Brin, her silent voice was crying in her mind, listen to what I'm saying, and trust him. I can't help you if you don't help me and anyone I bring to see you. Listen to me –

'Thank you Charlie,' he said, but he was still looking at Max and after a moment she pulled the curtain aside, ready to leave them.

'I'm sure I can persuade our patient of our shared concern for him, Miss Lucas,' Max said, and his voice was very level. 'You really don't have to give me a reference, you know!' and she caught her breath at the rebuke, again feeling like a raw new student, who had made a stupid answer to a simple question.

'Of course,' she said stiffly and this time she did go, letting the curtain drop behind her, but not before looking swiftly at Brin once more. But he wasn't looking at her at all. All his attention was fixed on Max and she felt bleak and lonely as she finally went away up the ward, leaving the two men together. She wanted Brin to feel better, to come to terms with his

34

injury in such a way that he would never again do anything as dreadful as he had the other night with those sleeping-pills, but she wasn't sure that she wanted any other doctor but herself to be the one to make him whole again. And that was a dreadful way for a doctor to be.

5

'Coffee?' Johanna said hopefully as at last the meeting broke up. 'Lee? You do agree that we need some sustenance of some sort to get us over that? Will you join me? We might manage to get something over at the Savoy.'

'Oh,' Lee said uncertainly and bit her lip. 'I'm not sure – I thought perhaps I'd see if I could find Harry, and then – well, it's almost lunchtime and –'

Johanna shook her head at her, smiling gently. 'Don't, my dear. I used to do things like that. It never made any difference. Made it worse, actually.'

Lee lifted her chin with a slightly defiant little gesture. 'I don't know what you mean, Jo –'

'Oh, darling, of course you do. This is me, Johanna, remember? Jonty's wife. If I don't know what it's like to be in your shoes, who does? I stood in them so long myself, after all –'

Lee couldn't look at her, keeping her head bent over her hands as she fiddled in her bag. She knew that Johanna was right, of course; it never helped to go after Harry, to seem to show an awareness of what he was doing. Oh, he'd be friendly enough if she tracked him down, charming even, but he'd tell her he couldn't have lunch, *so* sorry, *much* too busy, and would go off to sit and share his meal in the common room with whoever was young and female on the medical staff, while she went home alone to eat a meagre sandwich in the nursery with Stella, knowing he was snubbing her, and knowing too that *he* knew he need do nothing to comfort her. Because wouldn't she go on being sweet and good, refusing to make any sort of fuss, refusing to let him know how hurt she was by his silly philandering ways?

That was the trouble between them of course. Both knew the other so well that they could judge to a nicety what reaction would follow which action, and neither could bring themselves to talk about what had happened to them. There had been a time, once, when their closeness had warmed them both, but that had all seemed to dissolve into emptiness once Stella had been born. His interest in the children had dwindled as hers had grown and now they were like strangers, remote yet appallingly familiar, sharing a bed, sharing lovemaking too from time to time, but never sharing their real feelings or their real needs. It was a lonely way to be.

Now she lifted her eyes and caught Johanna's limpid sympathetic gaze and felt her lips tighten. Johanna looked dreadful, of course, old before her time and quite devastated; everyone knew that and said as much to each other in hushed tones, sympathizing in her widowed state and her obvious grief, but sometimes Lee couldn't help but wonder if, in a sense, Johanna didn't glory in her situation. Jonty dead was all her own, unlike Jonty alive, for then she had to share him with any number of women. And how she had hated that, and how she had fussed and wept and fussed again, so that everyone in the family knew of it. But now, she fussed no more, going about in her black clothes looking dreadful and yet somehow contented in her sadness; and Lee took in a sharp little breath through her nose and castigated herself for being so uncharitable. Of course Johanna mourned her Jonty wholeheartedly and of course she wished to have him back, even if he had been so cruel to her and so busy about other women's skirts. To think otherwise was to be very unkind indeed.

'All right,' she said impulsively, 'I'll come with you. Then we can talk about what this Benefit is to be and make plans. I could try to phone Letty from the Savoy, come to think of it, and perhaps go and see her this afternoon. Nanny is taking Stella to a friend for tea and then meeting Sally after school, and Michael's playing rugger till six, and I can be home well before that, so there's no reason why I shouldn't –'

'Lovely!' Johanna said. 'And I'm not meeting Claudia till after she finishes at the showroom, which probably won't be till after four. We have a cocktail party to go to at her future mother-in-law's hotel. She's in town for the weekend. Frightful woman, never stops talking about her war work with the evacuees – as though we didn't all do as much as we could – but there it is – Claudia wants me to go. So go I shall, but let's see if we can get some lunch at the Savoy. What do you say? It would be such a treat –'

'If we can get a table,' Lee said. 'It's getting impossible to get anything these days – I swear it's worse now than it was when the War was on – but by all means, let's try. How is Claudia? Is it a good match? Is she happy?'

'It's a lovely match,' Johanna said warmly, as they made their way down the stairs. 'He's a dear chap, and *very* eligible, from an old family. His place is in Norfolk and his father's made a very good thing of farming the estate all through the years, so Edward's come home to something worth while, not like some poor ex-officers. They've got a few thousand acres up there and Claudia says his father's been quite clever with money, so it's nice to know she's all right. With Jolly so set on medicine and no intention at all, as far as I can tell, of ever trying to make any fortunes, it's good to know I needn't worry about darling Claudia.'

'Oh, Johanna, my dear, you do sound so very old-fashioned! As if anyone these days worried about people marrying money! I was just wondering if Claudia was really happy – not whether she was doing well for herself. Though I suppose it's something she's getting married at all, as far as I can tell. Have you heard Barbara Burns going on about her two girls? Both in the WAAFs and had the most racketty time imaginable and certainly not intending to settle down now the fun's over, and Beattie Cowper is saying the same thing about her girl. And yet here's you sounding just like my darling Mamma used to about me, always going on about marrying well and how much money was there and –'

'She was right to worry,' Johanna said a little sharply as they came out into the rain of Endell Street and began to busy themselves with umbrellas. 'Getting a girl nicely settled is important. Wait till your two are of an age, and you'll see! You'll worry just as much as anyone else. Mothers always do.'

'I dare say you're right.' They began to walk, picking their way over the puddles. 'It's just that the War seems to have changed so many things – all the things that used to seem right everyone questions now and nothing seems sure any more and black's white and white's red and –'

'It's only surface change,' Johanna said sapiently. 'Just as it was after the last War, when everyone went wild on Armistice

Night and then the girls were a bit rebellious for a few months, and wanted to go on working and so forth, but it all went back to normal soon enough. Don't you remember?'

'Not really,' Lee said, as they stopped on the kerb of Long Acre, waiting till the traffic gave them space to cross to James Street so that they could push their way through Covent Garden to the Strand. Neither of them had even considered the possibility of finding a taxi, rare as gold dust these busy days, and they stood and stared across at the gaps in the buildings across the street, glad of the respite as they waited for the chance to move on. 'Not really. It seems like a different world, the past. I don't think I was ever there, not really. It's like I dreamed it.' She stopped, staring blank-eyed across the street, and then laughed. 'It looks the way Sally looks when she smiles.'

'Mmm?' Johanna peered at her under the edge of her umbrella. 'What was that?'

'The street, with those gaps. Like Sally's teeth, all blank. Odd really. I can't remember how that used to be either. It's as though it was always like this, all battered and ugly —'

'It won't stay that way for long,' Johanna said and pulled on Lee's arm as a space appeared in the traffic. 'Jolly never stops talking about what this Government's going to do, rebuilding and nationalizing and heaven knows what else. To listen to him it's going to be heaven on earth in no time, and everyone healthy and beautiful and no one needing doctors at all, except to advise them on staying well. He's quite embarrassing sometimes, he's such a supporter of that dreary little Attlee man.' She laughed then as they reached the other side and plunged into the narrow streets that led them towards Covent Garden. 'He says that people like us will be swept aside once it all happens. No more Boards of Governors, he says, no more lady bountifuls running things. Nellie's will belong to the patients and we won't get a look in. Dear Jolly,' she ended fondly. 'So silly sometimes! Not far now, thank the Lord. My feet are killing me. Heavens, what a stench of onions!'

'Apples too,' Lee said as they rounded the corner and came at last into the marketplace, where a few late porters were still sweeping up and the last fruit and vegetables were being loaded onto the vans. 'Oh, Johanna, do you remember how it used to be here? Pineapples and bananas and oranges and —'

'And roses and lilies and all sorts of exotic flowers from France and –'

'– And you could get all the fish and meat you wanted and butter and cheeses too, and all sorts of goodies and –'

'And you're going to make yourself so hungry you'll burst into tears when you see what the Savoy has to offer you for your five bob's-worth!' Johanna said and laughed again. 'The sooner they put an end to all that nonsense the better. I used to think rationing would end when the War did. Foolish me!'

'Foolish you indeed,' Lee said and tucked her hand into her cousin's arm as they hurried down Southampton Street towards the dryness and comfort of the Savoy, which even in these difficult times managed to produce a semblance of luxury for its beleaguered guests. Even a spartan post-war lunch seemed worth eating when you ate it in the Savoy Grill, and both women felt their spirits rise as they hurried there.

Katy had been sitting in the lobby for half an hour when she saw them arrive. She had been nursing her sherry for as long as she could, not wanting to have another before lunch if she could help it. Even in these days of shortages of food and drink you had to be careful of your shape; she'd noticed a most distressing tendency to thicken around the jawline and the middle these past few months, which was appalling for a girl of only thirty-two, and she had no intention of letting anything of that sort creep up on her unawares, even if it did mean having to be boring and dreary over how many drinks you had. And she took another sip from her almost empty glass and set it down again on the table beside her with a small sigh. Surely someone she knew who was fun would come pushing in through the doors soon? It was too absurd to be known all over the world as a leading film star and yet to be at so loose an end that all you could think of doing was sitting at the Savoy hoping someone agreeable would wander in. Too absurd –

And then she saw Lee and Johanna and sat very still, thinking fast. To acknowledge them or not? To attach herself to them for lunch or not? Which was worse? To be alone or to be one of a party of three women? God, how dreary *that* would be. But the decision was taken from her, as Lee glanced across in her direction and after a moment smiled in recognition.

It was a thin smile and less than spontaneous but a smile all the same, and Katy lifted one languorous hand in acknowledgement and watched as Lee said something to Johanna and the two women made their way across the crowded lobby towards her.

'My dear Lee, how good to see you, and how unexpected! I had no idea you ever frittered away your time in such gaudy spots as this!'

At once Lee felt she had been consigned to the ranks of the boring and the dull and the little spurt of anger that rose in her to add to that she had felt when she had first seen Katy sitting there, resplendent in green barathea and fox furs, made her want to turn on her heel and go. But that would have amused Katy hugely, as she well knew. So she offered instead a thin-lipped smile and said, 'I come here occasionally, when there's nothing more important to do', knowing it was a cheap little gibe that would have no effect against Katy's experience-toughened hide. After her years on the stage and in films, it would take more than Lee's rather feeble remarks to hurt that lady. And knowing that fact made Lee loathe her even more than she did, if that were possible.

'Oh, my dear, important!' Katy said and laughed, a tinkling practised sound that made people near by look round at her with interest. 'I promised myself years ago that I would pay no attention whatsoever to anything important, in my whole life, but concentrate only on what was delicious and amusing. And the Savoy is in that category. Or used to be.'

She made a little face then. 'It's threatening to become as tedious here as everywhere else, mind you. The people one sees in the place these days! Orderly-room sergeants and ATS lance-corporals, I swear, and dressed in the most ghastly clothes. You'd think people would have some decent items left from before the War, wouldn't you? One doesn't have to be a *complete* drab, if one tries.' And she glanced briefly at Johanna's heavy black dress and coat in a way that made it clear that her opinion of it was very low indeed.

'I had quite a lot of rather nice things from Schiaparelli, and some lovely Mary Bee clothes, but they were all lost when we were bombed,' Lee said, and couldn't resist the note of triumph in her voice. It was the first time that talking about the night her pretty house in St John's Wood had disappeared, in a

41

crump of high-explosive bombs that had left little more than a rubble-filled crater where London Pride and Rose Bay Willow-herb now grew, had given her any pleasure, and she revelled in it. 'So difficult, getting clothes right, isn't it? You look delightful as always of course. American, is it? A lovely costume.'

'Yes, I brought it over from California when I came last year.' Katy had the grace to look discomfited. 'Are you lunching? Perhaps we could –'

'I'm not sure,' Johanna said firmly. 'My daughter said she'd try to join us – if she can get away. So we'll have a drink and wait for her. Don't let us hold you up, though. *Do* go and have your lunch – I'd hate us to be the cause of your missing whatever they've managed to provide today –' And she smiled in a vague sort of way and nodded at Katy, and taking Lee's elbow in a tight grip led her away to the other side of the lobby.

Katy watched them go and made no attempt to join them. Miserable bitches! she thought, so sniffy and so boring. No wonder Harry had been so willing to have that fling the year before the War, just before she went to California; and her lips curved as she thought about that. Had Lee ever found out? Was that why she had been so sharp? They'd met once or twice since she'd come over last year to make that film for Letty, at dreary family affairs, but she hadn't been so edgy then. Perhaps if Harry had been there she would have shown a spark of spite then? But he never had, and now Katy let her eyes glaze as she thought about Harry.

It would serve Madam Lee right if she went to find him again after all this time; they'd been very close, the two of them, after all, and it could be fun. She had thought that perhaps he had been avoiding her, and had been amused by that, but not unduly perturbed. With a film to make and all sorts of new people to meet, she had had no need to rekindle old flames like Harry. But now the shooting was over, and the film out in the cinemas and the fun had stopped. So maybe she would, after all –

The thought of the film galvanized her into movement, and she got to her feet, pulling her fox furs around her shoulders and tucking her bag under one arm. That bloody film. Letty had promised her the moon and the stars to make the lousy

42

thing, leading lady, top billing, special privileges, massive publicity, the lot, and look what had happened. The film had had rave notices, and was doing excellent business – which was nice, considering she had a percentage of the box office receipts included in her contract – but she personally had been raked by the critics and that was far from nice. Supercilious bastards, she thought now as she made her way across the lobby towards the entrance to the Grill Room. Supercilious *English* bastards. No American critic would have dared to be so waspish about her performance. None of them would have dreamed of hauling her over the coals in that hateful fashion. But here they had, and she still stung as she thought of all they had said.

If only she hadn't signed that goddamned two-year contract! If only she could have gone straight back to Hollywood to set up a better deal the minute this fiasco was over, it wouldn't have been so bad. But as it was, here she was, stuck in bloody London where the rain never stopped and there wasn't a decent thing to eat or drink, let alone any people she could be bothered with, and another year to get through. She was making money all right; there was no shortage of that, with Letty in charge of the operation, but there was more to life than money, for God's sake. Like having the chance to spend it, and she marched into the Grill Room to eat her solitary lunch in a raging temper. But beneath her bad temper there lingered another thought. Harry Lackland. She really must winkle him out of wherever he was hiding and see what games there were to be played with him. He used to be quite good fun –

'I know,' Johanna said in a low voice as Lee faltered in what she had been saying about talking to Letty regarding the Benefit, as she watched Katy's narrow hips go swinging away, with the eyes of every man in the place following her too. 'It's maddening. Women like that ought to be – to be locked away. But never let them see they've hurt you, because when you do they only set out to hurt you more.'

Lee reddened. 'I don't know what you mean,' she said, and Johanna shook her head at her.

'I used to be just like you, blaming the women, blaming myself, blaming everyone but him. But it isn't anyone else's

43

fault, you know. Even if you did lock them away, it'd all be the same. Some men are like that – like Jonty was –'

She stopped talking and bent her head to look down at her hands and Lee looked at her and then leaned forwards and touched her wrist, impulsively.

'I know, Jo darling. Please don't let's fret about it. Men are men and – well, there it is. Not much we can do about it. Let's go to the restaurant instead of the Grill Room, and we'll plan how we're going to make money for dear old Nellie's and to blazes with everything and everybody else. What do you say?'

Johanna lifted her chin and smiled, a rather watery little grimace, but she nodded. 'Yes,' she said. 'Let's do just that. We'll go and raise some money for the hospital. That's more important than anything – and it'll be fun to do it.' And together the two women went to eat a rather leathery dried egg omelette filled with a few rare mushrooms, cocooned and safe in the fragile protection of their friendship. Just for a little while.

6

'Well?' Charlie jumped to her feet and then, realizing how unprofessional such excitement must seem, sat down again, perching on the edge of Sister's desk, and said again in as cool a voice as she could muster, 'Well?'

'*Very* well,' Max said, and went past her to sit in the chair behind the desk and reach for a report sheet from the rack in its corner. 'Very well indeed, in a psychiatric sense. I made no effort to judge his physical condition, of course, but at a cursory glance I'd say that was pretty good too.'

Charlie frowned and turned to look down at his greying head, bent over the report sheet which he was writing.

'I don't understand,' she said stiffly.

'Oh, I think you do,' Max said equably, not looking up from his writing, his hand never stopping its steady movement of pen over paper. 'You asked me to see your patient to assess his psychiatric condition, following a florid and, I am now certain, manipulative gesture. And I am happy to report that you need have no fear for his mental health. He is, in all the usual senses of the term, a sane man. Selfish, perhaps. Greedy and thoughtless of any needs other than his own, undoubtedly. But ill he is not –'

Charlie took a sharp little breath in through her nose, hearing the faint hiss even in this rather noisy little room, filled as it was with the rattle of trolleys from the ward and the voices of the nurses bustling about out there and the whine of the distant lifts.

'That's a very facile judgement, surely, on the basis of a mere twenty minutes of discussion with the man?'

'Ah, but there is more to my report than the mere twenty minutes spent with him, Miss Lucas.' Max reached for the blotting paper and carefully pressed it down on his report sheet. 'I am able to write here, as I have, NAD – nil abnormal

45

discovered – because I have spent over a quarter of a century now in my speciality, and I rather think I know more than most people about it.'

He lifted his eyes to her face and his lips quirked a little sardonically. 'More, I'd venture to suggest, than a young registrar, however gifted, who has only been a member of our profession for a handful of years and is still, in a very real sense, learning her business.'

The words were harsh, but his voice was gentle enough, but that made no difference to Charlie. She shot to her feet to stand, legs apart and knees braced, with her hands shoved deeply into her white coat pockets to glare at him.

'And I venture to suggest that you approached this case with some prejudice.' Her jaw tightened as she saw the look of amazement that spread over his face; a registrar to speak so to a consultant? It was unheard of: but she was too angry to care. 'Sir,' she added very deliberately, and stood her ground, staring at him as directly as he was looking at her.

It was Max who broke first. He had clearly been about to lose his temper but now he bent his head and with thumb and forefinger massaged both his closed eyes. There was a little silence between them, enhanced by the sounds from outside, and Charlie found herself thinking absurdly – now I know it's Friday! I can smell the patients' lunch – fish – poor Brin. He does dislike it so – and then Max looked up.

'I can see I must be careful,' he said. 'Come and sit down, Miss Lucas. No, don't glare at me in that fashion. It won't help either of us to understand each other better, and certainly won't do anything for your patient. And I'm assuming it is his welfare that concerns you above all else.'

She stood her ground for a moment or two longer and then nodded unwillingly. 'Yes,' she said, and her voice was a little gruff. And obediently she sat down in the chair on the other side of the desk and he leaned forwards, folding his arms on the cluttered surface to look at her.

'Now, my dear, hear me out, and do please *listen*. I've been dealing with emotional illnesses and psychiatric health in general for a very long time. And I have to tell you that the study of personality is something in which I am very well grounded. Your patient is a man with a particularly distinctive type of personality which I have met several times. Such

46

people are always of enormous charm. They are frequently, incidentally, good-looking as well, but that may not be relevant. The important thing about them is the way they beguile people. And the next important thing is the fact that they are very well aware of their effect on others, and use it. There's nothing reprehensible in that. Let me make it very clear that I'm not trying to make unkind judgements. Each and every one of us has to use such talents as we are given as best we can. And a talent to beguile is no more to be despised than any other. Unless it is used badly.

'But, unfortunately, he suffers from what often goes with this sort of personality. A rather, shall we say, childlike inability to brook any sort of frustration. The Brin Lacklands of this world want what they want when they want it.' He lifted his brows at her comically. 'They may not always know what it *is* they want, but they want it awful bad – did you ever read that poem when you were a child? No? Well, there's no reason why you should, I dare say. It's probably a very English poem and you grew up in America, I seem to recall. Anyway, to return to your patient. I have to tell you that his so-called self-destructive bid was a typical example of the sort of manipulative behaviour this sort of personality regards as reasonable. He wants something, and doesn't give a damn what he does to get it – and will usually go for the most theatrical methods. As I understand it, he wants to be treated by a particular surgeon at another hospital and you are having difficulty in making an arrangement for him. Hence this performance of his. He thinks that if he makes enough drama you will be forced to try even harder to get him what he wants –'

She sat silently, staring at him, trying to control the anger that still bubbled in her. How dare this dreary man talk so about Brin, her inner voice was raging, how dare he? He was being spiteful and stupid, not talking as a doctor should talk about a patient at all. He was just –

'Do you understand what I am explaining, Miss Lucas?' Max said gently. 'Your patient is using you – rather skilfully, I do admit, but using you all the same – and it is not in his best interests for you to let him do so. He needs, I would suggest, rather firm handling. He also needs to be disabused of this notion that he has been made very ugly by his injury. I looked

47

at that scar carefully and although it is by no means a thing of beauty and a joy for ever, it's nothing like as hideous as he maintains that it is. I've seen much worse on many of the patients who have been admitted here after air raids –' And then his voice seemed to dwindle and he stopped looking at her and looked down at the desk.

And now she could contain her anger no longer. 'Well, Dr Lackland, I must thank you for your opinion, no doubt, but I have to tell you that as a doctor in my own right – and however junior I may be and however ill-informed when compared to your own vast experience, the fact remains that I *am* an independent practitioner – I disagree with you very much indeed. I have looked after this man for some time now, so although my experience of medicine in general may not be as great as yours, my experience of this particular patient greatly exceeds yours. And I just don't believe you are right. He is not being manipulative, he is not selfish and – and he isn't what you said.' And now her voice began to shake, and she had to stop for fear of losing control and he looked up at her and though his face was blank there was an expression of new understanding in his eyes.

'You seem to have become more than usually interested in the man,' he said. 'Have you? It is possible for doctors to become rather more involved emotionally with an individual patient than perhaps they should.'

'No,' she said hotly and then as she felt her face redden got to her feet. 'No,' she repeated. 'I am interested in all my patients. It's why I came into medicine in the first place. I'm not like you – like so many British doctors, all ice and self-control. I care about my patients, all of them, and I don't care who knows it –'

'I stand rebuked,' he said and got to his feet, matching his action to his words. 'I've written my report, Miss Lucas, for his notes. Now I return your young patient to you. I know you haven't asked for any direct advice on his management but I shall offer it all the same. I wouldn't want to be in dereliction of my medical duty, however icy and self-controlled you might think me. I would strongly advise you to send him home to his family for a while to think about his situation and to face the fact that he does not need further surgery, and that however much he gets he is not going to end up with what he wants – which is a total restoration of his pre-injury looks. He has a scar, he'll always have a scar and no matter how you or I or anyone else fiddles with it, he'll never be happy with the result of any further treatment. Better to face this fact now than to go on as he is, trying to make people dance to his tune. If you don't tell him to do this then you'll be colluding in his fantasy of a totally restored face and doing him more harm than good.'

'Thank you,' Charlie said icily. 'I doubt very much whether I'll act on that advice but I must thank you for it all the same, I suppose.'

He stopped at the door, not looking round. 'Oh, Miss Lucas, do stop being so silly! You're not the first doctor to develop an absurd fascination for a good-looking patient, and I don't suppose you'll be the last, but for heaven's sake, do try to cover it up. It does neither you nor your profession any good at all to wear your heart on your sleeve in so obvious a fashion.'

'How dare you!' she cried and at once bit her lip. There was a limit to how far a member of the resident staff could go in dealing with even the most stupid of consultants, and she might well have overstepped it, but her anger overcame her native caution and she found her teeth lifting from her lip, heard her own voice and was aghast at what it was saying.

'How dare you speak to me like that? Just because you're a cold fish who never felt any hurt, who never had to face up to losing what mattered to you, you think you can tell other people how to cope with their sense of grief? That man is in a state of bereavement – if you can't see that you've no right to call yourself a psychiatrist. His looks have been killed – he feels as though he's inhabiting a dead body, and that's why he's so desperately unhappy! I've done all I can to get him transferred to the care of a plastic surgeon because this damned place doesn't have such a modern facility, and I would have thought a little help for the man from you wouldn't have hurt. But oh, no! You just preach about coming to terms with his loss – what do you know about such a loss? Who are you to –'

Suddenly she stopped, her words hanging in the air like palpable things as she stared at his still turned back, her face blank with horror. She'd forgotten. Oh God, she'd forgotten. Wasn't this the man whose wife had been killed in a flying

49

bomb raid? She'd been away on attachment at the maternity unit over at Stoke Newington when it had happened, but she'd been told and she could remember the pang of sympathy she had felt for this man she didn't really know but who had been left alone by a last stupid pointless flying bomb, sent on its way by an enemy thrashing around in defeat, could remember how very sorry she had felt for him – and how she had never thought about the matter again. And now here she was haranguing him about the effects of grief because she didn't like what he had said about a patient and –

'If you've quite finished, Miss Lucas, I must be on my way. You have my report and my advice. It is now up to you what you do. Good afternoon.' And still without turning his head to look at her he opened the door of Sister's office and walked out into the ward and she heard the sigh of the big double doors as they opened and closed behind him as she still stood there, frozen into immobility and hating herself and him in almost equal measure.

'So there it is,' Charlie said and couldn't look at him. Standing there beside his bed, her hands jammed into her pockets as usual, she kept her head bent, looking only at his hands folded on the red blanket that covered him. 'I had hoped that perhaps with his added support I might be able to overcome McIndoe's objections, but –'

'Miserable bastard,' Brin said, and moving fretfully drew up his knees to sit with his arms round them, staring furiously across the ward. 'What the hell do I have to do to get people to understand how *important* this is? Cut my damned throat and give them two scars to mend?'

Now she did look at him, sharply, for one moment hearing Max's words again at the back of her mind, but then, refusing to listen to them, shook her head. 'Don't be silly, Brin. You can't force people to do what you want them to do just by –'

'I'm not trying to force anybody anywhere,' he said and looked at her and as she caught his glance he smiled, that crooked smile that could make her feel so stupid and giddy. 'All I want is what any patient in this place wants – a cure for my ills. But no one seems about to give me one, or to care whether I get one or not –'

'That's hardly fair, Brin,' she said after a moment and he

50

reached out and patted her arm.

'Oh, I'm sorry, Charlie. You're right, of course. You care and damned grateful I am for it. If I didn't have you, I don't know what I'd do. So, tell me, what else did the old devil say? Miserable sod that he is. I should have known what sort of help I'd get from him. You should have seen the way he was at the VE night dinner. As cheerful as the hangman, so help me, sitting there crumbling his bread into pellets and saying not a dicky bird, I swear to you, all evening – a right misery –'

'I believe his wife was killed in a doodlebug raid,' Charlie said unwillingly, as angry with Max as Brin was but needing to be fair. 'I dare say it was a bad night for him. People remembered things that night – I know I did. I kept thinking about Cousin Mary, even though she didn't actually get killed by a raid, but it happened during one and –'

But he was paying no attention. 'So where do we go from here? I'm going to get into that man's hospital if it's the last thing I do, one way or another. If money won't help, then –'

'He's got all the patients he can handle,' she said, feeling a moment of chill. 'So it isn't a matter of paying. Anyway, the patients at East Grinstead don't pay, as far as I know. It's like us here at Nellie's – people in the open wards are treated free. They raise their money by voluntary contributions – and –'

'And then they can be lordly about who they'll treat and who they won't,' Brin said, furiously again, and he threw himself back against his pillows. 'Why shouldn't they take me on as well as any other patient? I need treatment, don't I? You said yourself that I did, so why refuse me the way he has?'

'I told you. I sent him the photographs, spoke to his secretary on the phone, but he was adamant. He said he had too much other more severe injury to treat at the moment and couldn't take you. In a year or two perhaps, when there's less work for him to do, now the War's over and there won't be any more of the sort of injuries he's been treating there –'

'A year or two!' Brin said with huge scorn. 'I haven't got a lifetime to waste! Damn it, I'm almost at my peak as it is! I'm thirty-five, not a baby of nineteen! I'd have thought on the grounds of my age and my occupation alone that ought to give me some priority over these kids he's filled his hospital with –'

'They were injured in the War, Brin. Airmen mostly and –'

'Well, I was injured in the War too, wasn't I? The fact that I

51

had a bloody bomb dropped on me instead of going off to drop them on other people makes me less important, does it?'

'No, but I can understand his point of view –'

'Well, I'm damned if I can.'

'You might feel better if you tried.'

'Like hell I will. The only thing that'll make me better is having the right sort of surgery to clean up this bloody mess that's been made of my face. It's my *face*, Charlie, for Christ's sake! I'm an actor – what am I supposed to do with my life, looking like this?' And he put up his hand and, with his fingers clawed, pulled at his scarred cheek and she reached forwards to take his wrist in her hand and gently pull it away.

'Don't do that. Hurting yourself won't make it any better. You have to learn somehow to live with yourself as you are – you'll drive yourself into a really severe depression if you go on like that, Brin. You really must learn to come to terms –'

'Did he say that?'

'Something like that.'

'Tell me exactly. I want to know every word he said about me – every single word –'

'He said he didn't think your face was as severely damaged as you believe it to be. That you ought to go home for a while to your family, and rest and use the time to think about –'

'My family!' he said in great disgust. 'Ye gods, the man's mad! Some bloody psychiatrist he is! He asked me about them and I told him what a shower they are. For God's sake, does he really think I'm going to go and sit in Haworth with *them*?'

'It might do you good to get the rest you need,' she said, hating the idea of having him go away but feeling obscurely that it was her medical duty to urge him to do so. However much she might have hated Max Lackland and what he had said, all the same he was a consultant, and it was Brin's right to be told what his advice was.

'Some rest I'd get there, with my father sitting round looking as though he's just waiting for the undertaker and my sister Sophie fussing around me like a hen with no chickens –'

'But she would look after you?' Charlie said.

'Why not? She's got nothing else to do. Ever since Ian was killed at Tobruk she's lived with my father and fussed over him, so she'd just fuss over me too, and I –'

'Has she no children?'

He shrugged that away. 'They'd only been married a few weeks when Ian died, and she never got round to children. So she'd treat me like one. My blood runs cold at the very idea. No, I'm going to get this lousy scar cleaned up, if it's the last thing I do – Charlie –'

He reached for her with both hands and seized her by the wrists, pulling her closer to him.

'Please, Charlie, say you'll help me? I can't go on like this. I want to work, to get back to my career – I've got to – time's running out for me. Please, Charlie, say you'll help me –'

'Brin, let go, for heaven's sake. The whole ward's staring!'

She felt her face redden as he pulled harder and she nearly lost her balance to fall over his bed, but she managed to stand her ground as he said even more urgently, 'Charlie? You won't pay any attention to that old fool of a nut doctor, will you? Promise me you'll talk to McIndoe and make him take me? Please? You've only sent him photographs and talked to his secretary, for God's sake – why can't you go and see him, make him understand what it's like to be me? You've got to help me, Charlie, no one else can. My life just isn't worth living the way I am. I mean it, Charlie, I'm not just talking. I mean every word of it. If you don't get McIndoe to fix my face then I just won't – I'll just give up. I swear it. Say you'll go and see him for me –'

What else can I do? she asked herself as she looked down at that face raised to hers, at the scar snaking its way across that smooth brown cheek and the lift at the corner of the mouth; what the hell else can I do?

'All right,' she said at last, feeling as though the words were being pulled out of her with forceps. 'All right. I'll go and see him.' And after a moment he grinned triumphantly and let go of her wrists and leaned back on his pillows, a smile lifting his uninjured cheek into contented lines, as the other one twisted into its usual sardonic shape. For the first time in weeks he looked pleased and happy. But Charlie felt deeply uneasy and far from contented. Max Lackland's words had stung her and now she couldn't forget them, as she looked down at Brin being pleased at last with the way things were going for him.

7

'Oh, my dear, no! Absolutely out of the question. You don't know what you're asking. I couldn't possibly.' And Letty leaned back in her armchair and settled herself more deeply into its embrace as though she had no intention of ever leaving it again.

Lee looked at her and then around the room and sighed. This was one place that never seemed to change. In spite of bombs – of which Albany had had its share – and the long fatigue of war, and shortages and dreariness in general, here in Letty's flat it was for ever 1935, when life was glittery fun and there was plenty to eat and drink and pretty clothes were everywhere and no one worried about anything more than the newest revue or the latest film and who was making the most delicious cocktails.

Except for me, she thought. I was worrying then about having babies and getting so anxious I was misery to live with, and now there they are, my Michael and Sally and Stella, and I ought to be so happy – but thinking about being happy meant thinking about Harry and she wasn't here to think about Harry. She was here to talk to Letty and persuade her to work for Nellie's.

The fire muttered in the grate, and a few embers fell in with a little hiss and rattle and Letty leaned forwards to look consideringly at her small stock of coal in the scuttle.

'Now, shall I or shan't I?' she said musingly, as though there was nothing more important to think about in all the world than the state of her coal supplies. 'If I put more on now, will I be able to light a fire tomorrow? Mrs Alf told me this very morning that for all her nagging the coalman says he can't come again for a fortnight, and it could get even colder and nastier yet, couldn't it? And it's still only October – What shall I do, Lee? To warm or not to warm? That is the question.'

'Put some on. I've got a few logs I've managed to get from Johanna. They've been cutting timber at Collingbourne, she said, and she's sending me some next week. I can let you have a few as soon as they arrive.'

'Oh, the joy of having relatives among the landed gentry!' Letty said sardonically and at once piled more coal onto the grate. It cowered there for a moment and then the flames leapt up from the embers and lit the room into a new cosiness. The light flickered on the old wood of the furniture, burnishing it to a richer sheen than even Mrs Alf, Letty's indefatigable housekeeper, could manage, and lifting the warm reds out of the old Turkey carpet on the floor.

'It's lovely to be here with you, Letty,' Lee said impulsively. 'It's like the War never happened, being here. It's all so warm and cosy – and you've hardly changed at all.'

And she smiled at the older woman, trying to convince herself she was telling the truth and knowing she wasn't, really.

Letty was looking older and much more tired than she had used to look. Once sturdy and solid, her familiar head with its square-cut grey hair held high, now she looked rather as though some part of her had fallen in on itself, leaving her a little shrunken and somehow hollow. She seemed to need fuel to fill out those narrowed cheeks with the fine lines which softened the skin to a papery delicacy, seemed to want warmth to lift her once vigorous body back into its old strength. She sat there and looked at Lee, her eyes, the only part of her that really seemed unchanged, glittering wickedly, and she laughed and shook her head.

'Stuff and nonsense. The flat may look the same, but I'm damned sure I don't. I'm old and I'm tired and it's time I turned up my toes.'

'Rubbish,' Lee said strongly. 'You're not that old. You can't be –'

'Sixty-five,' Letty said and made a face.

'Then you ought to be ashamed of yourself, talking about being old enough to turn up your toes and so forth. At sixty-five? Bless you, my father's five years older than you and he'd be ashamed to be heard talking so!'

'Ah, your father – he's a man of God, though, isn't he? They always stay young longer –'

55

'Pooh!' Lee said. 'He seems religious, I grant you – spends more time at the synagogue than he does at home, but I dare say that's as much because Mamma chatters at him so much as because of any deep piety. But seriously, Letty, you really shouldn't be talking so – so pessimistically. It's not healthy. Whatever's the matter to make you so low?'

Letty made a face again. 'I'm tired, I suppose. That Benefit I did for the war orphans – it half killed me. It's hell to get hold of so much as a length of flex to mend a set of lights and as for costumes – ye gods, it was like pulling teeth.'

'It was a marvellous show, though, for all that!' Lee said. 'I enjoyed it hugely. It looked lavish and glittery and – really, it was just like one of those marvellous pre-war things we all used to take so much for granted.'

'Well, most of the stuff we used I dug out from the various warehouses where I stored it, but it was on its last legs. Some of those costumes were in tatters, and they certainly can't be used again. So, if you're working your way round to trying to persuade me, dear Lee, to go through all that again, the answer is still no.'

'Oh, Letty, you really *don't* change a bit!' Lee said and laughed. 'All right, I am going to try to persuade you. I don't care how much you fuss and try to get out of it, I'm going to find some way to make you see how much we need you.' And she launched herself into an account of Nellie's pressing financial problems, painting a graphic picture of ailing patients waiting for admission, of gallant nurses and doctors struggling to cope with inadequate supplies of everything from syringe needles to actual beds; but all through it Letty sat unmoved, watching her with those glittering dark eyes, and smiling faintly so that her lined cheeks creased agreeably.

And when Lee at last ran out of breath and stopped talking she smiled even more widely and said sweetly but with definite finality, 'No, Lee, my darling. You're a dear girl, and your determination does you infinite credit, but no, no, *no*.'

Lee sat silently and looked at her, and Letty smiled amiably back and then leaned forwards to pour more tea for them both from the tray Mrs Alf had left there waiting on the low mahogany table where a blue faience bowl of bronze chrysanthemums glowed in the firelight. And then Lee sighed and said abruptly, 'Well, all right, if I can't persuade you to do it for the good of Nellie's, maybe you'll do it for Peter.'

Letty's hands stopped moving among the cups and saucers and the milk jug but she did not lift her eyes, and then she went on calmly pouring milk into tea and said easily, 'Peter?'

'You haven't forgotten Peter,' Lee said. 'And you can't pretend you have, so don't try to fool me, Letty.'

'Of course I haven't forgotten Peter. No one could. How is he?'

'Have you seen him lately?'

'If I had I wouldn't need to ask.'

'Nor have I. No one has.'

'What's the news of him then? You've seen Max and the Old Man?'

'We were all at the Governors' meeting, when we talked about this Benefit idea,' Lee said, and then lifted her hand as Letty opened her mouth to protest. 'No, hear me out. That's the point, you see. We talked about Peter as well as the idea of the Benefit.'

'Well?'

'The Old Man is dreadfully unhappy about him.'

'Aren't we all,' Letty said and leaned back in her chair again, turning her face away from Lee to look into the now steadily glowing fire. 'Dear Peter. It's a dreadful thing to know he's still so unhappy –'

'Max and his father – we all agree that he needs something to do. Something that would make him think about other things. Not just – whatever it is he sits and thinks about there at home on his own.'

Letty took a long slow breath and nodded, 'I see. I see it all. You think that if I do another Benefit I can persuade Peter to help me with it? That it would be some sort of therapy for him?'

'Why not? It might work.'

'Yes. It might.'

It might, it might. It had worked for Theo, after all, Letty thought. And suddenly it was as though almost thirty years had rolled away from her and she was a girl again making her first important film in the streets of London on Armistice Night. She could smell the acrid shreds of fog that had filled the air that night and the reek of heavy beer and gin in which the revellers had seemed to be wrapped, and could see Theo's face gleaming at her out of the darkness. Dear Theo who had been, and was still, so beautiful a man. That face that she had been the first to recognize as being so rich in potential was imprinted on the romantic imaginations of three-quarters of the women in the world, but he had been hers first. He had been a shell-shocked, deeply disturbed man and she had pulled him out of the morass into which the War had flung him and given him back to himself. And to other people, God damn it, and to other people. And now, here was Lee asking her to do it again for someone else. For Peter, who had worked with her and for her so steadily and devotedly for so many years before the War – and she was so tired, so deeply bone tired and those fleeting pains she had been trying to ignore in her belly for so long weren't as fleeting as they had been, and she was tired, tired, *tired* –

In the facing armchair Lee too was staring at the glow of the fire, also immersed in her own thoughts. Peter, she was thinking. Peter who had been so kind to her, who had helped her so much on that long frightening journey they had shared through Europe as the threat of war had grown darker and heavier. Peter who had taught her to find her peace of mind, who had found her beloved Michael for her, had helped her to bring him home. Peter who had loved her so much. More than Harry does, she thought then, more than Harry does. Maybe Peter still does want me, or maybe he could again? And then there would be someone to care for me, to hold me as though I mattered to him and not just because he wanted to please himself, who would look at me as though he saw me and not just a dull wife, who –

'Please, Letty,' she said then, not appealingly, not coaxingly, but very directly. 'Please, will you do it for Peter? He needs help so much. Whatever else comes of it, do it for Peter.'

And if the whatever else that comes of it is some sort of happiness for me then I'll take it, I won't turn my back on it. I'll learn to be reckless and live for me and think of what I want, just for once.

'If he says he wants to, then I'll have to,' Letty said after a long moment. 'But it will be for him and not for the hospital. Understand that. If he refuses then so do I.'

And if working with Peter again makes me feel better, less hollow, makes the pains go away for a while, then I suppose

58

it's worth it. Even though I know I ought to tell someone at Nellie's about how I hurt and get something done about it, I won't, because I know damned well what it is and I don't want to be meddled with. But working again with Peter will make me well again. And absurd though she knew the notion was, she felt better, suddenly, as a little surge of unfamiliar energy rose in her.

'Come on then,' she said, and got to her feet. 'The sooner we ask him the better.'

Lee stared. 'You mean – go and see him now? But why not phone? Or even write to him?' She was frightened, suddenly, of the thought of actually seeing him, frightened and excited too.

'That would be stupid,' Letty said brusquely but not unkindly. 'He'd not talk, or he'd tear the letter up, the way he is. The way I've been told he is, that is. If we're there, sitting there in front of him, he won't be able to say no, will he?' She laughed then. 'Any more than I managed to say no to you, sitting there, you wretch. Come on. Let's see if we can find a cab. It might be our lucky day. You never know.'

The last three games of Patience had come out as easily as melted butter oozing through hot toast, and he stared down at the piles of playing-cards on the table in front of him and thought – maybe if the next one does it as well it will be all right? Maybe then I'll find the courage to get up, go to the door, take my hat and call out to old Jenny in the kitchen that I'm just going for a stroll, to have dinner at a restaurant, go to a play, tell my father I'll see him at breakfast? And he reached for the cards to pile them together again, to shuffle them and re-lay them for a new game. And then pulled back.

And suppose it doesn't come out? Will I see that as yet another reminder that I have no right to be here, that I ought to be dead like all of them? I can't go on setting myself these stupid targets, I can't – it makes it worse, not better; and he got to his feet sharply, moving so quickly that he sent the table tipping and the cards spilling all over the carpet, but he made no attempt to pick them up. There would have been a time, long ago, when such untidiness would have offended his fastidious eye, when he would have had, willy-nilly, to get to his knees to collect them all together again. But now he paid no attention to such trifles. Now he didn't care what his surroundings were like. They could be as ill kept as he was himself, with his unshaven hollow face and his staring eyes and his hair ill-cut and straggling over his collar. His trousers, old flannels which had been worn out even before the War and which were now sagging and threadbare, hung on his thin shanks like rags and the old cardigan he wore had torn elbows, and he didn't give a damn. He almost seemed to revel in his own squalor, resisting fiercely any attempt by old Jenny to take his clothes to mend and press them and glaring at his father with those hot deep-set eyes when he said anything about getting him something better to wear.

He went to stand at the window as he so often did, staring out onto the street below, looking slightly to his left so that he could see the traffic of the Bayswater Road. Below him the stucco of the house front was peeling a little in the driving rain and he thought for a moment – Mamma. She would have been mortified to see her house in such a sad state, Mamma who had been so particular about details, who had been so warm and so dimpled and so altogether Mamma-ish, and he tried to conjure up a picture of her in his mind's eye, tried to see the round face and even rounder body that had been Miriam, the softness of her and the sweetness of her – but it failed of course, as did every attempt to think of anything other than that which he had to think of.

And now there they were again, marching past against the background of the Bayswater Road and its splashing pedestrians hunched against the driving rain and its swishing vans and lumbering red buses; the endless parade of figures that never left him. Skeletal, with dead eyes and shaven heads, shuffling along on their almost thread-like limbs, fragile inside the black and grey stripes of their cotton uniforms, looking at him as they went past him, their mouths open in silent shrieks, telling him, begging him, demanding that he do something, get them out, take them home again to real life where people ate food and lay in real beds and could sleep in the sure knowledge that they would wake next morning to live another day, instead of being dragged to a gas chamber to –

'No!' he shouted aloud and turned away from the window to look round the big room, at the familiar old furniture, massive in its Victorian rightness, the thick carpet, dusty in the corners now where old Jenny couldn't deal with it as the only servant left to care for the vast old house, at the huge dull mirror over the mantelpiece and the portraits of his mother and Johanna on her wedding day and the faded photograph of Tim, taken the day before he went off to France and –

'This is real, this is real, this is real.' He whispered it aloud the way he had taught himself to do. Somewhere deep inside himself he had known when he had come home that not until he could stop seeing everything around him as a wraith, not until he could reinvest the world with the solidity that he knew was still in it if he could only find it, not until then could he eradicate the visions that accompanied him all day as well as all night, the memories of Belsen at Celle in Germany and the months he had spent there in the last year of the War. And eradicate them he must, because if he didn't he would go completely and utterly mad instead of hovering on the brink as he now was.

'This is real,' he said again, and this time it seemed to work for a moment. The furniture in the room became more solid, stopped looking almost translucent so that the visions of the parade of shuffling figures that accompanied him all the time faded and almost vanished behind the glow of dusty polished mahogany and silver and crystal ornaments. 'This is real –'

So real that the door opened and creaked as it did so, and there was Jenny peering round it, pugnacious in her fear of alarming him, as she always was these days, never knowing how he would be or how he would react to her.

'Mr Peter?' she quavered, and he peered at her, almost startled, and said, 'Jenny?' as though he wasn't sure he recognized her, and her mouth drooped at that; she who had been a young nursery maid in this house when he had been born, who had known him all his life, to be greeted so!

But she made no comment, and just gave a little jerk of the head to indicate that there was someone behind her.

'Here's Miss Letty and Mrs Lee to see you,' she said, her old voice sharp and shrill. 'So you mind your manners and talk to them proper and I'll go and make them a nice cup of tea. Come away in, now, my dears, and I'll see if I can't find a bit of shortcake or something of that. I've been saving up Sir Lewis's butter ration this three weeks to make it, but I don't suppose he'd grudge it you, good soul that he is –' And she went

61

creaking away, her back bent and her head poking forwards, as Lee and Letty came into the drawing-room together.

Lee stood and stared at him and felt tears prick her eyelids and she said nothing, not trusting herself to speak. But Letty stood there, her old Burberry coat tied firmly round her middle and her rain hat pulled down ferociously over her eyes, staring at him with her chin up challengingly and then she said, her voice loud in the dim and over-furnished room. 'Peter? Ye gods, man, but you look ghastly! What have you been doing with yourself? Whatever it is, it's high time you bloody well stopped!'

8

'Well, you're tenacious enough, I'll give you that,' he said, and shot a sharp glance at her from behind the heavy rims of his owlish spectacles and then grinned. 'Clearly a lady who prefers not to take no for an answer – I should have realized you weren't English, but American. No Englishwoman would push at me this way. And I should know. I worked in the States. I was at the Mayo Clinic.'

Her face lit up. 'Really? I was born in Rochester, but the family went to live in Baltimore. I used to think of going to Rochester to train at the Mayo and then decided to go to our own Johns Hopkins. And then in the end I came here and trained at Nellie's, after all. It's odd how things work out, sometimes –'

'You're damned right it's odd. I was born in Dunedin in New Zealand and here I am working in a tuppeny ha'penny country hospital in Sussex.'

'Not so tuppeny ha'penny,' she said, almost shocked, and he laughed and nodded, pleased with himself.

'Of course it isn't. It was, but it isn't now. Famous all over the world, now, they tell me. And it'll be even more famous. Just you wait and see.'

'I've no doubt of it,' she said and looked consideringly at him as he sat there on the other side of his desk, his heavy squared-off fingers playing with a paperknife, and marvelled a little. He was such a heavy stocky sort of man, with his bullet head with its cap of smooth greying hair, neatly parted in the middle and slicked down with some sort of brilliantine, and his air of self-satisfaction. She had more sense than to expect surgeons to conform to any kind of physical pattern; the idea they were all thin and ascetic with long sensitive fingers and suffering eyes was a figment of romantic imagination, and she had always lacked that, but all the same he was rather unexpected.

'And that's why I can't take your chap,' he said. 'Because fame brings its problems, as you'll find out when your time comes.'

'I don't think that's very likely. –' she murmured and he shook his head, jovial and more self-satisfied than ever.

'If you never try, then of course you won't. But if you want to be good then believe me, you can do well. Most people, especially in this country, are so damned lazy and so un-ambitious you really have to be very wet not to overtake 'em. But be that as it may – I'm overwhelmed with work. Or very nearly. And I'm not taking any but the sort of cases that other chaps can't handle properly. I studied the photographs you sent me of your patient, and his injury isn't one that needs me. Find another plastic surgeon to look after him. There are plenty of people who could do a good enough job. It's not so bad a scar –'

'But they wouldn't do as good a job as you can,' she said and lifted her chin at him challengingly.

He accepted the compliment comfortably as though it were no more than his due. 'No, that's true. But they'll do it well enough. It's a simple enough operation, after all.'

'He's an actor. His face is too precious to allow for someone who'll only do it well enough. It's got to be done superbly well. And that means you.'

'And I've told you. I've got too much pressure on my ward to take such a patient. My guinea-pigs need every bed there is available. They're airmen, every one of them – or bloody nearly. If I brought in a civilian and that blocked a bed for one of these chaps, my name'd be mud. They'd have my guts for garters –'

She lifted her brows at that, and he laughed again. 'Don't look surprised. We run the place on very democratic lines, you know. None of your usual hospital spit and polish. These boys of mine – they have to face the prospect of a lot of surgery. Thirty, forty, fifty operations, some of 'em. And then I'm still having to tidy 'em up from time to time. You can't treat chaps like that as so much bed fodder. They're people who have lives to live while we try to give 'em back some sort of semblance of faces and hands. So, we run the place in a way you'd find a bit odd. Come and see.'

64

'I beg your pardon?'

'I said, come and see. You're obviously a stubborn girl, not going to take no for an answer easily – and I like that. Can't be doing with namby-pambies who grizzle and whine and don't stand up for what they want – but you can't get your own way this time. I'll show you why. When can you come and see?'

'To East Grinstead?'

'To East Grinstead. I'll be down there later today. Take a train from Victoria – they're pretty good these days – and anyone'll direct you to the Queen Victoria. It's the most important place in the town now – put it on the map, after all. Get there around four and I'll show you round, introduce you to my guinea-pigs –'

'You said that before – are they all being used for research, these patients?'

'None of 'em and all of 'em,' he said and got to his feet. 'Every patient I operate on is a one-off. I learn something for the next fella for each one I put a knife to. But I'm not one of these wallahs who are panting to get their names in print in the *Lancet* or the BMJ. None of that so-called research-paper writing for me, thank you very much. I've got far more important things to do. No, I didn't label them guinea-pigs. They did that themselves. Got a club – I'm the president – and a pretty good one it is. Good drinking, good yarning and good care taken of each other. You'll see. Four o'clock this afternoon. And now you've got to be on your way. I've got others waiting to see me –' And he stood up and nodded at her and she had perforce to get to her own feet.

'You still see some private patients here in Harley Street?'

He frowned sharply.

'Some. But I still wouldn't take your young man, even as a private patient. I saw the pictures, and I just don't think his is a case for me. I can send you to other reasonable chaps, as I've already told you –'

'No,' she said. 'No, he wants you. So do I. I just thought, if it was a matter of money for a private case – that wouldn't be a problem.'

'It isn't a problem with me either,' he said, and now his voice was a good deal sharper. 'I'm just not taking him. Now, four o'clock at East Grinstead? Or shall we leave it at that?'

'I'll be there,' she said hastily. 'Four o'clock sharp. Thank

65

you, Mr McIndoe. Goodbye till this afternoon.' And she went hurrying down the thickly carpeted stairs into the lavishly appointed hall with its oil paintings and flowers in big bowls and out into the October bluster of Harley Street to stand on the kerb for a while, thinking.

She had been so sure it would work the way she had wanted it to. It had been silly to be so certain, perhaps; his letter in response to her first approach to him, when she had sent him Brin's photographs, had been uncompromising enough in its refusal, but for all that, she had been sure that if she went to see him herself she'd be able to convince him.

And at first she'd been really hopeful as she'd sat in front of him and gone through Brin's history, explaining, showing even more photographs, pleading for her patient. But though he'd listened courteously enough, he still had said no. Brin wasn't a patient for him –

But then she cheered as at last she turned and set out to walk towards Cavendish Square in search of a little lunch before making her way to Victoria Station and a train that would take her south east out of London to the heart of Sussex. He may have refused so far, but he hadn't slammed the door entirely. To be invited to look at his ward at East Grinstead was a considerable step in the right direction; and to go there was as good a way as any she could think of to spend her solitary day off. So her step was jaunty as she made her way along the august pavements of the most famous medical street in the world. She'd get her patient treated by this man, somehow, she was absolutely sure of it. Because it was what she wanted more than anything in the whole world.

But by the time she was back on the train in the darkness of the early evening, chugging her tedious way back to Victoria, her spirits were a great deal less elevated. She sat in the corner seat of her compartment, staring out at the blackness that slid past the windows, seeing not the absence of light nor the faint reflection of her own face that gleamed on the dirty windows, but the faces of the men she had seen that afternoon in Ward Three at the Queen Victoria Hospital.

At first it had promised to be a cheerful afternoon. She had managed to find a taxi at East Grinstead station to take her to the hospital and had stood in the road with her back to the trees that fringed it with their amber and golden leaves, and the cheerful substantial houses warm with red brick and white paintwork and gardens alive with the vivid colours of Michaelmas daisies and late dahlias, staring at the place and liking what she was looking at. A handsome building, with lots of glass and a big central tower, it stood as a living memorial to the hopeful building boom of the 1930s when there was, in spite of the depression, money and time for the building of local hospitals like this. The fringe of temporary buildings and Nissen huts which had sprung up around it didn't detract from its self-assurance and it stood there, benign and calm in the afternoon glow of a sun that had at last managed to break through the overcast of the cloud, and seemed to promise the fulfilment of her hopes for Brin. McIndoe would never have brought her here if he hadn't meant to relent and accept him as a patient, she told herself as she made her way up the drive towards the main entrance. He couldn't be so unkind as to drag her so far for no purpose.

He hadn't; but it had been for his own purpose and staring out of the train window now she felt herself fill with a moment of fury at the way he had manipulated her. But there was admiration in her too; he had the sort of determined driving pushiness she had always found rather engaging, and whatever he did to get his own way, it was clear to her, even after so short an acquaintance, that there was no malice in him.

'Ah, Miss Lucas,' he had said, giving her that owlish stare through the heavy glasses as she was shown into his small cluttered office by a starched rustling nurse. 'Come to see my Ward Three, hmm? I can't show you myself – got a couple of cases to get to the theatres this afternoon, but one of Blackie's people will take you round. Good chap, Blackie –' And he had nodded at her and gone pushing past her on his way out of the office, clearly dismissing her from his mind, and she had remained standing there, uncertain what to do and with a slow tide of anger rising in her, when a head was put round the door. It had a round amiable face adorned with a broad smile.

'Miss Lucas?' it said and as she nodded and the face came further into the room and showed itself to be attached to a body as round as itself, and which was wrapped in a white coat. 'I'm Davey. One of the people who help Blackie – he'd come himself but he's tied up this afternoon and the Boss said

67

that you're to be shown round Ward Three. So I'm here to show you.' He had grinned then at the look of doubt on her face. 'I know I'm just an orderly, and you can see that and you're asking yourself what does an orderly know to be showing me, a lady doctor and all, round the ward? Well, I'll tell you, Miss Lucas, I know better than most. Not as much as the Boss or Blackie, I grant you, or Sister, but a lot. Been on Ward Three I have since it all started, back in '41 – five years hard I'll have done –' And he laughed cheerfully, and beamed at her and she couldn't help but smile back.

He had led her along wide clear corridors, talking all the time, pointing out to her with great pride various features of the hospital as they passed, and she went on smiling because his enthusiasm was infectious; and she nodded with all due expressions of admiration as he showed her where the pathological labs were, and where the theatres were and the corridor which led to the pharmacy and the other wards as though Nellie's weren't pretty much the same, albeit in a much older building and with less Vita glass about.

'And here we are,' he said with great pride as he led her out of the main building and through a covered walkway to a large hut. 'Ward Three, in all its gory –' And laughing delightedly at his own joke, he had pushed open the door.

She had stood and looked down the ward; a long room with tall windows on each side, and with beds ranked under them in the usual way, rather closer together than they were at Nellie's, but otherwise much the same. A good deal of dark green paint, enlivened in places with cream, and a ceiling that was a tracery of metal girders, bolted together. There was a coke stove with chairs set round it and there were a few trolleys and screens about, none of which was surprising. But still, it didn't feel like an ordinary hospital ward and she looked closer and saw the battered grand piano in the corner and the long table with what looked remarkably like a barrel of beer on it, with tankards alongside, and explicit pin-up pictures of the sort that she knew were commonplace in barrack rooms but which would have caused an uproar if they had appeared in Nellie's chaste wards, and blinked at the sight.

The patients too seemed to be very different. None of the neatly arranged bodies in beds that were so marked a feature of Spruce where she spent so much of her working days. Here they sprawled on their beds in postures which would have made Sister Spruce go white with horror and then scarlet with fury. They sat in groups playing cards or board games and in one corner someone was clearly working hard on a project that involved the use of cane and board and glue in great quantities and had spread it around lavishly. Some men were playing darts with a board pinned upon a screen, and another was tapping at a typewriter at a central table. There was a radio playing 'Music While You Work' very loudly, competing with a lot of laughter coming from a group who were clearly gambling – a totally forbidden activity in any hospital she had ever worked in – and altogether the place looked rather more like a private club room than the sort of hospital ward she knew. She turned to look at Davey and opened her mouth to say as much, and then closed it as she saw the great beam of delight that illuminated his face.

'Every doctor that comes here from outside starts off looking like you do right now,' he said with vast satisfaction. 'Dead dumbfounded, that's what. Really easy-going here, isn't it? None of your usual sit-up-and-do-as-you're-told stuff for our chaps, eh? But there, look at them – you wouldn't expect it, would you? Not with what they've got to put up with, and the time they have to spend here. Not that they're here all the time, of course. Pop out into the town, they do, when they want to, go on the occasional bender – though if they get too boozed up the Boss gives 'em the rough side of his tongue, I can tell you!'

'I imagine he does,' Charlie said weakly and turned back to look at the ward. 'I – can you tell me about these patients? About their treatment, that is?'

'Of course I can!' he said, almost indignant. 'Knows 'em all like the back of my hand, I do. Treated most of 'em in the bath unit, haven't I? Course I can tell you –'

And tell her he had, walking between the beds, introducing her to man after man, and she had somehow pinned a smile on her face and kept it there, not knowing how she did it. Because with all her experience of the disagreeable sights that parade each day in every hospital – and she had her fair share of them – she had never seen anything like this.

Young men, all of them, some very young – there were boys of little more than twenty or so, as well as more settled ones in their thirties, but generally youthful – they sat there and showed her faces so appallingly damaged that it was all she could do not to show her horror. Faces twisted with fire, with eyelids vanished and lips lifted in perpetual snarls and skins that looked like scratched and torn fabric that had about as much similarity to normal human skin as the tough boarded wooden floor on which she was walking.

And it wasn't only that; there were men in the process of having special pedicle grafts made. She could remember reading articles in her *Lancet* and in other medical journals of the technique; or the way in which flaps of skin and soft tissue were raised from bellies to be sewn to chests and then, once the new circulation had established itself, as it usually eventually did, were severed from their original site and lifted to be sewn on to an upper arm. And then when the slow development of a new blood supply there was complete, lifted once again to be attached to areas of the face which had been burned away.

So, there were men here with their arms raised in what seemed like absurd perpetual salutes, the weight of their limbs held in plaster cradles that stuck out at awkward angles yet which allowed the lumps of flesh attached to their faces to make an incongruous bridge between upper arms and cheeks. There were men for whom the pedicle end attached to the upper arm had been severed, so that the arm could be left to heal, leaving the pedicle dangling from the face like some obscene sausage, waiting to be removed in the operating theatres and tidied up once it was clear that a good union had formed. There were men with pedicles that had been grafted to noses which were still at the stage where the pedicle hung down like a human elephant's trunk. There were men who were without noses at all, with just gaping holes where they had been, and men with no lower jaws, and tubes emerging, snakelike and hideous, from the vast gaping spaces which were their mouths. There were men in bandages, so all-enveloping that they looked like mummies, and men who stared from perpetually open watering lidless red eyes at the world which had treated them so appallingly.

It smelled odd too, this ward. There was the usual scent of lysol and carbolic and ether but something more besides, a strange kitcheny sort of smell, and she realized after a while it was the scent of burned flesh; and still there was something

70

more besides. Flowers, of course, and – she thought, trying to concentrate on the messages from her nose in an effort to keep her pity for these desperately damaged young men from boiling over into tears – and something else. And suddenly she was a child again, out at Tiger Point at home, smelling the sea. Salt water. A disconcerting smell to find so strongly represented in the cocktail of odours that was the Ward Three atmosphere of Queen Victoria Hospital at East Grinstead in the middle of green Sussex.

And all the while as she and Davey walked along the long room he talked. He told her of how the men had suffered their injuries, and he told their stories in simple direct language that was more chilling than the most hyperbolic descriptions could have been.

'Flying a Hurricane, this chap was. Over the Thames estuary. Got hit by a Messerschmitt 109, baled out, but before he could get out of the cockpit, petrol tank went. Blew up, like, ate him up with fire. He'd taken off his goggles, 'cos he couldn't see proper with 'em – lots of the boys did that – and his gloves, so's he could hold the controls better, 'cos the gloves got in the way, so there wasn't much of what you might call protection. He says he could see his own flesh floating away from him when he was in the water waiting to be picked up. And the place they took him – usual sort of army hospital, you know, all done by the bleedin' book, shoved on tons of bloody tannic acid. Turned him into a right tortoise, that did. The Boss has been trying to clean him up ever since. Five years it's been and he's still in and out of here like the bishop's in and out of the actress. Sorry miss, didn't mean to be rude, but all the chaps talks easy here. You know how it is.'

'I know,' she said, and was proud of the steadiness of her voice. 'No need to apologize.'

'And this chap here – he got burned up inside his plane on the way down. Got out in his para eventually, and just as well he was in it. I mean, he was burned everywhere except where his harness covered him. Legs, arms, belly and all, skinned like a bloody rabbit. But his necessaries were all right, on account of the fit of the harness. When we got him here he was in a right state. They'd wrapped him in dressings at the first aid unit and they'd gone septic. He stank – my Gawd how he stank! We used to soak him for hours on end. The only way he

71

felt good that was, having his bandages floated off. He's been coming back for surgery for – oh, I forget how long. He's had about thirty-five operations now. Not the record but it's a respectable total.'

'Soaked him?' Charlie said, as much for something to talk about as for any real need to know.

'That's right. The saline baths. We pioneered that treatment here. Soak the chaps in running salt water we do. Hose 'em down – they love it –'

Which explains the smell of the sea, Charlie told herself as at last the circular tour ended and they were back at the door of the ward. 'Thank you, Davey, for showing me round,' she said. 'I appreciate it.'

'My pleasure, Miss Lucas. Hope you like it when you start work here properly like.'

'What – I beg your pardon?' She looked at him, her face blank and he gazed back, his smile fading.

'Sorry, I'm sure, if I got it wrong, but I thought that must be why you was doing the round? Applying for the job, like. We've got a vacancy for a houseman, you see, and I thought – especially as it's the Boss's idea that we ought to have the best-looking women round the ward. It's the least we can do for the lads, he says, and the nurses are handpicked for their legs and their – well, anyway, I thought, you see, that you must be up for the job –'

'Me, work here?' she said slowly and her eyes glazed as she grappled with the idea. 'As a surgeon?'

'There's plenty of work to be done, that's for sure,' Davey said feelingly. 'What with those chaps you've seen and the ones who keep coming back for follow-up. It's not as bad as it was, of course, when the War was on. We were getting so many new patients in them days we didn't know whether we were on this earth or Fuller's. But, the War over or not, we're still overworked as you can see. We've more beds in this ward than we've any right to have, but what can you do with so many chaps needing more surgery?'

'Yes,' she had said, her voice as flat as she could make it. 'Yes, I can see the problems. I'll have to think about it. Thank you, Davey –'

And she had gone back to the station, walking all the way because she needed the air, needed to rid her nostrils of that heavy smell that seemed now to pervade her whole being, and to think. And she was still thinking all through the journey and after she had arrived at Victoria, and found a late bus to take her back to Nellie's and her small room in the medical quarters.

It was clear to her now, as obviously McIndoe had meant it to be, that there was no way she could demand that he take Brin as a patient. His disfigurement dwindled to a minor blemish, no more, when compared with the sort of injuries she had seen this afternoon. But if those patients were treatable, it surely meant that Brin was too? Perhaps if she applied for that job that Davey had spoken of and managed to get it – and how many applications could there be for work so desperately uncongenial? – maybe she could learn enough to help Brin herself? It might sound like a mad scheme when he had been so adamant that he wanted only the great Archie McIndoe himself to operate on him, but perhaps he would accept her care, if she had been directly trained by the great man?

It was that thought that kept her awake till the small hours, and that made her dream restlessly for the remainder of the night. The possibility that she could herself give Brin the one thing he most wanted. A new face.

9

'Now, Letty, my dear girl, what shall it be? I still have some pretty good port left – never thought it'd last the War, but there it is, several bottles still skulking down there in the dark, and as drinkable a tipple as you've had any time this past ten years. Or would you prefer some Madeira? Got some of that too!'

And the Old Man is as jovial as *he* has been any time this past ten years, Max thought, watching him, and he caught Lee's glance as she, sitting on the Old Man's far side, saw him smiling at his father and he nodded at her, acknowledging her awareness of his thought and happy to share it with her. She too was watching Sir Lewis approvingly, glad to see him so happy.

He's almost too happy, she thought then as he leaned back in his chair at the head of his dinner table, at last leaving it to Victor to pour the precious Madeira which Letty had accepted. His eyes were glittering very brightly and there were smudges of hot colour high on his papery old cheeks as he looked round at them all, and it worried her. He shouldn't be so elated, not at his age.

Around her the old room glowed in the lamplight. Sir Lewis liked to use oil lamps to illuminate his dining-room on the rare occasions when he used it for guests, just as his beloved Miriam had so many years ago when they had first come to live in this big old house, and the faint smell of paraffin oil which pervaded the air merged with the smell of mutton and cabbage which had been the best dinner Jenny had been able to muster for them. But it wasn't a disagreeable smell. It hung over them like a gentle mist, sending them all back in time, distancing them from the harsh austerity of these difficult post-war years, and that, Lee thought, was no bad thing.

'I do wish Harry had been able to be here, Sir Lewis,' she said impulsively. 'It was so good of you to ask us, and I know he wanted to. But he had a case, and he just had to – well, you know how it is.' Liar, she was thinking. He had no case, he just didn't want to come here to dinner, and had said as much. God knows where he is tonight. Better I don't either, I suppose.

'If I don't understand, who does?' Sir Lewis said. 'One of his private patients, I take it?'

'I really don't know.' Lee was startled. 'I didn't ask –'

'It can't be one of Nellie's,' the Old Man said. 'I still get a list of all the day's work at Nellie's sent up every evening, you know, and they include the emergency admissions on it. There were no emergencies in Harry's wards tonight, so it must be a private patient. Probably gone to one of the clinics, I suppose. Ah, well, must make a living, mustn't we? Yes?'

And he looked at her sharply and becked his head and then looked back at Letty, and his eyes softened as he did so. His gratitude to her was so powerful that it almost exuded from him like a medium's ectoplasm, visible and palpable.

'It's good news about what you're doing to help old Nellie's make a living, Letty. It's much appreciated, and never you think otherwise. Why, without your efforts I can't imagine how we'd –'

'Come off it, Lewis,' Letty said rudely, but she was smiling and there was no rancour in her voice. 'You don't have to flannel me. There'd be some way of getting the cash you need, I dare say, even if I didn't do this Benefit. Anyway, it's not just for Nellie's that I'm doing it.'

'I know,' Sir Lewis said. 'But it's easier to say thank you for the plate than for the pudding on it. If you see what I mean.'

'I see what you mean. And you don't have to say thank you for either. I do what I do because I want to. And by God, I don't want to see a good chap like Peter going down the pan for want of a bit of effort. Silly devil!' And she glowered into her glass at its dark amber depths and scowled. But none of them were deceived for a moment; she was embarrassed and they all knew it.

'He won't now,' Sir Lewis said with great satisfaction. 'Not now he's got a job of work to do, and you to make sure he does it. It's what he's needed this past year, and I can't tell you how – well, let be. But all the feeling's there. Now, Max, m'boy, where is he? Hey? Been gone long enough now, surely?'

'My dear father, I don't time people when they go to lavatories!' Max said with mock severity. 'He'll be back in a moment, I dare say! Stop fussing!' But he was a little anxious too. Peter was so unpredictable that being anxious about him had become second nature for all of them, and still was, in spite of the change in him that there had been over the past couple of weeks. It was now almost ten minutes since he had excused himself from the table with a murmur and left the room, and Max too had been watching the door for him.

Almost as though he had been waiting in the wings for his cue the door opened and Peter came in after a perceptible pause; it was as though he had stood quietly on the far side of it for a moment to recruit his courage to come in, and when he did Max again felt the stab of pain and pity that Peter always drew from him now. He had at least dressed, putting on one of his pre-war dinner jackets, and he had brushed his hair so that it looked neat, despite its length, instead of hanging lankly over his forehead. His face looked even thinner over the blinding whiteness of his shirt and Max got to his feet and said easily, 'Let me get you some Madeira, Peter, old man. Rather good it is. Letty's guzzling it as though there's no tomorrow, so take it while the getting's good.'

'Damned liar,' Letty said equably, and pushed her chair back from the table and made an inviting gesture towards Peter. 'Come over here, Peter, and talk to me. Ignore these others. We have to talk –' And after a moment Peter obeyed, moving a little stiffly, as though he were out of practice.

As soon as he sat down Letty leaned towards him and began to talk animatedly about the Benefit. They would need a framework, she said to Peter as he sat there and watched her face, seeming to listen to her, some sort of chain on which they could, as it were, hang the many acts she thought of asking to take part. Had he any ideas? She herself had wondered about a pantomime structure with good fairies and bad fairies – or had he a better idea?

The others watched them both, while pretending to be immersed in their own desultory conversation about the weather, about the news in the day's papers, about the latest political decision, but all three of them were far more interested in Peter's and Letty's discussion than their own, and

76

after a while stopped even pretending to talk; they just sat and listened and thought their own thoughts as they watched the two heads close together in the lamplight. Letty's square grey bob and Peter's lacklustre mousy hair clinging to his skull as if to a child's, and yet making him look so very old –

She can do it if anyone can, Lee was thinking. Already the difference between the Peter they had talked to here, a couple of weeks ago, and the Peter who was sitting having dinner with them was a marked one. He looked cleaner, for a start, and in spite of his silence and his stiffness the blankness had gone from him. She had been actually frightened of him that afternoon when she and Letty had come to talk to him; frightened of his remoteness and of the odd look in his eyes. Now he looked only tired and ill and that was far from frightening. That just made her feel protective and caring towards him. She wanted to take him in her arms the way she did the children when they were tired and tearful, and rock him till he slept and then tuck him into bed, safe and warm, to wake the next day feeling himself again, feeling like the old dear Peter she had travelled with all those years ago –

Max too was feeling happier about his brother. What alchemy it was that Letty had he didn't know, but there it was. She had succeeded where he and his father and everyone else who had tried to prise Peter out of his bewildered misery had failed, and his gratitude, like his father's, ran deep. And then, as at last Letty leaned back, seeming well satisfied with their talk, he got to his feet.

'Far be it from me to be the one to spoil the fun, but I'm sending you to bed, Father. No, don't glare at me like that. You're tired and you're a fool if you deny it.'

The old man grunted but looked glad enough to do as he was bidden.

'And Lee, my dear, as soon as I've handed Pa over to Victor – if I can dislodge him from the kitchen and Jenny's no doubt lascivious attentions – I'll see you home and –'

'No need, Max,' Lee said, and smiled at him, as grateful as Sir Lewis for the chance to go to bed. It was getting late and she'd been occupied with the children all day, for it was Stella's birthday and that had meant a party, and she wanted her sleep. And wanted, too, to see if Harry was home yet. 'I've a little petrol, so I cheated tonight – brought the car. It's simply not

77

worth the misery of trying to get taxis these days. Shall I give you a lift home, Letty?'

Letty shook her head. 'No, thanks, my dear. It's not that far to walk, and I enjoy the exercise. I can do it in half an hour or so –'

'Heavens!' Lee said lightly. 'The energy! My feet would never forgive me if I demanded such a trek of them. Still, if you're sure –'

'I'm sure,' Letty said firmly and then as Peter spoke went a little pink with pleasure.

'I'll walk with you,' he said. 'I need some exercise too. I'll walk back, too –'

'Oh, no, Peter.' Sir Lewis sounded alarmed. 'It's much too far for you! You haven't been a bit well and you're as thin as a –'

'Pa, shut up,' Max said firmly. 'Peter, you walk. It's an excellent idea. I'll see you upstairs with Victor, Pa, and then I'm going. Goodnight, all of you. It's been delightful –' And moving purposefully, he removed his father from the room and Lee followed them too, stopping to linger for a moment at the door.

'Peter,' she said as she looked back at the two of them, still sitting by the littered dining-table. 'If I haven't said it before, let me say it now. Thanks for what you're doing for Nellie's. We do need the money so, and it's grand of you to make the effort for us –'

He looked at her in the soft light and then, amazingly, produced a sardonic grin and for one glorious moment it was the old Peter come back again. Thin as he was, haggard though he now looked, there was the wry smile that had been so much a part of him. There were the friendly eyes and the glint of laughter and she felt her own eyes fill with tears at the sight of him.

'Stop ladling out the butter, Lee,' he said. 'This is me, remember? You're just glad I'm doing anything, and to hell with whether it's for Nellie's or not.'

Letty guffawed then, loudly and rather coarsely, and Lee reddened and glanced at her and then said a little stiffly, 'Well, anyway, thanks. And I'll look forward to hearing more of the show and what you're planning. Good night.'

And she fled, to drive herself home in a state of some

confusion. She'd forgotten just how delightful a person Peter had been. Back in the days when they had travelled through Europe together she had been so wrapped up in her own feelings she had given little thought to anyone else. But now it was different. Peter, restored to his old self – and it now was beginning to look as though he might well be restored soon – would be a very interesting person to have around. And she finished her journey home in so abstracted a state of mind that she missed the turning into her own road, and had to reverse to get home.

It was cold as they went along the Bayswater Road, with tendrils of icy fog drifting over the railings from the park and muffling their footsteps on the greasy paving stones, and both of them had their collars pulled up against the chill and their hands, gloved though they were, buried in their pockets.

The silence between them was a companionable one, each lost in private thoughts, and then Letty said abruptly, as they came up to Marble Arch and negotiated the traffic to make their way through to Park Lane so that she could cut through to Piccadilly and Albany, 'I need some advice, Peter.'

'From me?' He sounded distant, his voice thin and more muffled than even the fog made reasonable, and she said more loudly, 'Yes, I do. Concentrate, now. Do as I told you before. Listen to every word, repeat it inside your head and then you'll hear me properly.'

'I'm sorry,' he said and turned his head to look at her in the dimness. 'How did you figure out that was the way to make things work for me, Letty? It does work. It really makes me hear. It stops the – nothing gets in the way when I do it.'

'I haven't directed actors for all my working life without knowing how to make people do as I tell 'em,' she said. 'Listen, Peter, I'm on the proverbial horns of a far from proverbial dilemma.'

He listened and it was almost as though she could hear him thinking her words inside his head. 'What dilemma?'

'To take a plateful of glory or not,' Letty said, and then more gruffly, 'I had this bloody letter, you see.'

Again the pause. 'What letter?'

'It's ridiculous, it really is. It wants to know if I'll accept an honour. And don't say "what honour?" or I'll spit.'

He managed a small chuckle. 'Then spit. I can't advise if you don't tell me what we're talking about. So, what honour?'

There was again a little silence between them broken only by the sound of their footsteps on the pavement and the swish of the passing traffic. 'They want me to be a Dame,' Letty said at length in a rather small voice.

'A Dame,' Peter said consideringly, and this time he laughed aloud. 'Like Dame Goody Two-shoes, in the pantomime?'

'Oh, God, that was my first reaction – to laugh and shout, "Lawks a mussy me, this is none of I –" But I don't know. I've been thinking about it a lot. I haven't said no, at any rate. But I have to decide soon. It's almost the deadline. It's for the New Year honours list.'

'Do they say why?'

'Services to theatre and the cinema,' Letty said and grimaced in the darkness. 'Not that I was ever concerned about either of them in the abstract. I mean, I care, but I cared most for my own dear old Gaff, and about the Shaftesbury while I had it. But I don't know – this brave new world they're building for us – I've heard there are plans for so many things. A National Theatre – now, there's a novel idea! They've had something of the sort in France for the devil knows how long – Comédie Française and all that – but here; well! The mind boggles! And then I think to myself, don't be such a bloody cynic. Think positively – and if they want to make a gesture towards the theatre, who are you to stand in their way, even if it does make you feel like a great fool?'

Another little silence fell and then Peter said with great firmness, 'Say yes.'

'Why?'

'Because it shows respect for the theatre. You're right about that. And because it shows respect for you. You deserve it.'

'Codswallop,' she said loudly and a passer-by looked up curiously at them as he went scurrying away in the opposite direction along Upper Brook Street into which they had now turned. 'I can think of umpteen people who deserve honours more than I do. You for a start.'

'Me? I deserve nothing.' He sounded savage suddenly and his voice rose. 'I deserve nothing, nothing at all. I stood by and did nothing. I'm alive and they're dead and –'

'Shut up,' she said in a very even voice, never altering the rate at which they were walking. But she pulled one hand out of her pocket and tucked it into the crook of his elbow.

She knew what he meant; he had told her at last, in long silences between painful halting sentences day after day ever since she had first gone to see him at Leinster Terrace to ask him to work for her, pouring out to her his guilt at all he had seen, his horror and his conviction that in surviving as he had, he had in a deeply traitorous way betrayed the people with whom he had shared the disgusting pain of that place in Celle.

'Shut up. We agreed, you were going to stop that. It was not your fault. You did all you could. More than most. More than I did, sitting here in safety and comfort. They only bombed us here. Here was clean and decent and peaceful compared with there. You owe no apologies. Stop making them.'

They walked on and after a while he took a deep breath, so deep that his body seemed to shake under the hand she still had tucked beneath his arm and then he said, 'All right. I promised. I won't talk about it again. Talk about Dame Goody Two-shoes instead. You be Dame Goody Two-shoes because it's right you should. Everyone would be very happy. Alf and Mrs Alf and Pa and everyone.'

She laughed then as at last they reached Bond Street and the last leg of their long walk. 'All right. I'll write tomorrow and say yes. I'll feel an absolute prune, but I'll do it. And we'll get on with the Benefit and settle down to making a really good plan for it. I thought perhaps – Katy. What do you say?'

'Katy? What about her?'

'She's here in London. Under contract to me for another year, almost. Champing at the bit a lot, because although *The Lady Leapt High* is taking good money at the box office the critics were a bit rude about her.'

She chuckled appreciatively in the darkness. 'One of them said, "The film indeed leaps high. Miss Lackland, however, manages little more than a bunny hop, which goes well enough with her pert nose and fluffy personality." Bitchy but rather apt, I thought.'

'What could she do in the show?' Peter said after another of his long pauses.

'Look pretty, be vivacious. Make 'em fall in love with her – all the things she usually does.'

81

'She's worth more than that,' Peter said, and suddenly it was as it had been at his father's dinner table; a curtain had pulled back and revealed the old familiar Peter of seven years ago. 'She used to be a damned good actress. I directed her, remember? I chose her out of the students at Guildhall to join the tour of Germany we did. She can *act*.'

'Then you shall direct her again,' Letty said. 'Whatever else we have in this damned show, we'll have a bit of class. A scene from Shakespeare, maybe? Yes, that's what we'll do. We'll have the wooing scene from *The Shrew*. They'll love that – I'll find her a lively Petruchio and we'll dress it well, and set it with all the glamour we can lay our hands on.'

'Yes,' Peter said. 'The wooing scene.' But the moment of renewal had passed as quickly as it had come; his voice sounded flat and dull again, but Letty was not worried. She hugged his arm close to her side as at last they turned into Old Burlington Street and reached the back entrance of Albany.

'I'll call her tomorrow. And you too. Come here again at ten, will you? We've work to be done. Can you get home again all right, Peter? Remember what I told you, how to stop the bad thoughts coming – think the better ones –'

'I remember,' he said. 'And they'll get me home again. Thanks, Letty. I – thanks a lot. I do love you, you know.' And he bent and hugged her and laughed softly in the darkness. 'Dame Goody Two-shoes –'

10

The hallway was big and square, with a highly polished parquet floor and a central table that was so glossy that it could have been used as a mirror. The windows glittered with cleanliness behind snowy curtains and the white paintwork that gleamed everywhere was immaculate. Altogether, Charlie thought, gazing round, the place looks as though it belongs in a shop window. I do hope Brin isn't hating it here; I do hope it isn't all as starchy and fussy as this hallway looks. I should have checked it for myself before I sent him here, but there just wasn't time –

A tall woman in the navy dress and flowing white veil of the hospital matron came padding softly from the far side of the central staircase, smiling frostily. 'Miss Lucas?' she said, in a low and obviously carefully modulated voice. 'May I help you? I understand you have come to see one of our patients. From Queen Eleanor's Hospital.' Her accent was so very refined and proper that she could hardly get the words out.

'Please,' Charlie said sharply, finding the woman's particularly careful enunciation of Nellie's full name grating. No one called the place Queen Eleanor's any more, for heaven's sake, she thought irritably. 'And I haven't a great deal of time –'

'It is rather irregular for – er – outside medical people to come and see our patients, Miss Lucas,' the matron said and tried to look down her nose at Charlie, but she stood very tall and stared the woman straight in the eye. 'We have our own medical staff, you see, and it really is not necessary to –'

'It is indeed necessary for me to see *my* patient, Matron,' Charlie said, making her voice as clipped as she could. 'I must discuss with him the strategy of his further care. Now, if you will please tell me where I can find Mr Lackland –'

'Mr Lackland! Oh! I hadn't realized that – well, I dare say we can bend the rules a little for *him*! Such a charming young man, and no trouble to any of us, in spite of his sad problem. *Such* a dreadful injury to so handsome a man. He was *so* nervous and tense when he came to us, but I'm sure you will find he has improved greatly in our care. Greatly. So much more relaxed and as I say, a most *charming* man, eager to help the staff in any way he can, so important in these times of difficulty, don't you agree? Yes, I'm sure you do – well, now he is probably in the lounge where our patients are able to foregather before lunch. We *do* try to give our charges the most refined atmosphere we can manage in these days of such severe staff problems. One is afflicted with the most slipshod people nowadays, don't you agree? *This* way, Miss Lucas, if you will just follow me –'

Talking all the way in her carefully strangled tones about the vital importance of maintaining good standards and the general dreadfulness of the sort of plebeian people she was forced to work with these days, the matron sailed ahead of Charlie like a galleon in full rig, taking her to a big room as ferociously clean as the hallway but with so much added daintiness in the form of heavily embroidered cushion covers on chintz draped sofas and chairs and china shepherds and winsome dog ornaments on low tables that Charlie felt as though she had been force-fed with honey. There were a few people sitting about in postures of some dejection, who visibly straightened themselves at the sight of the tall veiled figure who had appeared among them, but no sign of Brin.

'Perhaps the card room,' the matron murmured. 'His bridge is excellent and some of our better class of patients – I'm *sure* you know what I mean, Miss Lucas – some of them have started quite a busy little bridge club –'

But he wasn't there either, and finally, clearly put about now, the matron stopped a hurrying little nurse in the corridor that led to the sitting-rooms and asked her where Mr Lackland was to be found and the girl looked scared and muttered, 'Gone for a stroll in the garden, Matron, said you wouldn't mind –'

'In the *garden*? But no one ever walks in the garden in the mornings!' Matron sounded scandalized. 'Not at this time of the year. You know it's not allowed –'

'He went with Nurse Macmillan,' the other girl said and there was a spark of spite in her voice that puzzled Charlie for a moment, making curiosity push through her growing irritation. 'Shall I go and find them for you, Matron?'

'There is no need for anyone to go and find anybody,' Charlie said firmly. 'I don't suppose the gardens are that big. I'll find him for myself. Just direct me to the right door –'

'Our gardens are excellent,' the matron bridled immediately. 'This is the best appointed convalescent home in the town, indeed on the *entire* South Coast, I venture to say, both inside and out –'

'I'm sure it is,' Charlie said. 'But I can still find him for myself. Don't you come out, Matron – I wouldn't dream of taking you away from your duties –' And she nodded crisply at the tall woman and turned her back on her to look enquiringly at the nurse who pointed to the door at the end of the corridor.

'That'll lead you out to the rose garden,' she said, and added almost under her breath, 'And I'd look down at the far end if I was you – there's a summer-house –' And the note of spite was even more marked.

Charlie escaped into the chill November air with gratitude. The atmosphere of the place was overwhelmingly unpleasant, she told herself as she made her way between the dripping naked branches of the rose-bushes along a sodden grassy pathway; so desperately proper and fussy. Rigid as the hierarchy at Nellie's was, and strong though the discipline had to be, the place had a deep humanity about it. There was none of this strangled gentility there. Heavens, but Brin must hate it here, she thought again, full of contrition. I must tell him how sorry I am and find him somewhere better to recuperate. Or maybe it's time I eased him out of being looked after this way, altogether, time I got him back into his own flat, living a more normal life again. He can't go on for ever hiding away from life like this –

The rose garden came to an end, opening into a wide lawn dotted with several dejected rhododendrons and there, on the far side of it, she could see what she imagined must be the summer-house that the nurse had mentioned. It was a small structure built of undressed planks with a thatched roof and a trellis to which the dead branches of a clematis clung and she picked her way towards it over the soggy grass, wishing she'd worn more sensible shoes than the slight high-heeled ones she had put on this morning.

85

She had in fact dressed as carefully as she could before leaving London, not for a moment admitting to herself that she wanted to impress Brin with how interesting she could look once she shed her white coat, but aware all the same of wanting to make the best of herself. But now, in this wet Broadstairs garden where everything was dank and dismal her smart town suit looked more bedraggled than sophisticated and she was sure she had splashed the back of her stockings with mud; and since they were of lisle (she had no black-market contacts anywhere who could get her any precious nylons) the effect, she told herself miserably, must be less than alluring.

'Cheeky!' The voice seemed muffled and then there was a little squeal of laughter, and a breathless giggle and the voice said again, 'Cheeky devil – just like an octopus –' and there was a scuffling sound and Charlie stopped walking. The summer-house was now just a few feet away, but she could see nothing because there was no door to be seen and she walked round to the other side, peering as she went, seeking for the doorway.

And found it. In fact the whole front of the little building was open to the view beyond the lawn, where, when there was no mist to obscure it, there was probably a distant view of the sea. But Charlie wasn't interested in the view; only in the people she could now glimpse inside the summer-house.

It was shadowed in there, but she could just recognize the gleam of a starched white apron and cap and beside them a darker shape and then again there was that little giggle, this time cut off short and Charlie stood there frozen, hating herself for being there and yet not being able to walk silently away.

After a moment, she coughed, feeling wretched and like a character in a bad play, and at once the huddled pair in the shadowed summer-house moved and she saw the apron pull away, saw a pair of hands smooth it down, and then Brin's voice, that so familiar deep and exciting voice, said, 'Oh, lummy, caught in the – oh, glory be! No need to flap, silly girl. It's only my doctor! Good old Charlie! How are you? Why didn't you let me know you were coming down? I'd have laid on a real welcome for you! God, but it's good to see you!'

He had come bounding out and was standing beside her

now, holding both her hands in his and shaking them up and down, and his face was alight with real pleasure at seeing her, the uninjured side lifting into a delighted smile and even the damaged one seeming to look good. She stared at him and tried to collect her thoughts; she was wrong, she must be, he hadn't been locked in that great embrace with anyone, she'd imagined it, imagined she'd seen his hands wandering all over his companion, tugging at that white apron – there'd been no one there, it had been all her own silliness –

'Well, introduce me, Brin, do.' The voice sounded pert now and not at all breathless and Charlie turned unwillingly to look at its source. A girl with round blue eyes and a pink and white face surmounted by a froth of yellow curls stood there with her head on one side and her pink button of a mouth half open, staring back at her, and Charlie was suddenly very aware of her own dark thinness compared with this obvious prettiness and felt old and dull and dowdy. Even in her uniform the girl looked delectable, her waist small and tightly defined inside a wide black belt over which her bust pouted lavishly, and her slender legs clad in black silk. Clearly she had plenty of contacts to get her good stockings, Charlie thought absurdly, and then, as Brin said cheerfully, 'Oh, this is Nurse Macmillan, Charlie, a very naughty little handmaiden of Aesculapius who's doing her bit to improve my state of mind here. This is my doctor, Miss Lucas, little Mack, and we have to talk. So go and take yourself back to old Mr Pillbrow and see if you can revive the poor old devil in time for his lunch. If you see the battleaxe tell her I'm out here yearning for a sight of her – that'll keep her happy –' And he slapped the girl on her neat bottom and she giggled again and went obediently, looking back over her shoulder at him as she did so.

'Well,' Charlie said after a moment. 'I was worried that you might be miserable here! I took rather a dislike to the place when I got here and was feeling guilty for having sent you. Clearly I needn't have worried.'

'Oh, Charlie, it's dreadful!' he said cheerfully. 'A positive hive of gentility. Matron works so hard at being a grand lady that she convinces me she started life as a counter hand in Woolworth's. And the patients – they're really at the bottom of the world, believe me. Fussing all day about who's pinched their sugar ration and why isn't there any jam for tea, and who did what to who with which – ghastly.'

'You don't seem to be too unhappy, though,' Charlie said, hating herself for the waspish note in her voice as the girl disappeared into the house with a last wave at Brin. 'As far as I could see you were managing to console yourself pretty well.'

'Chap's got to do something to amuse himself,' Brin said and tucked one hand into her elbow. 'Come on. We'll walk round this benighted patch of unlovesome garden and you shall tell me all the news. How is it with McIndoe?'

But she couldn't leave it alone. She should have been as he was, insouciant and unconcerned, but that just wasn't possible. 'Is she someone special, that girl?'

'Mack? Ye gods, of course not! She's just number seven.' He chuckled and hugged her arm closer to his. 'I thought when I first saw that matron, I've got to do something about her, so pompous – it's unbelievable! So I set out to flirt with her, quite outrageous I was, but it worked! Eats out of my hand now, and then I thought – well, if I can captivate that old bag, even with a face like mine, let's see what I can do to other women here. And I've been flirting with 'em one after another. Promised myself I'd get every girl on the staff well and truly kissed before I left – and finish with the old bat herself –'

'Oh! Then it doesn't matter after all, your scar? You've proved to yourself that you can be as attractive with it as you were without it?'

'Oh no.' Suddenly he was serious again. 'It's one thing to flirt with silly nurses who've nothing better to look at than a scarred chap, because all the other men in this place are older than God and about as attractive, but it's quite another to deal with a career as an actor with this sort of handicap. I still want to know when McIndoe can put it right for me. You've fixed it, haven't you? That's why you're here? To tell me it's all arranged?' And he looked down at her eagerly, his eyes alight with excitement.

She looked back at him, trying to sort out her feelings and knowing she was a fool. From the moment this man had become her patient she'd been fascinated by him, and for the past few months positively obsessed. She who had always been too busy with her work, with her studying and her patients and her career to be bothered with men, to have been bowled over so very thoroughly – it was shaming, and her face reddened now as she looked at this man who had been occupying her thoughts for most of the time for so long and realized that as far as he was concerned she was his doctor, his ally, perhaps his friend – but no more than that. He did not see her in at all the way he saw girls with round baby-blue eyes and silly pouting mouths and fluffy yellow curls. They were for holding and kissing and for letting his hands explore as she had seen him in that summer-house exploring –

With an almost physical effort she pulled her thoughts back to the moment and to his question. If that was all she was to him, his doctor and his ally, then that was what she would have to be. To attempt to be otherwise was to be stupid in the extreme and that she must never be – or at least not so that it could be noticed by others. Bad enough that she knew herself to have been stupid. No need to display it –

'No,' she said. 'Not quite – I –'

'Not quite –' Brin's face flattened, every trace of the pleasure that had been there vanishing, and he stared at her with his mouth half open. 'No quite?' he said again. 'What does that mean?'

'I went to East Grinstead and saw the sort of work he does,' she said. 'Appalling injuries. A great deal worse than yours. I can see why he says he has no room for you in his ward. So would you if you could see what sort of people –'

'I don't give a damn about other people!' Brin burst out. 'Why the hell should I? Why does everyone try to make me feel guilty because I want to be well? Haven't I as much right as anyone else to be cared for? Are doctors now measuring the sort of treatment they give according to some sort of worthiness table? Are you going to start refusing to help people with – with cancer on the grounds that their cancer is only a little one and that other people have much worse ones? Doesn't it matter that both lots'll die if they're not treated? Doesn't it matter that I'm as unhappy and as disabled by my injury as a man with a much bigger one? What do I have to do to get across to you doctors that I'm miserable like this? That life isn't worth living? That I've got to be helped? Ye gods –'

'I know, Brin,' she said, and she spoke loudly, to over-whelm the almost shrill pitch of his voice. 'I know – I'm not trying to award scores for misery. I'm just trying to explain to

89

you why McIndoe won't take you at present. But I've got a plan. I'm going to try to work there with him –'

'You're leaving Nellie's?' His voice sharpened.

'Yes. I applied for a job at East Grinstead as a houseman – it's a step down as I'm a registrar at Nellie's, but it's worth it – and I'll train as a plastic surgeon myself. If he can't take you after I've done my stint there, then damn it, I'll operate myself. I'll have all the skills you need by then and –'

'Is that the best you can offer, you and your bloody McIndoe?' Brin roared and now his face was mottled with colour and the blood vessels in his neck stood out. 'All I need is a couple of weeks, surely – a simple operation and then –'

'Brin, it isn't as simple as you think. Your scar isn't as bad as many I've seen, but it is involved with several very delicate facial muscles. To operate on it successfully will take a lot of skill. I'm prepared to work at getting that skill for you. I can't do more. If you can't accept that, then –'

She stopped and turned away from him, and began to walk back towards the house. 'Then there's nothing more I can do for you. I'm sorry, but there it is. Either you wait till I can learn enough to be the surgeon you want, or you find yourself another practitioner to take care of you. I've gone as far as I can – I'm sorry, Brin, but that's the best I can do. It's up to you, now.'

11

The big room was dusty and cold and the peeling old green paint and the skylights, still crisscrossed with wartime sticky tape, admitted as little light as possible, yet for all that the place was crackling with excitement and Katy took a deep breath of the chill musty air and felt better than she had for a long time.

This was what she had missed, she now realized; the reality of work. It was all very well to be a film star and have all the fuss that was made of you going on, but filming wasn't real work, what with all the long boring waiting between shots and the fussing about camera angles and lights and microphones. Real acting started in places like this, rehearsal rooms where a show was put together, painful step by painful step, over long hours of concentrated effort which finally erupted into the high excitement of a long night's sustained performance.

And she looked round contentedly as all the frustration and loneliness of the last few weeks, ever since *The Lady Leapt High* had been released to such horrid notices, seemed to melt away and smoothed her already perfectly fitting slacks over her hips and pushed up the sleeves of her big baggy sweater – very American that, and she could feel the envious eyes of the other women on her and loved it – and settled down to enjoy her morning.

Across the room Letty was sitting with one buttock perched on the rough deal table that had been set up with a few battered bentwood chairs to accompany it, her head down over a sheaf of papers with smoke rising round it in a lazy tendril from the cigarette she had clamped between her lips. Her eyes were squinted against the smoke, and her hair looked ruffled and messy and her clothes – trousers and an old shirt – were far from exciting, though clearly well cut and expensive, yet for all that she looked good, and Katy grimaced a little at the sight of her. If I can look as interesting as that at her age, I won't complain, she thought. It's as though she's a spring, all coiled up and only just held in place, waiting for the least touch to explode into vigorous action.

Not like the man on the far side of the table, sitting quietly in his chair, and also watching Letty from deep-set shadowed eyes. Katy couldn't remember when she had last seen a man so thin; his features were so sharp they could have been carved out with a razor that very morning, and his head looked more like a skull with dead skin stretched, only just, to cover it than like part of a living man. His wrists, emerging from the big shaggy coat he was wearing, were as fragile as a bird's and his hands looked like great claws from this distance, fleshless and less than human. Yet for all his oddness, there was a familiarity about him.

Katy stared and frowned, trying to think who it was he looked like, and then as he turned his head to reply to something Letty said to him, recognition hit her like a shock wave. It couldn't be Peter, could it? She'd heard he'd come back to England after doing heaven knows what in the War, and wasn't too well, but she'd had no idea he was as changed as this, and she sat and stared at him, more subdued than she would have thought it possible for her to be.

To see Peter looking as sick as that made the War suddenly seem to have been important. Sitting in California all through the six years of fighting, working in films, going to parties, swimming and picnicking and being photographed wherever she went and whatever she did, the War had seemed to her to be little more than stints at the Stage Door Canteen and Bond Drives and public appearances at aeroplane factories; but looking at Peter now in a cold rehearsal room in Earlham Street in London's Seven Dials a full year or more after the War was over, the death and the horror of it became real to Katy for the first time, and she shrank back in her seat, and stopped feeling quite as good as she had. It was as though she were a child again, and a rather stupid one at that, who had suddenly learned to understand what being a grown up was all about. And didn't like it.

'All right, everyone, let's settle down, shall we? Settle down –' Letty called and the little knot of dancers who had been giggling together in a corner in the time-honoured way of dancers straightened up and pulled up their thick hand-knitted socks and came padding over to the middle of the room to collapse into elegant heaps at Letty's feet. The singers, who had been sitting by the old upright piano picking out notes and loudly complaining about its dreadful pitch, closed the instrument's lid and came across also to sit primly on the chairs provided and the rest of them, actors and speciality acts and musicians, arranged themselves behind them so that everyone was paying attention to Letty, who sat there calmly waiting for silence. And eventually got it.

'Right,' she said and took her cigarette from her lips and ground it out on the cocoa-tin lid beside her on the table. 'This is the first call for *Rising High*, the working title for a Benefit I've been asked to set up for Nellie's – Queen Eleanor's Hospital down the road. For your information, they badly need money for rebuilding a lump of the hospital that was bombed to a rubble and to reopen some wards they've had to close. They need at least ten thousand quid out of this effort which, even allowing for using the Stoll Theatre which has a capacity of two thousand two hundred and fifty seats and if filled to the roof at top prices can bring in a good deal, takes a lot of earning. There's a committee of ladies from the hospital' – and she nodded at someone who was sitting at the far end of the room, in a shadowy corner – 'who will be organizing a brochure in which they'll sell advertising space at no doubt vastly inflated prices' – there was a little titter at that – 'and they have other schemes for mulcting the audience of their cash. It's a good cause and they'll be working as hard as any of you. Right now, I want to thank all of you who are working for nothing. Your reward will be taking part in the best damned show I can devise for you, and the best quality audience you're likely to get this side of Paradise. I'll also make sure you get the highest level direction and music and all the rest of it. I'm producing and some of you will, I hope, remember the superb work of my old friend and colleague who also happens to be my cousin, Peter Lackland. He's working on this show too. Altogether, you'll be in good company. We've got David Crankshaw from the Opera House among our singers, James Fennel from the Guildhall School of Music to direct the orchestra, Irina Capelova from the Diaghilev company – and no need to be fearful of language

93

problems. She started life in Stepney as plain Irene Caplan, hey Irina? – and Katy Lackland, from the film side. Plenty of stars to share the limelight with you, you see, so I hope you'll enjoy yourselves.

'Now, I've set plenty of rehearsal time to accommodate those of you who are lucky enough to be in paying work, and we'll fit in as best we can with all of you. This first call is just to let us all meet each other and to give you an idea of the shape of what we're doing and to thank you all for your efforts.

'Right. The show, as I say, is called at present *Rising High*. Can't think of a better title, so there you are. It gets across the idea of a new hospital building going up, I hope. We want to do it as a revue knitted together with a story line – a bit different, you'll agree. And Peter's suggested we use the thread of the hospital's history. It was founded back in 1811, so there's plenty of history to use. He'll be researching it for us, putting a script of sorts together, with the help of Daniel Burke – you'll all remember the great hit he had with his play *Deborah* in '39 – and Irina who will choreograph dances to tell some parts of the history, and there'll be sketches and tableaux and songs; we're hoping to get some specially written music from James and altogether we should be on to a lovely original presentation. Any questions?'

'Yes – what time's tea?' someone called from the huddle of dancers and Letty grinned and turned her head to look into the shadows on the far side of the room and bawled, 'Mrs Alf! Naafi!' And there was an answering shout and then a clatter as a trolley was pushed out with a large and steaming tea urn on it as well as a number of thick white cups and plates of heavy sticky buns.

'I should have known not to keep you waiting for that,' Letty said and then, as they began to move with alacrity towards the trolley, raised her voice. 'As soon as you've got your tea, come and check with me how you're needed. Peter and I have our work sheets here and you'll be given your numbers and your calls. Tell us any problems you have with the rehearsal schedules as soon as you possibly can – all right, all of you –'

They scattered and there was a happy babble over which the constantly scolding voice of Mrs Alf, busily wielding tea urn and milk jug, could be heard, and Katy got to her feet and

94

moved lazily and with apparent unconcern, yet for all that very directly, towards Peter who still sat at the table looking down at the papers that Letty was now showing him.

'I'm not sure the original idea I had for her will work,' Letty was saying as she came up to them. 'I can't see how that'll fit into the theme. But I dare say I'll find something out of Shakespeare we can use –'

'I think we could still use the wooing scene, you know,' Peter said. 'It's about one person getting his or her own way over another – the whole play is, isn't it? Well, as I recall the history of Nellie's – and I've heard only odd bits here and there – the old man who started it all was a bit of a battler. With the right piece of linking script we could make it stand up. And she'd do the scene well. Given the right Petruchio –'

'Hello, Peter,' Katy said, deliberately making her voice throaty, and he looked up at her and the shock came new again. At this close range his eyes were quite dead, and the translucent frailty of him even more apparent.

'Katy,' he said after a moment. 'How are you? We were talking about you.'

'Saying good things, I know. You were always generous to a fault. Remember? That incredible universities tour before the War?'

'I remember,' he said, after another perceptible pause.

'We had a marvellous time. All those divine students, and the fuss about which plays they'd let us do, those ghastly Nazis – we had no idea why then, did we? And then we found out.'

'Yes,' Peter said woodenly, after the expected pause. 'Yes. Now we've found out.'

He seemed to be shrinking away from her, though in fact he hadn't moved, but Letty moved a little closer to him in an oddly protective fashion and said rather loudly, 'The wooing scene in the *Shrew*, Katy. We'd like you to look at it, work it up. I'll find you an attractive man to play opposite – could be good.'

'You'll direct it if I do it, Peter?' Katy didn't look at Letty.

'We don't know yet who's doing what,' Letty said shortly. 'No promises. Might be me, might be Peter. Will you do the scene? It's what we want. If you can't, of course –' And she left the implied threat hanging in the air and now Katy did glance at her and saw the watchfulness in her face and knew that Letty wouldn't hesitate to give her her congé.

And she didn't want to go. What had seemed when she first heard of it a bore, and only worth doing because it filled in some of the interminable dead time still left in her hated contract, was now a highly desirable activity. It offered not only a renewal of her first love of real theatre, but the renewal of an old acquaintanceship as well; an acquaintanceship that could, with a little judicious care, be ripened into something much more interesting. When she compared the man now sitting in front of her with the one she had known all those years ago, when she had been a brand new and very young actress, there was a marvellous challenge implied. The two had to be merged, made into a whole and more interesting *today* sort of man, and she, Katy, was the woman to do it. It would be fun –

And she smiled as bewitchingly as she knew how at Peter who, after that moment of delay that she now realized was characteristic of him, actually managed to lift the corners of his lips a little in response.

'If you'll excuse us now, Katy,' Letty said, loud again. 'We really must get on. Look, Peter, here's the basic story-board Danny worked out for me – you'll see that –' And she continued to turn her back to Katy so that Peter was hidden from her sight and she could no longer hear their conversation.

She stood still for a moment, gnawing her lower lip and then lifted her chin. She would walk round the table, talk to Peter again, in spite of Letty; and then as she raised her eyes she caught the direct gaze of the woman standing on the far side of the little group who had just emerged from the shadows.

'Oh!' she said, startled. 'What are you doing here? I didn't know you were a performer.'

'I'm not,' Lee said. 'I'm representing the hospital. I'm on the Board of Governors. Looking after the brochure and so on. Letty suggested I should come this morning, to see what was going to happen, meet some of the people –'

'How jolly for you,' Katy said, letting her voice drawl, and she threw a glance at Lee's neat suit and small dark hat that implied that they were exceedingly dull, though in fact they were chic in the extreme, and Lee flushed a little and looked away from her. Katy followed the line of her glance and saw

96

she was looking at Peter and flicked her own eyes back again to see on Lee's face an expression that startled her a little. She looked – what was it? Anxious and concerned, certainly, but there was something else there; a tenderness and an odd excitement, and then, as Lee looked back at Katy she saw the rest of it. The woman was as interested in Peter as she, Katy, was, saw in him the same possibilities, and suddenly Katy wanted to laugh aloud.

To try and coax Peter out of his state of misery and into the interesting here and now would be fun enough; to do so in competition with this pretty and well-dressed but undoubtedly dull woman would add to the delight enormously. She could think of nothing she'd enjoy more and she moved across to Lee, slid her arm across her shoulders, and said heartily, 'Well, those two are clearly *far* too busy to chat right now! Come and have some tea and we'll have a jolly cosy prose, just us girls together. You shall tell me *all* about how dear Harry is, and your children –' And she beamed at her, wanting to laugh aloud at the way the prospect of working on this show was improving by the moment.

'Er – thank you,' Lee said and let her lead her off to Mrs Alf's tea urn, chattering all the way, and Letty, well aware in spite of her apparent absorption in her conversation of what had been going on, watched them go and frowned.

'I hope I haven't made a mistake including Katy in this. She can be so malicious, damn it. She was always a rather selfish minx, but Hollywood ruined her – I swear she's up to something. I didn't have her living with me as long as I did without getting to know her in all her moods –'

Peter wasn't interested. He was still looking down at the call sheets on which they were working, absorbed and interested. He seemed to have come alive once more and the hesitancy in his speech had vanished.

'Oh, she'll do well enough,' he said. 'I can deal with her – I always did, and I can again. Look, Letty, if we aren't careful, we're going to overload the musicians. I know we're going to need them most of all, but all the same we can't call them as often as this. Look, what I suggest is this –' And he pulled a sheet of clean paper towards him and began to scribble a new pattern of rehearsals, and Letty sat there beside him and nodded, well able to dismiss Katy and her machinations from her mind while Peter was looking so much happier.

It's going to be all right, she was telling herself. It's going to be just fine.

12

She was sweating under her thin cotton theatre dress so much
that there were trickles between her breasts and running down
the centre of her back, and she turned her face to the nurse
standing behind her so that she could reach out and mop her
forehead for her, as though that would reduce her bodily
discomfort too, and then returned her attention to the pair of
retractors she was holding.

Her hands, smooth and glossy and amber-coloured in their
sheaths of rubber gloves looked alien to her, though she could
see her knuckles shining whitely through them above the
glitter of the chrome instruments, matching their appearance
to the strain she could feel in them, and she stared at them,
thinking: that's me, they're my hands – but she didn't really
believe it.

On the far side of the pool of light in which those almost
disembodied hands were so visible McIndoe's own hands
moved, swift and sure in their stubbiness, tying each minute
bleeding point with stitches so fine she could hardly see the silk
in his needle, and handling the instruments with such assur-
ance it was as though they grew out of his fingers rather than
being held in them.

'Concentrate,' McIndoe grunted. 'Your hands are shaking
and that's a bloody nuisance. Concentrate, woman, and be
still –'

Obediently she concentrated, consciously shifting the
tension from the muscles in her hands to those in her wrists
and forearms and her fingers, which had indeed begun to
tremble with their efforts, steadied and held the retractors
firm. The sheets of muscle she was keeping out of the way of
McIndoe's flashing needle remained just far apart enough for
him to work easily and he grunted again, a sound she took to
be approval this time, and moving in a gingerly fashion, she

straightened her shoulders. They were beginning to ache too, now, and she blinked the sweat out of her eyes again and thought – I'd never have dreamed plastic surgery could be so damned effortful. It's as bad as dealing with an above-the-knee amputation –

'Right,' McIndoe said. 'I'll have those retractors now. That's it – ease the muscles back and we'll see where the tucks have to be taken. Got it – shave it here – and here – and a little here – and yes – I'll have some number three catgut, Sister, unchromicized for this, and we'll be out of here. Nice, very nice – if that doesn't give the man better movement of the jaw, nothing will. Lucas, stitch that muscle there – yes, you. Time you had a go –' And he stepped back and his eyes glinted at her over the upper edge of his mask as Sister pushed a pair of needle holders into her hand, and she was at last released from holding those hateful retractors.

She looked down at the operative field in front of her, trying to see it as just a technical problem, a piece of tissue to be sewn, the way it was in other forms of surgery. When she operated on bellies and chests and limbs there was no obvious presence of a human being there on the table; just the vivid colours of a piece of familiar work; the dark green of the towels that edged the wound, the acid yellow of the skin painted with acri-flavine, the rich scarlet of the blood that streaked the whole; but this was different. There in front of her lay a human face, the eyes cotton-wool padded beneath the cap that was tied round the head and the gaping hole of the mouth filled with an endotracheal tube, but a recognizable face for all that. A face with its lower half flayed on one side, the skin folded back to reveal the torn muscles to which they were so painstakingly making their repairs, looking like so much meat on a butcher's slab –

'Well, get on, girl, get on!' McIndoe barked. 'I want my tea and I've a lot to do before the day's over, if you haven't –' And she glanced up at him, stung, remembering how much she too would have to do before she could drag her exhausted body to bed tonight and he looked back at her, his eyes bright above his mask, and she relaxed. The Boss's bark, they had told her, was much worse than his bite, and so she was discovering. His famous impatience in the theatre was aimed not at self-aggrandizement but at getting the best possible work done, and that was an aim they all shared, so she smiled at him, her eyes narrowing above her own sweat-damp mask and bent her head to the work.

Around her the theatre sounds, so familiar and comforting, accompanied the movements of her fingers; the soft susurration of the anaesthetic machine, measuring the steady rise and fall of the patient's breathing as the oxygen bag on it filled, emptied and filled again; the trickle of running water and the hiss of steam from the sterilizers outside and the click of the instruments on the trolley as Sister checked them, all made a counterpoint to the rhythm of her work, and she set the stitches delicately, moving as precisely as though she were dancing, sliding the curved needle through the fibres easily and gently, tying each stitch with its own careful knot; and slowly the muscle took its normal form, the gaping hole that had split it down so far that the underlying teeth could be seen, narrowing and finally closing to leave it looking as it did in the illustrations in her textbooks, smooth and red and with her line of sutures snaking elegantly across it. Now, it was the masseter muscle, running from maxilla to mandible; she could remember learning about it, long ago, in her first year as a medical student, enjoying the euphony of its name, and now it lay there beneath her hands bearing the clear evidence of the repairs she had made to its living fibres. It was an odd thought, that. That she had done something so powerful, so creative, was remarkable, and she stared at her handiwork and was cautiously pleased with herself.

'Very nice too,' McIndoe said and prodded the muscle with a critical finger and it resisted his touch and regained its smoothness, as soon as he moved his hand away. 'Very nice indeed. We'll make a plastic surgeon of her yet, eh?' And he jerked his head at the anaesthetist at the head of the table who laughed and said, 'If she survives you, Archie, she can survive anybody. She'll do fine –'

Standing there between the two men as Sister reached across to move the clips on the skin flap so that McIndoe could start replacing it across the naked muscle Charlie felt absurdly, childishly, pleased with herself. Praise from men like these was praise indeed; maybe this past few weeks of incredibly hard work and long hours had taught her something?

Certainly she would never have believed she could work as

delicately as she just had when she had first come out here to East Grinstead, and she looked down again at the face on the table, now rapidly becoming ever more normal, as McIndoe, working with his usual incredible speed, restructured and shaped the skin flaps, and felt a great wave of affection for the patient to whom it belonged. She would watch him very carefully as he recovered, tend his scar, make him look as good as she could – it was a warming prospect and for the first time since she had arrived here she felt as she used to feel long ago; calm and content and happy.

It really had been a miserable time, those weeks, and she looked back over them as she stood there beside McIndoe, snipping the catgut for him as he completed each stitch, seeing herself as she had been.

She had left Brin at the convalescent home in a towering rage; he had shouted at her, demanding that she take him at once to East Grinstead so that he could see McIndoe for himself and then, when she had refused to entertain such a stupid idea, had started trying to plead with her and when she had shaken her head at him, embarrassed at his obviousness, and had told him that unless he stopped she would have to leave, he had glared at her furiously and then turned on his heel and gone stamping away, leaving her there in the wet garden alone. And because even though she sent messages up to his room he had refused to speak to her again, she had had to walk out of the place, turning her back on him, miserable at having to behave so, never before having abandoned a patient in her professional life but not seeing anything else she could do.

And then having to honour the arrangements she had made to leave Nellie's and join the staff at East Grinstead, dealing with the farewells at the one and the newness of work at the other against a background of silence from him, had been dreadful. She had called the convalescent home the very next day after her visit only to be told by the Matron in a decidedly icy and yet somehow triumphant tone of voice that Mr Lackland had discharged himself the previous afternoon, and no, she had no idea where he had gone, and that had left her desolate. She had failed abysmally, both as a doctor and as a woman, and she hated herself for that.

How she had got through those exhausting first weeks at East Grinstead she would never know, but get through them she had, and now she stood in the main theatres, on this dark mid-December afternoon, feeling for the first time since she had arrived here that she was, after all, going to be able to cope. She may have failed with one patient, but she could still succeed with others.

'Right,' McIndoe said and pulled off his gloves and threw them on the floor as he went marching away from the table. 'Penicillin umbrella for this one for the next week – those teeth could give us trouble if we don't – and then get him back to his own hospital as fast as possible. I want that bed for a new pedicle graft for one of my air-crew boys. It'll be his last try at getting his nose right. The last two efforts we got gangrene, God knows why, but we did. This time I'm going to get it right, so help me Hannah, so we need that bed. Try to get this fella out before Christmas, Lucas, and we'll start those trims on Davy Smaul this evening as soon as you can get the theatre cleaned, Sister.' And the big double doors swung closed behind him and he was gone.

'I'll be ready here in three quarters of an hour, Miss Lucas' Sister said crisply. 'Nurse Hudson, Nurse Angers, you two get straight here and then go to your suppers. Peters and Dallas can set up for the evening list and I'll be back to take it. You can scrub too, Angers. Miss Lucas, *if* you please, the sooner we can get this man on his way the sooner we can all get on –'

The man was lifted to his trolley by the theatre porter who winked at Charlie behind Sister's back and she took charge of the complex tubing of the blood transfusion that was dripping into his arm – for he had bled copiously at the start of the operation – as a nurse took the other end of the trolley to see the man out and on his way to the ward, glad to leave the bustle of the theatres behind her for a while. Ten minutes in the ward, checking all was well, then a snatched cup of coffee and a sandwich in the common room and she could be back here ready for another couple of hours hard surgery before the day ground to an end in exhausted sleep. And tomorrow there'd be the usual mounting panic of dressings and ward rounds and theatre lists and more ward rounds and – she sighed softly and pulled off her mask and dropped it into the hamper before padding away alongside the trolley to the ward.

Usually she hated appearing there in theatre garb, knowing she looked absurdly young in her regulation white cotton dress and ankle socks and white plimsolls and that it was that which made the men tease her, but she was getting used to it. Apart from their appalling injuries, they were vigorous and healthy young men in whom the sap ran high, and she shared with the nurses the sort of attentions such men always paid to young women. They called her Charlie, loudly, and whistled at her, and the more daring ones pinched her bottom as she leaned over their beds, and though at first she had hated that, now she felt as the nurses did about it. It showed a man had hope for his future in spite of his appearance, that he hadn't given up trying; a pinched bottom and a lascivious leer and outrageous suggestions whispered into your ear as you performed a tricky dressing became experiences to be cheered, not reprimanded, indications of successful care.

The ward was full of its usual busy early evening hum as she got there, following the man on his theatre trolley, and she handed over the blood set to the ward nurse and stood there waiting for the theatre staff to get him into bed and safely tucked in, looking round and smiling a little.

The patients' taste in Christmas decorations was, to say the least, exotic. Paper chains and garlands hung from every available space and were looped dizzily round the metal girders that made up the ceiling, while a vast Christmas tree at the far end was so laden with parcels and baubles and homemade trimmings that it was almost impossible to see any of the green of its branches; but she could smell it, the sharp pungency of pine filling her nostrils and mixing uneasily with the usual Ward Three smells. There was a rather more evident reek of beer tonight, too, and she grinned as she saw the cluster of men in the far corner who, rather red of face over their bandages and sweaty of bodies, were busily putting together a special parcel amid great peals of noisy laughter. God help the poor nurse that was destined for, she thought, and then turned as the ward Sister came clacking across the wooden floor behind her.

'Ah, Miss Lucas – I've a letter here for you. I'm sorry – it actually got here this morning but the post clerk is new and didn't realize he should have taken it over to the mess for you. And I've only just seen it. Hope it isn't something madly important – I've told the post clerk in future to see to it you get your letters delivered to the right place at the right time, but there, you can't get any decent staff these days – now, you men, *what* are you up to there? I've told you before, I've had about as much of this mess as I can take –' And she went plunging towards the noisy group in the corner, who immediately went into a scurry of activity, as they hid away whatever it was they were busy with, leaving Charlie staring down at the envelope Sister had thrust into her hand.

The envelope was written in block capitals so that she couldn't certainly identify the handwriting and the postmark was blurred so that she couldn't read it, and she stared at it for a moment before pushing it into her pocket and hurrying over to the bed of the operation case, now safely ensconced and with the bottle from his blood transfusion glowing redly above his head on a stand, trying to concentrate on the matter in hand, which was ensuring that he was in good condition; but it was a difficult thing to do. All the time she examined him, checking his heart rate and his blood pressure, she could feel her own pulses beating harder and faster than they should in her ears and she was furious with herself. It was only a letter, damn it, and she couldn't even be sure who had sent it. Why get so excited? Calm down, do your job –

She hurried through her tasks; had to, unable to be comfortable until she could rip open the envelope and smooth out the pages inside, but then, when at last she had turned her patient over to the nursing staff and could go away to the mess to collect her meagre supper, she took her time. She sat in the corner of the big shabby room, withdrawing from the rest of the staff who were there chattering over their own meals and ate her sandwich slowly, not tasting it, but behaving as though it were something especially to savour, sipping her coffee as though it were a really fragrant brew instead of the repellent bottled stuff that was all that the hospital provided. And then when she had finished and couldn't delay any longer, she took the envelope slowly from her pocket and unwillingly opened it. And it was, of course, as she had known from the moment she had looked at it, from Brin.

'My dear Charlie,' his large erratic handwriting sprawled over the page. 'How I've the brass neck to write to you, I'll never know. Heavens, how badly I've behaved! To nag you so and then to sulk and fuss and go stamping off like a spoiled two-year-old – you don't have to say it. I've said it all to myself and more these past weeks. I've been saying it ever since I got here, the day after I was so hateful to you at that ghastly Broadstairs pest house. (It was awful, wasn't it? That Matron had lysol in her veins, I swear, but she adored me so she couldn't have been all bad, I suppose!) I went marching home like a stupid schoolboy and the moment I got here I knew I'd been an idiot. But there it was, I was here and there was no way Sophie was going to let me go straight back to London, which was of course what I wanted to do as soon as I got off the train at Haworth station! She took one look at me, being very much the big sister, and began to cluck like the most proverbial of hens and laid on so much in the way of food and hot water bottles and soft beds and general tender loving care that I couldn't escape.

'My father fussed too in his dour fashion and made me feel frightful. He's a good enough old stick, I dare say, but I can't pretend we've ever been as close as we might be. He's always been so wrapped up in his boring old Mill and local politics – and nothing is more boring than Yorkshire politics except perhaps Yorkshiremen, who are indeed a special breed – that talking to him was, for me, like climbing up the moors in bedroom slippers. And my dear, the weather here made it all seem so much worse! Tansy Clough (that's the family home, they've been living here for who knows how many generations, madly feudal) is all grey stone and bitter nights and not enough coal and what there is smokes so that you're kippered – but Sophie and Father have done so much to try to make it agreeable for me that I just got stuck here. Sophie has managed to get hold of some wood and so there we sit night after night, staring at the flames while my father nods over the *Yorkshire Post* and Sophie knits and watches me, anxiety on a plate! So, as you can see, I've had a rest as you suggested – but it's the sort of rest I imagine corpses feel they are getting, tucked into their graves.

'Anyway, here I am now, apologizing to you for being such a wretch and treating your kind efforts on my behalf like some sort of oaf. Of *course* you were right. I have to be patient, and if you feel you can eventually operate on me and make me look as I should, then I'll be forever grateful. So, please, *dear*

Charlie, this letter is to ask you to take me on again. I'm coming back to London – I've got to – can't stand it here another day – though quite what I'll do about a job I can't imagine, and I'd be so glad if you'd see me again, and make a plan for taking me in hand as soon as possible. I can hold on till the summer – that's when you'll be finished there at East Grinstead, isn't it? And then it'll be back to Nellie's and a nice new face for yours truly!

'Do say I'm forgiven and am once again the patient of the clever, dear and delightful Miss Lucas. Please, Charlie? Yours, grovelling and ever affectionately, Brinsley Brotherton Lackland.'

Slowly she folded the pile of thin sheets, over which his elaborate handwriting had sprawled in such profusion and slid them back into their envelope, and though she tried not to be exhilarated, it was impossible for her not to be. There she had been, not an hour ago, congratulating herself on having got over her obsession with this damned man and here he was again pushing her with one extravagantly written letter right back into the tangle of feelings she had lived in ever since he had first turned up at Nellie's as a patient. She was excited and dubious and hopeful and frightened and happy all at the same time; it was an exceedingly queasy mix of emotions and she wasn't sure she could cope with it again. She had, in a sense, got out of practice.

But for all she lectured herself as she left the medical staff room and made her way back to the theatres to scrub up ready for the evening cases, for all she went on telling herself off through the long hours as McIndoe snipped and shaped and smoothed and stitched, while she held his instruments and anticipated his needs as she had been trained to do, the excitement never left her. Brin was coming to London. Brin wanted to see her again. What more could she want? What more except, perhaps, a little peace of mind.

13

'Invitation!' announced the piece of paper pinned to the rehearsal room notice board. 'To all and sundry, near and far, the *Rising High* company in particular. You are all invited to my New Year's party, next Monday, 30 December, from 7 p.m. onwards, at Rules Restaurant in Maiden Lane. Sorry, no room for spouses or other attachments – we are a big company! RSVP on the attached sheet and say you can bring yourself, your appetite and your thirst. I'll look forward to dealing with them for you. (Signed) Letty Lackland.'

'That's a bit odd,' one of the dancers said, peering at it. 'I mean, why the day *before* New Year's Eve? Seems a funny sort of thing to do –'

'She'd have to invite those – what does she call 'em – spouses and attachments if it was on Tuesday night, wouldn't she? You can't split loving couples then, can you? And like she says, we're a big company.'

'Seems a bit on the mean side, all the same,' one of the other dancers joined in. 'There's my boy, just out of the army, poor darling – how can I not bring him? After all, serving his country all those years –'

'What, him, sitting out the duration in a cosy quarter-master's office in Aldershot? I should cocoa! Never heard a shot fired, he didn't –'

'He worked very hard! I shall ask her if I can bring him – she can't say no –'

'Oh, yes she can,' the first dancer said and leaned over and scribbled her name on the acceptance list. 'I tried that. Asked her if I could bring that super flight sergeant I met at the Stage Door Canteen – he's gorgeous! But she wasn't having any. Nice about it she was, very sorry and all that, but the original Rock of Gibraltar, believe me! Be sad if I wasn't there, she said, but she only had accommodation for the company – and let's face it, it must be costing her a bomb! What'll you do then? Come and join in or go out with your quartermaster?'

'I'll think about it,' the other girl said loftily and turned and flounced away. 'Got to discuss it with him, haven't I? Come on, I'm due at the Palladium in half an hour for an audition. If you want to go through that flower sellers' routine with me before I leave, you'd better put a move on –'

They moved away to the far side of the big room towards the piano, chattering like starlings all the time, to start their rehearsal, and Katy, who had been leaning quietly against the wall listening to them, quirked her lips. So dear Aunt Letty wasn't being amenable about bringing extra people to her boring party? Fine – then she wouldn't be asked. Katy would just bring him and see if even Letty had the brass neck to chuck him out. She'd be livid and watching her control that would be fun, and Katy hadn't had a great deal of fun lately, what with Peter being so aloof all the time and the rest of the company including no one of any interest at all. She hadn't even been able to see anything of old Harry, in spite of cultivating that tiresome Lee as she had. The last weeks had been nothing but work and Katy was getting decidedly bored. Ripe for mischief, that's me, she thought then and smiled brilliantly as the tall and very good-looking – but somewhat dull – actor who had been cast to play Petruchio opposite her came hipping his way into the room. He was the most boring of all, with his doggish devotion, and any moment now she'd give him the sharpest snub of his life. But not quite yet –

'Peter, this is ridiculous!' Letty said. 'I don't need you to work yourself to a streak, dammit! You'll be exhausted if you go on like this, and then what use will you be? Let me get an assistant for you – someone to take some of the donkey work off your back.'

'Not yet,' Peter said. 'Honestly, I'm coping well, really well. And I am enjoying it, you know. And wasn't that the object of the exercise?'

'It certainly wasn't to make you look like your own ghost! Are you sleeping properly? Eating as you should? Looking at you I'd say you weren't.'

'I'm sleeping incredibly well,' Peter said and lifted his eyes to her face. 'Can't you tell?'

She looked at him carefully, unhappy about what she saw. The smudges of violet shadow beneath his eyes were even darker than they had been and there was a pallor about his sunken cheeks that seemed to go right into him, to be much more than a mere surface attribute. But she had to admit that the deadness had gone out of his eyes. That opaque stare that had so chilled her wasn't there any more and he looked at her so birdlike and bright that she had to smile, and he responded with a sudden grin of his own.

'Well, yes, I can tell. You're different. But are you eating?'

'Dear Letty, it's very hard to get interested in eating the awful sort of stuff that we're offered these days. I mean, snoek and dried eggs – hardly conducive to greed, are they?'

'Maybe not, but you've got to eat all the same. I'll talk to Mrs Alf. She's got her fingers in more black market pies than anyone I know. She's even managed to get the most enormous goose for my party – the people at Rules nearly fell over with shock when she brought it in – and I haven't a moment's compunction about getting her to do something for you. Eggs and cream and good broths, that's what you need –'

'You get them and I'll consider eating them,' Peter said. 'Black market or not. It mayn't be very ethical, but who gives a damn about ethics any more, anyway?'

'Every inch the cynic, that's you,' Letty said but the jeer in her voice was a gentle one. 'All right. I'll try to sort things out as far as some decent food's concerned. And I'm also going to get you an assistant. No, don't fuss, man. I'm the boss here and you'll do as you're told and like it.'

'Dame Goody Two-shoes on the rampage,' Peter murmured. 'Power's gone to your head –' But he didn't argue any more, because he was indeed getting very tired, and that was not an agreeable way to feel. He'd thought that once the horror of his nightmares stopped he'd be completely well again, but it just wasn't working out that way. But all the same, he told himself as he settled down to putting Katy and Rollo through their scene so that Letty could see how they were shaping – all the same, be grateful. You're sleeping these nights, you're sleeping. And that is no mean achievement.

'Well, that'll put a nasty little spike into the Lackland guns,' William Molloy said with a deep satisfaction and slapped down the letter he was holding so that it lay precisely in the middle of the blotter on James Brodie's desk. 'I've tried to warn 'em, of course, but they don't listen to me. I'm just the secretary here, that's all, no one at all. But maybe they'll pay some attention to the Ministry of Health.'

Brodie picked up the letter and read it carefully and then sniffed and put it neatly back in the same place. 'I wouldn't pay too much attention to this, old man. It's the usual Civil Service chatter, stuffed with parties of the first part and parties of the second part and pursuant to the acts and so on and so forth. If you'd had as much experience as I have of dealing with these obfuscators you wouldn't get so excited.'

'I am not excited. I am merely pointing out to you that any money they raise with these junketings of theirs will be –'

'Will be used for the benefit of Nellie's. As I understand it, the show will be done some time in the summer. They need a lot of time to get all the people properly rehearsed, and free from other commitments, and time, too, to get the sets and their costumes organized –' He sounded very knowledgeable in these theatrical matters and blinked owlishly at Molloy. 'They are a very important part of any performance, you understand –'

'I've been to theatres before, you know. I'm not precisely an idiot. But I also know that these Ministry people mean business. If there's any money in the kitty when they take over, it goes to the Government, every damned penny, to use for their lunatic state medicine schemes. That's what that letter says – I can follow Whitehall English if you can't. And here are these Lacklands swanning around raising money left right and centre, telling people it's for Nellie's –'

'And so it is!'

'– when all the time it's going to go straight to the Treasury! They might as well pay voluntary income tax, these people, as –'

'And what do you propose? That we throw up our hands now and stop worrying about where we're to get money from? There are bills to be paid every damned day in this place, as well I know! Do I tell our good hardworking fund-raisers not to bother any more and let Nellie's fall apart? Do I let the patients go hungry and without clean linen – or turn them away altogether? And what about the new block? Do we

forget all about the fact that we haven't any proper pathological facilities and –'

'For heaven's sake, man, didn't you *read* that letter? Can't
you see what it says? Even if you get all the money in from this
stupid show and the new building started it won't be
completed before April '48 when the new scheme starts! It
won't be Nellie's money any more or Nellie's building or –'

'Oh, of course it will!' Brodie said and leaned back in his
chair to stare offensively at Molloy down his rather long nose.
'It's you who seem to lack the ability to understand what's as
plain as the nose on your face. There will still be a Nellie's, still
be patients who belong to Nellie's and who rely on Nellie's.
The only difference will be that we won't have to fuss so much
about where the money's to come from to keep the wheels
turning. The Government will provide all we need and very
nice too – so we might just as well start as we mean to go on,
and raise the cash we want to get our new block started. Can't
you understand that work commenced by April '48 will have
to be completed? But that work that's still in the planning
stage could be held over for heaven knows how long? If we
want to keep control here, then we let the Lacklands go on
beavering away at their fund raising. We need every penny we
can get and the sooner the better. I'm already looking at the
estimates from the architects and sounding out builders and
I've got all sorts of feelers into the Min. of Supply. The sooner
I get essential materials ordered the better – do you have any
conception what it's like to get a few simple basics these days?
If you don't, you ought to spend a few days with me – then
you'd know what there was to really worry about. I'm in
competition for cement and bricks and paint and all the rest of
it with every major building in London – because you can't use
your prefabricated Portal buildings here, you know! That's
what *I* have to fret over! It certainly isn't the fact that the
Government'll be taking over the running of Nellie's. It's the
fact that the Government needs a lot of prodding to get done
the things we need done now, that's the worry. Do stop
fussing, man, and get on with encouraging the Board to keep
on keeping on –'

'One thing you can be sure of,' Molloy said spitefully, 'is
that you'll be out of a job once they take over with their
damned scheme. You can start as many projects as you like

now, expecting to be busy keeping them going after Whitehall moves in, but it won't be so easy for you. They'll always need a hospital secretary here to keep the place going, but a bursar? You'll be as obsolete as – as a Focke-Wulf fighter, after Nye Bevan really gets going –'

Brodie laughed at that, a wide grin of real amusement. 'I don't think so, old boy. I'm afraid you can't get rid of me as easily as that. Just you wait and see how it'll all be – I've got myself well and truly sorted out, don't you fret!' And he bent his head over his desk, pulling a ledger towards him to signal the end of the discussion, and Molloy made a small disgusted noise, halfway between a snort and an exclamation and turned on his heel, and went. Bloody man, he thought as he slammed the door behind him. Bloody man!

And the bloodiest thing about him is that he could be right. Maybe I should be quiet about this letter, not stop the Benefit sub-committee from ploughing on, not alarm them unnecessarily. Once we've got the money, then there'll be time to worry about whether we had a legal right to raise it. Once we've got it. And he went into his office and slammed the door and spent the rest of the day reducing his secretary to tears as often as he could.

When the idea had come to her Lee wasn't certain. It was as though one moment such a notion had never entered her head and the next there it was, complete, down to the last detail of the plan she would need to carry it out.

And once the idea had come to her, there was no disposing of it. It haunted her, coming between everything she did, whispering at her as she sat and coaxed Stella to eat her greens and while she helped Michael with his homework or tried to teach impatient clumsy-fingered Sarah to knit.

She would get it all organized in advance, that was the thing. Don't say a word to anyone, least of all to Harry. Find a house to rent somewhere as near as possible to this one, so that the children didn't have to change schools. That would be the hardest part of it all of course; ever since the War had ended the demand for flats and houses in London had gone mad, as well she knew. Hadn't she tried to help any number of her friends to find places to come back to from their evacuation hideaways in the country? Everyone wanted to live in London again, and prices were lunatic. But all the same, with her father and her brother to help she'd be all right – both of them were sensible capable businessmen who had friends everywhere. One of them should be able to plug her into the network, find her the home she needed.

And once she'd got her house, she'd quietly furnish it. She had never used much of her own money, leaving it quietly to accumulate in her bank, for Harry, to give him his due, was not a mean man. He paid all the household bills with never a murmur, and equally quietly paid for all her clothes and other personal needs with never a moment's suggestion that she should use her own considerable resources. Well, now she would use them. She would furnish the house, once she got it, with the new utility furniture which might not be beautiful but at least was well designed and sturdy, and she could soon make a place look like home with her own collection of pictures and Victorian embroideries and –

She tried over and over again to push the whole absurd idea out of her mind, but it was impossible. Because over and over again the certainty rose that this *was* the answer; that to go on as she had been, fretting over him, lying awake wondering what time he was coming home, weeping bitterly at the sense of rejection with which he filled her, was lunacy. She was Lee Lackland, a person in her own right. She didn't have to tolerate this sort of pain, didn't have to be so humiliated all the time. She could manage well enough to care for the children alone. She had her parents still, after all, even though she wouldn't want to cause them distress of course, and she had her brother and his wife to turn to, and all the cousins and –

Not that I would, she told herself, sitting alone in the drawing-room one night after the children had gone to bed, after her usual lonely supper on a tray. Not that I would. I'd manage well enough on my own. Aren't I already on my own most of the time anyway? Why should I find life any different? It would be the same – only a bit better because at least I'd have my self-respect.

Self-respect? a little part of her mind sneered. How could you have self-respect if you did this? No one in the family has ever done such a thing before; could you live with the way they'd all whisper and talk and stare? And what about your friends, and the people you know who would talk and talk?

What about the children, and *their* friends and what they would say? Come off it, Lee Lackland! What self-respect could you possibly have if you did so crazy a thing?

It's not crazy, she told the little voice, sitting staring into the tiny fire that was all she could manage until a new supply of coal arrived. It's not crazy. It's just something that has to be done. And I'll do it.

I'll sue Harry for divorce; heaven knows I've grounds enough. And if that won't make me happy, at least it will put an end to the sort of unhappiness I've had for so long.

14

Letty stopped at the Southampton Street end of Maiden Lane, and with one hand tugged her coat collar closer to her ears while with the other she held grimly to her umbrella, which was struggling as though it were a live thing to escape and go sailing away into the wind. I must have been mad to do this, she thought, quite, quite mad. I'll go and find a phone box somewhere, ring and tell 'em I'm ill and can't come and to go ahead without me; they won't give a damn either way, and I can go home to have a hot bath and an early night and –

And then what? she jeered at herself. Just sail into the next rehearsal and face it out, all the fuss and drama and congratulations there'll be once they see it in the paper? This way at least I'll get it over and done with in one fast simple act, and they'll exclaim and open their eyes wide and that'll be that. You've got to go. Anyway, they're sure to make an awful mess of it all if you aren't there to keep an eye on everything. And you're paying for it, after all. So stop whining.

The wind came leaping even more boisterously round the corner, slapping her coat sharply against her legs and attacking her cheeks with exuberant wet kisses and she felt a sudden lift of exhilaration as a car with its headlights blazing came out of Maiden Lane and went rattling on its way up Tavistock Street. The wartime blackout regulations had long since been abandoned of course, but they had been stringent enough for her still to get a lift of sheer pleasure out of seeing the darkness shattered by light, and she tilted her head to gaze towards the bustle of the Strand and the glittering shop windows there, and then looked at the upper storeys of the Southampton Street houses, glowing rosily and cheerfully in the December night and thought: London: where else could I bear to live but here in my London?

Her exhilaration bubbled higher and warmer then and she

lifted her chin to the rain, holding her umbrella tilted over her shoulder so that she could feel the cool wetness of the sooty drops on her face, and took a deep breath. It was as though she could feel London all round her, could see it in all its sprawling immensity, grey and red under its pall of smoke and pock-marked with hideous craters and deadened buildings, but alive and stirring for all its weariness; could see herself standing there diminutive and wind-battered in the middle of Covent Garden in the middle of London, in the middle of the world that had survived the awfulness of the past half dozen years or so. She, like her London, was ageing and tired and consider-ably the worse for wear, but like her London, she had lived through a great many horrors and was still here to go on making plans, being busy, feeling alive.

It was a splendid way to be and to feel and she laughed aloud and turned sharply right to start her short walk down Maiden Lane to Rules, her doubts about her plans for the evening vanquished; she was giving a party to announce her elevation to a Damehood, and by God it was going to be a great party. She was whistling as she arrived and pushed her way past the old plush curtain that hung behind the entrance door and went into the cosiness of the bar beyond, as happy as she could remember being for a very long time.

The place was already humming with people, and smoke was thickening the air convivially as actors and dancers and musicians shouted at each other at the tops of their voices, and Letty grinned a little sardonically as she peeled off her wet coat. No one could make more noise than performers showing off, she thought, especially performers who all knew each other. Thank God I insisted it was to be the company only; otherwise they'd have brought all their out-of-work friends and this would have turned into one of those frightful, 'Hallo, darling, *how* are you?' and 'Hallo, darling, *who* are you?' affairs.

'Letty!' The small dark and very vivid Irina Capelova emerged from the crush of bodies and seized her wrist in a hot little hand. 'Thank God you're here. My dear, do come and rescue Peter. That idiot Don Portland – the stage manager chappie you brought in last month – is talking all sorts of nonsense about what happened during the War, and I swear Peter's about to go up in flames –' And she pulled her into the hubbub and through it to the far side where a small group were sitting at one of the round tables which had been set for the evening meal.

Letty saw at once that Irina had been more than right about Peter. He was sitting on the far side of the table, his face so tightly controlled that his skin looked like parchment stretched over a drum, and his eyes were glittering so that for a moment she almost thought he was in tears; but it was anger that was filling them with that flinty sparkle as he stared at Portland. His face, an unwholesome saggy one that made Letty think of a wax doll that had been left in the hot sun, was flushed and sweating and his own eyes were dull and fixed in comparison with Peter's as the words fell out of his lips, slightly slurred with the drinks he had obviously already taken in abundance, but clear enough to be well understood.

'– Not as though we got anything out of the whole bloody shambles anyway,' he was saying as Letty reached the table. 'I mean, here we are, never been worse off in living memory, no bloody food, no decent clothes to put on your back, not a dribble of petrol to be had off the black market and try to get a flat that isn't falling to pieces! No coal, no hot water, no bleedin' whisky or cigarettes without queues, rationing worse than it ever was, and what for? All because we went off to fight the Germans – and not such a bad lot, they weren't. Knew 'em well, I did, b'fore the bloody War – worked there for years, I did – decent enough chaps, in their own way. Efficient? I'll tell you! All the trains ran on time there, and what about those autobahns they built, hey? Fantastic, they were – I tell you, we could ha' done worse than be Germany's allies – better than these stinkin' Socialists we're stuck with now – they'll join us up to bloody Russia any minute, and you'll wish for a decent Kraut government then, believe you me – Should have left 'em alone to deal with their plans in their own way in '39 – Chamberlain was right, I reckon, all that fightin', what good did it do anyone? Those Sheenies brought it on themselves anyway – time they got what was comin' to 'em –'

There was a rattle as Peter lurched to his feet and his chair was tipped backwards, and Letty, seeing the dark flush that was now rising in his cheeks, moved forwards smoothly and said in a low voice that disturbed none of the people chattering so busily behind them but which the people at the table could hear easily, 'Portland, shut up. You're a drunken disgusting fool, and I don't want to hear another word from you, now or ever. Get out. You aren't wanted here now, and you aren't wanted in the *Rising High* company any more either. Keep away from us, or I warn you there'll be all hell let loose. Daniel –' And she flicked her eyes at the writer who had been sitting redfaced with embarrassment on Peter's other side. 'Daniel, take this – this lump of nastiness away. You can go out through the kitchens, I dare say – George'll show you –' And the young waiter who had been hovering with avid interest behind them shot forward willingly.

Portland got to his feet and stood leaning on his knuckles on the table to steady himself and peered at her blearily.

'Whassat? You can't chuck me! Done nothin'! Can't chuck me – have Equity on you I will –'

'Oh, get out,' Letty said disgustedly and pushed past him to reach Peter on the far side. 'You try and involve Equity in this and you won't know what hit you! I'll see to it you never work again. This is a charity show anyway, so Equity won't give a damn, and after the sort of things you've said here tonight in front of witnesses, it's unlikely they'd be interested in offering you so much as a torn paper bag in the way of protection. People don't go into battle for slugs like you. Get out – *now* –', and as Daniel, moving with alacrity, pulled on the man's elbow she took Peter's hand and firmly but not ungently pulled him away and back into the crowd standing around the bar, none of whom had noticed the brief altercation.

'I'll kill him,' Peter said in a flat expressionless voice and she pushed her hand into the crook of his elbow, feeling the muscles as tight as bowstrings beneath her fingers and said as matter-of-factly as she could, 'Don't be stupid. Characters like that aren't worth wasting spit on, let alone touching. Forget him. We'll get a new stage manager and he can go to hell his own way –'

'How can it be?' Peter's voice was still low, but there was more animation in him now. 'Is he just a lunatic or are there others like him? Can there be people in England who think that what happened there was – I mean, God damn it, trains running on time, compared with what they did at Belsen? Autobahns to compensate for gas chambers? How can a man with any head at all come out with such crap? How can it be?'

Letty looked at him briefly and then, as a waiter came pushing through the crowd, which was steadily thickening as more and more people arrived, she took a glass of wine from his tray and pushed it into Peter's hand.

'Drink up,' she said shortly. 'The toast is better days and better people.' She looked at him consideringly as he drank and then said abruptly, 'I dare say there are a few more like Portland and you might as well face that fact. You don't think you can get rid of a disease like Nazism just by winning wars, do you, Peter? Winning can be a difficult burden – it can make some people, like the Portlands of this world, think they ought to be getting something better than they have. Wars have to be paid for, but his sort don't want to cough up their share. He's a greedy, selfish bastard, so he hankers after the sort of regime that greedy selfish bastards think'll give 'em what they want. How else d'you suppose Hitler got ordinary Germans to join in? Because there were enough like him. And there are enough here in England still, God help us.'

'More like Portland?' Peter stared into his glass. 'Jesus, Letty, why did I bother to come back? I should have stayed there with them, battled it out with them, those people at Belsen. I should never have come back –'

She stood very still as the crowd eddied round them, as water moves round a rock in a stream, looking at his bent head and wanting so much to reach out and hold him close to comfort him. But it would be the wrong thing to do; how she knew that she couldn't be sure, but she knew it all the same, and acted on that knowledge.

'You make me sick!' she said in the most contemptuous voice she could muster, and Peter's head shot up and he stared at her, his eyes wide and shocked.

'What?'

'I said, you make me sick. Are you going to let a revolting slug like that Portland defeat you? Are you going to go crawling back into the hell you've started to get out of, because of what *he* said? If you are, then you deserve to live in hell and worse for the rest of your life. I'll wash my hands of you if you let a creature like *that* affect you.' And she turned her back on him and began to push away through the clusters of her guests towards the corner where a sweating barman was pouring out with great lavishness the wine she had ordered for her party.

For one dreadful moment she thought it hadn't worked; that he was just going to let her go, but then she felt his hand on her shoulder and it was as though a hot-water-bottle had been set there, so immediately warm and comforting was that touch.

'Sorry, Letty,' Peter said in her ear. 'You're right, of course. The man's a shit, if you'll forgive the barrack-room language.'

Somehow she managed to laugh. 'Forgive the language? Ducky, I was swearing better than that before you were born! Now for Christ's sake, get me a drink and let's make a party here. Look, there's Rollo just arriving – ye gods, will you look at that jacket? Where do you suppose he got it?'

'Wherever it was, he ought to put it back immediately,' Peter said and laughed and she looked round at him and knew there were tears in her eyes and didn't care at all.

'Peter, you're a great man, you know that?' she said, but so softly he might not have heard, but he certainly felt the warmth from her, for he gripped her shoulder more tightly and then, as though by previous agreement, they both turned to greet the new arrivals, Rollo at the forefront.

'Very nice, dear,' Peter said loudly, letting his eyes drift mockingly over Rollo's blue velvet jacket. 'Where's the skirt?'

Rollo made a moue and then grinned. 'Saving it up for you, dear heart,' he said. 'It's a nice full one and it'll do a lot to disguise those skinny legs of yours. Letty, darling, this looks like the best party *ever*. Positively pre-War. It's magnificent. The wine flows and the food, they tell me on the grapevine, is going to be something very special. Am I to believe roast goose?'

'Indeed you are!' Letty said jovially, and patted Rollo's cheek. His handsome face and cheerful open campness had always amused her, and amusing people were always welcome, but tonight she was doubly pleased to see him. 'And if you behave, I'll even let you have some bones to chew on. Oh, hello, Katy – how absolutely lovely you look –'

She did indeed look breathtaking and several people turned to stare and the chatter around them faltered as they gazed at her, taking in the sheath of gold lamé and the glitter of sequins on the squared shoulders and long sinuous sleeves. The neckline dipped daringly and above it her throat rose as

121

smooth and rich as a column of cream beneath a face as perfect as cosmetics could make it. Her eyes were wide and sparkling, her nose charmingly wrinkled, her hair a drift of curls and she smiled bewitchingly at Letty and said, 'Dearest Letty, the best aunt anyone ever had. I've been an absolute villain, and I beg you to forgive me.'

'My dear girl!' Letty opened her eyes wide. 'Whatever have you done?'

'I know you said there was no room tonight for spouses and attachments, but what could I do? Here's my poor darling bro sitting alone in his beastly little flat in Earlham Street with nowhere to go and all night to get there and I simply hadn't the heart to leave him to droop there in solitary like that. I've brought him to your lovely party, because he's so depressed, no job or anything to cheer him. So *do* say you'll forgive me. Will you?'

And she set her head to one side as pert as a robin on a spade handle in a winter garden and as certain of her welcome, and smiled enchantingly.

Letty looked at her, nonplussed, very aware of the sudden hush behind her as the rest of the company waited for her response. All week she had been regretfully but firmly refusing requests to bring special people to the party, not even accepting wives or husbands, for Rules, fashionable and popular restaurant though it was, was far from roomy. They had already overflowed the section that had been set aside for the party, and other diners, she knew, were muttering darkly about damned pushy theatricals making such a nuisance of themselves. And now here was Katy looking as delicious and as appealing as only Katy could, and challenging her.

Letty lifted her chin to look beyond Katy to Brin who was standing quietly behind her, seeming unaware of the tension that was surrounding him and looking round with an interested expression on his face. The scar that crawled across his cheek was livid in the soft light that came from the brackets on the walls between the clustered caricatures of the many notables who used the place and his eyes above it reflected the lamps' glitter. He was wearing an old but impeccably cut dinner jacket and soft shirt with a wider than usual black tie, and was standing in a relaxed and comfortable way with his raincoat hooked across his hands which were clasped in front of him.

Damn you, Katy, Letty was thinking. Damn you, painting me into a corner like this. Bringing someone with an injury like that, so that if I stick to my guns and turn him away I'm the biggest bitch in the world – but if I yield and let him stay, then I'm an even bigger bitch for giving my own nephew preference when I've turned away other people's equally valued relations. Damn you, damn you, *damn* you –

'Hello, Aunt Letty,' Brin said in a low voice, but it was a clear, well-modulated one and carried easily to the far side of the bar. There was no doubt now that everyone could hear him, especially as no one was any longer making any pretence of conversing, all listening avidly to the exchange. 'I haven't seen you since I can't remember when. You look just as I recall you, though, only better. Success suits you down to the ground. I do hope Katy was right, and that you don't mind me tagging along like this? I've been up in Haworth you know, with Father and Sophie – they send you their best love of course – and to tell you the truth, I'm bored out of my skull. I ache for a little theatrical gossip. It's as though I've been deprived of my life blood!'

He looked around at the people crowded around and smiled amiably, and they stared uneasily back – though some of the girls tossed their heads like startled and interested ponies as he caught their glances.

And then, suddenly, Letty felt as she had on her way to Rules, when she had stood on the corner and felt the pattern of London round her, seen herself as part of a great scheme in which she had a role to play, but over which she exerted no sort of control. It was as though there were other forces organizing her, and organizing life around her, using her for their own ends as the pieces fell satisfyingly into place, smoothed out and made a beautifully shapely design of the tangle in which she had found herself.

'No job, did you say, Katy?' she said clearly, letting her drawling voice lift so that she too could be clearly heard by everyone. 'My dear chap, how disagreeable! And a man of the theatre, as I recall –'

'Yes,' he said. 'An actor.' And then he lifted one hand and touched the scar on his cheek with one long forefinger, a fleeting regretful little gesture that made more than one of the watching girls catch their breaths as pity sent a sharp little dart into them. 'Heaven knows what hope I have of ever getting another job of course, but – well, to be with actors again would be like a transfusion, Aunt Letty. I'm sure *you'll* know what it's like to be away from all the things you most enjoy –' And his hand drifted away back to his raincoat.

'Can't give you a part,' Letty said brusquely. 'Not casting anything at the moment.' Very deliberately she didn't look at his scarred face, keeping her gaze fixed on his eyes. 'But I can give you a job. Had to send the stage manager off tonight with a flea in his ear. Disgustingly drunk and revolting with it. Won't have him anywhere near any show of mine, that's for certain, so I need a senior stage manager to take over. Can you cope with that? There are two ASMs to help you, but you'll have to help Peter too – our director. He's overworked, needs a lot of running around and dogsbodying for him. No pay of course – only expenses – it's a charity job. But after this show's over, I'll be back doing something commercial again, and people I've worked with happily in this show are obviously going to be well at the front of my mind when I come to set up future companies. So what do you say?'

Brin stared at her, his eyes a little narrowed and then slowly he smiled, and his scar puckered as his lips lifted.

'Dear Aunt Letty, that's the best offer I've had this side of last Christmas! To work for you for no pay'd be better than working for the whole Moss Empire at a hundred a week. Yes, please, I'd love to.'

Letty grinned with delight and moving past Katy as though she weren't there, set her hand into the crook of Brin's elbow and pulled him into the middle of the room.

'Listen, everyone! I want to introduce you to the newest member of the *Rising High* company – Brin Lackland, taking the place of the singularly repellent Portland, who had the brass neck to get stewed in the middle of *my* party, on *my* booze, and make a disgusting nuisance of himself. But someone up there loves us, because now we've got a much better chap. Now everyone, fill your glasses, and have fun. We'll be eating soon – and I'm going to have a rather personal and embarrassing announcement to make. No – shan't tell you yet! Right now it's drinking time, and Hello-to-Brin time –'

And she beamed round as people moved forwards to speak

124

to Brin and shot a glance over her shoulder at Katy who was standing at the door still, with no one paying any attention to her at all. It was such an unusual sight that Letty couldn't help laughing and Katy saw her amusement and reddened furiously. But Letty didn't mind that at all.

15

January blew itself out petulantly and gave way to a sulky, freezing sodden February during which everyone shivered and grumbled at the bitter cold because of the fuel crisis that had emptied all the coal stores. The cast of *Rising High* came to rehearsals so wrapped in scarves and mittens and heavy overcoats that they could only just walk through their paces; offering the director any sort of vivacity in performance was, clearly, out of the question. Tempers weren't helped either by the fact that many of them found themselves out of paid work, as shows closed because paying customers found no pleasure in sitting shivering in unheated auditoria, and managements held back from launching new productions until they could be sure of bringing in the necessary bottoms to fill the seats. Altogether it was a miserable way to start the New Year of 1947.

But as the weeks wore on and a few brave snowdrops started to appear in grimy parks and squares, through the palls of sooty snow that lingered everywhere, and sparrows began to scold each other furiously over nesting-places, moods lifted. The cold weather gave way to a more blustery cloud-scudding freshness and spirits rose as London came to life again. Every other street seemed to be partially blocked by builders' vans and lorries, and piles of bricks and cement mixers starred the gaping holes where buildings had used to be, promising newer streetscapes for the future. The city felt like a game old woman who had been sick almost to death, but who was at last getting better and stirring in her bed, shifting the covers, sitting up and taking notice and even putting some makeup on her sagging old cheeks. Or so Charlie thought as she went hurrying along Shaftesbury Avenue towards Letty's rehearsal rooms down at the Cambridge Circus end, almost in Seven Dials.

Not that there was any need to hurry. She could have taken the later train from East Grinstead and a bus from Victoria and still been punctual, but somehow she found it easier to kill time at this end, loitering along the Charing Cross Road and peering into musty old bookshops, trickling the minutes through her fingers to make them into hours, waiting till the exact moment when it would be permissible to climb the dusty cat-scented stairs that led to the big bare room where Brin was spending his days with Peter and those of the cast of the show who had been called to rehearsal and who could get there.

Silly to be so excited, she thought now, as at last she reached the Circus and her pace perforce slowed to a loiter. We see each other quite often now, after all. I ought to be used to it. But she wasn't, and she doubted she ever would be. Ever since he had returned to London from Haworth and pushed his way back into her life her obsession with him had grown, and she was embarrassed by it as much as anything. There was something so childish about being in love, she thought. It marched so uneasily with her vision of herself as a cool professional and practical woman. Surgeons intent on building themselves careers as plastic surgeons – as she now was – shouldn't dream and droop over a man like a character in a story in a woman's magazine. In-love-ness was for shopgirls and factory hands or for silly little junior nurses, not for serious thoughtful women like Charlotte Hankin Lucas.

And then she would castigate herself for her snobbery, for wasn't it a perfectly normal feminine thing to do, to seek a mate? It was high time she satisfied her biological urges, she would tell herself sternly, for she was approaching thirty, after all, and this obsession with Brin was Nature's way of prodding her into action. And then she would shake her head at her own silliness and set her mind to concentrating on her practice with the specimens of muscle and skin that McIndoe obtained for her, bending her head over her busy fingers in the circle of light on the work-bench in the histological laboratory.

That usually helped, because she was enjoying developing her manual skills. She knew that it was possible to be a deft and delicate surgeon even with fingers like bananas; she had already noticed that McIndoe's were stubby and far from the long-fingered supple image that so many people had of the surgeon's hands, but all the same it was useful to have small neat fingers like her own, and she was becoming quietly proud of the work they were capable of doing. Stitches of the finest cobweb silk put in with a needle so whippy and delicate that it could only be seen when the light hit it and sent reflections back, created repaired incisions that were a delight to behold and which would, she knew, have healed to a perfect hairline scar in living tissue. She had started by suturing clean cuts and then had moved on to the jagged tears that were so often presented to plastic surgeons, and then to the painstaking patchwork restructurings that were needed where burned tissue had to be replaced with grafts of different thicknesses from different parts of the patient's body.

And it was not only in her practice that she was beginning to excel; more and more McIndoe – a generous teacher – encouraged her to operate on her own cases, taking on increasingly difficult ones until she was sometimes being positively heroic in the range of work she was doing. She made big pedicle grafts and also learned to handle tiny Thiersch grafts; she remodelled burned-off noses and destroyed eyelids, reshaped torn lips and tattered ears, often having to do several such operations on one injured man. She would see her cases anxiously through the immediate post-operative days and supervise the crucial early dressings and then see them on their way to convalescence, their faces – and therefore their view of themselves and their world – quite transformed. And that would make her glow with content-ment, an experience powerful enough to push Brin Lackland well to the back of her mind.

But not completely. His welfare and her developing skills had become inextricably woven in her mind, so that she knew that her training would only be complete when she had operated on him and dealt with that wide scar that puckered his face and wrinkled his eye so interestingly. When she had smoothed out that pucker and disposed of that wrinkling then and only then would she be ready to leave McIndoe's side and start out on her own career as a mender of hurt faces.

That was her new ambition, the plan on which all her previous training and experience now seemed to be focused, so that in a very real sense Brin mattered to her not only personally but professionally too. His welfare was hers – and that made her feel both exhilarated and uneasy. To be so dependent on another person for fulfilment can't be healthy, her inner voice would murmur, and she would try to ignore it. But the anxiety was always there.

Today it sharpened her eagerness to see him, and after the hour had at last passed by – some of it occupied in buying a quaint old medical book published in 1890, from Foyle's bookshop – she made her way with a bouncy step to the door that led around the corner from the rehearsal room feeling everything about her with extra sensitivity; the icy wind slapping rubbish around the frosted gutters, and whipping her own cheeks to a glowing red, the smell of petrol and gas in the street from the nearby building site where a main had, as usual, been fractured – London seemed to smell of gas almost everywhere these days – and the rattle of traffic in Cambridge Circus, all battered at her senses. But she was content, for what better way could there be to spend one of her few days off than with Brin?

And today, happily, he seemed as pleased to see her as she was to see him. Sometimes he was sulky and almost offhand when they met, only gradually becoming more cheerful as their time together went by, but she put this down to the way he felt about what he was doing.

That even an unpaid job was better than no job at all was undoubted. He needed to be occupied and he was well aware of that fact, and to give him his full due, he was not a man who cared a great deal for money as money. He wanted to be a highly paid actor if he could, but only because the level of his cash reward would be an indication of the level of the esteem in which he was held by the public. All he needed now, however, was enough to live on and he had that. His little flat in Earlham Street, which he had rented for a number of years, was cheap and he was lucky to have it in these times of chronic housing shortages; his small income, drawn from the modest fortune his mother had left him, and supplemented by an allowance from his father, was enough to feed him. There were no costs to be met for clothes, for who could buy clothes when rationing was so severe that one was lucky if one's meagre allotment of coupons kept one in essentials like socks and underwear? So that was not a problem.

But the longueurs of the job he had were. Letty, he would tell Charlie furiously, had allowed far too much time for the production of this Benefit show. She had said it was because she had to fit in with the performers, all of whom were giving their services free and needed to earn their livings as well as to work at raising money for Nellie's, but as far as Brin was concerned, this was all nonsense.

'It's all so damned *tedious*,' he'd said the last time they had met, sitting hunched over the interminable cups of coffee or tea they would share in shabby Lyons' teashops whenever Charlie came to London. 'Peter sits there as silent as the bloody grave and only manages to dredge up some conversation when Letty comes in – I could die of boredom.'

'Not enough work to do?' Charlie said sympathetically, knowing how miserable she would be without her hours well filled.

'Oh, it's not that,' Brin said. 'They keep me belting around like a lunatic. There's plenty of work – it's just that there's no one to talk to as much as I'd like – though some of the dancers are rather delicious.' He had chuckled then, his mood improving suddenly. 'They don't talk much, or when they do it's just babble, but then, it's not talking I want to share with *them*.'

And Charlie had managed to say nothing and not to show that she minded these casual references he would make to flirting with the girls. She knew he did, that casual kisses and caresses in dark corners of the rehearsal room were an integral part of his life and was glad he talked to her so freely about it, seeing it as an indication of intimacy they shared. If they weren't close friends, rather than patient and doctor, he would be more discreet, surely? His free and easy chatter about girls was really a compliment, she would tell herself fiercely and it was silly to get these stabs of jealousy. The dancers meant nothing to him; they were just silly girls he played with and then forgot and she knew it. But all the same the jealousy did flare, often, and she hated it.

But on this bright and blustery morning it was different, and her belly tightened with pleasure when she walked into the rehearsal room and saw the wide and welcoming grin with which he greeted her. Today his mood was a good one and they'd have a lovely time, and she grinned back delightedly, not knowing how pretty her relief made her look.

'Charlie, I've got a treat for you today!' he said gaily. 'I managed to scrounge some chicken off the ration, would you believe, from that funny little shop in Short's Gardens, and this morning, before I came here, I put it with great reverence into Mrs Burroughs' hands with strict instructions to make something magic out of it. She mayn't be much of a cleaner of the flat, but she's a fantastic cook, I'll tell you, so come on. We'll have a super lunch *chez moi* and gossip.' And he waved a casual hand at the others and they went clattering happily away down the stairs.

Katy watched them go and then said easily to Peter, 'Chicken! Lucky devil – but he's not the only one. Peter, dear heart, I have been making the most outrageous sheep's eyes at the old man at Ley On's, and I've got a table! He's promised me all sorts of wondrous Chinese goodies if we turn up there in good time. What do you say? Noodles and the like should set you up for the afternoon, and you've got that big flower sellers' number to do, haven't you? And Rollo said he'd be in too, to do ours – and high time too, the lazy wretch – so we need a bit of sustenance.'

Peter looked up vaguely from the set designs he had been studying and Letty, sitting beside him, looked sharply at Katy too and considered for a moment opting herself into the planned lunch. The waiter at Ley On's restaurant wasn't the only recipient of Katy's outrageous sheep's eyeing, she thought; maybe Peter needed a little protection. There was no way, as Letty well knew, that Katy was doing anything but playing a game of flirtation with him to pass the time until she could go thankfully back to Hollywood when her contract was ended and promptly forget him, and Peter had been hurt enough.

She threw a quick glance at him now and thought for a moment and then relaxed. It was worth the risk; he was looking much better now than he had, his body becoming less fragile and his face filling out a little as at last he began to put on some weight, and he seemed to be amused by Katy, no more. Right now he was looking at her with a grin and seemed very much like the Peter of the pre-War years.

'It sounds delicious, but I did sort of tell Lee that I'd see her this afternoon, give her a bit of a progress report – the Committee are wanting more news now we're getting to about the half-way stage, and I want to know how they're getting on with the brochure and so forth. I really ought to –'

Letty made up her mind suddenly. Katy was doing more good for Peter now than she might do potential harm, she decided.

'I'll see her,' she said brusquely. 'I want to talk to her about this wretched paper shortage. They've sent out a damned Government circular limiting the amount that can be used for magazines and so forth, and I'm worried about our ration for the brochure. So you go and have lunch – I'll sort things out with Lee.'

'There!' Katy said gaily and reached for Peter's hands and pulled him to his feet. 'Noodles were written in your stars for you today, and who are you to fight the stars? We shall go and make absolute pigs of ourselves and to hell with the regulations. He'll charge us the legal rate for lunch and pounds and pounds for our pots of Chinese tea and we'll get far more than our share. Lovely and greedy! Do you mind being a black marketeer?'

'Not too much,' Peter said, and shrugged on his coat. 'It's a very minor form of villainy, after all. I've seen worse –'

'Haven't we all, darling,' Katy said, and tucked her hand into his arm and threw a glittering look at Letty. 'Give my best love to darling Lee,' she said, and took Peter triumphantly away, and he went happily enough, with more of a spring in his step than Letty had seen before, so that she began to regret her hasty decision to aid and abet Katy. That minx, she thought uneasily as she heard their footsteps receding down the stairs; will she hurt him? He's doing so well, and it would take so little to shatter him again. But it's too late now, and she heard the street door far below slam behind them.

In the event it was better for Peter that she had kept him away from Lee, she decided an hour or so later as she sat opposite her in the teashop near the rehearsal rooms. She was as well dressed as she always was, as perfectly turned out, but there was a listlessness about her that made the air between them seem to hang heavily and Letty looked at her bent head as she stirred her tea mechanically for far longer than was necessary

132

to dissolve the saccharin in it, and shook her own head in some irritation.

'Well, come on Lee, out with it,' she said. 'What's bothering you?'

Lee looked up, almost visibly pulling her mind into the here and now from wherever it had been.

'I'm sorry, Letty,' she said. 'Am I being rather dull? It's – it's just that I'm worried about this brochure business. We're going to need every penny we can get, and it's worth thousands and thousands to us to get that advertising printed. If we can't, then, really, the Benefit just won't be as worthwhile as it should and –'

'We've been through all that. I've told you, I'll fix it. I've got contacts. This is me, Letty, remember? I'm family as well as friend. Now, what's really the matter?'

There was a little silence and then Lee said baldly, 'I'm going to divorce Harry.'

'Oh,' Letty said after a long pause. 'Are you indeed?'

'I've found a house, and it's almost ready. I'll be moving in with the children a fortnight on Friday. It's quite a nice one. Very convenient for the children's schools and so on, and Nanny has said she'll stay with me, thank God. I was afraid she'd go all proper on me and refuse to work in a household where a divorce was happening –' Her voice trailed away and she returned to the stirring of her tea.

'What does Harry say about this? Has he agreed to – to give you grounds?'

'Give me grounds?' Lee laughed, a singularly mirthless sound. 'He doesn't have to give me any grounds. I've had them to hand any time this past two years. I shall just serve the papers on him. Or my solicitor will. As for what he'll say –' She shrugged. 'I really don't know. I'm past caring.'

Letty stared at her blankly. 'Are you trying to tell me you haven't talked about this?'

'What's the point, Letty? We're miles apart and – what's there to talk about? He spends all his time flirting with other women, rushing from one to another – if one refuses him then he seems not to care and turns to the nearest that will listen to him. It's one of the things that makes me feel so *sick*.' Lee's pale face reddened suddenly. 'He's so undiscriminating. It's as though anyone will do. As long as it isn't me –' And again she

133

bent her head, unwilling to meet Letty's direct gaze.

'Well, I certainly hope you manage to keep the children out of earshot the day you move out,' Letty said grimly. 'I imagine he's unlikely to just sit there quietly and let you pick up your luggage and go.'

'He won't be there,' Lee said drearily. 'He'll be away for the weekend. Says he's got a case in Sussex, near Brighton, to follow up and won't be back till late on the Sunday.'

She laughed again, that short ugly little sound that was so unlike the Lee that Letty had always known. 'He's got no imagination, has he? Brighton! I ask you – he's probably taking her to the Metropole with all the other seedy little weekenders –'

'Do you know who she is?' Letty asked, her voice as sympathetic as she could make it.

'Could be anyone. One of the nurses, I imagine. He's bedded most of them, at one time or another. No, don't look like that, Letty. I'm no fool. Not now, at any rate. I have been, for far too long. He's been rushing around women like – like some bloody rabbit for all this time and I've tried to pretend to myself it hasn't been happening. Well, I'm not telling myself any more lies. I've had enough –'

That Lee should swear, however mildly, was an indication of how distressed she was, Letty thought, and reached out impulsively to hold her hand on the table top. 'My dear, I'm so sorry. Anything I can do to help –'

'Thanks,' Lee said. 'I – it's the family I'm worried about. Old Sir Lewis and –' She swallowed. 'They were all so proud of you when you got your Damehood, and – and now I'm going to disgrace you all. There's never been a divorce in the Lackland family, ever, and I'm going to ruin everything. But I just don't know what else to do – I truly don't –' and tears began to splash off the end of her nose onto Letty's rather gnarled hand on the table. 'I'm sorry, Letty, so sorry. I hope there won't be any publicity – I hate the thought of it for myself enough – I hate it even more for you.'

'Never mind that,' Letty said bracingly. 'I doubt any of the papers will care at all. They're so short of newsprint these days that such matters won't concern 'em –'

But she knew she was lying. When her name had appeared in the New Year's honours list there hadn't been a newspaper of any political colour that hadn't made much of it. Her photograph had been everywhere, and now taxi drivers greeted her cheekily as Dame Letty when they picked her up, and strangers in the street nodded and becked knowingly at her. Oh, there would be publicity all right over a divorce involving a member of the Lackland family.

'Well, you know where I am if you need me,' she said, and signalled at the bored waitress in the corner for her bill. 'But meanwhile, the best advice I can give you is to talk to Harry as soon as you can. Whatever has happened between you, and however stupid he's been lately, he's still Harry. He used to be a good caring sort of chap, and somewhere inside he still is. Talk to him, and you might be able to sort it out –'

But Lee shook her head stubbornly, and despite Letty's attempts over the next fifteen minutes to persuade her, she was adamant. She was going to walk out of her marriage with all the dignity she could and that meant without saying anything to Harry.

Which means, Letty told herself grimly as she went stumping back to the rehearsal rooms, I'll have to talk to him myself. Wretched Harry, she thought furiously, remembering that golden afternoon more than a dozen years ago when she had stood in a Golders Green garden at their wedding, watching the adoration that hung between them as rich and as sensuous as the roses that had clustered on the bushes all round them, *wretched* Harry to hurt her so! By God, but he's a fool. And somehow I've got to try to get him back to his senses in time. If it isn't too late already.

16

'Oh, my God, but I wish Letty were here,' Peter said beneath his breath and looked rather helplessly from one to the other of them not knowing what to do.

If he'd had any inkling of what the problem was when Brin had phoned the rehearsal room and asked him to bring Katy to his flat, he would, frankly, have found a way to duck out of it. He was getting slowly better – there was no comparison between the way he had been before Christmas when Letty had first scooped him up and set him to work and how he felt now – but he was still frail, and he knew it. Over the weeks of rehearsal he had learned the importance of pacing himself both physically and emotionally. Now he regularly walked all round Kensington Gardens in the evenings, whatever the weather, and was eating heartily but he made sure that he lived as peaceful and ordered a life as possible, avoiding any attempts to pull him into social affairs, only going out sometimes to eat a meal in a restaurant with Katy when she could persuade him. To get involved like this with someone else's distress was more painful; it made him feel shaky, made the old veils of fear seem to come creeping back into his mind and that was something he couldn't possibly allow to happen.

'I'll try to see if I can find her,' he said now, and began to move towards the door, edging away a little gingerly and ashamed of himself for doing so. 'She ought to be here.'

'She told me yesterday she wouldn't be back at Albany until late tonight,' Brin said shortly, from the depths of his big armchair. 'She said she wasn't going to tell me where she was or who she was with because she wasn't to be bothered. Important family business, she said –'

'This is important family business too,' Katy burst out, sitting upright on the sofa on to which she had thrown herself full length to weep. 'How much more important could it possibly be?'

She began to cry again, not pretty tears of the sort she could shed on stage at command, but real tears, ugly ones which reddened her nose and distorted her face so that she no longer looked like a girl but very much a woman, and one who was beginning to age rather quickly at that. 'Oh, God, Brin, how could you not have told me how bad it was! If I'd have realized I'd have gone like a shot –'

'I told you, damn it!' Brin shouted. 'Don't blame me because you just didn't want to know. I feel bad enough about not going up myself and not telling Letty either, but how was I to know he was so ill? Sophie always fusses a lot – I thought she was just making dramas – how was I to know?'

'When did it happen?' Katy said, and rubbed her face to dry it, but the tears still flowed, roughening her eyelids and making them swell. 'Would there have been time to get there?'

'The telegram's over there,' Brin said and indicated the table. 'It doesn't say much.'

'Read it to me, Peter,' Katy said. 'I can't see clearly – please read it to me.'

Unwillingly Peter picked up the flimsy piece of paper and smoothed it.

'Father died six a.m.,' he read, his voice flat and expressionless. 'Tried phone you, no answer, call at once. Sophie.'

'Have you called her?' Katy said, turning to Brin and he nodded, still sitting slumped in his armchair.

'I called her,' he said, and now there were tears in his voice too. 'She was –' he stopped, choking a little.

'I'm not going to the funeral,' Katy said loudly and sat straight up. 'I can't bear funerals. I want to remember Pa the way he was last time I saw him, not in a bloody box and all those damned Haworth people staring and – I shan't go –' Her voice rose to a wail. 'I shan't go, I shan't –'

'She says she doesn't want us to come up. It'll – if we'd been there in time to see him it'd be different, she said, but as we couldn't get there, it'll be better if there's just a quiet funeral – and – they'll all gossip horribly if we turn up now.'

There was a little silence and then Katy said, 'Oh, Brin, we've been awful.'

'I know. Bastards. But – I just didn't believe Sophie. She makes such –'

'No she doesn't,' Katy said, and her voice became shrill again. 'We're just kidding ourselves. She expects us to behave right and we never do. And when she said Pa was very ill and we ought to go up we should have listened to her.'

'Well, we didn't, did we?' Brin shouted. 'We chose to stay here, all right? And now she says she doesn't want us to come to the funeral because we'd be an embarrassment. If the villagers thought we were in London and could have got there before he died, well – it'd make it miserable for her and for George and John. She's told people we were away at the time Pa got ill and she couldn't get a message to us and –' He got to his feet and began to prowl around the room. 'So there it is. She's sorting everything out and says we're not to worry. She sends her love.'

Katy began to cry again and after a moment Peter went over and sat down beside her and took her hand and she turned and clung to him, weeping even more bitterly.

'I feel such a beast, Peter – It's not that I don't care – I do – it's just that I hate illness and death. It was bad enough when Mother died and – I just couldn't get away fast enough. So I couldn't bear to go to Haworth when Sophie sent for us. I just couldn't, so I pretended to myself it was nothing to worry about and just refused to think about it and now I hate myself for it, I hate myself –'

'No sense in that,' Peter said, trying to sound as practical as he could, modelling himself on Letty. 'No sense at all. I made myself ill fretting over what I should have done and didn't and hating myself for it. Don't do it. Whatever happened, you can't unhappen it. Live with it, and promise yourself you'll be better next time –'

'There won't be a next time.' Katy drew a big shuddering breath. 'There's no one else but us, now, us and Sophie. George and John are both married and got children so it's all right for them. They've got other people to think about. But we, we're just ourselves. And – oh, hell!" And she pulled away from Peter and went to the door. 'I'm going to wash my face,' she said and disappeared and Peter looked after her and bit his lip, trying to decide what to do.

'Thanks for bringing her home,' Brin said. 'I suppose I should have just come round and fetched her, but I felt so – oh, hell and damnation!' And he went over to the window and stood there banging his fist rhythmically on the frame as he stared out into the street below.

That he was deeply distressed there could be no doubt; Peter had found him a rather difficult person to work with, polite and friendly enough but lacking any depth that would have made it possible for him to forge any sort of real friendship, but now there was no shallowness about him. He was grieving and wracked with guilt, and from all Peter could gather, a justifiable one. There was nothing anyone could do to help him cope with that.

'I'll try to find Letty,' he said now, getting to his feet a little awkwardly. 'You'll want to be left alone, I imagine. But Letty will want to know and I'll send her as soon as I can. He was her brother, wasn't he?'

'Yes,' Brin said, still staring out of the window. 'Her brother and my father. They weren't very close, but still, her brother –'

'Yes,' Peter said and went to the door. 'Tell Katy how sorry I am. I – I'll see you both when you're ready to – well, goodbye, Brin. My sympathy –' And gratefully he escaped into the street.

In spite of all the death he had seen, all the grief he had shared, he found each episode of bereavement as painful as though it had been the first he had encountered. The only thing to do, he decided, was to go to Albany. If Letty wasn't there he'd wait for her. Then he could hand over to her the responsibility for the two people sitting there in that little flat and hating themselves and each other, and go back to being quiet and peaceful and dealing with his own pain. I've had quite enough of that, he told himself defensively as he began to walk down Shaftesbury Avenue towards Piccadilly Circus; I'm entitled to try to escape other people's misery as much as I can, surely. But he wasn't really convinced by his own arguments.

The next few days were, to put it mildly, difficult. Once Letty had come back to Albany, rather grim around the mouth, and been told what had happened, he had thought his responsibility to the younger Lacklands had been discharged, and had gone back to work, grateful to be busy and trying not to think about them. But it wasn't easy, even though he was overloaded with details to look after in Brin's absence – whatever else Brin was, he was a hard-working man who had been a genuine assistant – and by the following Friday he was on the verge of exhaustion, both from actual work and from the way many of his own distressing feelings about death seemed to have been remobilized by what had happened to Brin and Katy.

He knew he was getting short-tempered and difficult to deal with; he saw the occasional startled expressions on the actors' faces when he snapped at them, or seemed slow to understand what was said to him, or explained something badly, and fear began to rise in him. Had his recovery from last year's awfulness been just a flash in the pan? Was he going to get ill again? For a while he contemplated giving up the job of director and going cap in hand to his brother Max to ask him to take care of him. He had managed to avoid that when he had first returned from Belsen, but now, because an old man who had been full of years and had a good and tranquil life had died peacefully in his bed, in his own home, he was like this. It made no sense.

It was on Friday afternoon, when he was trying to understand what Daniel had done to restructure the first half of the show in such a way that they could get in an extra number that had been offered to them by one of the better known dancers from Sadler's Wells, when his head was aching and it seemed to him that everything anyone said to him came to his ears through layers of thick mush, that Brin came back to work.

The door opened and there he was, with Letty standing just behind him. Peter was filled with a sudden sense of deep gratitude at the sight of her; she had been away for so many days, it seemed, almost a lifetime, and there she was, foursquare and solid, looking at him with that wonderfully familiar sardonic twist to her lips, and when she glanced at him some of the mist that had filled his mind seemed to melt and drift away.

'Letty,' he said, getting to his feet a little clumsily. 'And Brin. I'm glad to see you both –'

Letty was shocked. It was as though the past weeks of progress with Peter had never happened. There he stood as gaunt and as remote as he had been the day she had first gone to see him in Leinster Terrace and though he was properly dressed, there was once more that slightly ill-kempt look about him. He hadn't shaved today and the shadows seemed to hollow his cheeks even more. She saw the look of relief on Daniel's face at the sight of her too, and the way he lifted his brows expressively at Peter's back and she bit her lip. She had no right to forget that Peter still needed support and help. To have left him for so long without so much as a message had been unforgivable.

'Peter,' she said and came into the room. 'I should have called you. I'm sorry. I went to Haworth for my brother's funeral and –' She turned then and stepped aside so that the person who was standing behind her could come in. 'I've brought my other niece back with me. She's a dear girl and she's decided to take care of Brin. Says he needs a housekeeper, so here she is.'

She smiled then as Brin scowled. 'He, of course, doesn't think so, but Sophie does, and so do I. Anyway, it's time she came to London and saw a little of metropolitan life. Sophie, my dear, this is Peter. I've told you all about him.'

It was extraordinary how unlike Katy she was, and yet at the same time there could be no mistaking the fact that they were sisters. It was as though Sophie were a monochrome version of highly coloured Katy; where Katy's skin was rich peaches and cream, Sophie's was somewhat sallow; where Katy's hair curled wildly in entrancing tendrils, Sophie's sat neatly on her head in restrained waves. Katy's eyes spoke volumes of wickedness, while Sophie looked tranquilly at her world without seeming to show any special interest in what she saw. Katy's vivacity was in Sophie a dullness. But, Peter found himself thinking, it was a restful dullness and he managed a smile and found himself rubbing his stubbled cheeks with an embarrassed hand, not wanting to be seen by those cool eyes to look so dishevelled.

'How do you do?' he murmured after a little pause, and Letty looked at him sharply, concerned to hear that hesitation again, but his eyes were clear and he was looking at Sophie with interest rather than with that opaque stare she had found so worrying.

'I'm very well, thank you,' Sophie said and her slight Yorkshire accent made her voice sound a little flat. 'I hope you are.'

'Er, yes,' Peter said and then he blinked and added, 'I'm so sorry to hear of your loss.'

'Yes,' Sophie said collectedly. 'It was very unfortunate. Aunt Letty –' And she turned towards her.

'Please, don't call me Aunt,' Letty said firmly. 'It was bad enough having one of you doing that – when Katy first came to me. To have three grown people labelling me so makes me feel older than God.'

'I'm sorry,' Sophie said gravely. 'I'll try to remember. I was just thinking – I've brought some supplies from Tansy Clough with me. One of the farmers killed a pig, you know, so I thought I'd stock Brin's larder for him. Perhaps you'd like to come along to supper, and bring Mr Lackland here? I've plenty for all, and it would be good to be able to get to know each other a little better, wouldn't it? Families ought to stick together –'

'We're quite distant cousins, of course,' Peter heard himself saying and then was furious with his own idiocy. It had sounded so unkind and he opened his mouth to explain that he hadn't meant to be ungracious but Sophie nodded, still unsmiling but not appearing at all put out, and said, 'Oh, I know that. I've made quite a study of our family history, in my own way, but still and all we are cousins, and bear the same name, so I hope you'll come and have a meal with us.'

'Really, Sophie, must you fuss so?' Brin said, and his expression was still scowling. 'I'm sure Peter's got better things to do –'

'Not at all,' Peter heard himself saying, again to his own surprise. 'I'd love to come to supper. You're not fussing at all, Miss L—'

'Mrs Priestly,' Sophie said. 'I'm a widow.'

'I'm sorry,' Peter said, floundering a little in his embarrassment. This cool quiet woman was really having a very odd effect on him. 'I should have known – perhaps I did, but I'd forgotten. I was out of England during the War, you see, lost touch with –'

'There was no reason why you should have known,' she said and dismissed the matter as unimportant, turning back to Letty. 'Where will we find Katy? It would be nice if she came too, and perhaps if there are other cousins you'd like to invite them? Cousin Harry and his wife, perhaps? It's a very big piece of pork and I've brought plenty of good fresh vegetables from the Pighill's farm as well.'

'Sophie, for heaven's sake!' Brin was clearly mortified, and he snapped the words out. 'This isn't Haworth, you know, where everyone spends all their time in and out of each other's houses! You can't invite everyone to –'

'I think it's a delightful idea,' Letty said firmly. 'But I'm afraid it won't be possible tonight, Sophie. Katy is – she's gone out and most of the rest of the family are, I imagine, rather busy.' Her lips firmed and Peter looked at her, a little startled. What had happened to make Letty sound so annoyed? 'But some time in the future, perhaps, when we can get everyone together, it would be very nice. I'd like you to meet them all –'

'Well, if I can get another piece of meat down from Haworth we'll consider it,' Sophie said. 'But meat's hard to come by these days, as I'm sure I don't have to tell you. Well, thank you for introducing me, Letty. I'll look forward to seeing you if not the others at Brin's flat tonight, then, at about eight, with Mr Lackland. Don't be late home, Brin. You need a rest. You're looking quite peaky. Good afternoon, everyone. No, don't worry about me. I can find my own way back.' And she smoothed her gloves on to her hands, tucked her bag neatly under her arm and went, and they watched her rather dumpy little figure as it disappeared through the door, and quietly closed it behind her, not saying a word.

'Dear me,' Daniel said mildly, coming back to the group from the distance to which he had tactfully withdrawn. 'What a very pleasant lady! I wish I were a Lackland cousin, I can tell you. I can't remember the last time I ate roast pork.'

'Oh, give her a chance and she'll adopt you too,' Brin said savagely. 'She really is the absolute end and always was. How could you let her come down to London this way, Letty? It's too bad of you!'

'She thinks you need to be looked after,' Letty said and turned away, not wanting to discuss what she regarded as private matters before other listeners, but Brin was not to be stopped.

'*She* needs someone to look after is more like it,' Brin said wrathfully. 'I'll never get rid of her now, not if you aid and abet her this way. Ye gods, why do I have to be cursed with so dreary a sister as that? Look Peter, you don't have to come to

143

her ghastly supper party. I'll see to it she doesn't bother you again, and I'll have her on her way back to Haworth as soon as I can –'

'But I want to come,' Peter said, and turned away to pick up his papers. 'I like roast pork too, and what's more important I like your sister. She's a very pleasant lady, and you're very fortunate to have her to care for you. I'll see you later, then. And you too, Letty. Right now, I'd better go home and see if I can make myself look presentable. Good afternoon.'

And he went, quietly, leaving Brin furious and Letty looking after him with a startled look on her face. But it was not a disapproving one at all.

17

Sophie slipped into London life so quietly and so easily it seemed as though she had never lived anywhere else. That she had a gift for practical organization she rapidly demonstrated; despite the fact that the demand for flats and even hotel rooms was so intense that the merest rumour of available accommodation brought eager would-be tenants flocking, she managed to get herself a small flat in the building adjoining that in which Brin lived in Earlham Street. And then she arranged for a few of the smaller pieces of furniture from Tansy Clough to be brought to make it, as she said, 'more homelike – London furniture is flimsy stuff, isn't it?', put the sale of the old house in hand, and had effected her permanent move to London in a matter of weeks.

Brin furiously tried to dissuade her from doing it. 'Tansy Clough's been in the family for donkey's years,' he had shouted at her. 'And you'll be miserable living here, anyway. You're solid Yorkshire – London's not for you. You'll hate it here.'

But she had paid no attention to the implied sneer at her provincial ways and had gone on sewing – she was mending his shirts, systematically going through his wardrobe to 'fettle things up', as she put it – and said collectedly, 'I can't afford to live there on my own. You and the others are all entitled to your share – Pa left everything to be settled equally between us – and it's beyond me to pay you all out. Anyway, it's too big and cold and rambling for one person to live in on her own. It would be plain sentimental to do it, and I hope I've more sense than that. London suits me well enough, and you need to be looked after, that much is very clear. Will you just look at these cuffs – I've never seen worse fraying. Tsk, tsk – they should have been turned long since –'

And Brin had flung out of the room and gone off to sit

sulkily in the pub on the corner of Long Acre where all the dancers and out-of-work actors congregated to slouch their weekends away, not knowing how to get this tiresome sister to leave him in peace.

But then, as the weeks went on and not only were his shirts more agreeable to wear, but every aspect of his daily life became more comfortable as Sophie harried Mrs Burroughs into cleaner and more efficient ways, he stopped sulking so much. Sophie didn't pry into his private affairs, and was pleasantly unobtrusive except when she was needed; and he came to take for granted the way she would appear with groceries and fruit and vegetables she had managed to buy, by dint of much busy hunting around the small shops of Seven Dials and also sallies further afield into Holborn and the street market at Leather Lane, all of which greatly improved his diet. He looked sleek and contented, and gradually came to take it for granted that his older sister was now part of his daily life.

He was not the only member of the family to find Sophie's quietly efficient care agreeable. Peter, after that first supper party at which he had eaten more heartily than he could ever remember doing, soon drifted into a pattern of dining with Sophie on a regular basis. He would arrive at her small flat with a bottle from his father's cellar under his arm – and old Sir Lewis was so delighted to see his beloved youngest son looking so much better that he pressed his choicest vintages on him – and then would sit reading the evening paper in the drowsy clock-ticking potpourri-scented little living-room while Sophie moved around her small kitchen cooking for them. The clink of her pots and pans and the occasional breathy little humming of popular tunes that she would produce as she bent, absorbed, over her concoctions would come to him down the little passageway and often soothed him to such an extent that he would be peacefully asleep in his armchair when she came to tell him food was on the table. But he never felt uncomfortable about that; he would blink up at her and then grin and come eagerly to see what dish she had prepared, and she would sit and watch him with a half smile on her round face as he ate everything she put before him.

He was, she told him gravely, a pleasure to cook for, at which he would grin again and point out that anyone who could make out of that awful dried egg omelettes that managed to taste as near to the real French magic as hers did need never fear that she would fail to give her guests pleasure, and then they would drink their wine and talk a little desultorily of nothing very much at all. Just comfortable chat and long peaceful silences.

Peter was remarkably comfortable on those evenings as the days lengthened and the light lingered in the skies over London, making it possible to sit without lights on until ten o'clock or even later, and so was Sophie. Or so she seemed to be; it was not possible to be sure how she felt, for Sophie, unlike her younger sister, showed little of her feelings on her tranquil surface.

Katy, of course, did, and she was furious that Sophie had settled into London as she had.

'It was bad enough when we were children,' she stormed at Peter on one of the evenings when she had been able to persuade him to come out with her, and she had managed to book a table at the Ritz. 'She used to fuss after me, and nag me and complain about what I did till I nearly went mad. She was the main reason I left Haworth in the first place, and to have her here now, like this, to try to regain – it's too bad –'

'Nonsense,' Peter said firmly and looked down at his plate on which a minuscule piece of fish lay drably clad in a glutinous sauce. 'Don't try and tell me that. I was around, remember, when you first came to London. You said nothing then about wanting to escape from your sister. All you wanted was to get on the stage. Letty took you to dinner at Rules and I was there. I remember it very vividly indeed. And you never even mentioned Sophie then. So don't try to tell me that –'

'I didn't tell you everything about myself then, any more than I do now,' Katy snapped and pushed her plate away pettishly. 'This fish is quite disgusting. How they've got the brass neck to put it in front of people –'

'Your sister could show them how to do it –' Peter said without stopping to think, and Katy reddened with anger.

'Damn it, there you go again! On and on about Sophie! I told you, I don't want to talk about her! It's like having a bloody jailer watching you all the time!'

'You started to talk about her, not I,' Peter said mildly. 'So, it's really up to you. But I warn you, my dear, I shan't hear a word against her. She's a delightful person, and –'

'Let's dance,' Katy said abruptly and got to her feet, and held both hands out to him, her head tilted to one side and her face alight with that famous smile. 'We're both getting dreadfully dull, and we need to get rid of the drears! And I just love this tune –' And she pulled him on to the small dance floor as the band swept into an even faster version of 'I'm Just A Girl Who Can't Say No'.

'We must go and see this show,' she said as the music whirled them into action. 'Everyone says it's quite marvellous, and that the Oklahoma outdoor scenes are simply wonderful – how about next Saturday? I think I can wangle tickets –'

'Sorry,' he said. 'I'm already booked.' Prudently, he didn't say he had promised to take Sophie to see *Born Yesterday* at the Garrick, but she guessed and for the rest of the evening worked particularly hard at being vivacious and exciting. But she knew she was losing, because although he smiled and seemed to enjoy her sparkle there was an abstracted air about him, and it really was infuriating.

That anyone as dismal as Sophie could possibly be more interesting than she was seemed to Katy to be absurd, and to do her justice, most people would agree with her. For the first time in all her life, Katy was beginning to find that she could not beguile people as easily as she had been used to. For as long as she could remember, she had only needed to smile at people and look up at them in that particularly entrancing way of hers and they were, if not literally at her feet, certainly interested and excited by her. Now, the magic seemed to be less potent, to have become tarnished and even tawdry, and that made her uneasy. For it wasn't only Peter who seemed to be withdrawing from the charmed circle of her regard; Harry too was behaving oddly.

She had for some time now been running a mild affair with Harry. She had always had a special regard for him, not because she found him a particularly exciting person – in her more private thoughts she had to admit he had become a little dull, indeed, positively stuffy, with the passage of the years – but because he had been her first lover.

When she had come back to London to make *The Lady Leapt High* she had wallowed in nostalgia for the first few days, remembering herself as an eager young drama student and then actress in pre-War London; and a very important part of that nostalgia had been her involvement with Harry. He had been the man she had chosen to initiate her into the mysteries of sex, and when she remembered that absurd time in her draped and cushion-strewn sitting-room in her flat in Fulham, her lips would curve with reminiscent pleasure. He had been so startled, so very funny about it all – and yet so kind a lover, and she had been more than happy to re-establish their old closeness on her return.

And at first it had been fun. He had been as eager as she was to pick up where they had left off, when she had gone off to Hollywood to be with Theo Caspar (and that was one man she always refused to think about, of course; still smarting somewhere deep inside at the way he had, in her opinion, shamefully misled and misused her, though all that was ancient history now) and she had been well pleased to have another man to dangle at her fingers' ends. Many had been the times these past few months when he had phoned and she had been captious with him, refusing to see him, refusing his eager invitations to out-of-town weekends, preferring to coax Peter to go out with her, finding him more interesting altogether.

But now, just as Peter was becoming boring and making such a fuss over dreary old Sophie, Harry was being difficult too. Now, dancing at the Ritz with Peter, she remembered the last stilted phone conversations she had had with Harry and had to work hard to keep her face looking gay and amused.

He really had been incredibly stupid, she thought angrily, making those lame excuses about having to take over someone else's duties for that weekend. She had, in fact, thought once or twice about cancelling it herself; it was one thing to spend a long evening making love with Harry, quite another to spend a full weekend with him. When she'd agreed to go she'd been at rather low ebb and the idea had seemed fun, but within a few days of making the plan, she had decided that she would probably cry off at the last minute unless nothing better to do showed up. To have Harry doing the crying off, therefore, had been infuriating, to put it mildly, and she had made no effort to hide her anger.

'I can't help it,' he'd said, his voice on the phone clacking tinnily so that she could not judge his mood from his tone. 'I'm as miserable about it as you are – but –'

'Miserable?' she had snapped. 'I am not miserable – just irritated at having my plans messed up. You're not the only person who enjoys my company, Harry, and I'd put myself out to please you – even though I was too mannerly to point out to you that Brighton really is *the* most ghastly place – full of dreary typists and greasy little salesmen on the make, but there, it was what *you* wanted, and I like to see my friends happy – and now you announce as cool as you like only a few days in advance that you can't go! It's too bad of you – and I'll tell you this. You'll have to be very nice indeed to me to persuade me to make any more plans with you!'

'All right,' he'd said shortly, and hung up, leaving her amazed with the phone buzzing dully in her ears. No one ever did that to her, and her anger boiled over so much that she had banged the phone down on its cradle and sent a pretty ornament of which she was rather fond flying to land in shards of glass on the floor. Harry was really too boring, and so was Peter, and the show was boring and London was boring and if Letty didn't let her go back to Hollywood soon she would, she told herself, go stark raving mad – and just wait till Harry phoned again. She'd give him a blistering that would make him come crawling to her for forgiveness. She'd show him.

But Harry didn't phone again, not that week nor the week after, and Katy became more and more miserable as the weeks wore on. She even phoned Harry herself once, but his secretary had told her smoothly that Mr Lackland was operating, she was so sorry, she would indeed tell him Miss Lackland had called and ask him to phone back; but he had not, and Katy was certainly not going to call him again. And she sat at rehearsals and watched Peter, a much more relaxed and busy Peter than he had ever been, working contentedly and seeming quite unconcerned with her misery, and felt dreadful.

She might have felt a little better had she known how badly Harry was feeling.

When Letty had called him at the hospital and told him brusquely that he was to come to her flat that evening because she had to talk to him he had had no sense of foreboding at all. She was just Letty, a good dear old soul and an aunt a man could enjoy being with. Ever since the days long ago when he had come to London as a raw youngster and lived in Albany with her, she had been a special part of his life.

So, he had gone to see her happily enough, telling the young nurse from Casualty with whom he had arranged to have dinner that she would have to wait till nine to get her meal, and driving himself over to Piccadilly, whistling between his teeth. He had a weekend at the Metropole with Katy to look forward to, and this child from Casualty was really rather sweet and absurdly eager, and the fact that Charlotte Lucas, whose looks he had really liked very much indeed, had disappeared from Nellie's still resisting him, no longer rankled as it had. Altogether he felt tolerably pleased with life; even Lee was better to have around these days, no longer nagging him when he was late, or looking at him with those accusing long-suffering glances he found so dismal. Good old Lee, he had thought as he had parked the car in Savile Row to walk over to the back entrance of Albany. She's an awfully good sort really. Maybe I'll stay home a little more once in a while. If she wants me to –

Letty's attack on him was even more shattering because his mood had been so good. He had settled into the familiar old armchair facing hers and grinned and said easily, 'Well, my dear old aunt? What has my favourite Dame got to say for herself this evening?' and then his face had stiffened with amazement when she had said it all, in terms that were, even for her, remarkably forceful.

'Lee?' he had said at last, staring at her. 'Are you telling me that *Lee* is – I don't believe it.'

'Then more bloody fool you,' Letty said shortly. 'She's got every right to do it, and I for one don't blame her. Anyone with any spirit would have done it long ago – but she, poor wretch, seems to love you. I can't imagine why. If I were in her shoes, I'd be as likely to take a knife to you as anything else, but Lee's a lady and behaves like one, God help her. So, it's up to you. If you care more than a ha'penny for her and those splendid children of yours, you'll start to mend your ways. Damn it all, you'll not just *start* – you'll do it right now. You'll go and tell her what a bloody idiot you've been and you'll beg her to forgive you. Because if you don't do that then she'll be gone. You'll be left in that house completely on your own, and much good may it do you.'

He had shaken his head, bewildered, and then became suddenly angry. 'It's all nonsense! She's been filling you with all sorts of stupid talk – I don't know what's happened to her lately. All she does is nag and pry and –'

'Rubbish,' Letty said just as loudly, but without heat. 'Don't try that sort of line with me. You've been sniffing around the nurses at Nellie's like some sort of tomcat for years. Sickening! And round Katy – oh, don't look at me like that with such great cow's eyes! D'you think I'm blind and stupid with it? I'm as sharp as the next woman, Harry Lackland, and I know all too well what you've been doing. So let's not waste time with a lot of silly bluster.'

He'd said nothing, only sitting very still and staring at her and then he had felt the heat rise in his face and for one shocking moment actually thought tears were going to appear in his eyes. He took a deep breath at that, needing desperately to save his face as best he could.

'Oh, my God,' he said after a moment. 'What on earth do I do about it, Letty? I've been a bloody fool, haven't I?'

'If you want to keep your family, then indeed you have,' she had said, for the first time feeling sorry for him. He looked stricken, now, and his face seemed to have sagged a little from the bones of his skull. '*Do* you want to keep them?'

He had sat very still staring at her but not seeing her, and then said loudly, 'Bloody hell! Of course I do.'

'You're sure?'

'Yes, I'm sure. It's just that – oh, I don't know, Letty. She's just been so – Lee, I mean. She's been so – far away. At the beginning we were so close, it was as though when she cut her finger I felt it, you know? And then that wretched business of wanting children and the trip to Germany and Michael – I –'

He swallowed then and it made an odd gulping little noise in the quiet room. 'I hated him you know, when he first came to us. I did hate him and it was dreadful. She loved him so and I –'

'Do you still hate him?' Letty said, and now her voice was gentle.

He managed to smile then. 'Oh, no. Not now. It all changed when he saw Sally for the first time. I'd taken him to the maternity ward to see Lee and the baby was with her and his face – it was so odd, the way he looked. It was as though it was me I was looking at and he turned and came running to me and held on and wouldn't let go and well, after that it was all fine. But it had done something to us. To Lee and me, I mean. It all got so –' He shrugged. 'I really can't explain. She had the baby, and then after a while there was Stella as well and nothing seemed any fun any more –'

'Jealousy,' Letty said, almost disgustedly. 'You really are the end, Harry! You're supposed to understand these things, supposed to be a doctor who understands and knows how to cope and you can't even see your own childish jealousy for what it is!'

'I wasn't jealous!' he began hotly and then stopped and leaned forwards and rested his face in his hands. 'Oh, hell,' he said after a moment. 'Oh, hell and damnation', and then he really did begin to cry.

The little nurse from Casualty never did get her dinner that night, nor on any other night come to that. Harry sat with Letty till long after midnight, talking in a great flood, letting out all the stored up resentment of the past years, and she had sat in the dimness of the comfortable room lit by one small table-lamp, letting him talk and knowing how much he needed that catharsis.

And at the end of it he knew what he wanted for certain. He wanted Lee, his Lee, and no one else. But she no longer knew that, Letty had pointed out firmly, and had to be convinced of it. It wasn't going to be easy to stop her from leaving him, but at least he knew he wanted to keep her and that was half the battle.

But only half. Because Lee, he discovered when he left Letty and went home to St John's Wood to find her and apologize and talk, had a strength of resolve he had not fully realized was in her. It was going to be a long and difficult task to overcome it, and that was all he now cared about. He certainly never thought about Katy at all.

18

'I really don't think I can say that to him, Dr Lucas,' Sophie said, not lifting her eyes from her work. She was kneading bread dough with a steady thumping of her arms, turning and twisting it lovingly with her strong little fingers, seeming to relish its satiny texture and its resilience. 'It wouldn't be in my conscience to do it.'

'Miss Lucas,' Charlie said automatically, staring at the dumpy little woman with her brows creased. 'I'm a surgeon, not a physician. Not that it matters all that much. Anyway, people call me Charlie – look, I don't quite understand. You say you can't give Brin my message? Do you mean you won't be seeing him? Will you be leaving here before he gets home?'

'I might be. I usually do. He doesn't like to see me around when he gets in, so I generally leave his meal ready and then go back to my own flat. But of course I could stay to see him if there was anything special to tell him.' Now she did lift her eyes from her rhythmic kneading. 'But I won't stay to tell him what you've asked me to.'

'Then I shall leave him a note,' Charlie said decisively, and began to root in her bag for a pencil and some paper.

'I shan't deliver that, either,' Sophie said calmly. 'Indeed, I'd be very likely to throw it away.'

Charlie's brows came down almost to a point between her eyes, so sharp was the frown.

'I really don't understand you, Mrs – er –'

'Priestly. But people call me Sophie.' And she smiled at Charlie, a sweet three-cornered shaping of her small mouth, but her eyes were watchful. 'There now, I'll set this to rise, and it can go into t'oven in an hour and be fine and ready by the time I have to leave.' And she turned away from the kitchen table to set her covered bowl of dough on top of the warm cooker. 'I've a bit of fat and sugar left so I can manage a few buns for the lad as well. He likes my buns.'

Charlie took a sharp little breath in through her nose, feeling irritation begin to bubble in her. Talking to this woman was like trying to catch a cloud. But she was Brin's sister and as such to be treated carefully. She couldn't use her clipped I'm-a-doctor-and-I-know-best approach with her; not that it was one she used often, but sometimes when dealing with patients who were a little slow on the uptake it was necessary. And Sophie certainly seemed to be rather slow in some ways, however clever she might be with her bread and her buns.

'You must forgive me if I'm being a bit stupid, Sophie, but I can't quite see what the problem is about giving Brin my message.'

Sophie turned back to the table and balling both her floury hands into small fists rested them on the table top, and with rigid elbows leaned forwards to look directly at Charlie. The sleeves of her rather dowdy flower-printed summer dress were rolled up high on her round plump arms and there was a large white apron pinned round her, making her waist, which was less than slender at the best of times, look extra thick. There was a smudge of flour on one cheek and her usually neat hair was ruffled from the heat of both the afternoon and the atmosphere in the tiny kitchen. She should have looked rather absurd. But she didn't. She looked formidable and even a little frightening as she stared at Charlie.

'Let me make myself very clear, Miss Lucas. I'm not about to deliver your message to my brother because I don't think it's one he ought to get. And if you've the sense I think you have you'll think again about trying to get it to him yourself.'

Charlie shook her head, bewildered. 'Perhaps you mis-understood me,' she said carefully, enunciating her words more clearly as though she were talking to a foreigner. 'I said I had managed to arrange for a bed at Nellie's for Brin. That I'll be back on the staff there in a week's time, and that I can do his operation soon after that, and –'

'Aye, I heard you.' Sophie stood upright again, and reached for another bowl and began with great punctiliousness to measure margarine and sugar into it, and then picked up a wooden spoon with which to pound the mixture. 'And I know what it is you want to do. You want to operate on his face again. You want to try to make that scar look different.'

'Yes, of course. What else would it be?' Charlie was still mystified but now beginning to get more and more angry.

'It'd be a big mistake,' Sophie said calmly. 'You mustn't do it, really you mustn't.'

Charlie stared at her. 'Why not?'

'Because you'll be taking away from the lad the only protection he has. And heaven knows he needs it badly.'

'Protection?'

'Aye – protection!' Sophie slammed her bowl and wooden spoon down on the table and looked hard at Charlie. 'Can't you see how much that scar helps him? It gives him something to blame when owt goes wrong. If he can't get what he wants because he doesn't have the wit to get it, or the talent, or he's too airy fairy in his notions to stick at working for it, then he can blame his injury and feel better for it.' Her Yorkshire accent seemed to increase as she became more intense, though her voice stayed equable and she seemed as composed as ever; but Charlie was aware of a great deal of strong feeling in that compact little body and found it more than a little disturbing.

'But it's a handicap to him,' Charlie said, needing to explain to this silly woman what the problem was, even though it ought to be obvious even to her. 'He's an actor – an actor with a damaged face. How can he get decent parts looking like that and –'

'Ah, such stuff!' Sophie said, and suddenly, oddly, laughed. 'Eh, but he's a clever lad, that brother o' mine. He's even got you believing it, hasn't he? Well, he could always charm the birds off the trees, let alone the girls into the bushes. He hasn't changed from the time he turned twelve and found out what he had that the lasses liked so well. He's not handicapped from his acting by his face, Miss Lucas! He's handicapped because he doesn't have a great deal of talent. He's got a great deal of charm and fun in him and that always works wonders, but talent is something else again. My sister Katy, now, *she's* got talent. Too much. If it's not used, the way it hasn't been lately, it turns sour in her like milk and makes everything about her go all wrong. The sooner she gets back to some real work and can think about that instead of her own silly face the better off she'll be. But Brin, now, he's different. Our Brin is a good sweet lad in many ways, but he was always the same. Fancied more than he could have, do you see? He fancied this business of being an actor when he was a lad and saw Katy's pictures in all the papers, and there was nothing for it but he must go and try it too. I told him he'd be better off doing something else, and he wouldn't have it, but I wasn't far wrong. He never did get anywhere much – Katy was working as an actress in no time, but he? Not he. They saw he was no more than a good-looking lad with a lot of charm and they didn't give him the parts he wanted. Well, they still don't, but now he's got a scar to blame for it, and that helps. And here's you trying to take it away from him.'

She shook her head and returned to her bowl of sugar and margarine, slapping her wooden spoon noisily against its sides as she blended her ingredients together.

'You'll be doing him no service if you do that. So I'll not deliver your message, and I'm hoping you'll go away and not deliver it yourself either. It'll all come to no good if you do.'

Charlie sat there, not knowing what to do, and suddenly it was as though she could hear Max Lackland's voice. 'I looked at that scar carefully,' he had said in that cool spare voice of his. '– It's nothing like as hideous as he maintains it is –' And she had pushed her hands more deeply into the pockets of her white coat and hated him for being so dispassionate about Brin, when Brin was so full of life and excitement and pain and need – and she had refused to think of her own doubts about the severity of his injury, the way that the wrinkling of his eye and the puckering of his lip added to his attraction when he grinned at her.

None of that mattered, she had told herself, and she repeated it inside her head now. Other people's opinions of Brin's need didn't matter. All that was important was how Brin himself felt; and if he wanted his scar operated on then she was going to do it for him. She, who had spent these long months learning and practising, working all the hours God sent to be ready to do it for him, was going to operate and make him happy again. No matter what his sister said.

'Do you like your brother, Mrs Priestly?' she said abruptly, and Sophie looked up at her consideringly.

'He's my brother,' she said after a moment, and returned her attention to her bowl, to which she was now adding flour from a sifter, making clouds of white dust through which the sun slanted from the little window on the far side of the small

157

kitchen. 'Of course I love him.'

'I didn't ask you that,' Charlie said, her own voice as controlled as she could make it. 'I asked if you liked him.'

Sophie seemed to contemplate the question for a while, her hands still busy and then she said calmly, 'Parts of him are very likeable. Parts are not and need changing. I've done my best since my mother died to watch over him, grown man though he was at the time. She was the only one who might have made him see how daft he can be and made him change. I'm still trying to teach him, but I'm not too good at it. I'm beginning to doubt I ever will manage it. But I have to go on trying.'

Charlie's lip lifted at the corner in a small gesture of distaste. 'I see. So you see him as someone who has to be cared for. Someone to be taught like a helpless child. Not a man in his own right –'

'I would if he were a man. His brother George, now – he was a man before he reached seventeen. Grew up as fine and sensible as any could wish. But Brin – eldest son, d'you see, and a bit spoiled, I think. I've done my best, but there it is. He's not grown up yet. He'll have to be sooner or later. I'm hoping he can do it without too much hurt to himself or others – and he'll not be helped by having operations on his face.'

'I think he will,' Charlie said levelly. 'I'm his doctor. I have a training in these matters –'

And what do you know? You with no training at all? The question hung unspoken in the air between them and Sophie smiled at it.

'Oh, I know I'm just a country woman, never did owt much but stay home and mind an ailing mother and an old dad and watch over my brothers and sisters. Didn't even manage to stay married long, did I? But for all that, I've learned a little in my small world, Miss Lucas. And I've learned my brother's ways and needs and –'

'Learned your own!' Charlie said and stood up, unable to control her anger any longer. 'You've said it all, you know, even if you don't realize it. You've never done anything but look after people, and now, with no husband – and I do of course offer my sympathies there, that was very sad – and your parents dead – what is there for you to do? You've got to find someone else to look after, and you've chosen Brin – and if keeping him in his mutilated state keeps him helpless, well

158

that's the way it'll have to be. And never mind what Brin needs. It's what *you* need you're concerned about.'

'I thought about that,' Sophie said, amazingly, and smiled at Charlie. 'Oh, I thought about that a lot. There, that's the buns ready.' She looked down in satisfaction at the tray of buns she had set ready for baking. 'I'll pop those in the oven and then I'll make us a cup of tea.'

She turned to the oven and with a practised twist of her wrist set her baking tray on the top shelf and clicked it shut. She was smiling as she straightened her back and turned to look at Charlie again.

'Oh, yes, I thought about that. Was I making him worse coming here to take care of him? Laid awake at night thinking of that, and talked to Letty – she's my aunt – d'you know her? She's a wise woman, is Letty. Knows more than she realizes, and I put a lot of store by what she says. And she says as I do. He's got a potential, has Brin, but not till he finds out he can't get by, all the time, on charm and smirks. He's got to do some growing up like I said, and I'm going to teach him. I've plans for myself, one day, but I couldn't live with my conscience if I left him to stew in his own juice, now, could I? No, Miss Lucas, believe me – I'm not holding the lad back for my own ends. My ends are different. But I have my responsibilities too and I can't shirk them, now, can I?'

She spoke with such an air of sweet reason that for a moment Charlie was beguiled by her and she thought suddenly – Brin isn't the only one in his family with charm. She's got it too, and that thought hardened her mind against Sophie.

'You wouldn't be the first person to hide an ulterior motive behind apparently high-minded behaviour,' she said. 'The sort of people who maintain this–will–hurt–you–more–than–it–hurts–me, and I–have–to–be–cruel–to–be–kind and all the rest of those silly clichés – everyone that I've ever come across is seeking comfort for themselves in what they're doing. I don't see anything in you that makes me think you're any different. Brin is an adult in every way. He knows what he wants and he has every right to do what he thinks is best for himself. He doesn't have to defer to you in a matter that is, frankly, none of your concern.'

'Oh, I'm sure I do look like a meddling old woman to you,'

Sophie said. 'Though I'm not that old. Nearly forty, I grant you, but that's not so old. I've plenty of good living to do yet.' And a small smile hovered over the corners of her mouth for a moment and she looked down at the kettle she had just set on the stove top. 'But I assure you I'm not. I've thought of every criticism of myself that you have and a good many more. And I know I'm right. Brin has to learn to stand on his own two feet – and encouraging his silly vanity over this scar isn't going to help him do that, is it? He needs to be taught to be what he is, instead of daydreaming about what he can't be.'

'I can't see any point in continuing this conversation any longer,' Charlie said stiffly and stood up, collecting her bag and gloves together with slightly shaking fingers. If she didn't control herself very carefully she would scream at this maddeningly calm woman like a fishwife. 'I'll talk to Brin myself. You needn't worry yourself. I'll arrange this operation and he'll have it when *he* and *I* decide it's right. One patient, one doctor, and no one else's interference –'

'I shall still interfere as much as I can,' Sophie said and her voice was as calm still as if she were talking about the recipes she used for her baking. 'I dare say I'll not succeed, but I do have to try. I'd have hoped you'd see that, Miss Lucas. If you really care for him as much as you seem to.' And she gave Charlie so shrewd a glance that Charlie felt her face get red, and was glad of the warmth of the July afternoon and the hot little kitchen to give her an excuse for it.

'Good afternoon,' she said shortly, not trusting herself to say more, and went, leaving the heat and the drifting smell of freshly baked buns and yeast and sugar and the round slightly sweating figure of Sophie to escape into the petrol-reeking heat of Earlham Street, but feeling she could at least breathe there. How dare that woman talk to her so, how dare she meddle so unashamedly in Brin's affairs! It was appalling, outrageous, and as she went marching down towards Cambridge Circus she luxuriated in the fury that rose in her, fanning it with her thoughts, needing to express her anger with vigour.

Just wait till I see Brin, she thought. Just wait! I'll tell him all she said, every word, alert him to the way she's trying to take him over, run his life – oh, I'll tell him –

She reached the Circus and stood uncertainly on the kerb,

not knowing quite what to do. She looked at her watch and frowned; just three o'clock. Brin had told her when she had telephoned the rehearsal room that he couldn't talk then; they were up to their ears and he'd try to talk later, he'd said hurriedly, and hung up, and that was why she had gone to the flat. She had expected perhaps to find Mrs Burroughs, the daily help, there, and had intended to leave a message for him and then go back to East Grinstead to finish her packing ready for her return to Nellie's in a few days' time, having spent the early part of the day at Nellie's in discussions about the job she was to return to. Pleasant though it always was to see Brin, she had decided, the present heat wave that had clamped its evil smelly hand on London was more than she felt she could bear; it would be much cooler in West Sussex, that was for certain.

But now she knew she had to stay and see Brin, no matter how late he got out of the rehearsal. The sooner she warned him of his sister's dangerous attitudes, as she now regarded them as being, the better. He must send her packing, home-baked bread and all, that's what he must do, she thought grimly, and went across the road towards that all too familiar Lyons' teashop on the far side, to while away as much time as she could over stewed tea and leathery toast. Once again, just as she thought Brin's problems were on the point of being solved, a new one reared its head. It really was getting more and more difficult having him for a patient, she thought, as she ordered her tea from the counter and went to sit at a grubby marble-topped table. If only he could be just a friend. Or something more.

But *that* was an outrageous thought, enough to get a doctor struck off, and not to be entertained. But it was an agreeable thought for all that, and it stayed with her all the time she sat in the stuffy teashop, refusing to leave her in peace, while she waited to go and see him.

19

The sky over Cambridge Circus was a rich deep blue by the time she emerged from the teashop. She had managed to stretch the eating of a limp salad and a toasted teacake so long that the waitresses had begun to stare at her with curiosity rather than disapproval, but at last she thought that Brin must surely have left rehearsal and made her way slowly back to Earlham Street.

There was a light in the sitting-room window of his flat and she stared up at the yellow square and for a moment her resolve failed. Suppose Sophie was still there? Suppose she had told him of their argument that afternoon, had managed to bring him round to her way of thinking? They were brother and sister, after all, and she was only an outsider; and for a moment her mind conjured up a vision of the two of them sitting side by side and staring at her with cold hostile eyes, Brin's as remote and unfriendly as Sophie's, and she wanted to turn and run away and forget all about the whole business. She wanted to help Brin, wanted to be with him, but was it worth all this obsessive anguish?

She tried to stand apart from herself for a moment. There in the darkening street with its smell of petrol and rotting fruit drifting over from Covent Garden market, and its exhausted gritty heat, she tried to be as cool and objective as a sensible trained woman should be, but that didn't work. However hard she worked at being Miss Charlotte Hankin Lucas, MB, BS, she was still Charlie, standing and looking yearningly at the window of a man she cared about, and that realization made her feel such a fool that she moved sharply and hurried to the entrance to go running up the stairs to the front door of Brin's flat, refusing to think any more about what she was doing. She just had to do it, and stop worrying. Just *do* it –

There was an appreciable delay after she rang the bell, and

then she heard padding footsteps and the door opened a crack and an eye appeared in the space.

'Who is it?' Brin's voice sounded irritable. 'I'm in the bath, damn it –'

'I'm sorry, Brin,' she said, her confusion coming back in a great wave. 'It's me, Charlie. I wanted to tell you about the arrangements I've made for you –'

'Charlie?' he said and the eye seemed to brighten. 'Oh, yes – great. Look, come on in – only let me get back to the bathroom first –'

The eye disappeared and after what seemed to her to be a reasonable pause she pushed open the door; but she had misjudged it because she just saw his bare back disappearing along the passageway towards the bathroom. It was only a fleeting movement, but it was long enough to etch his body's shape into her mind; a long back and a narrow waist with a little damp curling hair between the hips over small tight buttocks which dimpled just above the swell of muscles outlined by the glint of water on the skin. Her mouth dried for a moment with embarrassment at the sight of him and she walked as quietly as she could into the living-room, not wanting him to know she had seen him.

Not, it appeared, that he would have cared anyway. By the time she had taken off her jacket and was sitting in as relaxed a pose as she could on the sofa with her bare sandalled feet stretched out under her rather crumpled cotton frock, he appeared in the doorway, rubbing his head with a towel. He was wearing only another towel tied round his waist and his skin shone damply golden in the lamplight. He smelled of good soap and bay rum and quite without volition her mouth spread in a smile of sheer pleasure as she looked at him.

'Hello Charlie,' he said rubbing away at his head so that his hair stood up in rather childlike damp spikes. 'You didn't say you were coming here when you phoned this afternoon.'

'I didn't know I was,' she said, and looked away from him, suddenly feeling very shy. Absurdly shy. 'I – I was at Nellie's all morning and I meant to go back to East Grinstead after leaving a message here for you but –' She swallowed, awkward again. 'I thought I'd better stay and talk to you. After what happened here.'

'After what happened where?' he said lazily and came and

sat on the sofa beside her. He too stretched out his legs and the golden hairs on the sun-browned skin glinted and she thought ridiculously – he looks like hot buttered toast.

'Your sister,' she said and then stopped, not sure how to put it. The last thing she wanted to do was sound like a whining child, telling tales; but he had to be told, somehow, and she stopped, trying to put the right words together in her head.

'Sophie?' Brin said and laughed. 'Did she try to stuff you with freshly baked cakes and jam and heaven knows what else? I found a great pile of buns and new bread when I got in. It's good stuff, I'll give her that –'

'She was baking them when I was here,' Charlie said and then took a slightly shaky breath. 'Look, Brin, I don't want to – sound like a meddler or a grizzler, but I did worry about what she said.'

He turned his body so that he had one elbow up on the back of the sofa and could look down on her and again she avoided his gaze, keeping her eyes fixed on his legs. He smelled even better now as his skin dried and the scent of soap – was it sandalwood? – was released into the warm air. It really was quite stupid to be so embarrassed, and she a doctor who had seen more naked men than she could remember! But this, whispered her secret voice, isn't just any naked man. This is Brin.

'Bloody Sophie,' Brin said, but there was no real rancour in his voice. 'Nothing you could tell me about her could ever seem like meddling. Not compared with the way she meddles with me.'

'That's just it, Brin.' She turned to him gratefully, able to look at his face now. 'I wanted to leave a message for you with her. To tell you that I think I can get a bed for you very soon at Nellie's and do your operation and she said –'

His face lit up and he leaned forwards and took her shoulders in his hands. 'What did you say?'

'I think – I can't be absolutely sure, mind you, because beds are at a premium, what with wards being closed – but I think that I can put your operation on the list in the next couple of weeks –'

'Charlie Lucas, I love you!' he cried jubilantly and leaned forwards and kissed her roundly, his lips warm on hers and she was so startled she could only sit there, her eyes wide open.

164

And then he was sitting upright again and gazing at her, his eyes looking as though someone had switched on a light behind them. 'I knew you could arrange it if anyone could – oh, I just knew it! You really are the best thing that ever happened to me since that bloody bomb fell, do you know that? I can't tell you how grateful I am –'

'You don't have to be grateful,' she said a little huskily, still shaken by the way he had kissed her. 'It's what I'm for. A surgeon, remember? But you can't be sure until I've done the op how it'll turn out. Don't be too excited yet, for God's sake. You could be disappointed –'

'I won't be!' he said jubilantly and threw himself back against the sofa, but now with one arm thrown casually across the back of it, just above her own shoulders. She could feel the warmth of him through the thin cotton of her frock as though he were radiating energy. And indeed his whole body seemed rigid with the excitement.

'It'll be a wonderful operation,' he went on and with the forefinger of his other hand traced the line of his scar from tip to lip. 'It'll be just wonderful. A simple hairline that'll disappear beneath a bit of Leichner's –'

'Leichner's?' she said and he laughed and dropped his arm so that it was across her shoulders and hugged her close.

'Greasepaint, my dear old ass, greasepaint! I thought everyone knew about that stuff.'

'I'm not an actress,' she said in a small voice, trying to pretend that the warm pressure of his arm on her back and shoulders was not making her breathless. 'I know about operations – I don't know anything about shows –'

Suddenly his arm tightened and she looked up at him, aware of a sharp change in his mood. 'Damn it all to hell and back!' he said loudly, staring across her head at the window beyond, his eyes wide. 'Oh, God damn it all!'

'What's the matter?'

'The show. I just wasn't thinking. It happens on Saturday fortnight – that's why it's all getting so busy now. We're coming to the end of it all and we've been running around like lunatics getting it all together – and if I'm not there – when do you want me to come into Nellie's?'

'As soon as I get a bed,' she said promptly. 'I'm pulling every string I've got and then a few – like I said, there are so

165

few beds and every surgeon in the place is clamouring. I was hoping next Monday. I've booked the theatre, at least – that's a step in the right direction.'

'And if I can't manage to be there on that day?'

She shook her head a little worriedly. 'I'd just have to start the string pulling all over again.' She looked at him, turning her head so that she could see him and at once her face flamed. He was really very close to her indeed. 'But, look, don't worry. If I can manage it once, I dare say I can again – and I can quite see you can't let the show people down. It'd be a dreadful thing to do if they need you –'

'I'm not worried about the *show*,' he said almost contemptuously. 'It's Letty. I'm looking to her to give me a decent part once this Benefit's over – that's the only reason I'm doing the job at all. And if I'm not there on the night it's my guess she'll get decidedly shirty. It's not even as though I could ask her to let me go – unless maybe *you* did –'

Charlie felt chilled for a moment and then shook her head. 'It wouldn't help, I don't suppose,' she said. 'She might agree with your sister, anyway, and then –' She stopped. 'And it's not the end of the world, for heaven's sake, if you can't take a bed next week. I'll just put my application in again and we'll see how we get on. It might delay things just a while, but you've waited so long already that another few weeks shouldn't make all that much difference –'

'Every bloody day makes a difference,' he said violently and then looked at her, frowning. 'What was that you said about not talking to Letty for me? That she might agree with Sophie? What do you mean?'

'That was what I came to tell you,' she said, uncomfortable again. 'I – it was this afternoon. Sophie said she couldn't give you any message from me and told me I shouldn't do the operation on you.'

'She said what?' he began wrathfully. 'She had the damned bloody cheek to say *what*?'

She drew a deep sigh of relief. 'Oh, Brin, I was so worried. I thought perhaps – I don't know. I thought perhaps I'd got it wrong after all. That maybe I was doing the wrong thing in agreeing to your operation. I mean, I don't believe that your looks are all that spoiled by that scar. In some ways –' Again she swallowed and then went on hurriedly, almost too

166

embarrassed to get the words out. 'In some ways it adds to your attractiveness.'

'Oh, Charlie, you are a dear girl, you know!' He was laughing now, and again his arm was holding her closely. 'You thought I'd do as my sister Sophie told me? Honestly, what do you take me for? She's a silly fusspot, and always has been. Oh, she means kindly enough, I dare say, but all my life she's gone on at me about what I ought to do and what I ought not to do. I pay her no attention at all and I'm just damned grateful you didn't either. You didn't, did you?' He reached round with his other hand and took hold of her chin, pulling gently so that she had to look at him. 'You *didn't* pay any attention to her waffling on, did you? You'll do my operation, no matter what she thinks?'

'Of course I will,' Charlie said. 'It's your decision and mine, not hers.' And she smiled warmly, putting all the reassurance she could into her voice and her expression.

There was a little silence and then he said suddenly, 'For a doctor, you're a good-looking girl, aren't you, Charlie?'

' "Thank you kindly, sir, she said",' Charlie said a little shakily and made no attempt to pull her head away from his restraining fingers. They were warm and agreeable on her skin and feeling the whisper of his breath on her face as he spoke, and smelling the hint of peppermint toothpaste in it was even more agreeable.

'You're a good pal to me, you know that?' he said. 'I've thought of you all this time as a really good pal. Never thought you were a bit like the other girls. But you are, aren't you?'

'In what way?' She was still shaky of voice, but it didn't matter.

'You like to be kissed,' he said and bent his head and kissed her very thoroughly and with a good deal of expertise, not that she, with her lack of it, realized that fact. His lips were soft and gentle at first and then became rather more urgent and she found her mouth opening under his in a way she could never have thought possible. She had been kissed before, on occasion, but no woman who has to do all the work necessary to get a medical training has much time for lovemaking, and Charlie, for all her twenty-eight years, was in many ways a very inexperienced person. Certainly she was no match for Brin, who had lost count of the girls who had shared caresses with him.

Perhaps it was the heat of the evening, perhaps it was the emotion that had built up in her all that afternoon, perhaps it was merely as basic as the fact that he was wearing nothing but a towel and a skimpy one at that; whatever the cause, Charlie found herself responding to Brin in a way that amazed her. He too seemed startled at first by the eagerness with which she reacted to him and by the way her hands ran over his bare chest and back, but he made it very clear that he was glad of it.

His kisses became even more urgent and his hands as widely ranging as hers and then suddenly they were no longer on the sofa, but on the floor and her dress was crumpled round her waist as her legs curled up along his back. She had no memory of kicking off her shoes, no recollection of shedding her underclothes, but for all that she had and was as free and comfortable in her movements as he was, now that his towel lay in a discarded heap beside them.

If she had thought about it all, she would have expected that this, her first experience of sex, would be a frightening one, painful even, but in spite of the fact that she had had so little experience of men, had never even enjoyed much of the sort of petting that so many of the girls she had known had talked about on long cocoa-drinking evenings at school and later at university, she found herself so eager and responsive that there was no pain at all, and no doubts. She wanted him, wanted to swallow him whole, almost, and there was nothing he could do to her and with her that she didn't welcome, and want even more than he did.

And when after what seemed to be only a few moments she found the new and marvellously sweet sensations that filled her whole body rising to an almost unbelievable level she shouted her excitement aloud and clung to his back so tightly, her head thrown back and her mouth pulled wide with tension, that the result was incredible. It was as though she were both floating and yet swooping, as though she were being buffeted by waves of softness that made her face flame with heat, and sent sweat running between her breasts, and even then it wasn't over. He went on thrusting at her as strongly as he had from the start, his own eyes tightly closed, seeming oblivious of her, and then it all seemed to start again inside her own body; the waves of feeling, the lifting excitement and at last the swooping satisfaction, which seemed this time to go on and on and on.

But at last it ended and she was lying there as breathless as he was, his weight slumped on top of her and her eyes staring up at the ceiling in amazement. Was this really happening? Or was it some embarrassingly explicit erotic dream from which she would emerge to discover herself in her narrow bed in the medical staff quarters at East Grinstead?

She closed her eyes, tightening them till sparks of red and orange light shot through the blackness behind her lids and hurt her, and then opened them again; and there it all was; the ceiling with its faint cracks made into maplike shapes by the shadows thrown by the lamplight, the outlined black of the window, and the floor hard beneath her. She, Charlotte Lucas, had behaved in a way that was totally out of character, totally appalling, totally dreadful, and she had never felt more contented in all her life.

20

The next few days seemed dreamlike to Charlie. She walked through her last few days of work at East Grinstead and seemed to the other staff and to her patients there to be the same as she always was, quiet, but aware of and genuinely interested in them and their doings, but all the time she knew she was only giving half of herself, if that, to what she was doing.

Even at the surprise goodbye party they threw for her in Ward Three, with the men sitting up in bed in their bandages and plasters, some with the battered faces of recent surgery, some with the dependent lumps of misshapen tissue which were half completed pedicle grafts, but all with friendly and affectionate expressions in their eyes, she stood there seeming to listen demurely to Archie McIndoe's flattering speech about her abilities, but without really hearing anything. Because all she was doing was thinking about Brin, running over and over again in her mind that incredible half hour in his flat and reliving her delight in it.

And it was the same when she left the Queen Victoria Hospital and went back to Nellie's as a new registrar on the surgical side. She walked through her work in a state of abstraction, coping well, operating on her patients, supervising dressings and checking charts, doing all that was necessary, yet not really there. Brin's face and Brin's voice and Brin's smell and touch and presence seemed to accompany her everywhere.

Brin himself, somewhat to her surprise, seemed to be able to be exactly as he had always been; friendly, charming but not at all loverlike. Since she had herself told him that was the way he ought to behave, she should not have felt any chagrin because he did; but all the same, there was some regret in her that he had found it so easy to be obedient.

She had gone back to East Grinstead that night, taking the bus to Victoria to catch the last train, and he had hugged her warmly and kissed her soundly as they had waited at her bus stop, and told her with real admiration in his voice that she was a spitfire underneath all that surface quietness of hers, and she had laughed, feeling oddly as though she weren't really herself at all, but an actress studying a part. She had told him that it was always dangerous to make assumptions about people on the basis of mere appearance and then had said, a little awkwardly, 'Look, Brin – if I'm to go on being your doctor, this – I mean this can't happen again.'

She had looked up at him then and managed a small smile. 'Damn it,' she had added softly.

'Why not? Didn't you enjoy it?'

'You know damn well I did. You don't have to ask. No – it's just that doctors aren't supposed to have – they aren't supposed to be as close to their patients as we were tonight.' She chuckled softly in the darkness. 'It's usually men doctors and women patients they worry about, the powers-that-be, but it's frowned upon this way round too, I imagine. We really oughtn't to see each other again except strictly as doctor and patient till after your operation is over and done with –'

She had expected him to argue about that and had been quite prepared to make some sort of plan to meet him quietly, knowing there would be no real problems about their relationship. Neither she nor he would ever talk about it, of course, so there was no real risk. And anyway, as a woman doctor she wouldn't be seen by even the most censorious of her colleagues as taking advantage of the special doctor–patient relationship. Such an idea would be impossible to them, she knew, for they could never imagine a woman taking the initiative in any entanglement, so it would be reasonably safe to go on from their starting-point.

But he had nodded in instant understanding. 'I hadn't thought of that – damn it, just my luck! Now I've really got to know you properly we've got to pretend we're the same as everyone else, all stuffy and drear. Never mind, my darling old Charlie. We can wait – let's get this damned operation over and done with and then we'll see where we go from there! Let me know if you can hang on to admit me to Nellie's till after the show, will you, as soon as you can? If you can't, then I'll have to go and try my wiles on the Dame. One way or another, I've got to have this damned scar dealt with as soon as possible. Goodnight, ducks – see you soon –', he had added as the big red bus came grinding to a halt beside them and then he had handed her up onto the platform and stood on the kerb waving to her as the bus took her on its trundling way.

She had stood there swaying as she held on to the strap over her head, peering out into the darkness at his diminishing figure and then had sat down, feeling deflated and suddenly very tired. He was right of course to accept so willingly the need to return to an arm's-length relationship, but all the same, it would have been nicer if – and then she had shaken herself and bought her ticket from the yawning conductor and settled down to make the long journey back to her lonely bed in West Sussex, thinking of Brin all the way.

And so it had been ever since; she thinking of him and he being very busy with his work and offering her no more than the shortest of cheerful and friendly but undoubtedly impersonal conversations on the telephone when she called him. She spent a good deal of time in the admissions office at Nellie's poring over the waiting lists and arguing with the clerk as she tried to get a new date for his operation, and when she managed to arrange for a bed to be available just ten days after the Benefit night, she was jubilant. Just another week to go to the show, and then the operation and he'd be over that, she estimated, within a couple of weeks and then, *then* they could be themselves again. And her eyes had actually misted with tears of happiness as she had contemplated a future in which episodes like the one they had shared on the floor of his sitting-room would be a nightly experience.

There had been a moment when she had suddenly stopped being quite so starry-eyed and found herself thinking of any possible outcome to their lovemaking. It had all happened so suddenly and been so spontaneous that she hadn't given any thought to that possibility, and now she tried to work out from her diary just how risky that night had been. Could she possibly, she asked herself, leafing through its pages crowded with details of patients and dressings and letters she had to write to other doctors, could she have been at a vulnerable stage of her cycle? But the relevant information wasn't there; she had not bothered to enter it, and after all why should she?

Women who were not making love need not concern themselves with such matters, and until that night she had been one of the unconcerned.

For a little while she had worried, trying her hardest to remember the necessary dates, and then had relaxed. She was almost certain that she had been within safe limits, especially as her body had always behaved erratically in such matters, sometimes refusing to function altogether for a while when she overworked and became too thin; all she could do was wait and see, she told herself, and firmly put the thought to the back of her mind. It was exceedingly unlikely, her doctor's mind lectured her woman's mind, that she had any cause for concern. Every doctor who had ever worked in gynaecological wards knew how difficult it was for many women living in active marriages to start families; a single experience like hers, the doctor said firmly, was unlikely to give rise to alarm. And the woman who was Charlie listened and believed, needing to have that to hold on to. And perhaps hoping, somewhere so deeply inside her that the idea was not accessible to her conscious mind, that there had been a risk, after all –

The hospital was now buzzing with talk of the Benefit that was to happen at last on the next Saturday night. The posters had gone up and glittering name after glittering name adorned it. There was to be ballet and opera, musical comedy and jazz, sketches and songs and dances and everything the most jaded of theatrical appetites could desire. The writer and the choreographer and the director of the show were of the highest calibre, and altogether, the staff told each other, it was going to be the hit of the year.

The only pity was that none of the nursing staff could possibly afford to go, because the tickets were to cost an astronomical amount, from ten shillings in the gallery up to the heady box-seat charge of fifteen pounds each. It was clear this Benefit Night was designed to solve Nellie's financial problems once and for all from the pockets of the extremely wealthy, and the nurses watched enviously as the more senior and therefore richer doctors bought themselves their tickets from the special booth that had been set up in the lobby, right under the Founder's statue.

A poster had been painted to hang across the front of the

173

building and it announced the Benefit to the public at large and also begged for donations to help Nellie's reach its target of twenty-five thousand pounds, and many were the shabby individuals who came scuttling through the doors to drop their threepenny pieces and sometimes lavish sixpences into the collecting boxes. But they didn't consider for a moment the possibility of seeing the show, for too few of the people of Seven Dials could afford threepence, let alone the price of a seat at the Stoll Theatre.

Two days before the show was to happen, Charlie was in the Casualty Department standing in for a junior houseman who had developed a raging toothache and taken himself off to the Eastman Dental Clinic in Gray's Inn Road. She had nothing else to do and though she had had a long day in the theatres, the prospect of an evening spent in Casualty seemed to be more agreeable than one spent sitting alone in the common room. She ached to talk to Brin, but that was impossible. They must be at a crescendo of busyness, she told herself, at this stage of rehearsals, and he wouldn't welcome hearing from her. He knew she had a bed for him next Wednesday fortnight and that once he was admitted they would have time to talk contentedly; so she told herself firmly that it wouldn't be sensible to make a nuisance of herself now, and settled down to read the *Lancet* at the Casualty Officer's little desk, hoping there wouldn't be too much to do.

The big clock ticking ponderously in the big terrazzo-floored waiting-hall and the occasional clatter of a nurse's heels as she went busily about the small dressing-clinic that was going on in the far corner was all the sound there was, for the department was unusually quiet tonight, and Charlie yawned and looked at her watch. Another half hour and the night people would be on duty and she could go to bed herself and tomorrow she could look forward to a short but interesting theatre list of minor surgical procedures, all of which demanded some concern for the cosmetic result; she was feeling more relaxed than she had for some time. Not since Brin –

The big double doors swung open and a woman in an expensive satin coat which was streaked with blood came hurrying in. A man beside her in full evening dress was holding her round the shoulders with great solicitude as she held a large and very bloody handkerchief to her face.

'Quickly, quickly!' he shouted as he came bustling into the big waiting-room. 'We need a doctor at once – oh, please, be quick!'

Charlie came out of the small office at the same time as a nurse went hurrying across to lead the woman into one of the patients' cubicles amid much fussing from the very agitated man and saw her settled on the examination couch. She was a young woman, certainly a good deal younger than her companion, and her eyes above her bloodstained handkerchief were wide and frightened within their frame of heavily mascara'd lashes.

'What happened?' Charlie asked quietly as the nurse stood aside to let her bend over the couch.

'We were walking along, talking you understand, going to a little late dinner after the theatre and suddenly, there's this piece of metal sticking out on the pavement! I step on it, it flies up – whoosh!' The man gabbled and Charlie cocked an eye at him, intrigued a little by his accent, which was clearly mid-European.

'I'm sure it wasn't your fault,' she said as soothingly as she could. 'These things happen – there are still all sorts of pieces of debris around since the bombing – we see a lot of such injuries. Now, my dear, let me look –'

As she gently unprised the girl's terrified fingers the man gabbled on, explaining that they had indeed been passing a patch of bomb damage when it had happened, that he had done all he could to stop the bleeding, but knew it was bad, had been so grateful that Nellie's was so close, so wonderful a hospital – so much all a hospital should be, such fine doctors, such noble nurses –

'Where are you from?' Charlie asked, as much to stem the flood of explanations as because she was really interested, and the man stopped and then said carefully, 'I came to England in 1937. I was a refugee, you understand, in 1937 – from Poland –'

'It's all right,' Charlie said gently. 'No need to be worried.' She could hear the fear in the man's voice and knew its source; so many people with European accents had been hounded by the ignorant during the War, had had 'German bastard' shouted after them, been spied on and been accused of being

175

spies. It couldn't have been easy for a man like this and she smiled at him again and after a moment he smiled back.

'I am so anxious,' he said simply. 'My wife, you understand –' And then as Charlie looked down at the girl whose injury was now at last clear to see as she had mopped away the blood, the man added in a low voice, 'Ah – this is my friend, you understand. My wife, she is excellent, a superb wife, but this is my friend whom she does not know –'

'Not a word shall she hear from us,' Charlie said cheerfully. 'Now, Miss—'

'Dorning,' the girl said in a muffled and very London voice. 'Jayne Dorning, with a "y". Is it all right, doctor? Is it going to be an awful scar? I can't have a scar, not in my line of work – I'm a mannequin, you know. I gotta look good –'

'She shows my clothes from my business,' the man said wretchedly. 'It is so important it is right, you understand, doctor? My wife, the business –' And he almost wrung his hands with anxiety.

The cut was a jagged and messy one, involving the side of the nose as well as the cheek and Charlie looked at it very carefully and then straightened up, nodding.

'You're in luck,' she said as lightly as she could. 'I've had special training in such injuries. I can mend that for you so that you'll never see the scar. Do as you're told about the after-treatment and you'll have no problems –'

By the time Jayne with a 'y' had been admitted to the ward and had waited long enough for her evening meal to have been digested, so that she could have an anaesthetic, it was gone two in the morning, but Charlie was lively and ready. This was the first real plastic surgery case she could call her own, the first she would do without knowing McIndoe was available to help out if necessary. It was a challenge, but not one she feared. She knew with a solid certainty that she could make this girl's pretty, if rather commonplace, little face look as good as it ever had.

And she also knew that doing this case would help her to be ready for Brin's operation. She was sure in her skill, confident of her ability in every way, but all the same, it was good to be able to limber up, as it were, to get herself into a surgical rhythm. By the time she picked up her first pair of scissors to trim the jagged tears in the skin, she was as relaxed and alert as she could possibly be, in spite of the lateness of the night.

It took her almost three hours to set the fine stitches, for the jagged nature of the wound demanded a delicacy of repair that was considerable, but slowly, as the face reformed under her fingers, her conviction in her own skills grew and stretched. When she had left East Grinstead she had felt herself to be a tolerably good plastic surgeon. By the time she had finished with Jayne Dorning she knew herself to be an exceptional one.

It was already full day when she at last saw her patient safely tucked up in bed on the ward and could go off duty, and she pulled off her theatre dress and climbed into her own slip of a cotton summer one and set out to go back to the doctors' quarters and bed, but as she went through the big waiting-room of the Casualty Department to collect the bag she had left there, she saw the man in the evening clothes sitting sleeping heavily in a corner chair, his head thrown back against the wall and his mouth open in an unlovely gape.

She looked at her watch; almost six in the morning. She shook her head over the man's silliness, and went to sit beside him to shake him gently awake.

'You'd better go home, hadn't you? Won't your wife start to get a little – shall we say worried? – if you aren't there when she wakes up?'

He stared at her wildly for a moment, clearly having no memory of where he was and then rubbed his stubbled chin as recollection hit him.

'Oh, my God, you are right,' he said hoarsely. 'It is late – it is early – I must go – the little girl – she is all right?'

'She's fine,' Charlie said. 'Absolutely fine. She'll wake up some time in the middle of the morning and you can come and see her. The scar will be fine, I promise you. I've done a really good job, one I'm proud of. In a couple of weeks' time, when she can put a little makeup on it, she'll be as good as new. In a few months even the makeup won't really be needed.'

The man seized her hands gratefully. 'What can I do to say thank you? You are so good to me, so very good – what can I do to be – tell me your name, doctor. I send you dresses from my factory, the best I have –'

'No need,' Charlie said and laughed, as she disentangled herself from his damp hot grip. 'I need nothing. I'll tell you what, though – if you want to be grateful – take your wife to see the Benefit. The tickets are expensive but it's a good cause – and your wife deserves a treat, I suspect.'

He grinned suddenly, an impish grin that made him look a good deal less battered and a good deal younger than he clearly was.

'You are wise as well as clever – a good doctor. At least you should tell me your name so that I can know who is my benefactor –'

'I'm Miss Lucas,' Charlie said, knowing he could find out from Jayne anyway. 'But remember, no presents! I don't accept them. I'm glad to have had the chance to repair so difficult an injury. Now, home with you! It's time you weren't here.'

And that is how it was that Charlie was able to be at the Stoll Theatre for the Nellie's Benefit on that Saturday night in July in 1947. She had meant what she had said when she had told the elderly Pole that she never accepted presents from patients, but when she found in her post an envelope addressed in spidery handwriting and containing a front stall ticket for the show, she knew where it came from; and because the money that had been spent on it was to be of use to Nellie's, somehow it seemed a present she could in all conscience accept. So she did.

21

Not only the theatre was bustling with excitement and glitter; so was a large section of Kingsway and the central curve of the Aldwych, for not since the War had begun had there been quite so glittering a London occasion as this. Every well-known actor and performer in town who wasn't on stage tonight was in the audience, as were large numbers of the sort of people who generally had their photographs in the *Tatler*. Lords and ladies, earls and honourables and every other version of county aristocracy had turned out in force, as had City people more famous for their money-making skills than for their birth, and well-heeled manufacturers and traders who had found the War less onerous than profitable. The committee the Board of Governors of Nellie's had put in charge of selling tickets had clearly done a superb job, for not a seat was to be had even at these exorbitant prices, and Charlie felt herself to be very fortunate indeed as with muttered apologies she pushed her way through the gawping crowds to get into the theatre.

She almost gave up the attempt at one point, so intimidated did she feel by the sort of people with whom she found herself surrounded as she broke through to the front; face after face was a deeply familiar one, even to someone who went to the cinema fairly rarely, and only read the *Tatler* at the dentist's, and voices too were familiar, for many BBC people were there. But then she lifted her chin and told herself not to be so silly; she had as much right as anyone else to be there, for wasn't she part of Nellie's, for which the whole occasion had been created?

And then she almost burst into laughter, for as she stood there uncertainly hovering on the edge of the pavement outside the big theatre, someone pushed past her and she turned her head to see her elderly Pole accompanied by a lady of his own age who was so round and so firm of figure that she looked as though she had been upholstered. He looked at her with his eyes wide and limpid and as though he had shouted it aloud she heard him begging her not to recognize him. She looked casually away, her face quite expressionless, and he went gratefully on his way, and she stood there staring after him, glad to see he had taken her advice. It was agreeable to see his elderly wife so happy – for the round face was beaming with excitement – while Jayne with a 'y' lay bored and irritable in a ward at Nellie's waiting for her pretty little face to heal. There is, Charlie told herself philosophically as at last she made up her mind and pushed her way into the chattering crowd of theatre-goers, a sort of rough justice in this world after all.

Her seat was a superb one in the centre of the sixth row and she settled into it comfortably, glad to be on her own so that she could look around her at all the magnificently dressed people instead of talking. For all that the country was in the grip of Attlee's austerity programme, everyone in the auditorium looked exceedingly well off, showing how deeply they had dug into pre-War wardrobes to shake out sequined frocks and feathered wraps and well-cut tailcoats. There were wide expanses of starched linen on chests which had for the past seven years been wrapped in khaki or airforce or navy blue, and an air of genuine frivolity everywhere which quite banished the faint odour of mothballs. Only the most churlish, Charlie told herself, could fail to find it all enormous fun. And she opened the brochure she had bought for the massive sum of ten shillings, because she had felt the need to make her own contribution to the evening's fundraising success, and wondered how they were all coping backstage.

Was Brin as excited there as everyone on this side of the curtain seemed to be? she wondered idly and considered the possibility of going round afterwards to see him. That could be fun, she thought, and her spirits lifted even higher as she contemplated so agreeable an end to her unexpected treat.

The hubbub backstage was almost at hysteria level. The wings were big and roomy, but the massive sets of the show currently running there occupied much of the available space, so the dancers, who numbered over fifty – Letty and Peter had decided from the start that lavishness was to be the order of the day for *Rising High* – were crushed and cross as the sweating stage staff tried to get them into some sort of logical order ready for their first entrance.

Brin was swearing as much as any of them as he physically pushed people into their right positions, checking them against the clip-boarded papers he held in one hand, but he was clearly enjoying himself all the same.

Peter, who was anxiously checking the lighting cues with the man on the board, because several of the smaller floodlight bulbs had blown earlier that day and been irreplaceable in spite of frantic searching in all the usual warehouses and shops, looked happy too in spite of the way minor problems were building up. One of the singers had had an attack of screaming fury because someone, he swore, had stolen his music (it was eventually found in the lavatory where he had left it), a dancer had twisted her ankle and the whole line had had to be rearranged in consequence because as luck would have it she had been one who had a small speciality section to deal with, and two actors who lived together had not turned up, sending notes to announce dolefully that they both had chickenpox, which necessitated the cutting of one sketch altogether, and led to an attack of acute bad temper from the actress who therefore found herself unwanted after all despite all the months of rehearsal and expectation. But Peter had dealt with it all, his face showing no sign of strain, dealing with each problem one at a time and refusing to be made frantic.

Letty, watching him even in the middle of her own frantic busyness, had relaxed. She had been genuinely worried that the whole thing would prove to be too much for him after all, and had been fully prepared to step into the breach and take over his work for the evening if necessary, but clearly it was not going to be. Good for Sophie, she found herself thinking, and then shook her head at what she regarded as her ridiculous tendency to behave like a mother hen and had gone off to help the heavily taxed old actress who was acting as wardrobe mistress for the night to kit out the *corps de ballet*.

Somehow, in spite of the hubbub and a sudden fuss over mislaid props for a comedy act and an episode of sulks from a couple of singers who had expected to be later in the bill than they actually were, everyone was ready when the orchestra at last struck up its overture music. Brin, now as ready as he was ever likely to be, had a moment to lift the small flap that covered a spyhole in the great front curtain and he peered out and felt a sudden pang as he saw the serried rows of eager faces turned towards the front. The sound of the chatter and laughter that came to him was muffled by the weight and thickness of the wall of velvet, and the music too sounded thin and tinny as it struggled past its heavy folds, but the excitement in the house came through as powerfully as though it were electricity and he tried to imagine how it would be to be poised on the edge of the stage, not to ensure others got on to it, but in order to appear himself. To face that audience, to show his own skills, his own presence – he took a deep breath and let the cover fall, blotting out the tiny vignette of a full house, and lifted his chin. 'Soon,' he whispered. 'Soon. When my face is right' – and then turned as Peter touched him on the shoulder.

'Ready?'

'Very ready,' Brin said and lifted his clipboard in a sort of salute. 'If they get anything cockeyed so help me, it won't be because of anything I've got wrong –'

'I'm sure,' Peter said. 'You've done a great job so far – I'm sure you'll finish it the same way. Right, two minutes to beginners – get the dance line on –' And the show slid into gear as at last the work and the worry and the fretting and the organizing of the past months gathered itself into a peak and *Rising High* exploded into reality.

It was amazing how well it went. The dance line was faultless, the long hours of drilling they had been put through – not only by Irina Capelova but by Peter and Brin too – paying handsome dividends. They moved as one elegant sinuous animal, their long legs in glittering tights working with a military precision, and their feathered heads above faces on which wide toothy grins were fixed as with glue snapping from side to side like clockwork. The music clattered and brayed and tapped from the pit below as the audience roared its appreciation and Brin, standing near the lighting box at stage left, caught Letty's eye and grinned with huge relief. After such a start, what could fail?

And for a while it seemed nothing could possibly go wrong, that all the problems had been dealt with well in advance as act followed act, linked by the sketches that told the story of Nellie's history and which followed the introductory dance routine, delivered in the rich and sonorous voice of Theo Caspar, who had arrived from America only the day before to make his own contribution to the evening. The audience, clearly enchanted to see so famous a cinematic face in the flesh, hung on his every word in an entranced silence and then burst into applause after every act with so much enthusiasm that all the performers came off stage scarlet with excitement and pride. And so it went on as the atmosphere backstage became ever more euphoric, with everyone loving everyone else with a fervour that even for stage people was remarkable.

They were just two acts away from the first half finale when the whole fragile edifice of excitement and confidence and success threatened to fall apart. The callboy had been sent to get Katy and Rollo into the wings ready to do their wooing scene from *The Taming of the Shrew* and she arrived first, her face under its makeup tight and closed with some sort of unreadable emotion. Brin looked at her and frowned, for even he had never seen her looking quite so bad-tempered. And then, as applause again broke out he turned to be ready to see Theo Caspar come off stage, his hand out to take from him the big red book within which his script had been cunningly hidden. Theo was grinning lazily as he reached him and nodded affably as Brin took the prop from his hand and then stopped short, staring over Brin's shoulder at Katy.

'Well, well,' he murmured softly. 'If it isn't dear old Katy! It's been an age since I've seen you – how goes the battle, coz? *Sweet* coz –'

'No better for seeing you,' Katy said, almost hissing it between her teeth and Brin turned, startled at the venom in her voice.

Theo laughed and then, as the next act, a troupe of famous jugglers who did amazing things with beach balls and Indian clubs, went running past him to go on stage, said, in the same soft voice, 'Still so sweet, my darling? Oh, it *is* a comfort to know that things don't change in this wicked world! London looks as grey as ever, the people here are as phlegmatic as ever, and Katy Lackland is still as much of a little bitch as ever! *Sweet* girl – I see you're playing your namesake in the *Shrew*. Such splendid casting. Dear old Letty, always gets it right, doesn't she?'

And he moved past Brin and with a very practised move swept her into his arms and kissed her soundly.

She struggled furiously and then, as at last she managed to get away from him, turned her head and with great inelegance spat into the dust on the floor.

'You make me sick!' she blazed. 'You disgusting old – old *queer*!' and Brin stared in fascinated amazement, taken aback not only by her rage and the look of sheer glittering loathing in her eyes but also the professionalism of the pair of them, for they were still talking in the whispers essential in the wings when the tab is up.

'Darling!' Theo almost purred it. 'I can think of a much better word for you! Several in fact. Let's start with the nice ones – like little tart and –'

She lifted her hand and slapped his face so hard that the sound of the impact reached the stage and one of the jugglers, momentarily distracted, almost fumbled one of his Indian clubs, and Brin hissed automatically, 'Quiet!' even though he was, if the truth were told, greatly enjoying the little scene. But Katy seemed unaware of him and turned on her heel to walk away and cannoned straight into Rollo who was standing immediately behind her, as wide-eyed with interest in all that was going on as were Brin and several other people who were standing in the dimness staring.

Quite what happened then no one could ever be sure of. Rollo went sideways, turning away from Katy in an attempt to dodge her headlong rush, and the sword which was part of his costume tangled itself between his legs and sent him sprawling against a flat that was propped against the wall, and it swayed dangerously. Then, as Brin flung himself at it to hold it steady, Rollo twisted again to avoid it, and this time landed heavily on the floor.

He lay there for a moment seeming almost stunned and then tried to get up, but as he moved his left leg he yelped with pain and again Brin called 'Quiet!' automatically.

People clustered round as applause broke out for the jugglers, and Letty appeared almost from nowhere with Peter close behind her. She took one look at Rollo, still on the floor, and at Katy, now standing still and horror-struck as she stared down at her leading man who was whimpering with pain, and

184

said crisply to Brin, 'Send the jugglers back on as soon as they come off – tell David in the pit they're to do an encore and then get the dancers on to repeat their first line-up routine. We can hold the *Shrew* another ten or twelve minutes that way –' And she knelt beside Rollo and with careful hands touched his left leg and tried to straighten it.

All the time Brin was obeying her instructions he could hear what was going on; Rollo in real tears of obviously agonizing pain and Letty's voice soft but commanding as she tried to help him and then her demand for someone to help her get Rollo out of his costume.

'He can't go on,' she said shortly. 'And he needs medical attention, so the sooner we get him out of this stuff the better. Peter, send a callboy out front to find a doctor. The house must be littered with 'em –'

'Max is here with Johanna,' Peter said swiftly. 'Somewhere in the dress circle – I'll get him –' And he vanished as Brin came back to stand eagerly beside Letty, tense with excitement as the jugglers, puzzled but obedient, went back on stage to start their encore.

'Who'll do the part?' he asked urgently, having to concentrate on keeping his voice low, so eager and anxious did he feel. 'Letty? Who?'

'No one,' she grunted, as gently, with the help of Theo who had said not a word throughout the whole contretemps, she eased Rollo out of his constraining doublet and then began to ease the hose off his now rapidly swelling left leg. 'You know quite well that this one we didn't understudy –'

'I'll do it,' Brin said, his voice seeming almost to ring in his own ears with the tension that was in him. 'I've rehearsed this one over and over, remember? Rollo wanted a lot of time, and so I held the book for them umpteen times – I know every move and every inflexion, I could do it exactly the way he did –'

Letty looked up at him briefly and then went on methodically helping to get Rollo into the bathrobe someone had brought from his dressing-room. 'Rollo?' she said after a moment. 'All right with you?'

'Fine with me,' Rollo was sweating under his makeup, his normally cheerful face strained and white. Clearly he was in severe pain. 'Be grateful if you would, old man – shit, but this hurts! I must have torn a hamstring again – I did that once before when I was a kid and it was just like this –'

'There'll be a doctor here soon. Can you relax so that a couple of the boys can pick you up and carry you, Rollo? Good lad – just take it easy, now.'

She got to her feet as carefully two of the male ballet dancers made a carrying cradle of their arms and eased the tall figure into it, their trained muscles rippling easily under their leotards. 'Katy,' she said then, not looking at her. 'All right with you?'

'Yes, oh yes, Letty,' Katy said in a small voice and then, in a little rush, 'God, I'm sorry! I didn't mean to be so – Rollo, I'm so sorry –'

She moved forwards and now her face was more easy to see and she looked stricken and Brin without thinking put a hand out to take hers and convulsively she squeezed it, grateful for the touch.

'Me too, Letty,' Theo said, his voice a little brusque. 'It was my fault. I indulged myself baiting Katy. It's an old game we play, but I should have known better – really sorry, Rollo –'

'Never mind.' Rollo was now leaning against one of his bearers, his face wet with sweat but seeming a little less agonized. 'Just get me out of here, for pity's sake, and let Brin get on with it –' And Letty nodded and the two dancers carried him away.

'Right, get into the costume, Brin,' Letty said and reached for the clipboard tucked under his arm. 'I'll take over here. It probably won't fit too well, but do your best –'

'As long as the doublet's a decent length,' Brin said. He was already hopping on one leg as he pulled off his trousers and now he tugged them off completely and threw them aside and reached for the tights and began to get into them. 'I'll not be too decent if it isn't – no jockstrap – oh, hell, turn your back, all of you – I've got to get rid of my underpants. They'll look awful under these –'

With help from Katy who was now in a fever of willingness to assist in an attempt to expiate her guilt, and with Theo fastening on his sword, he was dressed in the costume by the time the dancers were taking a bow to rather thinner applause. The audience was getting restive now, and wanted something different, and Brin lifted his chin and stared out at the great vivid expanse of brightly lit stage and thought – me. They want me, and I'll show them – wait till they see me – And then suddenly his excitement and confidence collapsed about him like a child's brick house.

'Oh, my God,' he said blankly. 'Makeup. I've got no bloody makeup on –'

'Sod makeup,' Theo said succinctly and pushed a soft-feathered hat into his hand. 'It's the acting they'll see, not your bloody face –'

'But –' Brin turned to him, almost piteously, and touched the scar on his cheek. 'But this – oh, Christ, how can I go on without makeup and with this?'

'Idiot!' Theo said. 'They'll love it – get on with it –' And he reached for the red leather book that held his script and walked forwards to go on stage as at last the music cue that heralded the wooing scene started on its way.

He hesitated only one more fraction of a second and then came back and leaned over Katy and kissed her cheek gently. 'Sorry, Katy,' he whispered. 'You call it quits and I will –' And then he was gone, marching on stage to rapturous applause.

But he did not do as he was meant to do and go to stage right to take his place behind the lectern that was set there for him. Instead he walked down to the centre stage and held up his hand to the still applauding house.

'Ladies and gentlemen,' he cried and at once the clapping stopped and they sat there hushed and expectant, row after row of pale oval faces gleaming in the light from the stage and turned upwards towards the figure standing there. Brin, who had moved further back so that he could see into the auditorium, felt a moment of such acute sick horror that he thought he was actually going to throw up there and then. His stomach seemed to move up into his throat as he caught a glimpse of the great composite animal that was a full house audience. It could, if it loved him, make him the happiest man in the world, make him feel real as he had never been in all his life; but it could also, as he well knew, become savage and turn on him, booing and jeering its hatred and boredom.

That such an audience as this very fashionable one was unlikely to behave so didn't occur to him at that moment. It was an audience and as such to be deeply feared as much as it was adored and needed. He wanted it and hated it in the same moment and for a brief second he actually contemplated turning and running away, had actually made a small sideways lurch, but then Theo's voice began and he stopped and listened, unable to move at all.

'Ladies and gentlemen,' he repeated in those golden, liquid tones for which he was so justly famous. 'Alas and alack, problems have beset us backstage! That fine and much loved actor Rollo Groom has been injured. We are not asking if there is a doctor in the house –' He laughed musically. 'We don't want the entire staff of Nellie's backstage – and actually we have already sent for such help. But we do want to announce that there is no need to fear you will be deprived of seeing the item that he and his enchanting co-star, our own lovely Miss Katy Lackland, were to give you. Because there is backstage tonight another fine actor – untried as yet, and unknown to you, but his time will come, as you will, I know, agree when you see him in the part he is to play for you. It is indeed a very remarkable thing that fate has decreed he take this role tonight as you will understand when I tell you that he is one Brinsley Lackland – a brother to our own dear Katy, and therefore – like your humble servant' – and he sketched a little bow –' a member of the family whose efforts in founding the great hospital of Queen Eleanor's we are here tonight to celebrate.

'So, ladies and gentlemen, I here give you another Lackland, eager to ensure that Nellie's, our own wonderful Nellie's, which has served London so faithfully for so long, will continue to be an establishment that is Rising High. In the wooing scene from Shakespeare's *The Taming of the Shrew*, here are Katy Lackland and Brin Lackland – welcome them as only a London audience can!'

And as the applause broke on his ears like a great flood of water breaking on stone cliffs, Brin, with Katy's hand firmly in the small of his back to push him on his way, went sweeping on to the vast stage of the Stoll Theatre.

22

At first Charlie had been so startled that she couldn't react at all. She had sat there in the middle of the sixth row of the stalls staring up at Theo as he rolled out the words and hadn't believed what she was hearing. It was one of those silly fantasies she sometimes drifted into when she was trying to fall asleep, she told herself a little wildly and closed her eyes, screwing then tight till they hurt, but she didn't wake, for when she looked again at the stage Theo was still there, making his announcement. But then he stepped back, merging into the shadows at the rear of the stage as Brin came on with Katy close behind him.

The audience began to applaud, rising to Theo's manipu- lation of them as obediently as one end of a seesaw rises to the fall of the other, and Brin stood there centre stage, quite still, with his head up, and that made the applause falter for a moment and then start again, and Charlie felt her own face get hot as she realized why there had been that moment of hesitation.

It was his scar. He looked pale and somehow less real than Katy, and Charlie realized after a moment of puzzlement that he was, unlike all the other people she had seen that evening, quite without any greasepaint. His eyes were dark enough to be clearly seen, however, and the lines of his jaw defined the shape of his face well, but the light, that cruel penetrating light in which the entire stage was washed, did more. It outlined the scar on his face in a way that made it more vivid than it actually was. It was the same clarity of view that she had when she looked at a patient under the special operating theatre lights which cast their careful and pitiless shadow-free glare on the area in which she was to work and she wanted to jump up and cry out: 'No – don't look – don't stare – we're going to cure that – make it better, get rid of it – please, don't look – don't look –'

But of course she sat still and then became aware that around her the applause was increasing, that some people were standing up to make it easier to thump their hands together and she stared round as one after another rose to give Brin a standing ovation that went on and on, until her head was ringing with the noise of it.

She looked back at the stage and this time saw Theo standing beside Brin, his hands up as Brin still stood there and made no move, and then at last the noise stopped as people sat down and prepared to listen.

'Please,' Theo said simply. 'Please – the wooing scene from *The Taming of the Shrew*!' and he stepped back and cried in a loud voice, 'Signior Petruchio, will you go with us, or shall I send my daughter Kate to you?'

Katy stepped back too into the shadowed wings as an expectant hush fell on the house and Brin still stood there. It seemed to Charlie that he would never respond, but then with a sharp, almost convulsive move he turned and walked upstage and at last, turning back to the audience with a swirl of his purple cloak, he began to speak.

'I pray you do. I will attend her here, and woo her with some spirit when she comes –'

The audience were rapt, and slowly, as the speech progressed, the icy amazement that had filled Charlie began to melt and she could concentrate on what was happening. He looked pretty good, she told herself, staring at him with as an objective a gaze as she could muster, even though it was difficult to be objective when her whole body was aching with awareness of how terrified he must be by his situation, and when she felt almost as though it were she herself standing there in a yellow doublet and hose and purple cloak waving a soft velvet hat around. But was it a good performance? She couldn't be sure, because now Katy was there, wheeling and marching about the stage like some small mad thing, her eyes snapping and her voice clear and loud in the silence.

She, now was indeed giving a superb performance. When she spoke it seemed to Charlie that she wasn't in a theatre at all, but was there in an Italian courtyard with this small termagant of a woman, eavesdropping on a private scene between two real people. Her eyes seemed to spark actual light and her

190

mouth moved with so much anger that the small hairs on the back of Charlie's neck shifted and then lay still as Katy listened and reacted to the words that Brin was throwing at her.

'– bonny Kate and sometimes Kate the curst, but Kate, the prettiest Kate in Christendom, Kate of Kate-Hall, my super-dainty Kate –'

The scene went on, and slowly the awareness grew on Charlie that while Brin was giving an accurate enough reading of the part, sure of his words and clearly comfortable with the moves he used, still there was not in him that fire that she recognized in Katy. She had met Katy once or twice when she had called in at the rehearsal rooms, and thought her, if she had thought of her at all, a rather silly woman, vapidly interested only in her own appearance and quite unaware of other people. She had been used to smile vaguely at Charlie when she saw her and then show no further interest, and Charlie had assumed that she was just another mediocre actress. Good to look at, a splendid clothes-horse, but little more.

But, she now knew, she had been quite wrong in that judgement. This woman was an actress of stature, one who could take an audience in her hand and tease it and soothe it, amuse it and frighten it, break its heart and steal its soul. She owned the audience and could use it in any way she wanted.

And tonight, it seemed to Charlie, she was using her huge talent to draw attention to Brin. Every one of her reactions, her moves and her looks thrown at him made the audience more aware of him, and more responsive to him. She was, in effect, creating Brin's performance for him, by giving him the centre of attention and leading the audience in appreciation of him, and as the scene built beautifully to its climax Charlie leaned back and could no longer look at the stage.

Katy has done something very remarkable, she told herself, sitting there in the dimness as the words rolled over her and Brin's voice, strong and confident now, delivered the last lines: 'for I am born to tame you, Kate, and bring you from a wild Kate to a Kate conformable as other household Kates. Here comes your father; never make denial. I must and will have Katherine to my wife.' She has made an actor of him, because really, he isn't very good at all –

But that was a thought not even to be considered and she thrust it away from her for ever, and leapt to her feet with everyone else as once more the applause broke out. She, like everyone around her, clapped until her arms ached and her palms stung, and cried out, 'Bravo!' and 'Bis!' and just shouted her appreciation as all over the theatre, in tier after tier of seats, Brin Lackland was given a response to his performance of Petruchio in a fragment of *The Taming of the Shrew* that no one there could ever remember hearing before.

Charlie gave up the unequal battle after trying for over half an hour to get past the stage door. It made no difference that she assured the almost frantic and very startled stage doorkeeper that she was a friend of Brin's, that she was expected – a lie she felt justifiable – because even if he had been willing to let her in, there was no way she could get past the crowd. They were packed in the passageway and on the stairs side by side, buzzing like bees in a hive, and no one at all, even with the best will in the world, could have got her through. It was as though the entire audience had decided that they had to come backstage to tell the hero of the hour just what a hero he was.

She struggled her way out of the mob of people besieging the stage door and escaped, her clothes awry and her hair in wisps on her forehead – for the combination of the warm July weather and the excitement had made her sticky with sweat – to go back down Portugal Street to the front of the theatre, and stood there for a while, needing to recover her breath as she listened to what was being said around her.

It was really quite remarkable. Did people usually hang around outside theatres so long after a performance like this? She had no idea, but doubted it. Yet here they still were, many of then talking animatedly about the excitement of it all, clearly unwilling to go their ways and leave all the glitter behind, and feeling suddenly very tired and dispirited Charlie smoothed her hands over her head and then turned and went walking away towards the hospital, a bare few minutes away.

What had promised to be a treat had turned out to be something rather disagreeable, even threatening, and she was puzzled by how alarmed she felt. Why should I? she asked herself as she went trudging round the Aldwych past the Waldorf Astoria Hotel, into which many of her fellow theatregoers were disappearing. It makes no difference to me that he was so huge a success, does it? Why feel so uneasy?

And because she had always been as honest with herself as she knew how to be she faced the question fairly. Is it jealousy? Am I unable to cope with a man who can get that sort of attention from a theatre full of strangers? But she could absolve herself from that. At one level she was genuinely glad for him, had been truly happy to see the way his eyes had gleamed with excited pleasure at the response he got. She grudged him no part of it, and no one could ever convince her she did.

But it wasn't really *right*, a corner of her mind whispered. It was Katy who had made him look so good. It wasn't him at all, was it? That's what makes you feel so uncomfortable about it all. If he had truly earned that ovation, that thunderous appreciation, she would be glorying in the fact. But it had been Katy who had deserved it. Katy who, showing an unselfishness that Charlie would never have believed possible, had given him that experience of adulation and that, Charlie told herself as at last she crept into bed and tried to settle herself to sleep, that is why I feel so bad. I'm not sure where he's going to go from here, because unless Katy is there and is in as generous a mood, will he manage to achieve that again? And if he doesn't, will he ever be satisfied?

Letty too was concerned, and her doubts sharpened even more when Mrs Alf brought her all the papers with her morning tea on Monday. She sat up in bed with her hair a tangle of grey on her forehead and read her way through adulatory notice after notice, and all the time her face was expressionless. It was, she told herself, every bit as bad as she had feared, and when at last she folded the last paper and got out of bed, leaving her tea untasted, to go and take her bath, her mood was a decidedly low one.

She spent a great deal of time on the telephone that morning, checking first to see how Rollo was, and was comforted to hear that Max had insisted he see Nellie's orthopaedic expert, Mr Fitzsimmons, later that day.

'I'll do, Letty,' Rollo had clacked into her ear when she finally managed to get his landlady to help him to the phone. 'It's happened to me before and I got over it then. Bit of a bind it happened in the middle of the show, though. Honestly, would you believe it? I hear he did well –' He tried to sound casual but Letty wasn't deceived.

'A bit too well for his own good,' she said acerbically. 'Seen the papers?'

'Mmm.'

'The people who covered the show weren't the theatre critics, of course,' Letty said. 'They sent their society writers and gossip people. So all we've got is damn all about what the show was really like, but all this stuff about our noble hero, mutilated by the fight against Hitler and now standing up to show his scars bravely and so on and so forth –'

'I was in the Fleet Air Arm, you know,' Rollo said very casually. 'Invalided out with asthma, would you believe –'

'I believe you,' Letty said gently. 'Never mind, Rollo. I'm mounting something new soon. I've decided that much – and I'll find you something that's just right. Just get well soon.'

'Yes,' Rollo said gratefully and she could feel him brighten even over the phone. 'I say, Letty –'

'Mmm?'

'You really are no end of a brick, you know.'

'Ba – poppycock,' Letty said vulgarly, swallowing the first word that had come to her mind, and hung up. But she felt rather good, all the same.

Peter shared her unspoken concern when she managed to reach him. He had been out, he told her cheerfully when at last she managed to get him to the telephone. 'Sophie had some coupons to spare and wanted some material for curtains. We've been all over the place and finally got it just round the corner at Whiteley's – isn't it ridiculous?'

'You're getting remarkably domestic,' she said, unable to keep the hint of acid out of her voice, but he just laughed comfortably at that.

'Aren't I just! You all right today, Letty? Glad it's over?'

'Oh, yes, very – I'm trying to find out how much they've made for the fund, but I can't get hold of Lee. Um – have you spoken to Brin this morning?'

'Brin? No – should I have done?'

Letty laughed. 'Oh, Peter, you really are wonderfully vague – my dear chap, haven't you seen the papers?'

'Sophie wanted to start shopping early,' Peter said and Letty grinned, imagining the look there would be on his face.

'Brin is a cross between Henry Irving, Garrick and

Beerbohm Tree, according to our more popular hacks. Listen to this –' And she reached for a paper to read him the headlines. ' "Scarred war hero takes theatre by storm",' she recited in ponderous tones. 'And here's another one – "An unflawed acting talent makes its mark" – and then a lot of stuff about the damaged face that shows its underlying perfection, and oh – this one's a real stunner. "The face that will launch a thousand heartbreaks." That one comes with a photograph of Brin looking quite unbelievably brooding and sexy. Charles Boyer isn't in it –'

There was a little silence and then Peter said carefully, 'Did I miss something? I mean, I heard the fuss, but I thought – well, people are like that. They love a loser, and seeing the understudy go on always gets 'em – and he is a rather romantic figure I suppose, with that face, even though he didn't actually get it fighting anyone –but I didn't think the performance was all *that* good.'

'It wasn't,' Letty said crisply. 'Competent, I grant you. Nicely walked, if you see what I mean. It was Katy who did it, of course –' She shook her head. 'Overcome with guilt, the wretched minx, making all that trouble in the first place, so she gave him the stage. It really was a classic piece of Katyism – I've worked with her often enough to know what she can do. If only she'd been in the same sort of mood when she made *The Lady Leapt High* as she was last night, we'd have got a fantastic performance out of her, but there, that's Katy. Unreliable.'

'Of course she is. The girl's a damned genius, but who ever said geniuses were easy to live with?'

'I certainly never did,' Letty said grimly and then sighed. 'Look, Peter, what do I do now? He'll expect a star part in the next Gaff production but I can't give him that, whatever happened last night. He just isn't up to it –'

'With that sort of publicity, Letty, my dear, there is every chance that someone else will try to snap him up,' Peter said and Letty brightened.

'Now, there *is* a cheerful thought! I like it – thanks, Peter. I'll call you later in the week. I've got ideas for a new production – this blessed Benefit's put the bit back between my teeth –'

'Surprise, surprise,' Peter said and laughed softly. 'Well, let me know. I need a job, after all.'

'Feeling ready for one?' She tried to sound casual, but it was difficult, and Peter laughed again.

'Sophie says I am,' he said. 'And I rather think you know, that I'll have to do as I'm told. She isn't someone you can argue with easily, quiet though she is.'

'*That's* all right then,' Letty said with great satisfaction, and hung up. Whatever problems she might still face with Brin, she told herself cheerfully, as once again she tried to get Lee's number, at least Peter's all right. I really think I can stop worrying about him at last.

23

When the phone rang again Lee looked at it, and actually
tucked her hands under her arms to stop herself from
answering it. I had enough yesterday, she thought defensively. There's a limit to what I can cope with; but then the
phone stopped ringing as Nanny picked it up on the nursery
extension and she relaxed. Nanny, lovely, fiercely loyal
Nanny, would gladly lie for her if she told her she didn't want
to speak to him –

But it wasn't Harry after all. 'Dame Letty,' said Nanny,
putting her head round the drawing-room door and preening
a little, clearly finding glory in answering telephones to
Dames and then, as Stella came bumbling past her into the
room, swooped on the small bundle and bore her protesting
loudly to her morning rest as Lee picked up the phone.

'Letty? You must be psychic,' she said. 'I was going to call
you.'

'I couldn't wait – do we have a total yet?'

'We do – a lovely one. The Board of Governors are going to
be exceedingly happy people, and exceedingly grateful. We've
reached our target and gone more than five hundred over the
top – £10,522 we made. Which means the appeal has to get only
another £9,500 or so and we've got our new block and a bit
more besides –'

'Only!' Letty laughed. 'Ye gods, when I think how long it's
taken and how tough it's been to get what we got, the mind
boggles. Still, I'm delighted you did so well. Congratulations.'

'Congratulations to *you*,' Lee said warmly. 'You've been
absolutely marvellous – we're enormously grateful and –'

'Oh, pooh,' Letty said rudely. 'Listen, Lee, I want to talk
about you. How are you?'

'I'm very well,' Lee said, on her guard at once.

'Hmm. And the children?'

'Oh, they're marvellous!' At once Lee became more animated. 'This morning Michael said that –'

'Dear girl, I bow to no one in my regard for your offspring, but I do not require a blow by blow account of every one of their winning little ways.' There was no malice in Letty's tone, but she was very definite. 'I wanted only to know you were all well. And Harry?'

'He seems fine.' Lee's voice was quite colourless.

'Oh, Lee, for heaven's sake, this is me, remember? Now, tell me. What's happening?'

There was a little silence and then Lee said unwillingly, 'Well, I'm still here.'

'Yes, I'd noticed that.' Lee could almost see the smile on Letty's face at the other end of the line. 'I'm glad.'

'It's only a – a temporary arrangement, though,' Lee said. 'I mean – the possibility is still there. Of going, that is. It's just that –'

'You agreed to try again?'

'I agreed not to move out for another month,' Lee said. 'That's all. The house is still there, the new one, but I let Nanny's brother and his family borrow it until the middle of August. They live in Newquay in Cornwall, and they were able to get a good amount from letting their house there to summer visitors, so Nanny asked if –'

'My dear, I don't give a tuppenny damn about Nanny's brother's domestic arrangements. I'm just delighted to hear you two are talking.'

'I didn't say that –'

'Then it's time you did. You've agreed to stay with Harry for a while – well, that's a good beginning. Now, for heaven's sake, use the time well.'

'Letty, please, I do wish you'd –'

'I know, mind my own business. Well, as far as I'm concerned I'm doing just that. Harry is an ass and often behaves like a spoiled baby but he's my nephew as well as a basically good chap and I really am very attached to him. He's like my own son, really. Silly, isn't it? Here I am with a great raft of nieces and nephews, and it's Harry I feel closest to – and that gives me permission to meddle, doesn't it? And –'

'He did very well, didn't he? Your other nephew, I mean –

I've never heard such applause –'

There was a little silence and then Letty laughed again. 'All right, my dear, I'll shut up. For the present. Yes, he did very well. With his sister's help, of course –'

'Yes.' Lee stopped again. It really was depressing, to put it mildly, how everything seemed to come back to Harry. Harry and Katy, hateful sneering Katy – and she shook her head at herself and said as brightly as she could, 'Darling Letty, I really must go. Stella's giving Nanny a bad time over her morning nap and I think I'll have to go and intervene. I'll let you know how the appeal goes in all the other directions – the garden fête in St Paul's Churchyard next month should bring in quite a lot and there's to be a late summer ball too – we should get our target. Thanks again for all you did for us –' And she cradled the phone gratefully and leaned back in her corner of the sofa.

Around her the house was still, for Stella had after all stopped crying, falling asleep with the suddenness of the very young, and there was nothing more for her to do until she went to collect Sarah from her nursery class at lunchtime, and she moved restlessly at that awareness. To have nothing to do was dreadful; she hadn't realized just how good for her it had been to have the Benefit to keep her working. While she had been bustling about over advertisements for the brochure and begging for cheap printing and all the rest of it, she hadn't been able to think so much about herself. But now, with the whole thing completed, the pressure of her own situation became that much greater.

She closed her eyes against that thought, but that just made it worse. All she could see was Harry's face with its patient pleading look on it and she snapped her eyes open again and stared at the expanse of sunny window that faced her. She'd have to make her decision soon; she couldn't go on like this. And heaven knew she was well aware of what decision she wanted to make.

She wanted to believe him, wanted to yield to his assurances that he was different now, that he had only behaved so badly and had all those sordid affairs of his because he had loved her so much and had been so miserable because she had seemed so remote – but still she felt uncertain. If only, she thought with a sharp little spurt of anger, if only I hadn't told Letty, and she hadn't talked to Harry. If he'd come to me of his own free will, it would have been different. As it is, I don't know if he really wants me, or whether he's trying to please Letty. She matters a lot to him and always has, and he'd do a great deal to make her approve of him.

And, Lee told herself, fanning the little spark of anger to make it stronger, needing the edge of its harshness to take the edge off her deeper pain, it's me I want him to care about, no one else. I want all of his love or none of it, that's the truth of the matter. And I just don't know whether he's telling the truth when he says I've got it – however much he spends all Sunday courting me, fussing over me, coaxing me, and however much he may rush to phone me while he's at Nellie's – and again the phone rang, urgently, and she looked at it, knowing that this time it was definitely Harry. Shall I answer it, let him talk, beg and plead again? Or shall I just ignore it, tell Nanny to tell him I'm out? It was getting to be a more and more difficult decision to make.

'Well, now,' Katy said with great satisfaction. 'That is what I call a right turn up for the book.'

'Isn't it just!' Brin said and leaned back and stretched his arms luxuriously above his head. 'Who'd'a' thunk it –' And Katy giggled and settled herself more comfortably at the foot of his bed. His breakfast tray lay on the rumpled counterpane between them and they were sharing its contents with a degree of pleasure in each other's company that they hadn't found since they were very young indeed and had tumbled about the hay loft at the farm above Tansy Clough, making old Wilf the cowman furious at the mess they made.

'Let me see it again,' she commanded and held out her hand, and he threw the piece of flimsy paper across to her and she smoothed it out on her knee and read it carefully.

'It's good for a first contract,' she pronounced at last. 'And they really seem to want you. To send a cable this long and with such a detailed offer – it's for real, no doubt about it –'

'It's marvellous,' Brin said and grinned lazily at her. 'Bloody marvellous – just wait till I tell 'em all –'

'Not yet,' Katy said sharply. 'Not quite yet – we want to make sure. Send 'em a cable yourself asking for confirmation by post – tell 'em it's got to be sent airmail right away or you'll have to accept another of the offers that've been made to you and –'

Brin shot bolt upright, sending the tray tipping dangerously and slopping lukewarm tea onto the counterpane. 'Are you mad? I'm going to send a cable accepting it, right away, that's what I'm going to do –'

'No you're not,' Katy said crisply. 'Now, listen to me. I know Hollywood, ducks. I've been there, remember? And they'll cut your throat for a nickel, hang you up to dry for a dime. You have to be as tough as they are to get on, play them at their own rotten game. Don't be a bloody fool and go licking their boots, wagging your tail in gratitude! If you do that they'll think you're not worth a row of beans. It's playing hard to get that matters – ask Theo –'

'Theo? You want me to talk to *Theo*? I thought you two hated each other –'

She shrugged that away. 'Oh, that's not important. We have our rows, always have, right from the start. But he taught me how to handle Hollywood, and he was right. He'll tell you the same –' She frowned then, suddenly thoughtful. 'Come to think of it, I suspect I recognize Theo's hand in this already.'

'How do you mean?'

'How is it they've heard so soon? It's Monday – the show was Saturday night. Even allowing for the time differences being in their favour and all that, how did they hear so soon what sort of reception you got and –' She looked down at the cable again and nodded with an air of great satisfaction. 'Of course this is Theo's doing! He cabled 'em and tipped them off. He's had it in for his studio for years, wanting to get out, but he's a touch too expensive now to say the very least, and the other studios haven't exactly been falling over themselves to pay the asking price for his contract. But if he gets someone good for one of the other big boys, they'll owe him, and he'll make sure he collects. Oh, he's a cunning bastard, is Theo, but you've got to hand it to him – he always gets what he wants. He got me out there to the West Coast as part of a scheme to get a part he wanted for himself, and now he's using you in the same sort of way –'

'I didn't know that – I mean, that it was Theo who got you to Hollywood.'

She laughed then, a rather thin little sound. 'No, I don't

suppose you did. I didn't exactly make a song and dance about it. Damnit, I felt such a bloody fool, I'd have died rather than let anyone know what he did to me, but now –' Again she shrugged. 'Now it doesn't matter so much.'

'What did he do?'

She looked at him briefly and then away and looking at her face in the bright morning sunlight that was pouring in through his bedroom window to fill the small area with golden light he thought – she's getting older. My kid sister, getting older. I suppose I am too, a bit –

'Made love to me. Oh, not real love, you understand. But all the chat and the attention and the sexy come on – and I fell for it. Like a bloody ton of bricks.' She looked at him briefly again and managed a grin. 'Stupid, wasn't it? There he was, a raging queen, and I fell head over ears for him and wanted him so badly I could – well, never mind. And it was just what the lousy bastard intended me to do. Do you wonder I get so livid when he's around? I could kill him every time I see him – and then – oh, then I get used to seeing him again, and we go back to being more civilized. But it isn't a thing a girl forgets that easily.'

'You're still in love with him,' Brin said, startled at his own prescience, and she went suddenly scarlet.

'If you ever say anything like that in public I'll kill you,' she said, and her voice was low and thin but it made him draw back a little into his pillows all the same. 'The way I feel is no one's goddamned business but mine – you hear me? And I'll tell you this much – I don't go in for falling in *love* with people. I may fall for sexiness but I don't get soggy with it and burble on about love. That's for the idiots, not for me. Other people drool over *me*, in case you hadn't noticed, and that's the way it's supposed to be. So don't you go trotting out any of that sort of romantic garbage about me ever again or –'

He put up both hands in a gesture of mock terror. 'All right, all right! Not another syllable do I utter, ducky. I don't give a damn anyway. I'm more interested in my own career than I am in your love life.'

'That's sensible. Keep it that way.' She seemed to calm down as fast as she had caught fire and once more wriggled comfortably into the counterpane.

There was a little pause and then Brin said, 'So you think

Theo told these people at this studio that they ought to take me? Why should he? It sounds crazy to me –'

'No, it isn't. It's the Hollywood way. And listen, ducks. Let's be clear about this. Getting this sort of contract may sound delicious, but it's not for real, you know – not for the big side of the business.'

He looked alarmed and opened his mouth to protest, but she shook her head impatiently. 'Oh, it's for real in that they'll take you out there, pay you the money, do the test and groom you and prime the old publicity machine and so forth, but whether it's a big career – that's another kettle of catfish. You'll have to do something good – and then – then, of course the sky's the limit, as long as you don't make any mistakes.' She looked bleak for a moment. 'I made a mistake, agreeing to let my studio lend me to Letty. That damned *The Lady Leapt High* did me no good at all –'

'You'll do all right, Katy, for God's sake!' Brin said. 'I mean, everyone knows you, you couldn't be more famous and –'

'Oh, yes I could. I've a long way to go yet. But I've learned a lot doing that rotten film. Like the importance of using every chance you get, and not getting cocky. Remember it too, Brin, if you want to make it in this lousy business. Never get cocky. I did, and I'm paying for it –'

She bent her head over the cable once more and then, slowly, her lips curved and she looked up at Brin with her eyes wide and very bright. 'Hey, I have me a sizeable idea. I think it's time we talked to Theo, what say you? Thank him nicely for tipping off the studio and getting them to offer for you and then suggest that maybe they'd like to go for a cuteness award.'

He stared at her, puzzled by the way she was getting less and less English the more she talked. It was as though even thinking about Hollywood imbued her with Hollywood ways and a Hollywood voice.

'A *cuteness* award?'

She clambered off the bed and reached for his dressing-gown from the chair and threw it at him. 'Come on,' she said. 'I'm going to phone Theo. He's leaving from Southampton tomorrow for New York – we've time to do a bit of parsnip buttering before he goes –' And she went out to the living-

203

room and he could hear her dealing with the telephone as he struggled into the robe.

By the time he reached the sitting-room she was talking to Theo and he stood leaning against the door jamb listening, and marvelling a little. This was a side of her he had never seen, this crisp businesswoman, and it was a revelation to him; and an agreeable one.

Ever since he had started on his attempt to build a career as an actor he had felt at a disadvantage because of his younger sister. She had got there first, she had taken the limelight first, she had succeeded first. There had been a sense of isolation in him as he had tried to push his way through into the damnably exciting, frustrating and eternally seductive business he had chosen, but now, listening to Katy, he felt the warmth of kinship. He had always had the ambition to succeed, the burning hunger for the stage that was even more important than talent, as he knew perfectly well, but deep down he had doubted, often, whether he could make it. When his long dreary years as an ENSA entertainer had ended in that stupid flying bomb incident he had been sick with terror that this was indeed the end of the road. All there was for him in the future, he had told himself despairingly, was working for his father and brothers in that hateful Mill in Haworth, and contemplation of that had sharpened his desperate need to renew his damaged face, to try again to make the bitch success bow her head to him.

But now, listening to Katy on the phone, the fear dripped away, and was gone. He had her support now, and he *could* do it, he knew he could, and he grinned at her as she winked back at him.

'I thought you'd like it, Theo. Tell 'em when you get there, then? There've been sisters who've made it, of course, but we'll be different from the Cummingses and the de Havilands and the Fontaines. We're one of each kind, so we won't be competing for lovers, or with looks, and we're going to be the closest pair in Hollywood – the columnists'll adore us and the Hays Committee will purr with all that cosy family life. Sounds good, hmm?'

She listened for a while, nodding and then said, 'Theo, you're a lousy bastard. Always was, always will be –' But there was no rancour in her voice. 'What? Oh, right. He's here.'

She held out the phone to Brin. 'He wants to talk to you.'

'Brin?' Theo said, his voice thinned and remote. 'Glad to hear they got in touch so fast. I told 'em to move it or everyone else'd snap you up.'

'It was – thank you, Theo,' Brin said a little lamely. 'It was very good of you.'

'Not good – realistic. Ask that spitfire sister of yours. She'll tell you what a jungle Hollywood is. I behave like a jackal when I'm there, and you'll have to do the same. This new idea of hers. Good for her, of course, first and foremost – it's a better studio than the one she's with and they'll be better for her – but it's good for you too. Nice big brother and sister act – it's different. And it's a help to ride on someone else's back, and she was good for you on Saturday. D'you know how good?'

'I'm sorry?'

There was a little silence and then Theo said, 'Well, never mind. Maybe you can pull it off on your own eventually. But at this stage you need Katy, so for God's sake hold on to her. When she gets bitchy – as she will, my friend, as she will – hold on. Don't let her get away and leave you. You need her –'

'Er – yes,' Brin said and frowned, a little mystified. 'Look, you know I'm really quite fit? I mean I know I have this scar, but I'm going to get that fixed. It's all arranged – but once that's done I'll be as right as ninepence. I mean, you don't have to worry about my health or whether I can cope. I don't need looking after. I've got one sister who does that, and I loathe it – one of the best things about Katy is that she doesn't fuss over me. I don't think I could cope if she did.'

'I doubt she's ever going to do that!' Theo said and laughed. 'And it wasn't your health I meant. Never mind. Just remember what I said. Stick with her – you need her – oh, and by the way –'

'Mmm?'

'Stick to the scar, too.'

Brin blinked. 'What did you say?'

'Stick to the scar. It's great – a major asset. You wouldn't have half the charm you've got for the studio without it. War hero – never let it go. I didn't.'

'You didn't what?'

Again there was a little pause and then Theo said lightly, 'It doesn't matter. It's just that I had my share of war the first time around. They made a lot of play on it, when I first got out to the coast. They'll do the same to you. However much you hate it, let 'em do it. Encourage it, even. It pays off. I'll see you in LA, old man. Let me talk to Katy again –'

Brin handed the phone over and stood by the window as Katy chattered and then, as she at last hung up, turned and said shortly, 'What did he mean, I need you?'

She looked at him consideringly, her head on one side, and then seemed to make a decision.

'Listen, ducks, you have a lot to learn about the business of acting. It's all tricks, you know. Tricks and now and again magic when the feeling gets to be right. Well, on Saturday night I got the feeling right and I made magic happen for you. Didn't you feel it?'

'I felt myself doing a good job,' he said a little stiffly. 'The best I could. And they seemed to like it.'

'It'll get better,' she said cryptically. 'And then they'll know what it is they're getting. That lot on Saturday – they didn't have a notion what they were seeing.' She shook her head. 'Never mind, ducks. Let it be. Just listen to what Theo said, if he told you you needed me. You *do* need me, so be nice to me. However tough I get, you *need* me. And I dare say I might need you, quite a bit. It's a bloody lonely place, Hollywood', and her face seemed to look old again for a brief second.

Beside her the phone trilled again and she picked it up.

'Who? Oh, hello, Charlie,' she said and then listened, her eyes on Brin and her brows lifted. 'I don't know – I just got here. I'll see if he's in – I haven't found out yet – hold on.'

She covered the mouthpiece with her hand. 'Do you want to talk to her?' she asked softly. 'It's up to you, of course, but if you'll take my advice you'll be out. She's crazy over you – anyone can see that – and you've got other things to think about right now, haven't you?'

He stared at her, frowning slightly, and then nodded.

'Tell her I'm out and you don't know what time I'll be back. And don't take a message.'

24

Charlie tried very hard not to believe it. She told herself that it was inevitable that he should be preoccupied with what had happened to him, that people in the theatre business would be fussing over him, offering him work perhaps, and there was certainly enough in the newspapers to feed that belief. It seemed impossible to open one of them without finding articles about him, and seeing photographs.

She would sit in the medical common room over her breakfast looking at those photographs and especially at the way no attempt was made to hide the scarred cheek, how indeed some seemed to go out of their way to display the way his eye puckered and his lips curled when he smiled, and doubts would curl their way into her mind, but she would push them away. There was nothing mysterious about it. He was heavily occupied, obviously, but he would turn up at Nellie's as she had arranged for him to do and then they would be able to talk, before she did his operation, and afterwards too, when she checked the dressings and took out her spiders' web stitches. It would all be fine, she was anxious for no reason – and she would close the paper and set about work, hurrying on her way to the wards and the day's business.

But the anxiety was there, and she found that after all she couldn't just wait for the day of his planned admission. She phoned his flat, often, but most of the time there was no answer. Once Mrs Burroughs had spoken, shouting loudly and obviously far from comfortable in dealing with the instrument, and she had tried to leave a message but despaired at the woman's inability to cope with that and arranged to call back. Then she had got his sister Katy and she said she didn't know where he was, and for a while Charlie had considered just going to the flat and knocking on the door. But she shrank from that. Suppose he was in the middle of some sort of interview or discussion about his future? That such interviews and discussions were a major part of his life at the moment she could not doubt; newspaper report after newspaper report made that clear, and she would read them and despair at the thinness of real news in these hot summer days, that made constant gossip about Brin so staple a part of the papers' diet.

Once, almost a week after the Benefit when she had still heard nothing from him, nor been able to reach him, she became so very anxious that she actually phoned Sophie. She had thought hard about that, remembering how angry the woman had made her, but it was different now, she told herself. Quite different. And anyway, all she was doing was trying to reach Brin –

But Sophie had been of no help. 'My brother?' she had said, in that flat Yorkshire voice of hers, when she answered the phone. 'Nay, he's not here, he lives next door, in his own flat –'

'I'm well aware of that,' Charlie had snapped. 'But I don't seem able to find him in and –'

'Oh, he's very busy at present,' Sophie had said. 'I'm told he's been offered any number of these acting engagements. I don't know what, of course, he hasn't told me. But his cousin, Peter, he's told me. I'd phone his flat again, if I were you. Or write him a letter –'

And Charlie had done just that, but it had made no difference. He didn't answer, and she told herself on the Wednesday morning when he was to be admitted that that was why; he had seen no point in letters when they were to meet so soon, and she had set about her day's work feeling better than she had since the night of the show. Today they'd be able to talk, today he would explain his silence, and all would be well.

At three o'clock the admissions clerk phoned her on Elm Ward where she'd been asked to deal with a difficult case of abdominal ascites which needed tapping, and she finished setting the last cannula carefully in place and washed her hands quickly, her pulses thumping slightly in her ears before she picked up the phone. He'd arrived at last, she told herself, working very hard at being calm. She'd asked the clerk to let her know as soon as he got here, and at last he had. A little late – he'd been told to come at noon – but he'd arrived.

'Miss Lucas? I've a bit of a problem. Your patient, Mr

Lackland – he hasn't shown up, and I've got an urgent request from Mr Fitzsimmons' firm. They've got a compound fracture they want to plate, and there aren't any beds anywhere, apart from this one on Spruce. Is Mr Lackland going to take it up? I can't really turn Mr Fitz down, you see. I mean, he's a consultant and –' She let the words hang in the air and Charlie stared sightlessly at the ledger on Sister's desk where she was sitting and thought – I'm just a registrar dealing with an unpopular speciality. She'd had enough trouble getting this bed against the disapproval of several of the senior surgeons who didn't regard the work she was trying to do as sufficiently important, and to block Fitz, the highly mercurial little orthopaedic consultant, was to court all sorts of trouble.

'How long can you hold the bed?'

'Well, till four, perhaps. But no longer. This patient's in Cas, you see, and though Sister Briar said she was going to try to clear her side ward for him, she's not too hopeful. She's got extra beds up as it is – I am sorry, Miss Lucas, I really am –'

'I'll call you back,' Charlie said decisively. 'If you haven't heard from me or the patient by four, then let the bed go to Fitz –' And she hung up the phone with a clatter and went half running over to her room to shed her white coat and pull on a jacket. She'd have to go to the flat, find him and remind him. The ass, she thought; he's forgotten. In all the excitement of the reaction to that damned show he'd forgotten the most important thing in his life –

And that was when she had to believe what had happened, when all her attempts at self-delusion collapsed.

She had run all the way to Cambridge Circus and then across Earlham Street, dodging the traffic by the skin of her teeth, because she was looking up at his living-room window to see if she could see him there, and gone running up the stairs to the first floor and banged imperiously on the door. After a long wait it was opened cautiously by Mrs Burroughs.

'Oh!' she said, staring at Charlie closely. 'Oh. It's you –'

'I've got to see Mr Lackland,' Charlie said peremptorily. 'It's important.'

The woman seemed to bridle and then looked uneasily over her shoulder.

'He ain't here,' she mumbled and tried to push the door closed.

'Then where is he?' Charlie set her hand on the panels and pushed hard in the opposing direction and the woman stood there dubiously, clearly not knowing what to do.

'He ain't 'ere,' she said again and took a step back, and Charlie was about to push the door open and just march in when she heard a door on the inside close softly, and the woman once again looked over her shoulder in the direction from which the sound came.

'Not here,' Charlie said dully. It was a statement, not a question.

The old woman looked relieved. 'That's it. Not 'ere. Like I said, 'e ain't 'ere –'

'And you don't know where he is.' Again it was a flat statement.

'No. 'E never said where 'e was –' And this time the woman looked flustered and began to push on the door again. 'I got my work to do,' she said, and there was a belligerent yet whining note in her voice. 'I'm 'ere to look after these flats, not to act like a bleedin' doorkeeper –' And this time she did shut the door and Charlie stood in the dim hallway looking at the blank panels and tried to pretend just for a moment that it hadn't happened. That she hadn't been aware of someone else there on the far side of the door listening, hadn't heard whoever it was hurry into one of the rooms and snap the door shut when it seemed she was about to push her way in.

She went back to the hospital, walking at a brisk pace, her hands thrust into her jacket pockets and her head up. People passing her saw a rather intense young woman, not pretty but interesting enough despite the fact that her face was expressionless, and paid her no attention at all, forgetting her as soon as they had passed her. But inside she was burning, actually physically burning as the knot that had become her belly creaked and tightened and sent waves of its tension spreading to her limbs as ripples spread on a still pond.

She went to her room, still seeming composed and quiet and put on her white coat and then went directly to the admissions office.

'Miss Burns? You can have that bed for Fitz. The patient has cancelled. I'm sorry to have wasted your time.'

'Oh, that's all right, Miss Lucas,' Miss Burns said with great relief and smiled at her, gratefully. 'I'll just let them know –'

And she picked up the phone. 'Wait a minute, and we'll see if we can rebook a bed for you. I shan't be a sec –'

'It doesn't matter,' Charlie said. 'He's decided not to come in at all. So I needn't bother you.' And she went back to Elm Ward to check how the ascites patient was getting on, and sat and talked to him for a while, soothingly, assuring him that the awful swelling in his belly would get easier once her treatment was complete, and managed to concentrate on what she was doing so well that later that evening during visiting hours he told his wife he had a really lovely doctor to look after him now, much better than any of the men.

She managed to finish her day in the same calm and competent fashion, dealing with dressings and drips and all the many odd jobs that fell to her usual work load and then went to the common room for supper, as though nothing at all out of the ordinary had happened that day, and she might well have managed to continue on that same cool level; if it hadn't been for Max Lackland.

He was sitting in the common room too, drinking his own after-supper coffee when she got there rather late, and since there was only one other occupant of the small room, she had perforce to speak to him. But she kept her conversation as remote as she could, simply nodding at him as she did to Daniel Shaw, the casualty officer, and murmuring 'Good evening', before sitting and concentrating on eating her vegetable soup and dry bread, trying to pretend she was interested in it.

Max cocked an eye at her and said pleasantly, 'I haven't seen you about here at Nellie's for some time, Miss Lucas! I thought you'd gone and left us.'

'No,' she said and managed to swallow some of the soup. It wasn't easy, for her throat felt as though there was a taut wire rope around it.

'Couldn't stay away, could you, Charlie?' Daniel Shaw said and reached for some bread. 'Isn't this cheese disgusting? Still, it's better than nothing. Did they feed you as badly as this at East Grinstead?'

'East Grinstead?' Max said, and cocked an eyebrow at her. 'You went there, did you? With McIndoe?'

'Yes,' she said, still not looking at him, wanting to behave normally and knowing she couldn't.

'Did very well, too,' Daniel said heartily. 'It's amazing how good she is, sir. She's giving me ideas, I can tell you. I was off sick with toothache a week or so ago, and this girl came in with a very nasty laceration of the cheek, so Sister Cas said, and Charlie here did as handsome a cosmetic job as any I've ever seen. She came back to Cas today for a check-up and I saw her – I really do congratulate you, Charlie. She was cock-a-hoop, she looked so good. It looked like no more than a scratch – and I gather it had been a real mess –'

'Well done,' Max said, and then spoke no more, sitting there quietly, to Charlie's enormous relief, until Daniel Shaw finished his disgusting cheese with gusto and every sign of having enjoyed it and went away complaining loudly about having to be on duty until midnight. And then Max said quietly, 'McIndoe –'

'Mmm?' Charlie was momentarily startled. His silence had given her the chance to retreat again into her own private world, where she was not thinking, not feeling. Just being. Every atom of her self-control was at work, keeping her mind blank of everything except her patient. She had been thinking about making one last round on Spruce Ward before going off for the night and Max's voice brought her back to the present, almost with a thump.

'You went off to do plastic surgery,' Max said.

'Oh. Yes.' Don't think, don't react. Just one word at a time, her self-control instructed her.

'Because of that young cousin of mine, Brin Lackland?'

'Because I was interested.' Careful, careful. Say as little as possible.

'And you discovered you have a talent for the work?'

'Yes.'

'I hear there are some very severe disfigurements to be seen in his wards.'

'Very.'

'Then you no longer see any need for Brinsley to have surgery?'

'I –' She swallowed, and got to her feet. 'He is no longer my patient.'

'Really!' Max lifted his brows. 'Quite fit again, is he?'

'As far as I know.'

'Good. You took good care of him, then.' He smiled at her,

212

and she looked away, not wanting to see that pleasant face. He looked too sympathetic in spite of the altercations they had had in the past and any sort of emotion like that was dangerous to her in her present state.

'I try to take good care of all my patients.'

'We all do, my dear. But we don't always succeed, do we? I look back on some of my cases and I hang my head in shame and disappointment. That is something doctors have to live with, isn't it? But you need have no such feelings about this patient. I'm told he gave a remarkable performance at the Benefit. Did you think so? I saw you there at the theatre, though you were too far away from me to speak to you, but I thought, when I heard what happened – you must have been very pleased. I hear he was a raging success. I didn't see him, of course, because I was in the other poor chap's dressing-room. He made the most dreadful mess of one of his hamstrings and now Fitz is trying to sort him out. But you must have been pleased to see Brin do so well without needing any further surgery.'

And then her control went, and her perception of him as sympathetic shattered as she took a long breath in through her nose, feeling the muscles of her nostrils pinch down with anger. 'Are you sneering at me, Dr Lackland? Telling me you told me so and that I'm a fool?'

He looked at her with real amazement on his face, because she was standing up now, seeming unaware of how she was staring at him. Her face was white with fury and her eyes seemed to be very dark in their sockets.

'Is that it?' she blazed. 'Are you sitting there mocking me because I've made a bloody fool of myself? Are you enjoying yourself, liking to see someone who once dared to disagree with you put down in the gutter where she belongs?'

'My dear!' He was on his feet, concern written all over his face. 'My dear girl, what did I say? Whatever is the matter? Please, sit down, let me –'

'Don't patronize me!' she flamed. 'So I was wrong and you were right! I concede that. You were right. He didn't need surgery and he isn't going to have it. You were bloody well *right*. But do you have to rub it in? Is that supposed to be good psychiatric practice, making people feel so – feel so –'

It was no use. The words were sticking in her throat, refusing to come any further, and she gaped at him and moved

213

her lips, trying to speak again, and then choked, and he came round the table and took her across the shoulders, and half led her, half dragged her to the door.

'You're not well,' he said firmly and his words seemed to come to her through a mist from a very long way away, echoing down long corridors. 'You are not well at all – come on – we can get you there – just hold on –'

The door swung in front of her, distorted and threatening, and the passageway beyond reared up and she thought the floor was going to hit her in the face; but then that voice came again, from even further away.

'Easy, easy does it. You can hold on – good girl – here we are – all right now, let it go. You'll feel better –'

There was a hand across her forehead, dry and cool and blessedly secure and she let it take all the weight of her head, which was suddenly enormous as the feeling rose and rose in her and then erupted into the most painful of retching. She was being sick, dreadfully, appallingly sick, and as her body heaved with the shuddering of her chest and belly muscles a part of her mind, her doctor's part, was saying conversationally; 'Now, why? Why on earth are you doing this, you who never vomit? When everyone else gets gastro-enteritis or seasick or whatever, it never happens to you. But now you are, now you are, now you are –'

She was sitting on the floor, her head resting against the door jamb and he was squatting in front of her, one hand on her wrist, and she lifted her head from its drooping position and straightened her back and heard herself saying aloud, 'Now you are, now you are –', and he patted the wrist he held and sat back on his haunches.

'Well, well! That was a nasty moment for you. It's hateful to be sick, isn't it? I loathe it when it happens to me. Bit better now? You passed out, too. All very vaso-vagal altogether – feel ready to get to your feet? I'll see you back to your room and then you can –'

'No,' she said and managed to catch her breath, wiping the back of one hand across her lips, a little shakily. Her mouth tasted tinny and yet dry, and her head was aching now. 'No. I can manage. I'll go on my own –'

'My dear, of course you need to be taken there! You're not at all –'

'No,' she said. 'Leave me be, for heaven's sake! Just leave me be', and she managed to look up at him as her vision at last cleared and lost the mistiness at the edges that had been so horrible. 'Please. Go away.'

He was silent for a moment and then stood up, brushing his knees with his hands.

'I'll send one of the nurses from Cas to you. Stay where you are till she comes,' he said curtly. 'You'll allow her to take care of you?'

She closed her eyes. 'All right. Only you, please go away.'

'I'm going. But I insist on a doctor's right to offer at least one piece of advice, even though it's obvious you don't want me to be involved in your care. But care you need. See one of the physicians tomorrow. Because someone ought to be looking after you. I may only be a psychiatrist, but I suspect that there is something far from right with you at the moment. Ellen –' He looked over his shoulder at the kitchen door. 'Keep an eye on Miss Lucas till a nurse gets here –'

And he went, leaving her sitting with her back to the lavatory door, her eyes closed and the common room maid peering anxiously at her from the kitchen.

She too knew there was something far from right with her at the moment and she didn't want to think about what it was.

25

Billy Brocklesby watched the last of the Governors go hurrying up the stairs to the boardroom, and chewed his lower lip thoughtfully. Trouble in the wind, he decided, that was what it was. Trouble in the wind. Every last one of 'em with faces as long as a fiddle and hardly a civil good morning for him among 'em, not even from Mrs Harry, who was usually as sweet as they came. She looked about the worst of them, come to think of it, white as your shirt and eyes like whatsit holes in the snow – and he shook his head and went back to his lodge and his cuppa feeling dispirited and irritable.

Upstairs the Governors were even more dispirited. One by one they settled themselves at the big table and arranged their papers as they talked in low tones to their immediate neighbours, lifting their heads sharply to look at each new arrival, and then going back to their conversations when they saw that it was not yet Sir Lewis.

Max arrived last and went directly to his father's place at the head of the big old table, and tapped the gavel on its stand.

'My father is far from well this morning,' he said shortly. 'I'm sorry to be late, but I had to see him first – he agreed to let the meeting go ahead without him.' He looked round at them and lifted his brows. 'You may imagine how he must be feeling to permit that,' he added drily and they stared back at him and nodded like so many mandarins. 'So, with your permission, as his deputy I shall take the chair.'

There was a murmur of assent and they settled to listen with an air of slight relief. Everyone was very attached to the Old Man of course, but doing business with him in charge was never as easy as it might be, for he was an irascible man, and getting hard of hearing. With Max sitting in his place there was every hope of getting this matter settled quickly.

'We'll get the routine business out of the way at once, I

suggest,' Max said crisply, 'so that we can have as much time as possible for the affairs that most concern us. Now, Mr Molloy, the minutes of the last meeting of the Board, if you please –'

They went through the minutes, through matters arising and through new appointments and routine financial reports so fast that it was still only ten thirty when Max leaned forwards and reached for the newspaper he had brought with him and had left lying to one side throughout the discussions.

'Now,' he said grimly. 'To this. You've all seen it, I'm sure –'

'Which paper have you got there?' Molloy asked. 'The *Graphic*? Have you seen the *Daily Sketch*?'

'That one too?' Max looked at him sharply. 'Any others?'

'Someone from *Picture Post* telephoned here yesterday,' Molloy said. 'I refused to talk to him, of course, and gave instructions no one else was to speak to the man, but you know what these gutter journalists are –'

'Slanging the press because you don't like what they say is no answer,' Max said. 'The *Graphic* is a respectable and responsible paper. We have to take what it says seriously –'

'Well, what does it say, after all?' Brodie spoke for the first time, leaning forwards in a relaxed and easy manner that still managed to obscure Molloy's view of the head of the table. 'That a lot of money was raised for the hospital. And so it was. There's nothing in that to cause any –'

'It's what I warned you would happen!' Molloy spoke sharply and leaned forwards too, so that the two men were sitting side by side in almost ludicrously matched postures. 'I came to your office months ago and showed you the Ministry letter. I warned you then that –'

'Now, gentlemen, gentlemen!' Max held up his hand as Brodie began to expostulate. 'Let's keep our heads. Getting angry with each other helps no one. What letter, Molloy?'

The secretary riffled in his file and brought out with an air of triumph a sheet of paper which was passed from hand to hand up the table to Max, and he took it and smoothed it and read it carefully.

'Hmm. What this says in essence is that all monies held by Queen Eleanor's Hospital and its subsidiaries and branches will, when the new Act that establishes the National Health

Service comes into force, be deemed the property of that National Health Service and within its control, and –'

'You see?' Molloy said with great satisfaction. 'I warned you, didn't I warn you, Brodie, that the money raised this past few months wouldn't belong to us any more? Didn't I warn you that telling people that they were giving to a charity was tantamount to lying to them when the money was going to the Government rather than to us? Didn't I –'

'I'm not sure I agree with your analysis, Molloy,' Max said. 'As I read this letter, the money the hospital holds will still be spent for the hospital, but not by the Governors. It will be the responsibility of the new administrators who run Nellie's after the Act comes in –'

'We'll be thrown out, then?' Johanna asked. She had been sitting silent, not sure she fully understood what all the fuss was about; she hadn't herself read the morning papers and had only what other people had told her was in them to go by. 'Are you saying we'll be thrown out because we raised money for the hospital –'

'No, of course not, Jo,' Max said irritably. 'We won't be totally responsible, I dare say, for every detail of running the place but there's no suggestion that we shouldn't still be part of Nellie's. No, the problem is that these newspapers are implying that the committee – that we were less than honest with the people who contributed to the Benefit. They say that all money being raised for hospitals now is inevitably ear-marked for the Treasury and that people should be told that when they are asked for contributions. It seems –' He squinted down at the newspaper in front of him. 'It seems that a Mr Alfred Damont who gave a personal gift of £1,000 as well as buying expensive space in the brochure that went with the show has complained about the fact that he was misled –'

'He wasn't,' Lee said loudly and then reddened as everyone turned to look at her. She had been paying little attention to the meeting so far, if the truth were told, still preoccupied as she was with her private concerns, but the mention of the name aroused her. 'He's a cousin of mine, on my mother's side, and very rich indeed. He was manufacturing cement and so forth during the War and he did very well – he's got a conscience about that, I suspect, so I asked him to help us. He bought a space in the brochure and then he told me we could have a cheque as well, because he thought it was a good cause. I certainly never told him it was for anything but Nellie's –'

'But did you warn him that the Government was to take over Nellie's and that the money would therefore come under their control?'

Lee stared. 'Of course not,' she said uncertainly. 'I had no idea that –'

'And that is precisely what this article says,' Max said patiently. 'That the people who raised this money did so in good faith, or so they imagine, but that it's time that fund-raisers learned more about the uses that their collections were to be put to to avoid the risk of cheating the public –'

'How can it be cheating the public to collect money for a good cause?' someone at the end of the table called out. 'This is the most arrant nonsense, and I vote we pay no attention to it at all – just nasty yellow journalists making trouble –'

'I don't think we can set it aside as easily as that,' Max said, with barely concealed irritation. 'There is a real anxiety here. People are saying, it appears, that they see no reason why they should hand over their own money for a hospital when the Government which is already taxing us appallingly is going to be responsible for providing all hospitals' needs out of the income derived from our taxes, after the Act comes in, and I can understand this anxiety. There are other good causes which won't be getting Government support and people may well prefer to choose to give it to them. The question we now face is how we deal with this situation. For example, do we give back all we raised?'

'Heavens, that would be impossible!' Lee said. 'Have you any *idea* how many people –'

'I know,' Max said. 'I asked the question simply to make the point that we *have* raised the cash, that we are now responsible for it, and have to think sensibly about what we do with it. Brodie, tell me how does the fund stand at present?'

'We've done very well, so far,' Brodie said, rather smugly. 'The Benefit raised well over ten thousand – a marvellous effort and the ladies are to be warmly congratulated' – there were murmurs of, 'Hear, hear!' – 'and with our other efforts – the jumble sale and the collecting boxes and the garden party and so forth, we've reached almost fifteen thousand. Then there is your good father's generous gift, so we have done exceedingly well and we're close to our target –'

'Mmm,' Max said and then slowly grinned. 'Then we've enough to start work, you'd say? Enough to put the new block in hand?'

'We've got more than that,' Brodie said promptly and threw a glance of sheer malice at Molloy. 'I thought it best to waste no time – I've got architects' preliminary ideas and sketches to show the Board and I've also managed to get promises of certain amounts of basic materials. Not easy, you know, these hard times, but I've managed it. I have the use of the cash in the Bursar's Own Fund, as you all well know, and it was in a good state of health – about a thousand to play with – so I used it, as I'm fully entitled, of course, to start the ball rolling. With some of the blocking that goes on here' – he carefully did not look at Molloy – 'I thought it best to be discreet. I was waiting for today's meeting to apprise the Board of what I've taken it upon myself to do, but this stuff in the newspapers has rather stolen my thunder.'

He gave a self-deprecating little smile that fooled no one. This was a man who held himself in exceedingly high esteem.

'But there it is. We could, if the Board give their consent, set the architects to work virtually at once. I've taken the liberty of collecting all the necessary paperwork for getting the permits to build and for further supplies, and it also occurs to me that Mrs Harry Lackland could use her good offices with her cousin to get us more, if he's in the cement business. If she goes to him, explains that the money *is* for Nellie's and we intend to spend it right away, before the new Act comes into force, so that no one in any Government office can stop us, that should allay any fear he may have –' He cocked an eyebrow at Lee.

'But if he's already complained to a newspaper that he feels he's been cheated, won't going back to him make him furious?' Johanna asked, before Lee could speak.

'No – because it will *prove* to him that we're acting as we always have, with total honesty and in good faith! We're not asking him for money anyway. Only for priority with orders of cement and other essential materials.'

'I'll go and see him,' Lee said. 'I'd have to anyway, to sort it all out – I can't have him thinking we've been in any way dishonest with him.' She smiled thinly then. 'My mother will be livid if I don't. I'll ask him. He's a good man and it's my guess he'll be willing to help, whatever these journalists may have said to him – or about him.'

'You see?' Brodie said. 'This apparent embarrassment could prove to be very much to our advantage! If we start building now, as I've made it possible for us to do, that will be clear proof to the papers and to everyone else that we were raising the cash for the purpose we said. And there's another thing about starting to build now. If we don't manage to raise all the rest of the money we need to complete the work before the new Act comes in, well, who'll be responsible? As I see it, the Ministry of Health will, won't it? They'll have to find the money to finish the job – either way, it will be finished, and Nellie's will have a new block, and this present Board of Governors will go out in what might be called a blaze of glory. The hospital will benefit, the patients will benefit, the Board will benefit!'

The ripple of approval that ran round the table was almost visible as people relaxed and began to smile at each other.

There was a little silence and then Max spoke. 'Well done, Brodie!' he said warmly. 'You've really done very well indeed! Saved the bacon, as they say. We'll put it to the vote then, that *we* set the building in hand as fast as possible for the reason Brodie gives us. Yes – a show of hands, please, to the motion – well, there's no doubt about that, is there? No – right, Brodie. Where are these architects' ideas then?'

No one paid any attention at all when Molloy, with a muttered excuse, got to his feet and left the meeting. They were all much too busy with the sketches Brodie had produced almost by sleight of hand from the briefcase at his feet of a new and elegant ward block to rise to the east of the main Nellie's buildings to care at all about him, and he went slamming on his way back to his office in a rage.

He'd got it wrong, damn it all to hell and back. He'd got it wrong. He should have taken that damned letter to the Board right at the start instead of lying low and hoping Brodie would hang himself with his own meddling. As it is, they think the sun shines out of his rear end, and there he'll be handing out the jobs and getting no end of approval from everyone who works on the project and –

At which point he stood very still in front of his desk and

stared sightlessly at the window. Perhaps that was what it was all about? He'd never trusted Brodie, never; the man was too self-satisfied altogether, and too well-dressed and – too well off perhaps? He handled a lot of the hospital's money, after all; who was to say some of it didn't stick to his over manicured fingers?

Molloy sat down at his desk and leaned back in his chair and thought for a long time, aware of but not listening to the sounds of the hospital around him.

There was the whine of the lift and the clatter of its ironwork and irritable shouts as people on the lower floors called up to previous users to 'Shut the gates!' There was the rattle of the trolleys bearing morning cocoa and malted milk from the kitchens to the wards, and the never-ending rush of busy feet as doctors and nurses, physiotherapists and X-ray staff bustled through their hectic day, all of them set on one thing only; the needs of the patients of Nellie's. That was how it had always been here. People who worked within these walls did so because they cared. They weren't there for their own good, but for that of Nellie's and the frightened, sick, needful people who hid under its brick and cement wings amid its carbolic scented chrome and terrazzo.

So it was, and so it always had been, Molloy told himself, and no self-important jumped-up bursar like Brodie was going to change that, and with a very definite movement he pulled the telephone towards him. It was his duty, he told himself, his bounden duty to do something about this. He couldn't let that oily character, who was even now sitting up there in the boardroom telling them all to do what he wanted them to do, and having them agreeing like so many sheep, get away with his trickery. *Someone* would have to look into the matter.

And though Dr Max had said the Old Man wasn't well, everyone knew how his family fussed over him. He was a tough old chap, well able to look after himself – and to look after Nellie's too. No one else cared more about the place than he did, Molloy told himself as he heard the distant ringing of the telephone at Leinster Terrace and waited for an answer. If *he* thinks there's no harm in what's going on, well enough. I'll not say another word about it and let Brodie go on as he is, even if he's lining his own fat nest very nicely while he's at it.

But if Sir Lewis sees it the way I do, then it'll be a very different matter indeed.

26

Charlie sat very straight backed against her pillows, embarrassed at the way she had been almost forcibly tucked into the bed in the little cream and green painted room by the officious Sister in charge of the staff sick bay and tried to tell herself that all this was just nonsense. There was nothing at all wrong with her. She was just a self-indulgent fraud who needed nothing more to cure her than an immediate return to work, and she looked at the face of the man who was bending over her so closely, trying to see some sort of agreeing expression on it, but he just sat there, his head bent as he listened to his stethoscope and murmured, 'In – out – good – again –' and she looked away.

But this time she caught the frosty glance of the Sister who was standing beside the bed in the approved manner with her toes turned out and her hands clasped against her snowy apron and an air of such forbidding disapproval that Charlie had to close her eyes against it. She thinks I'm a fraud, too, she told herself and felt a spurt of anger at that. Who was she, dessicated old twig that she was, to make judgements about a patient?

'Thank you,' Dr Forester murmured and gently pulled her pyjama jacket across her bare breasts and gratefully Charlie rebuttoned it, feeling less threatened now that her nakedness was no longer on display. 'Well, now, we needn't keep you here any longer, Sister. I've finished my examination, so you can safely leave us alone', and he smiled at Sister a little crookedly and Charlie thought – I like you! You don't like that miserable old battleaxe either –

'Thank you, sir,' Sister said woodenly and went to the door. 'I will be in my office should you require any further assistance. Dr Lackland's notes are there on the locker', and she clicked the door behind her and they both sat and listened to the clack of her footsteps, receding self-importantly along the corridor.

'Terrifying, isn't she?' Dr Forester said and reached for the notes and opened the folder on his knee. 'I suspect that she was chosen specifically to frighten all her patients into good health, to get them back to work as soon as possible.'

'I rather think so, too,' Charlie said. 'I think it's worked for me. I can't wait to get away from her – and I'm fine, aren't I? A complete fraud –'

'That depends on how you interpret the meaning of the word fraud,' Dr Forester said and closed the folder containing her notes and held it on his knee with his hands crossed over it, so that he could sit and look at her. He had a pleasant face, square and solid under an almost bald head and he wore round glasses through which his eyes, as round as the frames through which they peered, were warm and friendly. She let her own glance slide away, suddenly afraid she would cry if he was too nice to her.

'It means there's nothing wrong with me. That I had a silly conniption fit as my old Boston nursemaid would have called it, and the sooner I get back to work the better –'

'Not quite, my dear,' he said very gently. 'Not quite. You do realize that you're pregnant, surely?'

She closed her eyes against the knowledge that had been beating at her for so long and said loudly, 'No!'

'No, you didn't know, or no, you would rather not know, or no, you aren't? Which is it?' He still sounded friendly, but there was a firmness that could not be resisted in his voice and she still kept her eyes tightly closed, needing to exclude him and all his words as well as his face.

'No, it isn't possible –' she said and then caught her breath, knowing how ridiculous that sounded. 'I mean –'.and then she opened her eyes and stared at him miserably. 'I mean, it shouldn't be possible.'

He shook his head, smiling a little. 'I'm afraid Nature is infinitely more clever than any of her children, my dear. Whatever method you tried to use to circumvent her, you failed. Most people do, in my experience.'

'I didn't use anything,' she said and took a deep shuddering breath. 'It was all so – unexpected, so –'

He frowned sharply. 'This was against your will? Have you

been abused by someone who –'

'Abused?' She laughed then, a sharp little sound in the stuffy room with its high iron bed and forbidding scrubbed furniture. 'Oh, yes, I've been abused. By myself. No, don't look at me like that – it's too complicated to explain, and I'm sure I – the thing is, I just don't see how it could have happened. Once, damn it! Just *once* and I'm pregnant? It can't be –'

'Oh, but it can,' Dr Forester said. 'And it is. Haven't you noticed the changes in your breasts? You can't tell me your nipples have always been so well provided with Montgomery's tubercles? You remember your obstetric training, I imagine? You were taught how "the nipples darken, enlarge and develop small white protuberances rich in lubricating lanolin"? I'm sure you do – and as soon as I saw those, my suspicions of the correct diagnosis for your – what was the phrase? conniption fit? – charming – were confirmed. The nausea and vomiting, the fainting – now, when was your last period?'

'I'm not sure.' Suddenly she reddened, deeply ashamed of this evidence of her own improvidence. How often had she sat in obstetric clinics in her student days and felt the frisson of irritable disapproval that went through the doctors whenever a woman said that she didn't have so simple a fact clearly marked in her memory? Women who didn't know every detail of their own bodily cycles were sneered at by doctors, were regarded as simpleminded, almost, especially if they had pregnancies they didn't want. Women who behaved as Charlie had –

'I'm not being stupid,' she flared, staring at Dr Forester's mild round-eyed gaze. 'I just don't *know*! I've always had a very erratic cycle and anyway, I wasn't – there was no reason to watch it. I wasn't – there was no regular – I wasn't – oh, damn it all, it was only once! Just once! How can I be pregnant after just one episode when so many women complain they can't conceive when they try for month after month, year after year? It's mad, it can't be – there has to be some other reason for the symptoms –'

'Whenever it happens it only takes once. One single cell out of the many millions Nature sends on their way – my dear, I am sorry. I don't want to pry, of course, but if it will help you to talk about the situation – is your – is the man in this married?

Is that the problem?'

'No,' she said and closed her eyes again. 'No, he's not married. Nor likely to be', and she opened them again and looked at him bleakly. 'Certainly not to me.'

'But surely, when he knows that there is good cause for marriage and –'

'It wouldn't make the slightest difference if he did know,' Charlie said, angry again. 'And he bloody well is not to be told! He doesn't care about me, so why should he care about –' And she set her hand on her belly, and thought confusedly – there isn't just me to care about: there are two of us – and then snatched her hand away as though her own skin was red hot and burned her, refusing to pursue that thought any further. 'I absolutely forbid you to tell him!'

'Such an injunction is hardly necessary,' Dr Forester said and smiled so widely that his eyes almost disappeared into the folds of skin around them. 'I don't know who the foolish man is, do I?'

'You think he's a fool as well as me?' Charlie said bitterly. 'But not that he's as big a fool as I've been –'

'I think he's a fool for not valuing you more highly than it appears he does,' Dr Forester said, his smile still lingering at the corners of his mouth. 'You seem to me to be a very valuable and charming person. I've seen you around the hospital and I know your work is well thought of by your seniors, and you are a handsome woman. Any man who doesn't cleave to a girl like you who clearly cares for him has to be an idiot –'

'I don't care a fig for him,' Charlie said fiercely, and still Dr Forester smiled.

'No?' he said gently. 'You don't strike me as a woman who would fall into bed with a man she didn't care for. There are women who do that, who behave like the sort of men I most despise, but in my experience they are few. I certainly don't think you're one of them – I think you love the man who has made this baby for you. Don't you?'

'Love?' She laughed again, making that same barking little sound. 'I don't know what it is. I've been obsessed, I'll grant you that. I've been so stupid and so –' And then the tears started, slowly at first, trickling down the sides of her nose and then coming faster, wetting her cheeks and filling her nostrils so that she could hardly breathe, tightening her eyes agonizingly. The sobs grew inside her like heavy greasy bubbles made of thick film that stretched and pushed and heaved against her body and thrust at her ribs painfully until they burst into great retching noises that tore at her throat and felt much the same as last night's sickness had felt.

For a while he sat there and watched her, benevolent and uncritical, and then as the sobbing grew louder he reached forwards and held her hands, and gradually her control, which had slipped away totally, came back. She was able to draw a few deep breaths and shakily reach for her handkerchief from her bedside table and wipe her face and eyes with harsh stabbing little movements which displayed her self-loathing so clearly it was like a shout echoing in the ugly little room.

'No,' Dr Forester said firmly, and pulled her hand away. 'You're not to treat yourself so harshly. You are by no means a bad person, and by no means stupid, and by no means all the other accusations you're obviously throwing at yourself. You're a woman who's been betrayed by her own body, and that is a fact that should excite the sympathy of a doctor, not criticism. Think as a doctor for a moment, my dear, and forgive yourself.'

'How can I?' she said drearily, her voice husky with the remnants of her tears. 'I behaved like a – like –'

'Like a woman who loved. Oh, all right, like a woman obsessed with love if that's how you prefer it. There's little difference as far as I can see. You've done nothing wicked, nothing wicked at all. Nature has, as she usually does, abandoned your personal welfare to her own imperious demands –' He smiled again and took back the hand she had pulled from his grasp. 'As you see, I have a taste for the literary view of life. We little creatures walk under Nature's huge legs and peep about – that's roughly how the quote goes, isn't it? Perhaps not, but you can see what I mean, I hope. That Nature in her wisdom took hold of you and played this trick on you. You're amazed that you conceived as the result of one experience of coitus? I'm not. I have come across the same phenomenon many times. A woman who has a deep emotional attachment to a man and who is for whatever reason swept into sharing the act of love with him is so overwhelmed by her own hormones that she ovulates in

228

response to the experience and thus conceives –'

She had been staring at him and now she managed a watery smile. 'You make me feel like a rabbit,' she said. 'I remember learning that they don't have cycles like the higher animals, like us. They just respond to the stimulus of sex and that's why there are so many rabbits –'

'Precisely! Dr Forester beamed at her. 'You understand perfectly! And in purely biological terms, it makes excellent sense, don't you think? I fear Nature slipped up a bit giving most women these regular cycles that mean they can only conceive at certain times – much more effective to have women react as you clearly did, and to conceive as a direct reaction to lovemaking instead of almost accidentally, if the times of lovemaking and ovulation happen to coincide –'

'I'm sure all this is very interesting in an academic sort of way,' Charlie said and sat up more straightly, rubbing her hands over her tousled hair in an effort to restore her tidiness and with it her sense of *amour propre*. 'But it doesn't convince me – look, is there any possibility that you could be wrong? I don't mean to be rude, but you're a physician and not a gynaecologist and –'

'I'm not wrong, my dear. I'm the father of four splendid young things, a well as a physician. A man, too, you see, and I'd lay my professional life in any bet that said I was wrong about this pregnancy. But of course you have a definite point. You *do* need the care of a gynaecologist and I'll arrange this morning for Mr Croxley to come and see you and –'

'No!' Charlie said and bit her lip, trying to think. 'If you're quite sure –'

'Of course I am,' he said kindly. 'And so are you, aren't you?'

She ignored the question. 'If you're sure, then it's stupid to try to deny it. I've got to think – I can't let people here know. I can't. I couldn't face them and –'

'You need good care, my dear, and I insist you get it. You may be a little anaemic already – looking at your pallor I can't be sure, but I suspect it and I'll arrange for some blood work to be done – so don't think I'm going to wash my hands of you, just because I'm not a gynaecologist and you're not married and so worried about your reputation –'

'Of course I'm worried about my reputation!' Charlie flared

at him. 'It's all I've got, isn't it? A doctor of ill repute is hardly likely to be able to practise anywhere she can do any good and – I'll have to go on as long as I can. The fewer people who know what's happening to me the better – so I can't see Mr Croxley here at Nellie's – I can't –'

He reached forwards and took her shoulders between his hands and gave her a little shake. 'My dear, I am so glad!' he said and there was very strong emotion in his voice.

'Glad? What about?'

'You're taking it for granted that you will bear this child.'

She stared. 'What else can I do? If you're so sure you're right and that I'm pregnant –'

'There are those who meddle with Nature,' he said and leaned back, as though he was ashamed of his momentary display of emotion. 'Especially some doctors.'

She blinked and now she stared not so much at him as through him as the import of what he was saying sank in.

'I hadn't considered that,' she said slowly, still with her eyes glazed.

'Then I'm very sorry that I even mentioned the possibility,' he said and there was a little anxiety in his voice. 'Though I imagine it would have occurred to you eventually.'

There was a little silence and then she shook her head. 'No, I couldn't. I – I may be very angry and hurt and – and a lot of feelings like that, but it's happened and I don't think I could – no. It wouldn't be right, however difficult everything might be. However much easier it might be to do as –. No.'

He took a little breath and it was loud in the small room and then he smiled at her. 'Now, my dear, to practical problems. You need to be looked after, of course, and to make plans for your confinement. Let's see if we can work out when this baby might be expected to make an appearance.'

She sat and watched him as he made notes, checking the possible dates of her last period against the date she gave him of that evening in Earlham Street and then he nodded.

'A spring baby,' he said with satisfaction and smiled at her, those round eyes mild once more behind his glasses. 'The second week in April or thereabouts', and she let her eyes move to the small window behind him where the heavy metallic blue of the sky brooded over Nellie's.

April next year? That was an eternity away from the hot city

230

she was living in now: 1948 would never come. She'd be dead by then, and all this would be a sick joke, over and forgotten.

'April,' she said.

'When does your appointment here end?' He sounded brisk and efficient now.

'Here? At Nellie's? At Christmas if I want it to, though it was suggested I could continue for another six months if I wanted to –'

'But you said you don't want people here to know of your situation?' He peered at her through those owlish glasses. 'Then I suggest you seek a new post for next year, and leave here when you're about twenty weeks pregnant. You're a well-made girl and if you dress sensibly there is no reason why you shouldn't conceal your – um, your private concerns till then. Full skirts, you know, and a slightly larger white coat –'

'You think I should go on working?'

'I imagine you have to,' he said a little drily. 'Mothers have to eat.'

'I have money,' she said, almost dismissing that. 'I inherited a sizeable income – but –' she shook her head. 'I couldn't bear not to work. I'd go mad, I think.'

'I think so too,' he said. 'For the first few months anyway. But after Christmas find yourself somewhere quiet to stay, buy yourself a wedding ring and go away to have your baby quietly. You won't be the first woman to be widowed before she's wed, and you won't be the last. That's my advice to you, my dear. Stay here as long as you can and then reappear somewhere else as Mrs Lucas. No one will question that, and you can maintain your reputation and eventually, if you choose to, return to your profession.'

'I'm not leaving it,' she said vigorously. 'I've – he's not going to steal that from me too.'

'Well done,' Dr Forester said and leaned forwards and once again took her hand, but this time he shook it. 'You are a splendid young lady, Mrs Lucas,' he said and smiled. 'I do congratulate you. I truly expect you will produce a most delightful child who will give you much pleasure. Let's be happy about Nature's gift instead of angry, shall we?'

'I'll try,' she said and then once again sat up more upright. 'Please, don't call me Mrs Lucas. It's happened and I'll do the best I can – but I don't want to tell more lies than I must –'

'I'm sorry. I was – perhaps anticipating the future a little. I'm sorry. Now shall I talk to Mr Croxley for you, quietly? You can trust him, you know.'

'No thank you.' She reached for the dressing-gown that was lying on the chair beside her bed. 'I'll make arrangements for myself. No, don't worry. I'll see someone. I know the sort of care I need, and I'll see I get it –'

She stood up and he helped her get out of bed and she stood there, barefoot beside him, tying the girdle of her dressing-gown.

'Then I'll tell Sister Battleaxe that you can leave her prison, shall I? You're feeling tolerably well, I take it?'

She laughed a little grimly. 'As well as can be expected.'

'Good, I'll write up some blood tests for you, so that you can take the results to whichever consultant you choose, and – well, I'm always here if you need me.' He held out his hand once more and this time she shook it with real gratitude.

'You've been very kind,' she said. 'I'm – please accept my apologies if I was at all rude.'

'You weren't. Far from it. I've only one regret, actually.'

She lifted her brows at him, questioning.

'I'd like to get my hands on that bloody man who left you like this. To knock some sense into him. He obviously has no idea what he's letting slip through his half-witted fingers. Goodbye, my dear. And very good luck to you.'

And to her amazement he bent and kissed her cheek briefly and then went, quietly closing the door behind him.

27

Max had spent over two hours with Miss Curtis since lunchtime and was, to say the least, tired. It wasn't the amount of work they'd done, though that had been considerable; it was the sheer effort of dealing with her enthusiasm for him and her fierce protectiveness of him. There were times he could shake her for being so solicitous, but of course he couldn't do that. She was a hardworking and efficient woman, deeply concerned with his and the hospital's welfare, and for that reason had to be tolerated. But it wasn't easy.

His tiredness did make him irritable with other people, however, even though he was as always very controlled with Miss Curtis, and when Brocklesby put his head round the door of the small office and announced with an air of great portentousness that he would like to have a quick word with Dr Lackland, if he didn't mind, sir, on a matter of importance, private like, he made no effort to stop Miss Curtis when she surged to her feet with great outrage and told Brocklesby shrilly that he had no right to disturb Dr Lackland in his private office when he was busy.

'If you have any messages to give the doctor,' she said firmly, ushering Brocklesby out of the office like a hen with an intrusive duckling to get rid of, 'you can tell me', and she closed the door firmly behind her so that Max could hear no more, but he didn't care, glad to be rid of her for a few moments.

He leaned back in his chair and stretched. He'd be able to leave in another hour or so, God willing, and after going straight to Leinster Terrace to check on his father – whose high colour and over-bright eyes had worried him a good deal this morning – he'd be able to get home and to bed for an early night.

He certainly needed it; he'd been sleeping badly and though

that was something he ought to be used to by now, the nature of his sleeplessness was changing. He found himself thinking more and more about Charlotte Lucas, and less about Emilia, though thoughts of her still threaded their way through his days and nights.

The thoughts he was having about Charlotte upset him a good deal. He had always prided himself on his tact, his ability to enter into other people's feelings, to empathize, help them to feel better; was not that the essential gift of the psychiatrist, after all? Yet with Charlotte Lucas all that failed. With her he was tactless, harsh, unfeeling; he must be, for why else would she always react to him with such hostility? He still could feel the sense of cold rejection that had filled him when she had so peremptorily refused his care the other evening even though she had been obviously ill. And his anxiety had sharpened as he thought of that illness, and wondered what it was that made her so pale and hollow-eyed.

He shook his head to rid himself of these obtrusive thoughts and turned back to the letters still remaining to be dealt with, irritably aware of the voices of Miss Curtis and Brocklesby locked in some sort of wrangle outside his door and he was about to get to his feet and go out to see for himself what was going on when she returned to the room, snapping the door behind her, with her colour high in her cheeks and obviously very put about by what the hall porter had said to her.

'That man,' she said in ringing tones that prodded into greater intensity the faint headache Max already had, 'is extremely rude, extremely.'

'I'm sorry,' Max said wearily, not sure whether he was commiserating or apologizing. 'You can make a complaint to the Secretary of course, if you feel that's necessary. The portering staff are part of Mr Molloy's department. I can't intervene, of course. What did he want?'

'That's the thing – he flatly refused to tell me, said it was personal and none of my affair, and if I wouldn't let him in then he'd keep his information to himself. I told him if he had any information you needed it was his duty to tell you, and that he could make an appointment if he wanted, but he was just thoroughly rude and still wouldn't say what it was you had to be told and said if anything happened as a result it would all be my fault and –'

'Well, I dare say it will all sort itself out,' Max said vaguely, bored by her chatter and by all the fuss. 'Now, if we can finish these letters, I'd be grateful. I want to get away as soon as I can –'

At once she was a whirlwind of busyness and he tried to relax and not let her get on his nerves so much, but it wasn't easy; everything about her set his teeth on edge this afternoon, but he bent his head and began to dictate, and she sat there, her pencil whispering importantly on her notebook and her lips pursed with concentration, as he got the words out as quickly as he could.

One of the letters demanded a long case history to be outlined, and he was doing his best to concentrate, but it grew difficult as he became aware of distant sounds outside his door. There were calls from one voice to another and the loud rattle of the lift gate and the sound of rushing feet and at last his irritation boiled over and he threw back his chair in a temper and went to the door and flung it open.

'What the blazes is going on out here?' he called as he went out into the corridor. 'I'm trying to work and I can barely hear myself think with all the racket that's going on –'

'Oh, you're there!' someone said in a surprised tone and he peered into the dim light of the corridor, which had windows only at the far end to illuminate it. 'I understood that you'd left and no one could get a message to you –'

'Who's that?' Max said sharply and then as the figure moved closer added, 'Oh, Brodie! What *is* the matter? People shouting and running –'

'I thought someone had told you,' Brodie said again and he looked uncertain and confused, very unlike his usual self. 'I'm afraid, it's not good –'

'What isn't good? Damn it, man, what is going on?'

'It's your father, Dr Lackland. I got a message to say he had arrived and that he wanted to see me and Molloy at once and –'

Max stared at him. 'My *father*? Here? But he can't be! He's not well enough! I told you that this morning – he's ill, or he'd have been at the Board of Governors' meeting.'

'That's the point, Dr Lackland. When I heard he was here, I didn't believe it either, but then my secretary assured me he was, that he'd gone up to the boardroom and seemed very agitated, and that I was to see him – and when I got there –'

235

Max had come out into the corridor now and was walking quickly in the direction of the staircase and the boardroom and Brodie fell into step beside him.

'When I got there I saw at once he wasn't well and sent for the physician on duty tonight. Dr Forester's out of London for the weekend, it seems, and so is Dr –'

'Why wasn't I told he was here?' Max said savagely as he reached the stairs and ran up them two at a time. 'What were you all thinking of not to let me know?'

'I was told you weren't here,' Brodie said again. 'Or at least I think that's what he – Brocklesby –. When I said someone was to find you, he said he'd tried to get a message to you and he couldn't, so there was nothing anyone could do –'

'Brocklesby?' Max said, and frowned, as he at last reached the boardroom door and pushed it open, and then stopped short on the threshold and stared at the tableau that met his shocked gaze.

His father was lying on his back on the floor and breathing heavily, making thick stertorous noises in his thoat. Kneeling beside him was Charlotte Lucas, leaning forwards as she listened with great concentration to her stethoscope. Grouped behind her were Molloy, his face quite flat and expressionless as he stared down, and Brocklesby, who had a look of avid excitement on his face. Another porter stood on the other side with an oxygen cylinder on a stand, and he was also leaning forwards in a state of excited interest, while beside him a nurse stood poised with a kidney dish in one hand and a dressing towel in the other.

It seemed to Max that the whole scene was imprinted on his vision in that split second of looking and indeed it was to be a long time before he would forget every detail of it. But then the stillness of it broke as Charlotte looked up and said to the porter, 'Now – let me have the mask, and nurse, turn the oxygen on to about – yes, that will do – no more at the moment.' And the nurse moved forwards and broke the pattern of immobility that had held Max in the doorway.

He started forwards and knelt at his father's other side and looked down at him, taking in the flushed cheeks and the half-closed eyes and the thin lips drawn back and specked with shreds of spittle. His breathing was erratic and loud still and carefully Charlotte fitted the oxygen mask over his face and held it in place.

'What's happened?' Max said shortly and reached for his father's bony wrist, seeking the pulse. It fluttered a little under his fingers, uneven and restless, and he said, 'We'll need some Coramine – have you sent for some?'

Charlie nodded and lifted her chin to indicate the nurse who at once leaned forwards and presented her kidney dish. 'I've drawn it up, Miss Lucas,' she said breathlessly. 'It's got an intravenous needle –'

'Thank you,' Charlie said and then looked briefly at Max. 'Shall I? Or would you like to –'

He shook his head at once and she pushed back the sleeve on the old man's jacket and with an expert twist used it as a tourniquet to tighten the upper arm, as she stroked the tissue of the forearm towards the elbow. Slowly a vein bulged in the crook of the elbow and she took the syringe from the nurse's dish and moving with great deliberation slid the needle into the snake of blood vessel that meandered beneath the papery old skin. She drew back on the plunger and then, as blood made the translucent contents blush pink released the sleeve and slowly made her injection, as Max remained there, kneeling and watching.

'I'll try the amyl nitrite now, nurse,' she said then, and the nurse reached the dish towards her again and she took from it the little bundle of gauze that held the ampoule ready. She snapped it beneath the old man's nose and again they watched as he inhaled the fumes, and beneath Max's fingers the pulse seemed to steady and thicken a little as the breathing deepened and became less noisy.

'I think he'll hold long enough to get him to a bed,' Charlie said at length. 'Dr Tillotson's on his way from the Surbiton Branch, and the senior medical registrar will be here as soon as he can get out of Buttercup – he's got someone there in a diabetic coma and –'

'It's all right,' Max said and his voice was harsh in his own ears. 'You're coping well. No need to rush for anyone else. What happened?'

There was a little silence and then Molloy said uncertainly, 'He – ah – he got here on his own. I was surprised – thought Victor would be with him but it seems that the Old – that Sir Lewis had managed on his own. He told me he'd sent Victor away before he got up and came here – said he'd have stopped him and he was determined to get here no matter what –'

'Why?' Max never took his eyes from his father's face. He was lying very still, but his colour had improved a little and his pulse seemed steadier. 'What the hell was he doing here at all? I don't understand –'

'I knew he shouldn't be here.' Brocklesby could contain himself no longer. 'As soon as I saw him come in, all shaky and on his own, I knew it was all wrong, and I said to him, "Oh, Sir Lewis," I said, "what are you doing out of your bed when anyone can see with 'alf an eye 'ow poorly you are." That's what I said, and all 'e said was, "Get Molloy, tell him I'm here as he asked me to be, and I want Brodie and I'll be in the boardroom and get on with it." So of course I did, and I tried to come and tell you, sir, private like, as your father was here and looking poorly but that there Miss Curtis she wouldn't let me in and it wasn't my place to be giving the likes of 'er messages, was it?' And he stopped to draw breath, clearly full of the importance of his role in the afternoon's events.

'I wasn't sure it was up to me to be letting you know, anyway, sir,' he added then with a sharp sideways look at Molloy who was still standing staring down at Sir Lewis on the floor. 'I mean, I was told to fetch them, not you, but I thought it my bounden duty, sir, seeing the Old – that Sir Lewis looked so poorly and you being his son and all, but there, I couldn't get to tell you, could I? And then I heard the noise as he passed out like and I knew I was right, but it was too late then, so –'

'Molloy.' Max looked up and stared at the thin man who was still watching Sir Lewis's face with a sort of hungry anxiety. 'What does Brocklesby mean? Why did my father tell him he was here as you had asked him to be?'

Molloy said nothing, but his face seemed to get even more putty-coloured than it was and after a moment Brodie said quietly, 'As I understand it, Dr Lackland, from what your father said before he – before his collapse – Mr Molloy had telephoned him and told him he should come.'

'I had no idea he was so ill!' Molloy said loudly and his voice seemed to ring a little in the big echoing room. 'No idea! How was I to guess he'd be so foolish as to – as to send his man away and just come here on his own? I couldn't know that, could I?'

238

'Why did you send for him?' Max's voice was still quiet and controlled but they could all hear the rage in it and Molloy lifted his eyes for the first time to look at him and seemed to shrink inside himself at what he saw in his face.

'I was worried!' he said after a moment, trying to sound natural, relaxed even, but managing only to seem truculent. 'I believe that there are things being done in Brodie's department that are wrong and against the interests of the hospital and I couldn't see any other way of sorting it all out. There you were all at the Governors' meeting, lapping up every word he said and ignoring me when I could tell you, when I could – so I thought I must tell someone, and I knew Sir Lewis was the one. He's the only one who cares about the place as it should be, the only one. Everyone else is after their own interests, him and – and the Board and –'

He spluttered into silence and Max stared at him, his face as expressionless as ever and then turned away to look at his father again. If he had spat his scorn at the man who stood there dithering in front of him it couldn't have been more obvious and Charlie stirred uneasily at Sir Lewis's side and said, 'Dr Lackland? Is he fit to move, do you think? Or do we get a bed brought here and try to settle him first before moving him? I'd be glad of your opinion –'

Max leaned over his father again and with a simultaneous twist of her wrist and her head she disengaged her stethoscope from her neck and gave it to him and he glanced at her and nodded gratefully and took it and with steady fingers pulled back the old man's shirt again and settled the stethoscope into his ears so that he could listen.

He straightened up at last and said shortly, 'I'm not expert enough to agree to moving him. And anyway, he's my father – it's hard for me to – I can't think as objectively as I should. Your opinion, Charlie. I'd be glad of it.'

He'd never called her that before and at the sound of her own familiar name on his lips she felt a sudden surge of pity for him, as well as for the old man who lay there between them. He looked, for all his grey hair and his lined face and the squareness of his shoulders, like a small boy, lost in his uncertainty and fear of the future, and she reached out and took her stethoscope from him and touched his hand briefly and said quietly, 'Of course you can't. I'll decide for you.

Brocklesby –' and she looked over her shoulder at the hovering porter. 'Go and fetch a bed from Spruce. Tell Sister we'll be on our way, and need the side ward to be ready. Nurse, you wait here and help us get Sir Lewis into the bed when we've got it. Dr Lackland –' She looked at him again, swiftly, and once more touched his hand. 'Max. Go and wait in the side ward, will you? We'll be there as soon as we can. We'll manage better, I think, on our own –'

Obediently he got to his feet, still with that indefinable air of lost childhood about him and she watched him go towards the door, and then returned her attention to her patient as Brocklesby went bustling in front of Max to hold the door open.

Max stopped when he got there and after a moment of standing with his head bent turned back and said loudly, 'Molloy, Brodie, I'd be grateful if you remained at the hospital for a while. It's important I talk to you both, I'm sure you'll agree. Once my father is in bed and settled in the ward, I'll be able to talk to you. Please wait for me in my office, if you'd be so kind.' And they both nodded, as he stared bleakly at them and then left, closing the door quietly behind him.

For Charlie the next half hour was as intense a one as she had spent in all her medical career. Although she was now a surgical registrar she had done her share of a physician's work and dealing with a coronary attack of this sort – and she was sure that this was what had happened to the old man – was not new to her; but she had never before had to deal with anyone quite as eminent as the chief of staff of her own hospital and she was painfully aware not only just of the responsibility she bore for the old man's life – which was after all, always there, with every patient, and one she had grown accustomed to bearing – but also of the burden of Max's fear.

This man who had made her so angry in the past, who had seemed to her to be all that she most disliked in a colleague, had displayed his vulnerability and his love for his father with so much simplicity and need that she had dissolved in the face of his distress. It was as though he was a different man, not at all the one who had baulked her request to help with Brin – she marvelled in a corner of her mind, as she helped the nurse to undress the comatose old man and get him safely into the bed that had been wheeled into the boardroom to collect him, that

240

that had ever really mattered to her – and who had seemed to taunt her that night in the medical common room. He was just a man fearing the loss of someone he loved. And she, who had suffered so many such losses herself, felt his pain as keenly as if it were her own.

They got Sir Lewis into bed, lying safely flat and with his head turned to one side to avoid the risk of his choking himself with his own lax tongue, and she leaned over him once more as the porters and the nurse stood poised to take him to the side ward of Spruce. His breathing was not so noisy and a little more even, she decided, and when she checked his pulse that too seemed to be holding its own. Perhaps, she told herself optimistically, he would survive? When she had first seen him, arriving hotfoot from the ward where she had been doing a dressing on one of her amputation patients, she had been deeply alarmed, doubting he would last more than another few minutes, but there was a toughness in this old man, a resilience that despite his age and his weakness seemed to linger and tie him to life, and she touched his papery old cheek and thought passionately, please, get well – please don't die. She wanted him to live as much as she had wanted her own parents and Cousin Mary to have lived, felt a need for his survival, even though she hardly knew him except as a remote and important figure who was part of the hospital, just as she was, but not part of her own life in any way.

And for a while it seemed as if somewhere deep in his mind he had heard her appeal and made a conscious decision to live, for when they reached the side ward and Max saw him again he seemed a little less deep in his unconsciousness, seemed to be breathing more easily and they stood there on each side of him, she and Max Lackland, looking down at him with real hope in their spirits.

And then he opened his eyes suddenly and seemed to stare at her and then turned his head and looked at Max and frowned and brought his head back to stare up at the ceiling.

'Miriam?' he said loudly, 'Miriam?' And then closed his eyes again, and his face smoothed and lost its blank look, seeming just for a moment to be a younger more vigorous face altogether.

'Miriam –' he murmured, so softly that they barely heard him and then, with no fuss and no drama at all, simply stopped

241

breathing altogether. It was almost a minute before they realized that he had, in fact, died, so quietly and so elegantly had he done so.

28

At half past nine Max at last left the side ward to go back to his office and see Molloy and Brodie.

He had been quiet and controlled all the time, efficient and courteous in his dealings with everyone and especially gentle with Sister Spruce who very uncharacteristically burst into tears when she realized Sir Lewis had died. She had been nursing at Nellie's for thirty-seven years and had worked with him for much of that time and his loss was a keen personal one, and watching Max comfort her Charlie felt her new liking for him deepen and grow. He seemed to be able to put aside his own distress in order to help others cope with theirs and that, she told herself, was remarkable.

And later, when his sister Johanna arrived, her face white and shocked and full of remorse because she had been at a theatre and for that reason hard to track down, he had soothed and comforted her too, and seen her on her way to Leinster Terrace where the family was to congregate, in the care of her daughter, who had come with her, promising to be there as soon as he could. He had spoken to his sons, telephoning them at the Surbiton branch, where they were both on three-month attachments, telling them of their grandfather's death, and reassuring them that there was no need to come rushing back to London; he would let them know about the plans for the funeral, and then had phoned his brother Peter, and arranged to meet him at the Leinster Terrace house as soon as he could get there, asking him to take care of Johanna, who was on her way to him. And then, still calm, he had again turned his attention to the hospital staff.

Dr Tillotson had needed much reassurance, for the senior physician had arrived in a state of considerable agitation at having been so far away from Nellie's when his own chief and good old friend had needed him. Brocklesby had to be told yet again that he had behaved exactly as he should and no, no one was angry with him. And finally a procession of other Nellie's people who wanted to say their own goodbyes to a man they had all known and liked for so long that they had regarded him as virtually indestructible had wanted to shake his son's hand, and offer their condolences.

Throughout his face remained closed and unreadable and Charlie, busy though she was in dealing with the formal details that always had to be sorted out when any patient died in such circumstances – the old man's death within so short a time of arriving at the hospital from his home might make it necessary for there to be a coroner's inquest – found herself worrying about him. He had shown no emotion of his own, in spite of being surrounded by loud expressions of other people's and that could not be good for him, she thought, and tried to say as much to him.

He stood there beside the bed in the side ward, now empty and crumpled, for Sir Lewis had been borne away on a rattling old trolley beneath a purple pall to the mortuary to await the last details of care that could be given to him before he was finally in his grave, his head bent as she spoke, not looking at her.

'I do think you should – that you need to let go a little,' she said, almost timidly, but emboldened by her concern for him. 'I mean – when my parents died I thought the right thing to do was to be strong and private about how I felt, but it wasn't – it was Cousin Mary who showed me that. She made me cry even though it was so long after, and I remember wishing I'd done it sooner. And when I lost her and that was awful too, at least I didn't wait to show it. I cried a lot –'

'Can you wait here for a while?' he said abruptly, and now he did look at her, a sharp little glance from beneath his tightened brows.

'How long?' She was startled, and didn't know quite what to say.

'Not long.' He sounded a little grim now. 'I have to deal with Molloy and Brodie. I told them to wait in my office, remember? I must see them. It won't take long at all, I do assure you.'

'Well, yes – I mean, if you want me to.'

'I rather think I do,' he said and went away and she sat down on the edge of the bed, staring out of the window at the rich indigo of the summer evening sky and marvelled a little at herself.

She had given no thought at all to her own very pressing dilemma for several hours; ever since Dr Forester had confirmed her fears she had been obsessed with herself, had walked through her work so abstractedly that it was amazing she had done no harm to any patients. All her thinking had seemed to be focused on her own body, and most specifically on that segment of it that lay between her umbilicus and her knees. There was a new life within her, a minuscule life that had an existence of its own, yet which was totally dependent on her for all its needs. Dr Forester had been glad, he said, that she had not considered the way out to avoid the demands that some in her situation and with her special knowledge and access to remedies, would have selected, and she had been adamant in her assurances to him that she would not think of it at all.

Yet, of course, she had; it had been impossible not to. When she contemplated the future when that new life was no longer minuscule and hidden but a separate lusty bawling thing that would make its presence very much felt to all around, it became a terrifying thing to be avoided at any cost. The thought of a quiet visit to one of the people she knew inhabited some of the glossier rooms in Harley Street, the passing over of a plump cheque and the end of the fear and the difficult future, had seemed a seductively attractive possibility.

Yet now, for several hours, she hadn't thought at all about that possibility or any others, had actually forgotten what had happened to her, and she stared at the window and thought confusedly – but I've *got* to think, got to decide. I can't just drift on. I've got to decide. I wish Dr Forester hadn't even mentioned the idea. But she knew that he had been right in telling her that it would have come to her anyway, and however it had entered her mind, it needed to be dealt with. But she closed her eyes against that knowledge and tried to recapture the freedom from her self-obsession she had had ever since she had answered the emergency call to the boardroom.

She saw it all again; the old man lying crumpled on the floor, her own almost automatic reactions, the way she had so urgently thumped his chest to restart a heart that had seemed to have stopped, the way he had at last begun to breathe again, the whole attempt to keep him alive. It had in the end failed, but at least she had tried; had there been anything more she could have done to save him? Reviewing all her own actions she was able to reassure herself that there had not and she relaxed her shoulders, sitting there on the old man's empty bed, and whispered to the indigo sky, 'I did my best –'

And then a strange thing happened. She saw inside her head not the old man who had died in spite of her efforts, but a child, an infant, lying there on the floor in the boardroom. Sir Lewis had been eighty-three, full of years of living, some good, some bad, but busy living, yet when she tried to think of him all she could see in her mind's eye was a baby who had experienced no life at all, lying on the heaped clothes that the old man had worn, and she shook her head angrily at her own absurdity. It was a ridiculous image, but all the same it wouldn't go away and she closed her eyes once again to look at it more closely, trying in a confused way to understand what her own mind was trying to tell her, and hazily she began to understand.

In working so hard to save an old man's life, she had stopped thinking about destroying another; he had been eighty-three years old and the baby within her wasn't yet eighty-three days old, yet they had shared their dependence on her. She had done her best to save the old life, the well-lived one, the tired one; could she do less for the new untried one that lay there between her umbilicus and her knees, waiting for her to decide on its future, on whether it was to have one at all?

Behind her the side ward door opened and she drew a deep shuddering breath and turned to see who it was, and was almost surprised to see Max standing there. Absurd though it was, she had forgotten he had asked her to wait and she stared at him, her eyes wide and blank for a moment, and he came and sat down on the bed beside her.

'Thank you for waiting,' he said.

'That's all right.' She knew she sounded inane. 'Have you – ah – is it sorted out with Molloy and Brodie? I wasn't quite clear about what had happened there. I mean, why Molloy sent for your father?'

'Nor was I,' Max said grimly. 'I am now though –' And he

was silent, staring down at his hands which were loosely clasped in front of him.

'Do you want to explain?' she ventured, needing to say something and not sure what would be best.

He drew a deep breath. 'Molloy – the man's paranoid – I'm a psychiatrist and I didn't see it. He's paranoid. And that was why he sent for my father. And Pa, being Pa, came because he told him there was damage being done to Nellie's. Nellie's mattered more to my father, I think, than his own life did. After us, his own family, there was nothing so important –'

His voice drifted away again and she sat silent, still not knowing what to say to him. He was showing agitation now for the first time; she could feel it coming out of him with the heat from his arm which was so near hers as they sat side by side on the rumpled bed.

'I still haven't explained, have I?' he said then, abruptly, and rubbed his face with one hand, as though he was trying to brush away his fatigue. 'It was all to do with the raising of the money for the new wing. That Benefit Night – Molloy had it fixed in his head that Brodie, who is the Bursar and so handles a great deal of Nellie's money, was misbehaving, and stealing from us. It's all nonsense, of course. Brodie showed me all his ledgers, every one of them – I'm no financial wizard but I know real honesty when I meet it, and Brodie's honest. He's an enthusiast and he's rather showy and glossy, and people like him always raise the ire of people like Molloy – the timid little men, thinking everyone's trying to harm them, to rob them. They hate the energetic excited ones, the generous ones. They're the sort who have to cut everyone down to their level, instead of trying to lift themselves to better ones.'

'What's going to happen to Molloy?' she asked, not so much because she wanted to know – she was still rather hazy about what the whole affair was about – as because of her feelings that he needed to talk about it. 'Has he apologized?'

'For killing my father?' Max said bitterly and then frowned. 'Damn it, I have no right to say that. Pa was old and ill – he was likely to die anyway. I don't suppose Molloy precipitated it by more than a few weeks or even days. And Pa would have wanted it this way, dying while he was busy with Nellie's affairs – no, Molloy didn't apologize. He's chosen to go.'

'Go? Where?'

Max shrugged. 'I stopped being a caring doctor, Charlie, and didn't ask him because I just don't care what he does. He just said that under the circumstances he couldn't stay here, that he was going to leave and that he'd send his resignation in the morning. And I agreed, for the Board. His deputy'll have to manage until we find someone else.' Again he rubbed his face. 'Let's not talk about it any more. I've had enough of it all – I want to talk about something different.'

She had been as taken aback this time by his use of her familiar name as she had been the first time he'd used it, and was sitting quietly, her own hands folded on her lap, unable to say anything. It wasn't all that strange that he should speak to her so familiarly; in the medical common room at Nellie's everyone was on first-name terms; however formal they were in the wards in the patients' hearing, in their private lives they were well aware of their dependence on each other and knew how important it was to break down barriers; yet for all that, it was odd to hear this particular man speak so to her. They had, after all, been at such odds with each other – and she stirred uneasily, ashamed suddenly of the way she had behaved to him.

It was as though he had read her thoughts, because he said, 'I wanted to tell you – I wanted to explain – I meant no harm the other evening. I wasn't trying to – what was the word you used? I wasn't trying to taunt you about Brin Lackland. I'm not like that. At least, I never have been and it's been worrying me because you were so angry and so hurt and –'

'I'm sorry,' she said, and her throat tightened, making her a little breathless. 'I'm so sorry – I shouldn't have spoken so. It was unforgivable of me. I know now you were right. I think I knew it then, and it – I was hurt, too, you see. I just hit out I suppose, and you were there, so –'

'I didn't mean to hurt you.' He looked at her and now she could see the distress in him clearly. It was as though all his grief over his father had been shifted to her, and to the little scene they had played out in the staff dining-room. 'I truly didn't –'

'It wasn't you who hurt me,' she said. 'It was just you who got the flak – it was Brin.'

She was never to understand why she did it, why she let the gates that guarded her from the world fall so easily, but the words were there in the air between them even before she had realized she was saying them.

'He made love to me, and now he refuses to see me. He tells people to lie to me, to say he isn't there in his flat when he is.' She contemplated with a sort of calm surprise the fact that she was telling Max this and then added to her amazement by saying, 'And I'm pregnant.'

He stared at her, his face quite smooth, and then said, 'Oh, my dear, I am so sorry.'

'Not as sorry as I am.'

'He – I'm not surprised.' He seemed to be picking his words. 'He – it was what I think I tried to explain to you when I first saw him. A personality type which – I mean, it's no reflection on you he behaved so. He's just that sort of chap.'

She managed a smile. 'You told me so?'

'No, I'm not trying to say that –' And then he stopped. 'I'm sorry. I suppose I am.'

'It doesn't matter. You're right. And I'm very much in the wrong.' The smile widened and became a laugh, but there wasn't any amusement in it. 'A woman wronged – it's a charming phrase, isn't it? Another way of describing a bad 'un – I'm a bad 'un –'

'You don't believe that.'

'I don't know what I believe.' She wasn't smiling now, just sitting with her head down and staring at the blank dark window. 'I'm a bloody fool. I know that. To let myself be taken in by such a one –'

He shook his head. 'You weren't taken in. That implies he set out to – to ill-treat you. He didn't, any more than I imagine you set out to be a victim. It happened because you're the people you are, not as a result of any sort of premeditation. It was just that he's the sort of man he is, and you're the sort of woman you are. Rather warm and caring, I think, and with depths you probably didn't know yourself that you had –'

'Thank you. You're very kind. I can see why you're a psychiatrist.' And she looked at him and again managed that small strained smile, not wanting him to think she was digging at him.

'I'm not speaking as a psychiatrist,' he said. 'Just as a man. A rather lonely one who needs to be liked. It worried me a good deal that I had somehow forfeited your liking. That was why I wanted to talk to you. To get rid of that – I'm glad I have. I need that much comfort –' And he looked over his shoulder at the empty bed behind them and said, 'I'm going to miss him dreadfully. In lots of ways he was my best friend. We talked a lot – especially since Emilia died.'

'He was a good man, everyone used to say –' She tried to find words to comfort him, but he brushed them aside with an almost violent little gesture.

'Good, bad – it doesn't matter. He was my Pa –' And then tears appeared in his eyes and lifted above the lids and trickled down his face and she reached out and touched him, feeling her initial embarrassment slip away as easily as his tears slipped down his cheeks and he bent his head so that she could put her arm across his shoulder and hold him, and he sat there quietly weeping, making no move to wipe away his tears.

How long it was they sat there she didn't know. He wept quietly, with none of the harsh sounds that she herself had produced when she had at last cried for her own parents, and she felt there was a dignity in his grief that helped her to express some of her own for what had happened to her with Brin; and she was not surprised to discover that her own face was wet with tears or that they were as quiet and unforced as were his.

Eventually he moved and lifted his head and took a deep breath and got to his feet and went over to the washbasin in the corner and methodically washed his face, splashing cold water over it and drying it as though having to cope with a tearstained face was something he did every day of his life.

'Thank you,' he said after a moment and turned and smiled at her. He looked better now, much less pale and tight. 'I'm grateful.'

'You needn't be.' She held out her hand for the towel and he gave it to her and she in turn washed her face, glad to feel the cool water on her hot cheeks and eyes.

'I haven't felt so relaxed since – I don't know when,' she said, surprised. 'I'm in this awful mess and I feel good –'

'Of course you do. Crying is what we all need a great deal more than we allow ourselves. I try to make my patients cry as much as possible.' He grinned fleetingly. 'They don't like it a lot at first, but once they discover how good it is, they become quite enthusiastic.'

She hung up the towel neatly, embarrassment creeping back into her. 'I think I must go. I have an early list tomorrow –'

'What are you going to do?'

'What? Oh, a couple of appendices and a rather tricky cleft palate on a baby and –'

He laughed aloud. 'No, my dear. Not about work. About yourself.'

'About myself?' She stopped and considered and then smiled at him. 'Oh, I'm going to have a baby,' she said. 'Your father made that decision for me.'

'My father?'

'It's hard to explain – but looking after him and trying to save him showed me how important it is to do the same for this baby. Whatever Brin did to me, this is a person –' And she set her hand on her belly in an unconsciously protective movement. 'So, I'll be the same with it as I was with your father –'

He seemed to understand, for he just nodded. 'Good. But don't say *it*. Think of he or she – it'll help you.'

'He or she?' She pondered that and then nodded. 'Yes, he or she.' She had reached the door now and she stopped and turned back to him. 'I don't need to say it, I know, but – you won't tell anyone?'

He shook his head, unoffended. 'No, I won't tell anyone. But will you tell me? Will you come and tell me how you are, when things get difficult? I imagine they will from time to time. And I'd like to know how you are – how you're coping.'

'I'll tell you,' she said. 'Goodnight. And my condolences.'

'Thank you,' he said. 'Goodnight, Charlie', and at the sound of her name again the warmth rose in her and she went to bed to sleep soundly for the first time since that night in Earlham Street when it had all started – and as she fell asleep she murmured to herself. 'Not it – he or she. He or she –'

It was a good thought, better than she would have believed possible.

29

'I rather think,' David Lackland said to his brother as they arrived at St Paul's Church in Covent Garden, 'that Gran'pa would have enjoyed this.'

Andrew, always very literal in all his reactions, looked at him witheringly. 'Ass! No one could possibly enjoy their own funeral. They're dead.'

'Gran'pa would have done.' David took off his neat bowler and tucked it under his arm in the approved manner as they moved from the brilliantly lit churchyard into the dimness of the cool church. 'Perhaps people ought to have their funerals before they die so that they could get the benefit of it – you could leave the burying bit till later, couldn't you? It'd be nice to know who cared enough for you to turn out. They cared about Gran'pa, didn't they? Will you just *look* at all the people there are here! Half London, I reckon – and isn't that a newspaper cameraman over there? By that pillar? At a funeral – ye gods, but the old man'd have been tickled pink!'

Andrew was still arguing with him in whispers as the two of them made their way to the front where the family pews had been set aside, and watching them Letty thought – nice boys. But what a pity neither of them looks like Max – and she gazed about her to see if she could see their father. But there was no sign of him yet, though the church was filling rapidly.

A few rows to one side of her she saw Harry and she craned her neck a little hopefully, and then, as she got a clearer view, let her lips curve happily. To see Lee there was very gratifying; she looked as uneasy as she always did when she was in a church – with her Jewish upbringing Lee still found it somehow shocking even to set foot in a place of worship that was not her own (and after all, Sir Lewis's wife, Miriam, had been Jewish too) but she was there, and that boded very well indeed. If those two weren't on better terms, surely she

252

wouldn't have turned out, even for old Sir Lewis? Lee might have come to the churchyard to show him respect, but not inside the church. She must have done that to please her husband and Letty nodded to herself contentedly as she contemplated her nephew and his wife.

Harry seemed to become aware of her gaze then, because he turned his head directly towards her and smiled at her; a smile so wide and so full of – what? – relief, Letty decided, that it seemed as though he were sitting in their own private patch of sunlight. He inclined his head slightly, indicating, and Letty followed his direction and saw that Lee's hand was held in his, on his lap, and she looked back at Harry's face and returned his smile as widely as she could, putting on once more the necessary expression of funereal solemnity.

Across the aisle another uneasy group sat, clearly as Jewish as Lee, and Letty looked at them and then remembered; the Henriques clan, the ones who owned that great chain of chemists' shops and who were so amazingly rich and successful. What were they doing here? And then she remembered that they had been cousins by marriage of the Old Man and nodded approvingly. It was good and right to see so many people turning out to pay their respects to him.

Someone tapped her on the shoulder and she turned her head to see Peter just behind her and she smiled at him too, and then even more widely as she saw him stand back to make way for his companion, Sophie, to enter the pew before making his own way to the front of the church and the pew reserved for the chief mourners, where his sister Johanna sat with her children and David and Andrew. Really, she told herself, thinking about Sophie and Peter arriving together, things are looking up for this family; and then she grimaced a little at the irreverence of thinking such a thought at a funeral and she restored her own expression to a suitably melancholy one.

Not far from her, resting on its trestles, Sir Lewis's coffin, rich with brass handles and gleaming wood and almost masked with flowers stood large and mute and she stared at it, remembering the Old Man with affection. Although they had shared the same surname their relationship had been far from close; though they had met at Lackland family affairs and been on polite dining terms, and she had become quite involved with them for a while in the long-ago days just after the Great

War when she had first found Theo, the links between herself and Sir Lewis's family had been tenuous, and as she sat there listening to the organist indulging himself luxuriously with a piece of sombre Bach she let her mind slip into genealogies, working out just how she had been related to Sir Lewis.

Her father hadn't been a Lackland; he had been Wilfred Brotherton, but for some reason Letty had now quite forgotten he had changed his name to his wife's when they had married; Sophie, her mother, had been born a Lackland, the daughter of old Bartholomew and therefore the grand-daughter of the grand old man himself, the one who had founded Nellie's so long ago, Abel Lackland. Now, Letty thought as the organ rumbled its long low notes all round her, how was Sir Lewis related to him? But she couldn't remember who his parents had been and pushed the thought away. She and Lewis had been distant cousins; no more than that, and now she sat here in a cool dim church on a brilliant July day bidding him goodbye –

And I don't feel too marvellous myself, she found herself thinking wryly, aware once again of the dull ache that so often came to plague her belly these days, and refused to think any more about that. It's morbid to be concerned about your own innards, she told herself stoutly as at last the music changed and the congregation got raggedly to its many feet; this was the time to think about the good old departed, not the about-to-depart-sometime-in-the-future, and she opened her hymn book and settled herself to enjoying the ceremony. She always enjoyed services in church. There was a lush theatricality about the language of the Book of Common Prayer and the readings from the King James's version of the Bible that appealed to her dramatic nature, and today was no exception.

By the time the whole thing was completed and the congregation was lining up behind the coffin to make the melancholy procession to the corner of the churchyard where Lewis's grave waited she was feeling tranquilly content. Not happy to see the last of Sir Lewis by any means, but aware that he had had a good and long life, and was being turned off with all due pomp and circumstance; and she found herself humming Elgar's funeral march beneath her breath as she came blinking out into the sunshine.

The interment went smoothly as the vicar stood there

beside the grave with his cassock flapping about his knees and the birds trying to shout him down and then, as the gravediggers took over, grunting a little over earth baked hard and dry by the long heatwave under which London still sweltered, and the mourners turned to make their way back to the front of the church, she felt the mood of the occasion lift, and looked about again for people to whom she would like to speak.

Max was there now; and she went over to him and took his hand and shook it and kissed his cheek and he nodded at her, a little abstracted but clearly glad of her attention.

'I should have thanked you sooner, Letty,' he said.

'My dear chap, whatever for?'

'For what you've done not just for the hospital but for Peter. Pa was very pleased, you know, very pleased. To have seen Peter as well as he is before he died – I think that made him feel good –' And he lifted his chin to look about for his brother, and saw him standing talking to the dumpy figure of Sophie, beside a rather bedraggled-looking rhododendron.

Letty followed his gaze. 'He'll do, I reckon,' she said with satisfaction. 'He's taken no end of a shine to that niece of mine. What's more important, she's taken a shine to him. Very Yorkshire, our Sophie. I don't think you need worry any more about Peter. Not if Sophie's decided to take him on. She'll ruin him, of course. Make him quite helpless. When Sophie's around no man has to wipe his own nose. She was born to look after people, especially male people.'

'Well, perhaps Peter's earned it,' Max said and then nodded as his sons, still together as they always were, touched his elbow and tipping their hats at Letty, made their way to the gates of the churchyard. 'I must go, Letty. I ought to be back at the house before most of the rest of you get there – you will come, won't you? You are expected –'

'Perhaps,' she said, unwilling to leave the sunshine, and stepped back. 'Don't worry about me. You've got enough to do. My condolences, dear boy. But he had a good life.'

'Yes,' Max said and went away, collecting Johanna, who was looking pale and very sorry for herself as she drooped on her son Jolly's arm, and Letty stared after them and shook her head. Pity Johanna had turned out to be so useless, she thought with all the contempt of the clever woman for the merely

255

pretty, and then went to sit down for a rest on one of the wooden benches that lined the pathways. To watch other people go, in their own time, and then join on behind them would be agreeable. And she needed to catch her breath, to get rid of the ache.

There was a little scurry along the path and she watched, a little amused. A newspaper reporter and a photographer, unless she missed her guess, she thought, trying to talk to Brin and Katy, and she watched, her eyes narrowed a little sardonically. She had seen them arrive and been amused to see how thoroughly Katy had thrown herself into the role of mourner. Her black silk shirt and suit of black barathea were the smartest Letty had seen for a long time, and were clearly imported from somewhere a good deal less austere than England was at present, and the whole outfit, surmounting the sheerest of silk stockings over the most elegant of high-heeled suede shoes, and topped off by an extravagantly veiled little hat of the most delicious prettiness, was designed to make people stare. And then when they did, Katy looked back at them with haughty disapproval. Oh, thought Letty, but she's enjoying herself!

And so, she decided, was Brin, as she watched him bend his head to talk to the reporter who stood a half head shorter than he was, and almost on tiptoe with the excitement of having the chance to talk to the man who had been labelled Hollywood's Next Heart-throb in every popular newspaper on Fleet Street. He too was well dressed, in a sombre suit with the most sparkling of white shirts set off by his black tie and bowler, and he held his head to one side so that the scar on his cheek could be seen easily in the sunlight. There was no doubt but that he had an air of distinction and of something else; of bravery and insouciance and impudence – it was a heady mixture. Now that he was so self-assured and aware of his own attraction, it was no wonder people were so eager to stare at him and talk to him and that the photographers hung about waiting for him even if doing so meant crashing funerals.

The last of them now were leaving, and as the churchyard at last emptied, Letty sighed and got to her feet. It would be as well to go back to the house after all; she hadn't wanted to, not finding it agreeable to eat funeral baked meats – and she turned the words in her mind, relishing their archaic sound – but

256

there, it would be expected of her, and she liked old Max and Peter. They were entitled to all the family support they could get at this moment in their lives and she went stomping on her way up King Street towards St Martin's Lane. Maybe luck would be on her side and she could find a taxi soon –

Charlie had meant to go into the church, to be part of the congregation proper which followed the old man to his grave, but when she had reached the gates of the churchyard she had seen him just ahead of her, and her courage had completely deserted her. She had turned and fled back along the street in the direction of the hospital and when she had at last allowed her steps to slacken she was almost there.

But then she had stopped and thought and turned round again, very deliberately, and gone back. To refuse to attend the funeral of a man she respected just because a man she could never feel any respect for ever again was there too, was to be chicken-hearted in the extreme; she had set out to go to Sir Lewis's funeral and go she would.

But when she got back to the church the service had already started, and she couldn't bring herself to walk in in the middle; it would have seemed too ill-mannered altogether, and she had stood in the cool shade of the doorway, staring unseeingly at the notices on the board there and listening to the sounds that came out of the doors; the reverberation of the organ and the rather querulous singing that for all it lacked in tunefulness was agreeable to hear, and the professionally resonant voice of the vicar; and then, as the service had ended had slipped along the path and stood quietly in the shadow of the wall to let them go by. The moment had passed to be part of it all; but that didn't matter. To be an onlooker was quite enough. Sir Lewis wouldn't have cared either way, she decided, not from any basis of close knowledge of him, but because of the sort of person Max was. His father could never have been the man to take offence at someone watching his funeral, rather than taking an active part in it.

When Brin went by, he didn't see her; he was talking with some animation, albeit in whispers, to his sister but she could see him clearly and she stared at him, trying to see the man she had loved so much that she had lost all sense of her own value and dignity, hoping that it would all be gone; that his treatment of her since then had somehow managed to shatter the feeling she had. But her hopes were ill-founded. As soon as she saw that face, saw the liveliness of its expression and the way his eyes glinted in the sunlight her belly tightened in the old familiar way and she felt sick; but whether that was with excitement at seeing him or disgust with herself for feeling as she did, she couldn't know.

She watched them all go, saw the little flurry of excitement at the gate where the newsmen were taking pictures of Katy and Brin and didn't emerge until they had gone at last, hurrying up King Street. She saw Letty follow them and then, when she was sure everyone had gone, stepped out into the sunlight herself.

But when she reached the gate she found that the newsmen were still there as the photographer was packing up his equipment and almost without thinking she stopped and said casually, 'Who was that you were talking to?'

'See tomorrow's *Sketch*,' one of them grunted. 'It'll all be in there –'

'Newest dreamboat that was, with his sister. Brinsley Lackland.' The photographer seemed more communicative. 'Where *do* they get these names? I ask you – Brinsley! Bet he was born plain Ted or Joe –'

'I don't think so,' Charlie said. 'He told me it was a family name. One of his father's uncles –'

'If you know who he is, why did you ask who we were talking to?' The photographer squinted up at her and grinned. 'Checking up on us, are you?'

She managed to laugh. 'No, not really. Just couldn't be sure I'd seen him properly. He was at the hospital, you see – I work there –'

At once the two men relaxed. 'Nurse, are you? Lovely, you girls are, really lovely! From round the corner? Nellie's?'

'That's right,' she said. 'Nellie's.'

'Was he there long?' The reporter seemed interested now, pulling his notebook from his pocket. 'Was he there for treatment to that scar of his?'

She looked at him and tried to think what to say and then, deliberately, shook her head.

'No – something quite ordinary –'

'Oh.' He put the notebook away, uninterested now.

'Nothing I can use then?'

'Oh, I don't know,' the photographer said. 'Saying he was cared for at Nellie's – that'd make it nice. Human, you know? Coming to the funeral of one of Nellie's doctors and all. But all he talked about to us was Hollywood and all that. Off tomorrow on the *Ascania* from Liverpool, he said – lucky sod. No rationing there they tell me. Imagine – all the grub you can eat and giving the whisky away. Ah, well, we can't all be born good-looking, can we? Goodbye, nursie! Take good care of the patients, and when I turn up there with a black eye and a thick head next week, be nice to me!' And she managed to smile at them and watched them go, then turned to walk slowly back to the hospital, pulling off her black beret and shaking her hair free to cool her head as she went.

Going tomorrow. Tomorrow. And obviously with no intention of letting me know, or saying goodbye or – and she felt her eyes prickle with tears as she thought about that and hated herself for her own weakness. If he didn't care why should she? What was he in her life, any more? Nothing, less than nothing –

And then her hand slid across her belly as it so often seemed to these days and she bit her lip. Brin might mean nothing to her any more – or so she might try to convince herself – but what about he-or-she waiting there so quietly to be born? Wouldn't he-she want to know about who his-her father was? Would he-she ask questions, demand reasons for his absence? What could she say to him-her, if she had never told Brin?

This was a question she had asked herself many times in the past few days, ever since Sir Lewis had died and she had made up her mind to hold on to her baby, no matter what happened. Did Brin have a right to know he was to be a father? Shouldn't he be given the option of being involved? To keep silence was surely to rob him of his just due, of the chance to behave as a man should and –

No, she had told herself fiercely over and over again. No. I'm using no blackmail of any kind. If he couldn't work out for himself that this was a possibility then he isn't worth worrying about. He's forfeited any right he might have had to share in this baby. It isn't his at all. It's mine, all mine – and she had warmed to that thought, found a great deal of pleasure in it. It wasn't going to be easy to get through these next months, to make her plans, to protect both her own reputation and through that the welfare of her child, but she was going to do it. To be Charlotte Hankin Lucas alone and independent and waiting for her child was a good and special thing to be. No worrying about Brin Lackland and his rights in the child was to be allowed to spoil that; and as she reached Endell Street and the main entrance to Nellie's, she lifted her chin in sheer exultation and ran up the steps. She had an evening's work to do on her wards, and plans to make for the future. Let Brin go off to his career in Hollywood tomorrow. She didn't need him and she never really had.

And for that evening at any rate, she really believed herself.

30

But as the days became weeks and they in turn pleated into months, her certainty wavered many times. At the end of long days on the wards, when her back ached abominably and her head spun with nausea – a problem which hit her rather badly when she was in the third month of her pregnancy, and just didn't go away as it should have done – self-pity would rise in her like a thick greasy tide and make her want Brin so badly it was like a physical thing. Then, she would lie on her bed in the doctors' quarters, trying not to retch and would hate herself for being so obsessed. The man was bad, bad, why let him hurt her so much?

But another part of her mind would tell her to stop being so silly and hysterical; he hadn't been bad, he'd just been himself; shallow and casual, perhaps, uncaring of others' needs and feelings, but without any real malice. Just a stupid but rather beautiful man with whom she had allowed herself to become infatuated. To hate him now because of her own foolishness was hardly fair, she would tell herself, and turn over in her hot bed and try to sleep, knowing that alone could relieve the nausea and the self-absorption that so plagued her.

Surprisingly, Max Lackland became a great help to her. He stopped her one afternoon in the corridor as she hurried from Spruce to Elm wards, a bundle of patients' records under her arm and said, 'Charlie – you look, if you will forgive my saying so, quite dreadful! You're overworking, and I rather think not eating enough.'

She had stopped and stared at him and then rubbed her hair off her damp forehead. 'I'm all right. It's the heat – I'm too worn out by it to eat –'

'I know.' His sympathy had been genuine and immediate. 'Hell, isn't it? And to think we all complained in the winter when it was so bitterly cold for so long – but all the same, you've got to take care of yourself. You've certainly got to eat. I know a rather nice little place you can get something that'll tempt you, however hot you are. When are you off tonight?'

So it had started, their occasional quiet little dinners in a small restaurant in Greek Street, where they offered her Italian dishes that even when made of meagre English rations, which had dwindled steadily all through the year, still somehow managed to taste of the south and which made it possible for her to overcome her queasiness and eat. And he would sit across the table and watch her, slowly turning a glass of wine between his hands and smiling slightly.

They would talk as well as eat. That was a great comfort for her, for there was no one else, apart from Dr Forester – who politely and carefully avoided indicating in any way when they met around Nellie's that he knew anything at all about her – who knew what her situation was. To have someone to talk to without reservations, to tell of her hopes and her fears and her plans and her doubts made her feel much better.

Her plans were good ones – he told her that approvingly when she had explained how she had at last claimed back her Lancaster Gate house, which had been requisitioned by the Government to be used as a branch of the Ministry of Information during the War but which was now once more all hers, and how she had made an elegant little flat out of the ground floor which had access to the garden.

'It's too big for just two of us, me and a baby – the whole house I mean. And it's not like the old days when there were hordes of servants to take care of it. There'll just be me, though I hope I can get someone to be a sort of nanny and general help. And I'm going to have the rest of the house made into flats and let them. There's such a shortage of places to live these days it'll be a good thing to do, and it's better than living on my own in a mausoleum.'

'It'll help with income too, I imagine.'

She shook her head at that. 'I'm rather well off, actually,' she said almost apologetically. 'Cousin Mary left me far more than I need –' She had brightened then. 'But that means the baby has a future, doesn't it? He-she'll be secure –'

'He-she will have you,' he had said gravely. 'And I rather think that in the long run that will be of more importance than any amount of money. Not that it isn't useful. Mind you, the way this Government's going, they'll have every penny out of your pockets and into theirs in no time.'

And they would talk then of politics, of what was going to happen to medicine under the great new National Health Act, which both she and Max approved of in essence, unlike a great many of their colleagues at Nellie's who regarded socialized medicine with appalled horror, and about the shortages and strikes that were making England so uncomfortable in this long hot summer of 1947.

She left Nellie's at the end of November. She had been feeling less and less well, and the consultant gynaecologist who was looking after her, and who had agreed to deliver her baby in her own flat with the aid of a midwife from St Mary's hospital in Paddington, told her firmly that she must stop, and she didn't argue with him. She had become thinner than she should be and the baby was beginning to show rather more than was comfortable. She wore a girdle at work, and an oversized white coat but was uneasy at the way some of the senior nurses looked at her so quizzically, and also, she was far from happy.

A period of self-assurance that had carried her through the late autumn seemed to be succeeded by a period of great depression and she even wondered for a while if some of it was due to the country's wedding fever. It seemed that no one around Nellie's talked of anything but young love and honeymoons, as the Royal Wedding filled the papers day after day until Charlie felt that if anyone else mentioned Princess Elizabeth and her romantic sailor groom she would scream at them.

So she left Nellie's and settled into her flat, and for a couple of weeks the novelty of arranging furniture and hanging curtains and sorting out where in her small kitchen her dishes should go sustained her, but that was succeeded by the worst time of all.

She had not realized how much she had relied on her work to keep her on an even keel and without it she floundered through the days, tearful and irritable by turns and far from her usual cool and sensible self.

It was Max who helped her through that. He had telephoned her one evening quite unexpectedly, early in January, and asked her to come out to dinner and at the sound of his voice on the phone she had burst into tears and he had made soothing noises and hung up and then, twenty minutes later, had appeared on her doorstep with a package under his arm.

'I imagine you have a kitchen here,' he said cheerfully. 'I've brought my own dinner, and a little something for you too. Can't drain your rations, can we? I have friends in illegal places, fortunately. Where's the stove?'

She had tried to protest at first and then given up, for he had been cheerfully firm, and had moved purposefully about her shiny new kitchen, which truth to tell she had hardly bothered to use for more than the making of tea and toast, and then set in front of her a piece of grilled fish and mashed potatoes which, she realized, were exactly what she wanted. She had wolfed it and he had said nothing all through their meal and then, pushing aside the dishes, had told her firmly that she was to tell him of all that was worrying her.

And though she had resisted at first, had felt he was treating her as though she were one of his neurotic patients, he had persevered and at last she had let it all out; her rage at both Brin and herself, he for being so selfish and shallow, she for being such a fool as to believe him, and he had listened and said little.

But at the end of it all she had felt amazingly better. They had reached her sitting-room by then, for he had made coffee and brought it to her and when she had said all she could she had fallen asleep, there in the corner of the sofa, and woken stiff and startled in the small hours to find he had covered her with a rug and was himself sleeping in an armchair on the other side of the room.

They had both laughed when she woke him, and she had given him another blanket and settled him on the sofa while she went to her bed, and in the morning she had made breakfast for them both and he had gone away, shaking her hand and telling her that she'd be fine now; and so she had been, to her enormous relief and gratitude.

For the remaining weeks of her pregnancy she became tranquil. She slipped into a pattern of daily living that was comforting in its regularity; a morning walk in the park on the other side of the Bayswater Road among the naked trees and shivering birds and the spikes of early crocus and daffodils pushing their way through the cold dark earth, a light breakfast in her cosy kitchen and then the morning spent over

264

her knitting and sewing, for she had decided to make the baby's clothes from the things she had found in Counsin Mary's trunks in the attics. Old silk dresses and cotton chemises were cut up to make rompers and pilches and old cobwebs of knitted woollens were unravelled to be reknitted into matinée coats and shawls and bootees, and slowly she became adept at her making over and as the pile of small garments mounted she was filled with a deep contentment.

Her afternoons were peaceful too, for she dozed them away, her wireless on softly beside her bed as she listened to 'Music While You Work' and talks about ornithology and cathedrals and cookery and even 'Children's Hour', and in the evenings there were books to read and more radio – she became an addict of 'Dick Barton, Special Agent', and 'ITMA' – and sometimes, quiet outings with Max. They would go to theatres and cinemas and more of their little Soho dinners and, as Max said, she began to bloom as a pregnant woman should.

But in the last two weeks of the pregnancy she became restless again. The sewing and knitting were finished, the small room she had prepared for the baby lay waiting with its old cot repainted and its cupboards filled with the results of her handiwork and all she could do was prowl uneasily around the flat, waiting impatiently and yet fearfully for the time to come; and then her fears were sharpened by two separate events, both of which alarmed her a great deal.

Her midwife called her in the first week in April and told her that she had fallen and broken her ankle.

'I'm so sorry, Mrs Lucas,' she said. 'I thought I'd be in plaster and able at least to look after some of my special patients, but it's no use. I've got to go into the hospital, they've just told me, and have an op on it – it's too silly – I'm so sorry –'

And then the next day, before she'd even had the chance to think about finding another midwife to take care of her at such short notice, the second blow fell.

The secretary of the consultant obstetrician who had been looking after her telephoned to tell her that she was very sorry, Mr Mills-Topham would not after all be able to deal with her confinement, since his wife had to have her appendix out and he had cancelled all his work for the next three weeks in order to take her on a convalescent holiday.

'And since your baby is due before he comes back, he feels it would be better to transfer your care to his colleague, Mr Harris,' the woman said smoothly. 'Mr Mills-Topham regrets any inconvenience but he's sure you'll understand –'

'But I don't *know* Mr Harris,' Charlie had said blankly, standing with the phone held so tightly in her hand that her knuckles shone white, and the baby leapt in her belly in seeming sympathy with her anxiety. 'I can't be looked after by someone I don't even know!'

'Well, I'm afraid that is how it has to be,' the secretary said sharply. 'I'll give you Mr Harris's telephone number and if you call him as soon as you go into labour he'll come and see you. And of course you have your midwife, haven't you?'

She did the first thing that came into her head, which was to phone Max. He listened to her account of her dilemma and said at once that it was absurd to try to find new people to come to her confinement in Lancaster Gate, that she would be much better off coming into Nellie's to have her baby.

'I wasn't best pleased with your plan to stay in the flat anyway,' he said. 'I know most women do have their babies at home, but you – it's different for you –'

'No husband?' she said bitterly.

'It's nothing to do with that. It's everything to do with your health and your age –'

'My age? What do you mean?'

'How old are you?'

'Thirty – last month –'

'An elderly primagravida,' he said and then laughed at her intake of breath. 'My dear, you know I'm right. For a first baby, it is a bit older than it might be, isn't it? You'll be better off here. Safer. So will he-she.'

'But to see everyone – people will know.'

'Yes,' he said. 'People will know. They know you and they'll be interested in you. Dr Forester will see you and be interested in you. So will Mr Croxley. So will we all. We look after everyone at Nellie's but especially we look after our own. You're one of ours, aren't you? And you told me, once, that you weren't going to do what Dr Forester had suggested and buy a wedding ring and tell lies about yourself, weren't going to pretend to be married or widowed or any of those other – what was your phrase? – shabby little subterfuges. Was that

266

promise only for other people? Not for Nellie's people?'

She stood silent, the phone against her ear, hearing him breathe and trying to think and within her the baby shifted and heaved and her belly hardened against the pressure and she felt the tension in her back, a dull aching, and thought – not long now. Soon, soon – and then, sharply, nodded her head.

And though she hadn't said a word he took a deep breath that was clearly audible through the phone and said, 'You will then? Come here?'

'I will,' she said. 'As soon as I start. Will – will you arrange it all? I don't think I want to try to –'

'I'll see to it that they expect you in Maternity,' he said reassuringly and then, suddenly, 'I'll be fifty this year, you know.'

'What?'

'My next birthday. It'll be my fiftieth.'

'Oh.' She didn't know quite how to respond and said the first thing that came into her head. 'So what? I mean, how nice –'

'That's all right then,' he said obscurely and hung up and she stared at the buzzing phone for a moment, puzzled. It was very unlike Max to be so inconsequential.

Whether it was the anxiety that she now felt about having to go to Nellie's to have her baby, or whether it was because the time had arrived in the natural order of things, she was never to know, but twenty-four hours later, at three in the morning, she knew she could wait alone in her flat no longer.

Methodically she collected the last few items she might need to add to her prepared bag and put on her coat and then phoned the taxi rank at Paddington station. There were always taxis there at any time of night, and when she told the man who answered hoarsely that she had to be taken at once to Nellie's, he said cheerfully, 'Right, ducks. On me way –'

And when he arrived fifteen minutes later he took one look at her and immediately began to fuss over her like the most excited of mother hens. His anxiety and his pride in his task amused her so much that when she arrived at Nellie's she was feeling far less anxious than she had been when she had first phoned there and told the midwife on duty of the progress of her early labour and been told to come in at once. As the taxi driver almost carried her into the main hall, the very prince of solicitude in every way, she laughed and thanked him and protested as he refused to take his fare and watched him go, her mind far less preoccupied with her state than it might have been.

But she was brought back to the present with a sharp reminder as another contraction began and she sat there on the bench where the night porter had left her while he went to find the midwife on duty who would admit her to the maternity ward, and tried to relax. What was happening to her was normal, a normal, natural physiological process. There was no need to panic, no need to fight it, her doctor's mind instructed her woman's mind just as it had been used to; simply relax, it said, let it roll over you, it has a vital function; it is making a pathway open for him-her –

But it was a big and painful contraction, the biggest so far, a deeply creaking sensation and she felt the sweat running down her face as she sat with her back held in an arch and her chin up, breathing deeply through her nose as through the mists of sweat in her eyes she could see the tall bronze figure of the Founder's statue, and needing something to help her cope, seeking a focus on which to fix her concentration as the contraction tightened and hardened till she thought it would break her in half, she found it in the small plaque at the statue's foot.

'Abel Lackland, Founder and Benefactor of this, Queen Eleanor's Hospital for the Sick and Needy and Old and Young and Especially for the Mothers of Covent Garden and its Environs. Blessed be his Name.'

'Blessed be his name, blessed be his name,' she murmured, concentrating on it, staring fixedly at the plaque, and then slowly the wave of the contraction began to ease and slide away and she let her back slump, and lifted one shaky hand to wipe her face. Blessed be his name, I'm through that one, she thought and peered at her watch. She'd better note how often now; that had been fifteen minutes since the last, wasn't it? Yes, fifteen minutes – and then the midwife arrived with the porter and in a wave of carbolic scented kindness took her on her way to the maternity department on the third floor, rattling up in the noisy old lift in the sleeping hospital, and chattering cheerfully of banalities all the way.

But Charlie kept the phrase that had helped her through that big contraction in her mind and when the next one came, as she sat on the edge of the bed to which the midwife had taken her she used it again, closing her eyes to recreate behind her lids the image of the big blank-eyed statue. 'Blessed be his name, blessed be his name –' she murmured rhythmically and it helped amazingly, making the pain seem so right and natural that it ceased to be a pain and became a powerful and exciting sensation instead.

For the rest of the night, as the pains came more often, first at ten-minute intervals and then at five and at three-minute intervals, she used the same technique. The midwives fussed over her, and so did Mr Croxley when he arrived and she smiled vaguely at them and nodded and did as they told her, but thought all the time of the silent figure down in the main hall, so secure and stolid, so comforting in its stillness, and murmured that absurd phrase in its absurd rhythm inside her head.

At nine o'clock, as the day got under its busy way at Nellie's, with the first of the people arriving for their outpatient clinic appointments and the consultants' big cars decanting them at the front steps, as nurses and physiotherapists and cleaners and radiographers and engineers and cooks and porters and the ever-demanding patients slid into the business of their day, Charlie's baby at last emerged with one last vast push from her weary body, her chin tucked so hard into her chest and her face so distorted with the effort that she looked like a tortoise, and immediately bawled very loudly indeed at the indignation of being swung up in the air by the feet. Charlie gasped and laughed and cried and said, 'Blessed be his name –' – which the Irish midwife took as a prayer and greatly approved of – and stared at the streaked and bloody object with the furious face that screamed at her and at his new-found world with a sort of amazement. Had she made that? Had she really made *that*?

'Ah, 'tis a fine boy – will you look at his great bits and pieces then?' the midwife said. 'A bonny, bonny boy, and all complete in every respect. Well done to you, Dr Lucas, well done indeed –' And she wrapped him in a sheet and gave him to Charlie who stared at him in even greater amazement as they bustled themselves at her other end, no longer aware of anything but him.

She'd done it. She, Charlotte Hankin Lucas, had done it, and virtually on her own – and she held the baby to her face, not caring that he was thick with the yellowish wax in which his skin had been covered in her womb, not caring for the blood that matted his hair, and crooned odd little noises at him which meant everything and nothing and which he understood perfectly. For at last he stopped bawling and closed his newly opened eyes and slept.

'I'd forgotten they come this small,' Max said, leaning over the crib and staring at him. 'And so neat – what will you call him, Charlie?'

'Mmm?' She turned her head back to look at him, for she had been staring dreamily out of the window at the new leaves that were appearing on the plane tree just outside. 'I hadn't thought about names. Isn't that ridiculous? But I have now.'

She smiled and stretched. 'It seems so right, somehow. I'm calling him after Nellie's.'

Max lifted his head and looked at her, and said carefully, 'After Nellie's? Don't you think a chap might find life a little difficult with such a name?'

'Ass,' she said and chuckled. 'I'm calling him after the man who *founded* Nellie's. Abel Lackland. He's entitled to be called Lackland, after all.' She looked out of the window again for a moment, and then back at Max and grinned, a slightly sideways little grimace that had some pain in it, but an insouciant one all the same. 'Abel Lackland Lucas. Sounds good?'

'Very good,' Max said and looked at the baby again. 'And you never know. One of these days he might be even more of a Lackland.' But he didn't look at her as he said it.

All round them Nellie's went on as it had for the past hundred years and more, providing and caring and trying its best for the people who lived and worked in the tangle of narrow London streets that surrounded it.

Soon it would no longer be the Nellie's everyone had known it as for so long. It would be just a part of the shiny new National Health Service in a shiny new post-war England where the want and the inequality and misery that had been so much a part of Covent Garden and Seven Dials and Hungerford and Clare Market and all the other London warrens of long ago would seem like long-forgotten bad dreams.

No more disease, no more misery, promised the new order. No more Nellie's dependent on the goodwill and the effort of the people who had built it and run it and fretted over it. Just a Government department it would be now, not one family's domain.

But there would still be Lacklands and Lucases, because they always went on. No matter what happens to institutions and systems, people go on and on. So the statue of the old Founder down in the main hall stood there stolidly as above his head the newest of his clan and of his once much-loved and long-forgotten Lilith's clan started out to make the world his own.